A CASTLE FROM ASHES

Castle in the Wilde – Novel 3

SHARON ROSE

To Joshua,
who brought the joy of another son to our family.

CONTENTS

MAPS

Map of Lavaycia
As commissioned by King Rithdon

❧

Map of the Wilde
As drawn by Duchess Fenoesh

Fountain Isle
River Thane
Vixicat Lair
The Wilde
Tower Woods
River Vale
Selta
Duchy
City of
Purthellia
Maerton
Duchy
Prushane
Duchy
Fennish
Duchy
River Joynlen
Portlen
Duchy
Othair
Duchy
The Lands of
Lavaycia
River Chazim
N

Fountain Isle
River Thane
Vixicat Lair
Cave Rapids
The Wilde
Tower Woods
Lavaycia
N
W
E
S

CHAPTER 1

S ir Thomas stepped over gnarled roots, quiet as a lynx. Trespassing. At least, Duke Maerton would call it that.

Unfair to name it a crime when he just wanted to see what little remained of Kaituer Castle. 'Twas not as though he could further harm the desolate ruins at the forest's edge. Broken walls and towers—the very emblems of defeat—stood resilient in the twining mist. No man-made sound reached his straining ears. Just his horse tearing up a mouthful of grass behind him.

Thomas paused beside one of the trees where forest crept near the shattered walls. Strange that so little of their stone remained. Carted away, according to the local who had pointed out the ruins from a distant hilltop yesterday. Used to build random structures and even parts of Maerton Castle.

A tingle crept up the back of Thomas's neck, though he still couldn't lay hold of what bothered him about that friendly local. 'Twas strong enough yesterday that he'd turned down the man's offer to guide him to the ruins. He checked his back again and still found no hint that he'd been followed.

The flaw of coming alone—only one set of eyes. But telling anyone where he was bound would have only led to puzzled stares, predictions of rain, and warnings to stay away. They didn't understand. He *needed* to see Kaituer Castle.

'Twas nothing like the edifice he'd imagined when his father told him the old stories. He could make out the keep's location, but only by its corner towers and the crumbling walls that clung to them. One tower still bore a parapet. Had it been spared by chance or choice? The ground floor windows were not much wider than arrow slits. Three tiers of arched, gaping holes must once have been stately windows of upper chambers. A tree branch skewered the tower through the second-floor gaps. Nature's creeping growth assaulted the remains that had not fallen to King Carleeton's trebuchet and decades of scavengers.

Thomas had thought a near view would suffice. It didn't. That roofed tower...could it be the one where his grandfather had slept? Surely, the grandson named after Lord Thomas had a right to enter.

He was here anyway. Duke Maerton and his objectionable son, Lord Ivan, wouldn't know. Besides, the place must be considered common land if the locals took the stones at will.

Thomas strode through clinging grass—taller than it looked and hiding broken stone that threatened to trip him. He headed for an archway, doubtless once an interior passage. Judging by fresh scrapes on the weathered rock and newly exposed surfaces, someone must have been scavenging lately. Thomas clambered over a tilted slab and crossed an exposed floor, misshapen by the elements. He passed through the arch and found a staircase. Nothing fancy—probably backstairs. At each landing, he made his way into the tower chamber. In the first, a tree limb had entered through one tall window and left by another. Each bare circular room contained a small fireplace. The mantels must have been fine, for only chisel scars remained.

In the top chamber, Thomas lingered. Just another bare room. Hooks mounted high on the curved wall may have supported the tapestry mentioned in the old stories. He rested his hands on a cold stone embrasure and stared out the north window at mist-shrouded tower trees. Had his grandfather stood here looking at Tower Woods? Before he'd known it would become his home in exile.

What was that sound? Like a rock shifting and maybe a stumbling footstep. Another scavenger, perhaps, but no more footsteps followed. A tingle crept along his spine again.

Thomas peered through the gaping doorway. The two corridors that branched off at right angles remained as lonely as ever, one blocked by a collapsed roof, the other open to blue sky. The sound must have reached him from below.

Regardless of who might be out there, he didn't want to be seen. Some days, he grew heartily tired of the blond hair and long nose that marked him as a Kaituer. He darted from the doorway to the staircase and ran down, keeping his footfalls soft the way he'd learned in his youngest days. He paused at ground level beside the last wall that could hide him. Not a sound to be heard. Perhaps a stone had simply chanced to fall as time weakened its support.

Thomas passed through the archway. He'd taken but one step beyond it when an arrow hissed past his shoulder and ricocheted off the wall.

He dropped to the uneven floor. A foot nearer, and that arrow would have pierced his neck! Rubble was not enough cover. Not with all those dark windows of the other towers. Three angles to shoot from. He scooted through the archway and snatched up the fallen arrow. From a partial crawl, he burst into a sprint for the staircase. He could not leave the way he'd come.

At the first landing, Thomas dashed into the tower chamber. The shocking truth kept thrumming down his nerves. Someone was trying to kill him. He tucked the arrow into his belt, then leapt onto the limb and worked his shoulders through the gaping window. He checked all sides and above. No one in view, but he was still within range from one tower.

He grabbed the nearest branch and dragged himself upright

beyond the tower window. The limb, he crossed at a speed that made his nickname believable. By the time he reached the trunk, he had spotted his horse among the trees. Thomas descended, bounded over obstacles, then jerked loose the tied reins of his startled horse. No sooner had he gained the saddle, than his horse's hooves pounded the ground in frantic retreat.

Some relief in that, though he shouldn't spook his own horse. After a moment, he straightened from leaning over the withers and slowed his mount from a gallop to a fast running-walk. "Easy, my lad." Thomas scanned the woodland. Neither horse nor man in any direction...that he could see, anyway, through the mist and drizzle. He drew his cloak around his shoulders and flipped the hood up.

By the horse's stiff ears and sweat, it must be convinced an evil fiend was on their trail.

Thomas patted his neck. "I think you lost him, lad. Let's find that cart track back to the market." Murmuring soft words to the horse helped his own pulse to slow but did not ease his frown. That arrow in his belt...it had a barbed iron point. Meant for large prey. Or a person. Him.

No matter how he turned it in his mind, there was no other conclusion. And indeed, he did nothing but turn it through the entire ride back. Mist evaporated as the sun neared its zenith. Fair skies couldn't soothe his worries, but afternoon sun dried his cloak by the time he reached the vendors. He reined his horse back to a slow walk so he could scan faces.

'Twas a strange market, with the typical border tensions wherever Maerton Duchy edged Tower Woods. No village, just space for carts—several of which had already left, for this was the second afternoon of the two-day market. Surprising that Duke Maerton even set up a market here, considering how much he loathed the very existence of Tristelle Duchy. The commoners weren't much better. Bartering had been more akin to skirmishes at first, though 'twas calmer now. Thomas nodded to one of the friendlier folk, who had once told him that Duke Maerton forbade fighting and paid vendors to bring wares here. Which would seem like an attempt to make peace with his neighbor— were it anyone other than Duke Maerton.

Thomas studied each face as he rode, seeking the man who had offered to guide him to Kaituer Castle yesterday. Nowhere to be found now.

"A belt is no place for an arrow," someone from Maerton said, more question than comment.

"I chanced to find it on the ground. Do you recognize it?"

The man shrugged at the odd question. "Looks like any other arrow."

A common design here, then. No surprise. Thomas left the market on the north end, where the People of the Woods always camped. Tristellians, they were called now, though they didn't take to that name. Rough awnings stretched between trees to shelter the firepit and the benches around it. Beneath them, Thomas caught sight of Captain D'Jorge. Though his back was turned, 'twas impossible to miss his brown hair queued at the nape and hanging to the hem of his jerkin.

Thomas's horse whinnied, and the captain swung around. He raised his eyebrows at Thomas in mute question.

Thomas dismounted and tied his horse with the others, considering how best to answer that question. Privately. He met D'Jorge's eyes and tilted his head toward the stream. No one would find that strange. Thomas paused by the gurgling water to drink a few handfuls, then walked a little farther with his friend.

"Where have you been off to for so long?" D'Jorge asked.

Glancing around to make sure no one was near enough to hear, Thomas said, "I went to see what's left of Kaituer Castle."

"Did you now?"

Thomas drew the arrow from his belt and handed it to D'Jorge, who inspected the point. "This hit the wall next to me when I was leaving."

D'Jorge pursed his lips. "Barbed to do more damage when it's removed." He wiggled the tip, and it came off. "Or to stay inside and cut further with each movement."

"I know how arrows work."

"Mm." He shoved the shaft tight into the socket of the iron tip. "You should also know how unwise it is to ride alone in Maerton Duchy, but apparently you don't."

Thomas let a sheepish quirk lift the corner of his mouth. "Didn't."

"Glad to hear you learned something. Kaituer Castle, of all places. What possessed you?"

"That's what worries me." He looked aside, then back at D'Jorge. "I suspect I was lured into a trap."

D'Jorge dipped his eyebrows and waited.

"I met someone in the market yesterday. Claimed he was a lad when Lord Thomas was sent into exile. He offered to show me the castle. I went as far as a hilltop with him. He was set on taking me the rest of the way right then—even though 'twas late."

"If you smelled a weasel yesterday, why did you go today?"

"It seemed safe enough to set out early, and thus avoid that eager guide. My father told me all the stories his father had told him, and I wanted to see it. Alone. Few people live in this woodland, so 'tis easy to remain unseen." He shifted. "I was just planning to look at it from the cover of the woods."

By his sideways smile, D'Jorge knew how that ended.

"Anyway, I went up the one tower that still has a roof." Thomas frowned. Those scraped rocks...

"What?"

"Now that I think about it, I suspect some of the rock had recently been moved, perhaps making it easier to enter." Thomas shook his head. "When I left—just as I came out into the open —someone shot that arrow. It struck the wall an inch from my shoulder!"

"Did you see anyone?"

"Nay. I dropped immediately to take cover, but I was within

range of at least three towers. So I grabbed the arrow—I don't really know why—and darted back inside. There was a tree that had grown through the second-floor window, so I climbed out on that." Thomas smirked at D'Jorge's grin. "I know—Sir Squirrel. But that blocked me from two of the towers. Then, I ran to my horse and returned. No one followed me."

D'Jorge was silent for a moment. "Many vantage points, but only one arrow. No pursuit. 'Twas one perpetrator, and he didn't want to be discovered. Hm. What was the name of your would-be guide?"

"He never told me."

"What did he look like?"

"On the short side. He wore a cap, with a bit of gray hair sticking out. A red nose like older men get sometimes. Not well-dressed, but he had a horse." Odd for the poor to be mounted. "He had a habit of doing this." Thomas rubbed his thumbs along the sides of his index fingers.

"Did he have a bow, quiver, or wrist guard?"

"Nay. I doubt he shot the arrow. I now suspect that he was tasked with getting me there."

"Which would mean..." D'Jorge gripped Thomas's shoulder to turn him and began walking. "...that someone who wants you dead knows you are here. I want you right in the midst of us while the Tristellian vendors pack up and head back into Tower Woods. If you do the asking, they would gather all the faster."

Strange comment. D'Jorge was one of Duke Tristelle's captains. Not forceful, but his words were obeyed. Thomas's title of *sir* was just a *thank you* from the king for saving his life. It didn't carry authority. Granted, the People of the Woods were his friends since birth, but they liked D'Jorge too.

Duke Maerton entered his son's private study without knocking.

Lord Ivan sent a sharp look over the top of his book, then closed it and rose. "Good morn, Father," he said, offering a proper bow. He crossed to a bookcase and placed his volume on the shelf. "You are always welcome here, of course, but a knock would be appreciated. This *is* my private study."

"Nothing is ever entirely private. Always remember that. Where have you been these past three days?"

"I rode west. Just seeing to the family holdings."

"For which I employ a steward."

"True." Ivan went to the shelf of tea tins and selected one. "Yet, it is well for him to know that we are also aware of what occurs on our land. And of course, there are some things we must tend to ourselves."

Tiresome games, but Ivan liked such talk. Maerton put enough impatience into his words to get an answer. "Such as?"

Ivan measured tea. "I heard a rumor that Sir Thomas has an interest in Kaituer Castle, and that he uses the market days as an excuse to ride about on our land." He lifted a kettle from the brazier, which he often kept hot in the fireplace, and poured water into his steeping pot.

"Were you so unwise as to confront him?"

"Certainly not. Indeed, I did not actually see him riding our land, so perhaps it is no matter."

Maerton settled into a chair beside the tea table and watched the steam twist from the spout of the steeping pot. He gestured to the bookcase along one wall. "In your unexplained absence, I perused the titles that interest you. Quite a collection on the subject of teas, herbs, and all manner of flora."

Ivan regarded him a moment. "It *has* been an interest of mine for a few years now, as you well know."

"Also, some medical texts, which is *not* a well-known interest of yours."

"Ah, but there is a close relation, for I find it fascinating that many herbal teas can treat ailments."

"And poison."

Ivan produced his gentle laugh. "Do but consider my endless curiosity. I would like to try every plant in the gardens and woods in my tea mixtures, but alas, nature is not always kind. If a plant is a known poison, I prefer to learn that *before* I sample it in my tea."

"You have a fine collection of explanations to complement your unusual library."

"Having endured malicious whispers in the past—though never about tea—perhaps I am more inclined to prepare. I would think that you would approve, my dear father. Did you know there is even a leaf that causes apoplexy? Imagine the tragedy if one so young as I consumed it by accident."

Malicious whispers...must he bring up his mother's broken neck? "It has been five years since your mother died. The whispers were forgotten when new events took possession of every mind. 'Tis a useful technique if used subtly—less so if you refer to the very thing that should be obscured."

Ivan snorted. "Not nearly as useful as silencing the tongue that whispers." He poured a little tea into one cup, tasted it, then filled both cups. Handing one to his father, he said, "This is a new blend, which I think covers the bitter notes of certain teas quite well."

"What meant you about silencing the tongue?"

Ivan smiled—again, a gentle expression, which he had cultivated over the last few years. "I just mean it was a relief that Hettie died when she did. You remember her—the woman you made use of to control Prushane. Until she started babbling both sides of the lie."

Indeed, her death had been the only beneficial event in those dreadful months. Maerton sipped his tea.

"And worse," Ivan said, "learned what my mother said to me on the stairs before she...fell."

Maerton almost choked. "What?"

"It must have been Hettie shrieking my mother's last words in the church that day. And Princess Ellabeth had been at her cottage door only moments before. Bad enough that the demented hag started babbling nonsense about switched babes. Starting in on mother's death…" Ivan gentled his voice. "Perhaps she secretly wanted to ensure that her own death would not be of the sadly lingering sort."

The physician had said she died of apoplexy. Maerton's gaze lifted to the shelves of tea tins.

Ivan laughed. "Worry not that I would keep anything dangerous here. But we were speaking of tea. What think you of this blend?" Ivan took another drink from his cup.

"'Tis quite palatable," Maerton said. He needed common talk as much as the heat of the tea, for Ivan's words chilled him. If they meant what they sounded like…

CHAPTER 2

Lady Sareen's stomach fluttered. She hated doing unconventional things. How did one even know if a lie would sound believable?

The pantry maid must have been the unsuspicious sort, for she packed up the picnic luncheon Sareen asked for and brought it up to her bedchamber, along with a thick woven cloth to sit on.

Behind the closed door, Sareen unrolled the red-checkered cloth across her bed, tucked two gowns and her under linens into the folds, then rolled it back up and tied it again. A little chubby-looking. Would others notice? She grabbed her brushes and such from her vanity—and worried again over her own image in the mirror. She had donned an older, pale blue riding habit and sensibly braided her black hair. A good thing her mother was away, for she would certainly notice Sareen's uncharacteristic appearance. Would servants? Would they try to stop her if they did?

Sareen stuffed her toiletries into the picnic basket, then laden with basket and bundle, snuck down the back stairs and out a side door that led to the stable. What a relief that she got through the stable door without needing to try out the next version of her lie.

A stable lad gawked at her.

"Run and fetch Adonna for me," Sareen said, keeping her words light and airy, "then saddle one of the riding hacks." When he set his shovel aside and hastened away, she released a tense breath. Struggling to manage a basket and bundle while keeping the skirt of her riding habit out of the muck, Sareen found her horse's stall, and hooked the basket over a peg beside it—then had to keep the mare's inquisitive nose out of it.

Adonna soon arrived and curtsied. "Did you want to go riding, my lady?" Her gaze flicked to the blanket beneath Sareen's arm.

The curtsy had revealed that Adonna wore a split skirt. Good. No need to delay for her to change clothes. "Aye," Sareen said, "for a little surprise picnic with a few friends. Not far, but I don't want to ride alone, so you may escort me once you've saddled my horse."

Adonna smiled and opened the stall. However odd she thought this venture, she loved being asked to tend horses. Sareen knew how it felt to be shoved into a mold, so she gave Adonna what she loved—a stable task usually assigned to the men. She was only seventeen or so, but taller than Sareen, and she tossed the saddle onto Sareen's mare as smoothly as the lad did onto the hack. She strapped the bundle behind Sareen's saddle, and the lad managed to anchor the basket behind the other. The women mounted and left the castle through a side gate without attracting attention...or at least comment.

Sareen took a bridle path to make her escape less obvious. When it connected to the road, Adonna, who had been riding behind, quickened her pace to reach Sareen's side. "My lady, where are we bound?"

This was far sooner than Sareen wanted to tell the truth. "Does it matter?"

"It isn't my place to ask, but it does seem strange to set out so early in the morn with a picnic lunch when you said it isn't far."

"Well...it will be far before we eat the picnic, but I didn't want a formal escort or a maid who's more proper than I am."

Adonna tittered like she didn't know what to make of that and hoped it was said in jest.

Sareen tried to form an arch smile and failed. "I know. I never do things like this. I hoped you would understand and... and help me...or at least not ruin my adventure."

"'Course, I'll help you! A body needs a fling now and then."

Sareen smiled. Though her mother didn't approve, her cousin Beth had been right about being kinder to servants. Now, when Sareen needed an ally, she had one. "Let's pass this cart, shall we."

'Twas the first of several carts they outdistanced as they pressed on northwest. Sareen usually traveled this route followed by a carriage bearing luggage, a maid or two, and often her mother, for the Duchess of Selta did not enjoy riding. Doubtless, Sareen would be longing for a carriage before she reached her destination. But no matter how she ached, she was doing this.

They bypassed the turnoff that meandered through fields and woods to the manor where she would normally spend the night. Instead, Sareen followed the direct route that the couriers used. 'Twas well before noon when they left the shade of the forest. A good thing, for many miles lay between her and the travelers' cottage.

"My lady," Adonna called from her proper position a length behind. Adonna quickened her mount and reached Sareen's side. "My lady, the horses tire, and this..." She spread a hand and gazed over the grassland. "This is the plain. Certain, we are not even in Selta Duchy anymore!"

"True. We've crossed the border of Tristelle Duchy." Sareen drew her reins back. "We'll walk the horses again for a while. We are not likely to meet many travelers along this stretch, and it gets dustier out on the plain. You may ride beside me."

"Uh...the picnic..." Adonna seemed unsure how to continue.

"We should reach a common stop along the stream by midday. There is a comfortable place for us to eat, and the horses may drink and graze."

"Oh. Um, then what?"

"I'm bound for Tristelle Castle." Sareen dipped her head. "I'm sorry I couldn't tell you before."

Her eyes growing rounder by the second, Adonna asked, "Does anyone know?"

That breathy question made Sareen feel like a guilty child. "Nay."

Adonna uttered something akin to a moan. "My parents are going to be right fussed."

"They won't blame you. The stable lad knows you went with me."

"That won't make it better. I know the duke and duchess are away, but your youngest brother isn't. He'll raise a hue and cry as soon as the household realizes you are gone."

"Lord Dermont left the castle before I did this morn." Sareen tilted her head toward their lunch. "A maid packed the basket, so that will be known too. With luck, no one will be surprised I'm gone until I don't come back in time to dress for dinner. I told the pantry maid to pack enough to feed four, and two of them young gentlemen with hearty appetites. That should give us plenty for the journey."

"Oh, heavens! They'll be running all over the duchy searching for you."

Likely there would be talk. Sareen's mother would scold, because it seemed that being a grown woman counted for nothing at all if one still lived in her ancestral home. Annoying, but bearable, for all would know of her safety long before she must endure her mother's complaints. Dermont, though...he'd worry and have to search. She hated serving him such a trick, but leaving him a note would have ruined everything.

"'Tis not as though we hid," Sareen said. "I got a few strange looks from people heading the opposite direction. I'm sure Lord Dermont will discover which road we traveled."

Adonna knit her straight eyebrows in silence for a time, then asked, "Is there something...not right in the mansion?"

"'Tis not that, exactly." Sareen sighed. "More like something that...that is on its way to going wrong, and I don't know what to do about it. I need to talk with Duchess Tristelle, but 'tis hard for her to travel just now, so I'm going to her." Of course, that provided no reason why she didn't journey there in a conventional manner, so she hurried on before Adonna could ask. "'Twas not well done of me to trick you into this journey. I'll share everything I brought, since you couldn't prepare. If you'd like to turn back now, I would understand and not be angry. But, well...I know you've no ambition to become a lady's maid, but if you would stay with me as maid for now, I would much appreciate it."

"Oh, certain, I would never be so unkind as to leave you now, my lady. Besides..." The corners of her mouth twitched. "'Tis better that I didn't know what you were up to, for no one can blame me for not telling."

Sareen laughed. "Thank you, and indeed, my horse thanks you too."

"Aye, the poor thing, for I know well you couldn't get her saddle back on if you took it off tonight. But how shall we make do? Is it not a three-day journey? And we've not so much as a tent."

"Three days by carriage, aye, but Duke Tristelle had a travelers' cottage built at the final marker, which I hope to reach by nightfall. Couriers reach it in a day's ride. We can sleep there."

"What is a travelers' cottage?"

"A resting place when the road is long and there is no village. Just a simple structure, with a common room between two bedrooms. There's a well and paddock too. A hovel, by my mother's standards, but it has everything one needs for a night's stay."

"'Tis a good thing, for neither of us has ever ridden as long or as far as the couriers do."

True, but at lunchtime, Sareen was all the more confident. They could do this. Her legs ached when they stopped for dinner, but after the cold meal, they rode on. The sun sank low and sat just above the horizon when they finally approached the cottage. Sareen doubted she would even be able to stand when she dismounted.

Tristan followed the road over the crest of a hill. He shifted his legs to slow Dauntless. Beside him, Captain Cotrell did likewise. This simple travel, with only a couple men riding behind, reminded him of his untrammeled days—before he bore the title *Duke of Tristelle*.

A fair sight met his eyes, one that he would never tire of. Beyond the village, Tristelle Castle rose majestic, graced by twin, blue-peaked towers. None would call it wild now, for the orchard thrived and the nut trees in their straight rows had forgotten they once strove with underbrush. Wide, groomed roads divided the forest, lanes served fledgling farms, and cobblestones kept the village streets from turning into rutted mud. Though the castle's demesne was now well-groomed, the structure itself looked the same. In his heart, it would always be the Castle in the Wilde.

Cotrell pointed to one of the cottages at the edge of town. "They've finished thatching that roof since we left."

"We leave for a week, and the village grows," Tristan said. "Happens every time we visit the east villages or go down to the sea. More so, if we weave through Tower Woods."

"Disappoints you so, doesn't it?"

Tristan chuckled, for Cotrell knew how much it delighted

him. Perhaps someday he would take this land for granted, but he hoped not. He exchanged greetings with the villagers as his party rode through, but he didn't linger today. It had been too long since he'd seen Beth and Robin.

East Road curved around to meet Castle Gate Road, which provided an unobstructed view of the imposing gatehouse in the south wall. The portcullises were raised within their arches as befit a castle in prosperous peace. A voice bellowed, "Duke Tristelle approaches," and a few trumpet notes followed to announce his return. A bit of pomp that he'd finally gotten used to. Besides, it usually brought his wife and son to his arms that much faster.

By the time Tristan dismounted in the bailey, his son pelted across the courtyard on chubby legs, shouting, "Papa!"

A nursery maid ran behind, calling, "Master Robin!"

Tristan hastened up the terrace steps to catch Robin before he reached the top one—running *down* stairs not being the lad's greatest skill. Tristan swung him high, delighting in his joyful squeals, dirty face and all. Settling Robin snug against his side, Tristan climbed the last couple steps.

"Pray pardon me, my lord duke," the maid, Evie, said, curtsying. "He got away from me before I could clean him up." She held a wet napkin, still intent on her mission.

"Let her wipe you," Tristan said, turning Robin, "for there is no hiding that you've been eating berries and honey."

"And cream too," Robin said.

"Ah. We must not forget the cream."

Though Robin submitted to the imposition of having his face and fingers wiped, the dark spot on his chin remained.

"What have you done to bruise your chin?" Tristan asked.

Robin glowered. "Suzanna grabbed me and made me fall."

Suzanna...the other nursery maid. Tristan raised an eyebrow at Evie. By her incensed look, she must have a different version.

"He ran off when he saw the tower door open," she said, "and

Suzanna caught up to him as he started climbing the stairs. She never meant for him to fall, but he wouldn't stop."

Tristan directed a serious look to his son. "Then, you should have answered that you bruised your chin because you ran from your nurse. Do not blame others when you disobey." Robin's lip protruded at the firm words. "You know you are not allowed on the tower stairs unless an adult holds your hand. I have told you this."

Robin sniffed. "I wanted to see if Mama was coming home."

That required another look at the maid, who said, "My lady duchess has gone to Tower Woods. Sir James mentioned something about a land dispute."

Tristan hid his disappointment. James approached behind the maid now, and he would know more. "You and Suzanna may take a rest."

Perhaps Evie tried to cover it with her curtsy, but her closed eyes and sigh suggested that a rest was long overdue.

"Welcome home, my lord," James said.

His voice always engendered calm within Tristan. "Thank you, James." Just between themselves, he and James maintained their styles of address from before Tristelle Duchy was created. It gave the castle a much homier feeling. It had also been the only means by which he could convince James to accept even the simple title of *sir*, though he deserved it as much or more than any Lavaycian recipient of that title. They walked together into the mansion's hall. "What took the duchess to Tower Woods?"

James glanced to a servant. "Bring tea to the library." He turned to walk there beside Tristan. "Apparently, some dispute arose between a young widow and her neighbor about the ownership of a field, which had been cleared by both her late husband and said neighbor."

"Which of them sent for us?"

"Neither. Another who had business here carried word, thinking the affair was getting out of hand. Duchess Tristelle left two days after you did, so I expect her back soon. I'm not sure how far off the road this plot lies, but she had a guide and her guard, of course."

Tristan strolled to one of the leather chairs by the library hearth and settled Robin in his lap. All hope of talking with James was lost, for Robin had much to tell—the litter of puppies in the kennel being the primary topic.

Amidst the many suitable exclamations and questions Tristan uttered, he remained aware of James's patient amusement. The tea tray arrived, with scones and a child-sized mug of milk.

James set a cushion beside the wooden box Robin had claimed a few weeks ago. "You may use this as your table, Master Robin."

Robin climbed down from Tristan's lap. "'Tis not a table. 'Tis my *desk*." He knelt on the cushion, eying the scone that James was placing before him.

As he reached for it, Tristan said, "You forgot something."

"Thank you, James."

"Sir James," Tristan prompted.

"Thank you, Sir James."

"Well said."

Robin took the biggest bite of his scone that his small mouth allowed, and finally, Tristan could enjoy a little refreshment and hear news from James of affairs at the castle and village. Nothing that his capable steward hadn't already dealt with.

"How fared your travels, my lord?" James asked.

"The cottages damaged in the storm have been repaired or replaced. I'd say the villagers are in finer spirits than they were before the storm, what with new or stronger abodes than they had, and possibly with the pleasure of joining together for the work. They are nigh finished replacing the market stalls. The old wood was so rotten, I'd say the wind did us a favor tearing them down."

"What of the elderly widow who didn't want anyone touching her roof?"

Tristan laughed. "I didn't know what was happening at first, but 'twas the funniest thing. It seemed one of the village women took it into her head to visit the widow's granddaughter in another village and offered to take her along. Their wagon no sooner rounded the bend in the road, than all the village women swarmed into her cottage to take everything out, and men crawled up on the roof to strip the rotting thatch. They'd stored all the fresh thatch, straps, and wickers in some sheds nearby. I'd wager, every able body in the village had a hand in getting it done. 'Twas all finished, and the cottage cleaned and restocked, by the time the two women returned the next afternoon."

"And what thought she of that?"

"She climbed down from the wagon all fussed and fuming, demanding to know who had done it and what sort of mess they'd left her things in. The men stood around, begging her pardon, till one of the women got her to look inside. She started wiping her eyes, mumbled a fair bit, then managed to say, 'I thank ye kindly. 'Twas right decent of ye, and don't set no store by aught I said afore.'"

James smiled in his calm way. "May all who grow cantankerous in old age, have such fine neighbors."

"Indeed. Makes it easier to bear when I've had to deal with a wily farmer, who lets his bull wander and then demands some form of payment from those who never ask for stud service. By the way, I happened to chat with Toby Burk on the way back. He tells me he's read all the books in the school and wishes there were more for adults who have already learned to read."

"I suppose that lad has grown into a man," James said, with a shake of his head. "Now you'll have to buy more books on top of paying the schoolteachers."

"A pleasing enough expense." Tristan set his teacup aside and handed his napkin to Robin, who stood at his knee again. "Wipe the milk from your mouth before you climb on me."

He rubbed his face with the napkin, then crawled into Tristan's lap. "When is Mama coming home?"

"I know not. Shall we climb the tower to see if she has reached the plain?"

A smile bunched his cheeks. "Aye, Papa."

Tristan took Robin to the tower's spiral stairs and positioned him at the center, where the steps were narrowest. The lad raised no objection to holding his father's hand as he boldly began mounting the steps. Huge compared to his short legs. When he slowed, Tristan carried him the rest of the way, with Robin's arms wrapped around his neck.

Narrow windows let in shafts of light as they climbed above the mansion's roof. On the top floor, sunlight flooded through the ring of windows below the tower's peak. The sun was lowering to the Great Sea beyond the wooded valley. Lovely as always, but the southward view drew Tristan. Grass rippled across the plain at the breeze's whim. With his long vision, he could make out the dark border of Tower Woods that edged the grassland.

Robin twisted in his arms, looking this way and that. "Do you see her, Papa?"

"Not yet. Down you go." Tristan set the lad on his feet, then took the covers from the ends of the distance glass and bent to its eyepiece, while Robin ran circles around the tower's perimeter. Through the glass, Tristan found the inn he'd had built on the far side of the plain. A couple of horses rested in the stable's rear yard, and the coach stood beside it. She must have ridden into the woods from there. With only two horses in view, she had not returned yet. He swept the glass slowly eastward, for a track followed the woodland. Depending on where she left Tower Woods, she would likely traverse it. Ah, there! A sizable party headed toward the inn...and two riders wore flowing skirts. The duchess and her maid. Even at this distance, the sight of Beth warmed him.

"I see your mother, Robin."

He stopped running to hop with his hands lifted high. "Rah!"

Tristan chuckled at the hint of Moorelin in the lad's cheer.

"She's still a long way off. She'll probably be home about this time tomorrow." She was riding slow. Not that there was any need to hurry, since she was sure to reach the inn before sunset. But she was a few months with child. 'Twas about this time when her last pregnancy had suddenly ended. He did not want to see her in tears again.

Since he was here, he may as well scan the plain. Queen's Road followed the central stream eastward. Within range, a travelers' cottage stood beside a mast with signal flags to indicate when a message waited there. No longer was it strictly necessary, since his people—once considered foreigners but now called Tristellians—were legal citizens of Lavaycia. Still, letters were sometimes left there if speed was not important. 'Twas hard to see much beyond that, but a tiny dark smudge on the road suggested that riders approached the cottage from Selta Duchy. Nowhere else did anyone stir.

Tristan turned the glass back to his wife and followed her progress. A small hand touched his thigh.

"Are you still looking at Mama?"

He glanced down. "Aye, Robin."

"We miss her, don't we, Papa."

Tristan picked him up again. "That, we do."

CHAPTER 3

Sunlight teased Sareen's eyes. She dragged herself upright from the mattress in the travelers' cottage and clung to the bedpost. Her legs and back objected to every movement.

Adonna sat on the edge of the other bed, wisps of her brown hair sticking out of yesterday's braid. "Do you know how much farther we have to travel?"

"About half of what we covered yesterday."

"Thank the heavens for that!" She stood. "'Twould be better to walk the horses today."

"Indeed! If they were to trot, I swear my legs would shatter." Sareen hobbled after Adonna into the common room, and bracing her hands on the table, lowered herself to a bench. A dozen scenarios plagued her about what her brother might be doing. Everything from him having no idea what had become of her, to his imminent arrival, determined to take her home. Though she wanted nothing but rest, that worry made her stop Adonna as she laid kindling on the hearth.

"Nay," Sareen said, "I'll not linger for a fire." She opened the picnic basket, which rested on the table. "We'll be comfortable at Tristelle Castle all the sooner if we make do with tepid water now."

After a cold breakfast, they set out with the rising sun at their backs. How long the journey stretched, with the hard-packed dirt road disappearing into an endless sea of grass. So monotonous, Sareen couldn't pay attention to it anymore, especially as the sun snuck overhead and began to tease her tired eyes.

An awkward motion grabbed her attention, and her horse nickered. Its gait felt off. "Oh, no. What now?"

Adonna dropped back and watched a few steps. "Better stop. Your mare has cast a hind shoe."

"What? How?"

"It happens." Adonna shrugged. "There's a few rocks poking through the dirt, here and there. Probably caught it." She turned her horse to walk back along the road, as she studied the ground. "Here it is." She dismounted and picked it up.

"Can you put it back on?"

Adonna stared at her. "Nay, my lady."

Feeling utterly stupid, Sareen said, "But she can keep going, right?"

Adonna licked her lips. "Well, aye, but…she's worn shoes for so long, her hoof will be tender. You'd best ride my horse, and I will lead your mare."

They made the change, though with nothing to stand on, Sareen could barely get her aching leg high enough to reach the stirrup. Their pace grew slower than ever. A couple times, they halted so Adonna could check the bare hoof.

Time to stop pretending. "She's limping worse, isn't she?"

"Aye." Adonna stroked the mare's neck. The poor thing rested her weight on three legs, favoring the bare hoof.

What to do? Continue and maybe permanently lame her horse? Continue alone and send someone back to tend the mare? She couldn't leave Adonna out here, but it didn't seem right to abandon the mare either. How much farther was it? Sareen stood in her stirrups and shaded her eyes to scan the grassy horizon.

Was that movement way off in the distance? "I think I see the roof of a coach!"

Sareen called out, and Adonna shouted much louder, but the coach did not slow.

"They cannot hear us," Sareen said. "Quick, untie the blanket." As soon as it was free, Sareen shook it out, heedless of her falling clothes. She waved the red and white cloth high above her head till her arms hurt. Still, the coach did not slow. She sank back into her saddle. What were they going to do?

THOMAS TRAILED behind Duchess Tristelle's party as they returned across the plain. He'd offered to lead the duchess's riding horse...something to do that didn't require talk. He just couldn't get his mind off troubles. Bad enough that someone wanted to kill him, then he'd learned last night of the land dispute and the duchess's judgement. A faulty decision.

Not that he blamed her. 'Twas sometimes impossible to know a matter when two of the People of the Woods contradicted each other. Nothing was ever written, for most were illiterate. The duke or duchess tended to give half to each party in these cases, but Thomas was nigh certain that at least one person had figured out how to make use of that. Now, he had done it again, obtaining half of a field that a widow needed to provide for her children. And maybe worse, the man who purloined half of her property would be working in the field without even a fence to separate them.

But what could Thomas do about it? He couldn't contradict the duchess. She had the authority. And what was he? Nothing but a target.

Thomas released his clenched jaw—again. No matter what consumed his attention, that thought kept recurring. Tower Woods had once been dangerous, but for the past few years, he'd felt safe there. He could even attend the royal court and parties given by the nobles of Lavaycia. And then someone shoots an arrow at him. 'Twas a good thing he had learned watchfulness as a lad. It seemed he would never be free of that need.

He continued his slow scan of the grassland. West toward the cliffs rising from the sea, ahead to the blue peaked towers of the castle beyond the carriage, and east toward—what was that wisp of red? He stopped the horses and watched. Red and white, like a signal banner, yet flipping too fast and low, as though it were not mounted on a staff. Indeed, if not for his long vision, he doubted he would have seen it.

He glanced toward the entourage. He'd let them get too far ahead to bother with telling them where he was bound. He was nigh Queen's Road. An easy trek to see what was flapping and determine if it meant anything. Wixxy, the duchess's horse, seemed to think poorly of his decision to turn, but after a moment, she stopped hanging back and eased into a running walk beside his own mount.

He soon spotted two horses on the road, and if he wasn't mistaken, a woman—nay, two women. What could they be doing out here, with no escort in sight?

The black-haired one turned, probably hearing his approach. Was that Lady Sareen? He quickened the horses. Indeed, it was. He could tell when she recognized him, for her stiffness melted and she pressed a hand to her chest. Her smile couldn't have charmed him more.

When he drew close enough for speech, she said, "Oh, Sir Thomas! You cannot imagine how happy I am to see you!"

"My lady, how do you come to be out here all alone? That is... how may I serve you?" Why could he never speak smoothly like the noblemen did? And why were clothes lying about on the road? He forced himself to look at her again.

She lost her ecstatic expression. "I, um, my horse threw a shoe, which has rather stranded us here. I thought I saw a carriage...and needed to signal...but I only had this and..."

The partially folded cloth hung from her lap, and a gown peeked from it. Her plainly dressed attendant gathered linen things from the road.

Thomas nodded. "Quick thinking, then, to use your, uh, luggage roll." An undergarment had snagged in the roadside weeds. Should he pretend he didn't see it? What if she needed it? He cleared his throat, and when the maid looked at him, he pointed.

Sareen followed his gesture too, then turned a shade redder.

He dismounted. "Perhaps I should look at the horse." He went to the far side so the women could tend to their things without his eyes on them. He stroked the mare's neck and murmured to it. 'Twas already clear what was wrong.

The maid seemed bothered that he approached it. "'Tis just that she cast a shoe and we walked her—without a rider. I've checked her hoof often, but she's not used to it bare."

"Perhaps if we wrap it, she'll come along with us easier."

"Do you have something to wrap it with?" Sareen asked.

"Nay, but you do. May I cut a strip from that cloth before you tie it up?"

"Of course." Sareen accepted the reins of his two horses. "Isn't this Wixxy? Duchess Tristelle's mare?"

"Aye. The duchess rides in her carriage today." Thomas drew his ornate dagger and focused on his task.

The maid proved more helpful than he expected and secured the wrap with a thin luggage strap. She straightened and studied her handiwork. "We'll have to keep a watch on it, for I daresay it will slip."

"You know horses," he said.

"I ought to, for my father is the stablemaster at Selta Castle."

They coaxed the horse to walk, but she didn't budge. Sareen, who had dismounted, gave the handful of reins to Thomas and took the mare's bridle. "Come along now. Don't coddle yourself." She strolled along the road, and her mare gave up balking.

"I think she will do," Thomas said after watching a few steps. "If you care to mount Wixxy, we can lead your mare."

"Aye. 'Tis a relief that you were leading Wixxy." Sareen gripped the saddle, lifted a foot, then flinched. "I fear I'm rather sore from a long ride yesterday."

"May I lift you, my lady?" He'd seen Duke Tristelle lift his duchess, and a few other men lift women to the saddle, but was he being presumptuous?

Lady Sareen looked a little self-conscious but said, "Please."

He hoped he would do it right. He gripped her waist, and she jumped a bit. He lifted too strongly but got her to the saddle. "Pray pardon my clumsiness. I haven't done that before."

As she situated herself, she smiled and said, "The first time my cousin tried, it took him two attempts to lift me high enough. I don't think my pardon is needed."

Ah, Sareen. Most ladies would have raised their noble eyebrows and uttered a politely distant *think nothing of it*. They only tolerated him because the king and queen had granted him a courtesy title...a nigh worthless syllable. But Lady Sareen...she could smooth rough spots into something natural—even pleasant.

The maid got herself into the saddle, so he mounted and they set out, albeit slowly. With a lady at his side, he should be making conversation. Thomas swallowed. "What brings you to Tristelle Castle?"

"I, uh, wanted to visit Duchess Tristelle." She looked away from him to the road ahead. "The duchess cannot easily travel to me, so I decided to come to her...and uh, I didn't want to deal with all the fuss that usually attends a lady's journey."

"Think not that I would blame you for traveling light," he said. "I didn't mean it to be an awkward question for you."

She sighed. "I suppose *I* made it awkward, for everyone at home will make a to-do over it. I daresay they will tell me I ran off like Princess Ellabeth before she became the Duchess of Tristelle."

He laughed. "From what I heard, she didn't take her maid or travel along Queen's Road."

Lady Sareen tilted her head and raised her delicate black eyebrows. "I like that point. It may even prove useful."

Much easier for him to smile when she sounded a bit mischievous. "When did you set out, and from where?"

"Selta Castle, yesterday morn. We reached the travelers' cottage at sunset." She closed her eyes for a dramatic shudder. "I had no idea how long that ride would take, for I've never traveled the courier's route." She glanced over her shoulder. "Oh, dear! Is that hooves I hear?"

"Indeed." The steady beat was clear now and approaching fast.

"I suspect my brother may be looking for me."

The pursuing horses came into view. "Then let us stop," Thomas said, "so we don't appear to be fleeing."

They turned their mounts sideways, to make it obvious they lingered. The approaching riders slackened their pace. Indeed, Lord Dermont led, with three other men following.

Judging by his wide eyes and flaring nostrils, this wasn't going to be pleasant. Before he even reined in his sweating horse, he snapped at Thomas. "Did you aid her in this escapade?"

A noble misunderstanding in the making! Thomas calmly replied, "When I discovered a lady stranded with a lame horse, you may be certain that I aided her."

"You've no cause to rant at Sir Thomas," Lady Sareen said. "Though you may wish to thank him for assisting me."

Lord Dermont crimped his lips and gave Thomas a scant bow from the saddle. "If you aided my sister, then I do thank you. Pray, let a day of worry explain my hasty assumption."

"Surely you have not galloped heedlessly all this way," Sareen said.

"Nay, of course not." He turned his winded horse and began to walk it around them, much like the other riders were doing a little farther back. "I thought I glimpsed a signal cloth and worried there was cause for alarm."

"Ah." Sareen pointed at the blanket. "I swung that when I saw movement ahead, which is what drew Sir Thomas to my aid. Let us continue on, rather than wasting time with circling."

She turned Wixxy to continue west, but Lord Dermont rode forward to grab her bridle. "You are returning with me at once."

"I shall not!"

Lord Dermont gritted his teeth and drew a long breath before whispering, "Do you have any idea the scandal you are creating?"

From her other side, Thomas said, "No one in Tristelle Castle will think it odd that you escorted your sister to visit her cousin. And since Duchess Selta did not accompany you, they will not be surprised that Lady Sareen chose to ride. Rather, they will welcome you, give you rest and fine food, and have the farrier tend to Lady Sareen's horse."

Lord Dermont stared at Thomas for a moment, then released the bridle and let his horse walk with theirs. Considering the layer of dust that covered every inch of him, the castle probably sounded quite good.

"Please do not be angry with me, Der," Sareen said. "You must know I couldn't tell you, but I didn't hide it either. I took a maid and traveled known roads."

He snorted, then turned back to address one of his men. "Return to the travelers' cottage for tonight. Tomorrow, ride back to the castle and give word that I am escorting Lady Sareen to Tristelle Castle. Say nothing more, save that the lady and her maid are in good health."

"Aye, my lord." The servant turned eastward.

Lord Dermont returned to his sister's side and spoke gently to her. "I'll not harp at you, but you *could* have told me."

"You would have insisted that I wait for Mother to return."

He grunted. "If you had refused that advice, I would have escorted you. This is about Lord Ivan, is it not?"

Thomas shouldn't ask, but he'd seen Lord Ivan dancing with Sareen at a ball the Duke and Duchess of Selta had given. And when they weren't dancing, Ivan hovered. "What about Lord Ivan?"

Sareen turned her eyes to some distant point. "He wants to marry me."

Thomas went hot all over. And the reason shocked him.

CHAPTER 4

Tristan offered Beth his hand to assist her in alighting from the carriage. When her feet stood firm on the rock of the castle's bailey, he lifted her fingers to his lips. "Welcome home, my lady wife."

"Ah, Tristan." She breathed the words so soft he could barely hear them. Greeting his wife under scores of eyes was never satisfying.

She laid her hand on the arm he offered, and as they ascended the terrace steps, she said, "I had thought to be home before you. When did you arrive?"

"Yesterday." He sensed the slight alteration in her movements, only present when she carried a child.

Her smile now rested on their son, who fidgeted between his nursery maids until she reached the courtyard and held her hands out to him.

Robin darted forward as Tristan murmured, "Remember." That slowed him enough to avoid colliding with his mother's legs...barely. Beth stooped to lift Robin, and Tristan boosted him from behind as words tumbled from the lad.

Beth hugged Robin tight. "I missed you too." After a moment, she set him on his feet, and the three of them strolled through the mansion's arched double doors. In the hall, Beth sank into one of the indigo cushioned chairs before the black marble fireplace, and Robin climbed into her lap. By unspoken agreement, she and Tristan let him rattle on for several minutes.

A footman arrived, bearing a silver tea tray, and the housekeeper followed.

Tristan motioned them toward the ground floor salon and said, "That is enough greeting for now, Robin."

One of the nursery maids stepped forward with her hand held out. "Come along, Master Robin."

He stuck his lip out. "Nay!"

Beth's eyes widened. "I know you missed me, dear, but run along now. I'll come up to the nursery after a while. Then we can have a long chat."

A storm lurked behind his eyes, but he crawled down from her lap. His little feet thumped the marble floor as he tromped away with the nursery maids.

Beth stood and took Tristan's arm again, leaning close as he escorted her into the salon, where the housekeeper was making tea. A few candles glowed from the fireplace mantel, for the windows faced only east.

"My sweet Robin seems to be getting a little out of hand," Beth said.

"Aye. His maids tell me he was 'a bit tiring,' to use their words, while we were both gone. They claim he is better since I came home. Granted, he is too young to understand, but *better* is not the word I'd use to describe how he talks to Evie and Suzanna. I have made a change. He is now to address them with the title of Miss, and he is to receive nothing he desires unless he asks with due courtesy."

By the housekeeper's raised brows and compressed lips, she too must feel something needed to be done. She soon poured the tea, and Tristan nodded dismissal.

Beth frowned as she leaned back on the ruby velvet cushions

and sipped her tea. "I wonder if a child so young can understand the idea of respect yet."

Tristan sat beside Beth on the couch. "I suppose it is a progressive understanding. I think it unwise for us both to be gone for several days together. I wish you had not left while I was away."

"I needed to, Tristan. I thought I could settle the dispute in a day, but both parties were so irate and beyond reason that I had to try to get information elsewhere." She huffed. "Which I could *not* obtain, so in the end, I had to divide the land equally between them. Believe me, I have made no friend of that widow! And now I come home to this."

"'Tis not how I intended to greet you." He took the cup and saucer from her and set them on the tray. "Perhaps tea can wait for a moment." He slipped an arm behind her and whispered, "For indeed, I have missed you." She relaxed in his embrace, sliding her fingers into his hair as he kissed her slow and gentle. "Is that a better welcome, my love?"

She traced a fingertip along his jaw. "Much better."

He rested a hand against her belly. Not large yet, but firm. "How fare you?"

"All seems well. I have been careful not to overexert, though it makes me fear I am being absurdly delicate." She straightened as he reached for her tea. "One would think I could relax with all the assurances I've heard that normal activity cannot harm my babe."

"I doubt that being irritated with yourself will make it easier to relax."

She uttered a little laugh. "You have a point." She took the cup he handed her. "How went your trip to the eastern villages?"

"The rebuilding is nigh finished. Not too much vexation to spoil the successes."

Beth shook her head. "Doesn't that always seem to be the way of it? Next we'll hear of some problem down the valley."

Tristan quirked an eyebrow. "Not a problem exactly. At least not yet."

"What now?"

"You recall that there has been a good deal of seepage below the western end of Vixicat Lair?" When she nodded, he said, "Captain Wellinstine tells me it has found a channel and now flows as a hot spring into a pool and then down toward the sea."

"Oh." She frowned. "Is it...like the healing waters of Fountain Isle?"

"Not like those in the cavern, but I understand that it eases one to soak in the pool."

"Hm."

"You sound much as I feel about it. 'Tis both wonderful and worrying. I'd like to see if I can convince the Lady Havella to leave her isle for a couple days to visit the pool. Her advice would be useful."

Beth nodded and took a bite of one of the glazed lemon cakes awaiting her on the tray. A knock sounded.

"Enter," Tristan said.

Captain D'Jorge came in and took a quick glance around the room. "Pray pardon me for disturbing you. I wondered if Sir Thomas was with you. I gather you have not seen him?"

Why did he frown so? "Nay. Is something amiss?"

"He hung back as we crossed the plain. I know he seeks time alone, but...someone tried to kill him in Maerton Duchy."

Tristan drew a sharp breath. "What?" He was on his feet almost before he realized he moved.

"Worries me, though it shouldn't here," D'Jorge said. "I'll go up to the tower to take a look."

"You cannot see the woods from there," Tristan said. "Take Captain Cotrell and retrace the road to the plain. I'll check the tower." He turned to Beth. "Pray excuse—"

"Never mind that." She shook out her skirt as she rose. "I'll go up to the nursery."

From the tower, Tristan spotted the cluster of riders with his long vision. It saved him time searching the expanse with the distance glass, and soon, he had it focused on faces. Three riders abreast in the lead. Tristan's muscles eased, for one was Thomas. The other two? Lady Sareen and Lord Dermont. What would bring the children of the Duke and Duchess of Selta to visit with no advance letter? Three more riders behind must be servants, plus an extra saddled horse. That could indicate a problem. How had Thomas come to be riding in their company?

That question mattered little. Not nearly as much as someone trying to kill Thomas. Tristan wished now that he had demanded an explanation, but it had seemed more critical to find Thomas. Tristan leaned against the window frame, absently watching their slow progress. They stopped, and one of the servants dismounted. At the glass again, Tristan focused on the man, who bent over the riderless horse's rear leg, hidden by the tall grass. Then, the front riders and the maid resumed their journey at a faster pace. Two horses trotted, but Thomas's and Lady Sareen's bobbed their heads with their running walk. Which meant she was riding one of Tristan's Moorelin-bred horses. Enough pieces now fit. Thomas's delay must be due to offering aid rather than danger. But what had happened in Maerton Duchy?

Tristan would gain no answer here. He descended the tower, sent a servant to carry word of the approaching guests, and found Beth in the nursery with Robin, once again enjoying his normal sunny temperament.

Beth raised a questioning eyebrow to him.

"All is well. Thomas is riding with Lady Sareen and Lord Dermont, so we will have dinner guests."

DUKE MAERTON PAUSED in his castle's bailey, for his captain was striding directly toward him. Odd, since he had reported this morn with the others.

The captain reached him and bowed. "My lord duke."

"What is it?"

"I've heard a rumor—one you may wish to know of."

Maerton waited.

"It came from the border market. From one of our guards who attends it in homespun clothes. 'Twas said that someone shot an arrow at Sir Thomas Kaituer."

"Is this being bandied around the countryside?"

"Nay, my lord, nor even around the castle. The guard overheard it from Tristellians, but he has told only me."

"Exactly when and where did this happen?"

"We know not. Sir Thomas attended the market's first day but was gone the next morn. He returned past noon, with an arrow tucked in his belt. Someone commented, and Sir Thomas asked if the man recognized the arrow. An odd question, that. Then a bit later, all the Tristellians started packing up early, so the guard kept near with his ears open. He heard that someone had shot an arrow at Sir Thomas but nothing more."

"Why didn't you tell me this morn?"

The captain blinked as his lips parted. The pause seemed too long. "Others were present."

Maerton's steward, the stablemaster, and Lord Ivan.

The silence lengthened, and the captain shifted. "I, uh, didn't think you'd want to give such a rumor a chance to sprout here."

"True, for rumors often suggest faulty assumptions. Anything else?"

"That is all, my lord." He bowed, then departed as Maerton walked through the arch in the low, inner wall that divided the bailey from the courtyard.

Maerton crossed it and ascended the steps to the mansion entrance, his knees alternately objecting. The pain was nothing compared to this rumor. Particularly the captain's reluctance to state it before others. Which meant he considered it...damaging. Maerton angled across the imposing hall toward his library, casting about in his mind for other explanations. A vain attempt.

He expected the library to be empty, but when he crossed that threshold, he found his son—seated at his desk. "What are you doing?"

Ivan flipped a page in the ledger. "Just perusing the accounts. Never hurts to have a second set of eyes review the steward's records and calculations."

"Do not overstep." Maerton gestured, for Ivan was slow to vacate the duke's chair.

He rose with a faint smile. "Certain, I shall not, but I am of age, and the estate will one day be mine. Far in the future, doubtless, but I should know the way of things. 'Tis not as though I suspect you are hiding something from me."

Maerton rested a hand on the chair back and met Ivan's cocked gaze. "Are *you* hiding something from *me*?"

No shift at all in his demeanor. "Whatever do you mean, Father?"

"Someone shot an arrow at Sir Thomas Kaituer."

Ivan shrugged. "What has that to do with me?"

Dismissal with no surprise. "It occurred on a border market day."

"Naturally." Ivan moved around the desk as Maerton sat down. "'Tis only the market that brings him near our land. Anyone who wished to fulfill King Carleeton's decree against the Kaituers would do it then."

"You were absent from the castle on those days."

Ivan settled into a chair and shrugged. So smug, he looked. The expression did not blend well with his oddly set eyes.

Maerton leaned across his desk. "Understand this. There is one thing that would bring the scandal of your mother's death back to every mind. Another death that implicates you."

"Sir Thomas is not dead, and I am not implicated."

"You are the only person who *wants* him dead. The only

person who speaks of an obsolete decree when both the church and the crown declare him innocent. If he dies from any cause, you are automatically implicated. He *must not die*. Is that clear?"

The clock ticked loud twice, thrice, before Ivan said, "Aye, Father. Worry not."

The very calm of Ivan's voice increased Maerton's worries. He leaned back in his chair. Had he gotten the point through? If not, was there any way to do so? Ivan had ceased the rages of his youth, but now that he controlled his passions, he was that much harder to read.

Ivan nodded toward the few sealed letters lying on the desk. "The courier brought those from Purthellia."

Maerton glanced at them. The top one bore the mark of his lawyer above the seal. 'Twas likely it pertained to Navayn Manor, the ownership of which was now contended. A matter that caused Ivan considerable angst. Not that Maerton liked it either. He broke the seal and read.

The duke tossed the letter onto the desk. "The argument that Prince Maerton obtained the Navayn estate by conquest has been set aside."

"Why?" Ivan demanded. "They defied the king."

"This *they* you refer to was not the holder of the title. Only the cousin of Lady Navayn, and he only held the land because her son was not yet old enough to take charge of his inheritance."

"But she wed Duke Kaituer, so her son, Lord Thomas, was a Kaituer and condemned. Thus, his estate fell to the Dukes of Maerton."

The current duke sighed. "We have been through this, Ivan. Stop mixing the arguments. The cousin defied the king, but Lord Thomas went into exile, thus leaving his estate vacant. An estate he inherited from his deceased mother—not the Kaituers— which Prince Maerton then occupied. King Carleeton's decree only granted the Kaituer lands to the House of Maerton. No doubt, that would have included Navayn Manor if Lord Thomas had been executed. Instead, he produced a son and surviving grandson."

Maerton tapped his knuckles on his writing pad. "Admit it, Ivan. If this inheritance didn't fall to Sir Thomas, you would not care."

"He is conniving to steal part of my inheritance. Why should I not care?"

"He has, in fact, never spoken in the matter," Maerton said, "nor penned a single word. 'Tis King Gairith who requested a judgement from the courts. This really is not surprising. My father knew our claim to that estate was weak. He even named me Naviad to hint at a past relationship with that noble family, though none existed."

"If he gains that estate..." Ivan rose and paced. "Do you not care?

"Certain, I care. 'Tis my brother's home." In truth, he was loath to surrender any portion of his lands, but he would not tell Ivan that. Nor what he feared most.

"What are you going to do about it?" Ivan asked.

"Raise another point. Keep the lawyers plodding slowly through the morass. Navayn Manor is not a very profitable estate, but it can bear the cost of endless lawyer fees. That will keep Sir Thomas out of Maerton Duchy for years to come."

Ivan halted and stared, as though arrested by those ordinary words. What did that mean?

CHAPTER 5

Sareen's welcome was much as Sir Thomas had predicted. Beth greeted her with an embrace and the touch of their cheeks. Behind her, Duke Tristelle inquired of her brother the reason for their visit, and she inwardly cringed over what he might say.

"Oh, nothing of great matter," Lord Dermont replied, "except that my sister was longing to see Duchess Tristelle again…and never has cared for the tedious carriage journeys our mother insists upon."

What a good brother! That explanation could work no matter what the servants let slip.

Beth smiled on Sareen with all the affection of a sister. "We will have such a delightfully long chat after dinner! Which draws very close, so let us go upstairs."

Dinner was cozy, with just the duke and duchess, Sareen's brother, and Sir Thomas. Sometimes Sareen wished Sir Thomas talked a little more, but when he did, his words were calmly sensible without the dramatic compliments of the young men who attended her parents' parties. The relaxed conversation made her problems seem less daunting.

By the time dinner ended and the two ladies settled down for a private talk in a guest chamber, the urgency of her escape did not seem quite as necessary. Sareen nestled in the corner of the curved sofa. Where to start?

Beth settled in the opposite corner, shoving cushions around behind her back. "Ah, now we will be able to have a sisterly chat." She pulled out a round pillow and tossed it to the middle of the couch, then finally leaned back. "Ugh! 'Tis already getting hard to find a comfortable position."

Sareen picked up the pillow and studied the leafy design embroidered in shades of green on silk the hue of a golden sunrise. She smiled when she found what she was looking for, then pointed to it. "There it is. Your signature flower shape, masquerading as a leaf."

Beth softly laughed.

"You have the best taste of anyone I know." Sareen let her gaze wander over the pale-yellow walls and soft green curtains. "I love this bedchamber. Warm wood instead of stately marble. The amber in the mantel carving is beautiful any time of day, but tucking candle jars behind it was pure genius. They make sunshine at night."

"Thank you, my dear."

"If ever I have a fine house, I'll ask you to help me choose the décor." She kept her tone light, but her smile went all crooked.

Beth raised her brows. "If ever? What do you mean?"

"I'm twenty-three, you know."

"Certain, but...'tis not as though you are ancient. I seem to recall you saying how glad you were not to be pushed into marriage at eighteen."

Sareen fingered the long black curl artfully draped over her shoulder. "I was glad then. It seemed to give me more of a choice. What with Master Wissent's genealogies up-ending all the marriage traditions, things needed time to settle." She shrugged. "But in the end, they settled back into the same place as when I first read his genealogies. I'm too closely related to all the ducal houses of Lavaycia. All accept Maerton—and Lord Ivan is determined to wed me."

"Oh, my dearest, *no*. Sareen, tell me you are not actually considering such a thing!"

"I have to consider it. His father has asked mine—again. My parents held the proposal off for a time because Lord Ivan had not yet fully matured. But one can no longer say that of him, and he courts me directly now. Sooner or later, my father must say aye or nay."

"He won't force you, will he?"

Sareen shook her head. "Neither way. He doesn't say so, but I don't think he much likes the match. My mother..." Sareen let a long breath out. "She thinks I should marry Ivan."

"A man suspected of murdering his mother? What possesses her?"

"She says that suspicion is not fact. He was never even charged with the crime because there was no evidence."

"I was with him in the church that day," Beth said. "I saw how he reacted when I pointed out blood on his hand from a scratch. I am absolutely certain he thought I meant his mother's blood was on his hands. I've never seen anyone look—and sound —*so guilty*. And when that uncanny voice started shrieking..." She shuddered. "He really did look like he was being haunted."

"You told me yourself 'twas a person very much alive."

"Certain, but that doesn't change how Lord Ivan reacted. I will be convinced until my dying day that he killed Duchess Maerton."

"I know. And I am so afraid you are right. But my mother says you likely misinterpreted because he was behaving so badly, dragging you into the church as though he could force you to marry him." Sareen sent a pleading look to Beth. "Please don't be angry with her."

Beth shrugged, though she looked miffed. "She's not the only one to say that, but if his behavior—which *was* atrocious—was the cause of my upset, does she want her daughter wed to such an unprincipled man?"

"People say he has changed." Sareen began tracing the embroidery on the pillow with a fingertip. "I see what they mean. He doesn't break out in rages anymore, and he talks like a gentleman. Showers me with pretty compliments and dances well."

"If you didn't sound so disinterested, I'd ask if you've grown fond of him."

"I cannot imagine loving him. I'm trying to figure out if I can live with him."

"*Why*, Sareen? There are other noblemen courting you. I saw them at your parents' ball a few months ago."

"Let's face it. I don't love any of them, either. Maybe I'm just cold-hearted."

"You're not, though." Beth laid a comforting hand on Sareen's arm. "You are warm and kind and loving."

"Then, maybe I can have some children and shower love on them. That rather points to the need of a husband. And if I must wed a man I do not love, then it may as well be Ivan."

Beth looked like she was going to cry. Small wonder. All the up-ended traditions gave her a perfect, loving husband—and left the worst possible husband for Sareen. Finally, Beth asked, "Why Ivan instead of another?"

"Well... Please don't think I'm grasping or power hungry." Beth chuckled as Sareen faltered, which made it easier to continue. "It's just that I've always expected to be a duchess. I know it was never guaranteed, but since my very youngest days..." She splayed her fingers on the pillow. "I just knew I would be. Really, I have tried to see myself wed to the lord of a lessor estate, but it just doesn't seem right. I would spend the rest of my life feeling...feeling like I'd taken a wrong turn and ended up in someone else's house."

Beth pursed her lips. "That would be uncomfortable."

"I know you don't see Lord Ivan as often as I, but you must

have noticed some changes in him. Is it possible that he is different within?"

"I'm sorry if you are hoping for that," Beth said, "but I don't believe it. Partly because, as a royal duchess, I know some things about Duke Maerton, and *certain*, Ivan is his father's son! More than that, I've seen Lord Ivan paying much attention to you and your family, while other guests are invisible to him. In my opinion—and I acknowledge I could be wrong—Lord Ivan is pursuing what he wants. Once he gets it, he will no longer need to be kind to you. I dread having you end up like his poor mother, almost locked away in her rooms and so nervous when her husband was near."

Sareen had barely ever seen the late Duchess Maerton. Beth would know more. "Do you think the whispers were true? That she was mad?"

"Hard to say for sure, but things were not normal in that family."

"I wonder sometimes if Master Wissent is right about the dangers of interfamily marriage. I know he is a remarkably learned physician but, well..." Sareen licked her lips. How could she say this?

"'Tis all right to talk about it," Beth said. "I lost my second babe, and then people started saying that proved he was wrong. But he never said unrelated marriages would make every pregnancy—every child—perfect. He just said problems would be less likely." When Sareen didn't respond, Beth's voice grew earnest. "I know you could if you wanted to, but *please* don't marry a first cousin."

Sareen hid her disappointment. There were no answers here either. At least she could sit in companionable silence with Beth. At home, her mother never ceased trying to persuade.

After a while, Beth said, "I was wishing, a few months ago, that Lavaycian nobles hadn't intermarried for so long...wishing someone had broken the dictates earlier...and then it dawned on me. Our children will wish the same thing if we don't make the changes ourselves. It needs to be more than just me. All the nobles need to look as wide as possible when they seek husband or wife. Would..." She twined her fingers. "Would you like me to take you on a pleasure trip through Moorelin?"

Sareen flashed a smile. "That would be great fun, but I don't want to live there."

"Selfish though this is, I don't want you to live there either. The last thing we need is more miles between us."

Sareen managed a bit of a laugh. "Truly said. How could I hop on a horse and run away to my heart's sister if I lived in Moorelin?"

"Run away?"

"That's what I did, but please make light of it if—*when* you hear the rumors. In truth, Dermont didn't catch up to me until after Sir Thomas found us with a lame horse, nigh stranded in that sea of grass. Just me and Adonna, who is more of a stable lass than a maid. Never was I so happy to see anyone!"

THOMAS FOLLOWED Lady Sareen with his eyes as she and Duchess Tristelle ascended one of the curved staircases in the hall. Dinner had been pleasant with Sareen. Usually, those who dined at the duchess's table gathered in the salon afterward, but not tonight, apparently. Disappointing.

Duke Tristelle was saying something to Lord Dermont, but he rested a hand on Thomas's shoulder, turning him to walk with them toward the library. Had he stared too long after Lady Sareen? An evening with her brother would have to do. He was a decent sort. Not that any of the nobles paid much attention to Thomas, but at least Lord Dermont wasn't haughty.

An oil lamp burned on the library desk, etching the marble sculptures with deep shadows. The duke lit a candle at the oil flame and set it to its mates in the candelabra. Thomas took another candle to the mantel. This had come to be a favorite room to Thomas, where most of his private talks with the duke took place. Whether flooded with morning light and a breeze, or filled with golden flames and the scent of beeswax, it always whispered of acceptance. Of home when he had none. The duke somehow made up for the father and brother stolen too soon from his life.

Through Tower Woods and across the plain, Thomas had wished for nothing more than to sit here with the duke and tell of the arrow that troubled him. Impossible with Lord Dermont present. More so, when Fullsham entered with a tray and poured them each a glass of wine, then withdrew.

The men settled into the leather armchairs, as Lord Dermont asked the duke what he thought of Lord Ivan's character. The idea of Lady Sareen wedded to that creature made everything else insignificant.

"I cannot abide him," Duke Tristelle said, "but you must know that I'm biased. He disdains my wife, whom he once tried to force into marriage. If he noticed my existence, he would disdain me too. He also likes to believe my duchy should be his."

Lord Dermont shrugged. "The Tower Woods portion of it, I suppose. You know well that you are the newcomer in Lavaycia, and I cannot believe you lose sleep over his opinion of that. But I, too, have my biases." He quirked a corner of his mouth. "According to my mother, I will never believe anyone is good enough for my sister. What think you of Lord Ivan's other dealings?"

"Does he *have* other dealings, beyond pursuing your sister and garnering your mother's favor? He ignores every woman in the room, save those of Selta. Intolerably rude."

"To which my mother says, he cannot show favor to another woman when he is courting my sister."

"He could show courtesy without showing undue favor." Duke Tristelle took a sip of wine. "As for the five duchesses he ignores, two cast their duchy's votes and the other three will never advise their husbands to vote in Lord Ivan's favor. Granted, his father will remain the Duke of Maerton for many years yet, but Lord Ivan is foolish in relationships. He seeks only those that will give him what he wants. Once he has obtained the object of his desire, I doubt he will expend more effort upon it. Though he may demand much from it."

Thomas's stomach grew ever tighter. How could Duke Tristelle call Lady Sareen *it*?

Lord Dermont frowned. "Must you refer to my sister as an object?"

"Only in this case, for I suspect that Lord Ivan views her as such. In fact, views all of us as objects. He guards his expressions—which never reach his eyes—but I have seen surprise when others show gentler feelings."

Lord Dermont shifted in his chair, making an odd sound in his throat. "'Tis not right to judge by physical flaws. Even the peculiar set of his eyes. I gather one lid does not work quite right."

"That is not what I mean, and I think you know it. Are you making excuses for what already bothers you?"

Lord Dermont's shoulders shook. "Indeed, I am," He took another sip from his glass. "To see if one of us can talk the other out of them."

"Neither of us seem inclined to," the duke said.

Lord Dermont finally looked toward Thomas. "What of you, Sir Thomas? I cannot fault you if your bias exceeds ours, but can you speak on Lord Ivan's behalf?"

"Nay." He smirked at his own tone. "Nor hide my surprise that you'd ask it." So much, he wanted to say but couldn't. "Why not ask one of his friends?"

Lord Dermont blinked, and it took him a moment to answer. "I'm not sure I know of...anyone who would call him friend."

"Then that should provide you some answer." Thomas met Lord Dermont's gaze until the duke broke the silence.

"Considering how attached my wife is to Lady Sareen, please grant me an in-law's fondness for your sister and allow my unrequested opinion." The duke waited for Lord Dermont to incline his head, then said, "'Tis hard for me to envision Lady Sareen comfortable in marriage with Lord Ivan."

"Comfortable?" Lord Dermont murmured. "Interesting word choice." He lifted a brow. "Fitting, I suppose, for my father once told me that when you are not being shockingly direct, you are as diplomatic as Sir Layton."

Duke Tristelle leaned his head back to laugh, a sound as infectious as always.

A little wine dampened Thomas's finger as he chuckled, for he had barely drunk from the narrow glass. At least the mirth loosened his tension.

Lord Dermont finished the wine he had been sipping. "I'll ask you to excuse me, for the last two days have been exhausting."

He rose with the words and gave a slight bow as the duke said, "Rest well," and Thomas murmured, "Good eve." They both waited for the library door to close behind him, then Thomas rested his head against the chair's back and let a breath slide out.

"I was unable to greet you earlier," Duke Tristelle said. "Welcome home, Thomas."

Much-needed comfort...the softened voice, the dropped title, the word *home*. 'Twas as it had been when Thomas first came to this castle. Here, he could address the duke as he always had. Thomas let his smile form. "Thank you, my lord."

"You had me worried this afternoon. Captain D'Jorge came looking for you—not realizing you had gone to aid Lady Sareen—and blurted out that someone shot an arrow at you."

"'Tis true. That news seems to spread like mist through Tower Woods."

"Rumor will not do for me. Tell me what happened."

Thomas shared the details, then waited, taking a sip from the glass he kept forgetting.

At last, the duke spoke. "Who shot that arrow?"

"I know not, but I can think of only one person who might want me dead." 'Twas unwise to accuse—only here did he feel safe enough to do so. "Lord Ivan."

"If you suspect the heir of the House of Maerton, why wouldn't you also suspect the current Duke of Maerton?"

A valid point. Thomas thought on it. "He disregards me. Much the same as they all do, for I am not...noble as they are. He simply does not think of me at all. Lord Ivan mocks as though there is some need for him to...make me less than I am."

"A vain attempt on his part. You are more noble than he."

Thomas tilted his head, acknowledging the compliment. "In my heart, aye, but the rest see only the decree that stripped the House of Kaituer of nobility. I am not significant enough for Duke Maerton to seek my death."

"What of the duke's brother, Lord Sathe Maerton? How does he treat you?"

"He nods if I am near enough to bow to him. We don't have conversation, but nor does he turn his shoulder on me."

"Mm. Forgive the question, but have you made any enemies I wouldn't know of?"

Thomas laughed. "If so, I don't know of them either."

The duke grinned. "You never have been the contentious sort, but 'tis easy enough to cause offense." His voice dipped. "Especially if one must judge disputes."

"Are you thinking of the widow's field?"

"Aye. Were you present when Duchess Tristelle gave her decision?"

Thomas shook his head. "We happened to join up with her party as they left Tower Woods."

"Have you knowledge of the agreement between the widow's husband and their neighbor?"

"Not of any agreement. I knew the family and that they raised forest grain. 'Tis easy to imagine that they wanted to extend their field, but hard to believe they would have traded away any portion of it for one season of labor. As for the neighbor...did you know that he is Warten—the same man you gave a portion of Berry Hill to a couple years past?"

The duke's black brows darted together. Doubtless he recognized the similarity of the disputes.

"He also provided wood for trough repairs at the mill," Thomas said. "I know not how he may have been paid, but don't be surprised when he claims half ownership of the mill."

The duke snorted. "You think he would try the same ploy a third time?"

"I know not. He is a skilled hunter, but folk used to complain that he demanded too much in trade for meat and skins. Now he owns fruit and grain fields—neither adjacent to his home site— and I fear a widow has been robbed. I do not want it to happen again." Thomas angled his head. "Forgive me if I speak too boldly. I mean no disrespect to Duchess Tristelle, for she could not know him."

"Should I assume that you have not told her of this?"

"Nay, too many others were nigh. It would have sounded as though I dishonored her."

The duke seemed to ponder the play of candlelight in his wineglass. "These disputes are troublesome, creating no good for anyone. Agreements could be written, but adults cannot read, nor do many send their children to learn that skill. They could use coin to complete their dealings at once, but they don't value coin, particularly north of the River Vale. Speaking of which, was the border market peaceful? Other than you being shot at?"

Strange that Thomas could chuckle over that. "It was. Besides, the arrow was shot at Kaituer Castle."

"Is your longing to see it now satisfied?"

"For now, it must be, though it would interest me to find the graveyard. I could not even tell where the burned village once stood."

"Plan your next visit as a group event, with Duke Maerton's permission. I know you like some solitude, but there is safety in numbers. 'Tis fitting for your position that you be attended. Choose a squire."

"I do not really have a position."

"You have more than you realize, Thomas. You speak of others disregarding you, but you also disregard what standing you do possess. Do not ride alone."

"Aye, my lord." Thomas rolled his lips. "Do you...suspect Lord Ivan, as I do?"

The duke shrugged. "I suppose, but that means little. Even if he is behind it, another hand could strike. For now, you can only remain watchful. There is no evidence to support an accusation."

CHAPTER 6

Duke Maerton took his last bite of eggs, as his son caught the servant's eye and pointed to the door of the breakfast parlor.

The man glanced toward the duke, who nodded dismissal, then he departed, closing the door with a soft click of the latch.

Lord Ivan refilled his coffee cup from the silver pot on the table. "I have been pondering the matter of Navayn Manor, Father. I think you should let it go."

What fancy was this? Maerton picked up his own cup and watched Ivan over the rim. His heir placidly sliced off another piece of ham, as though he hadn't just made a dramatic change of face. "Indeed? What prompted that conclusion?"

"As you said yesterday, 'tis not profitable. Since our gain from it goes to lining the pockets of lawyers, why bother?"

"'Tis not *that* unprofitable. It also provides my brother's livelihood."

"Uncle Sathe does not seem to care for it. He spends little time there, and the steward tells me the house is in need of repair."

In truth, his brother slept at home more often than away.

Why did Ivan make it seem otherwise? "Lord Sathe travels on my behalf," Maerton said, "but Navayn Manor is still his home."

"As to that, his oversight could be accomplished more swiftly by a younger man under the management of our steward. 'Twould cost far less than the allowance you pay to my uncle."

Maerton brought his empty cup hard to the saucer. "Are you suggesting that I throw my brother out of his house *and* cut off his allowance?"

Ivan lowered a forkful of ham to his plate and refilled Maerton's cup. "So sentimental, Father? He really is of no benefit to us. His visits do not seem to bring you much pleasure."

"Ivan!"

His heir passed the cream and sugar to him. "Father?"

"Dishonoring your near family dishonors your own house and your *self*."

"Ah, I did not mean you should send him off in rags. Doubtless, you will give him whatever allowance you deem fit. He could choose a house that suits him better. Smaller perhaps, for many of the rooms of Navayn Manor are closed up. Then, we could be rid of the double irritation—a house that none of us truly like and bickering lawyers."

There had to be more to this. "Just yesterday you were adamant that you would not give up any portion of your inheritance."

Ivan swallowed his ham. "True, but then I realized that I would likely be forced to. I would rather do so by my own choice than have it wrenched from my grip by spineless lawyers. You could pen magnanimous words and perhaps gain some goodwill among your peers."

Saving face? That might be enough to explain it. If Ivan was finally acknowledging that the opinions of the other dukes mattered, so much the better. "I'll think on it." Maerton poured cream and stirred his coffee. "The stablemaster said one of the horses you took west was lost. Why did you not tell me?"

Ivan had the rare grace to look sheepish. "Hoping it might

return, I suppose, for 'twas my own fault. I must have tied it poorly. Wandered off, or perhaps was stolen."

A vague answer, soon followed by Ivan's departure. Odd that he would part with a horse so nonchalantly, yet it did not seem to connect with anything else. As for Navayn Manor...that idea held some merit. Maerton must visit his brother. 'Twas true that he didn't enjoy Sathe's visits to Maerton Castle, but he could not tell Ivan the reason. Sathe often seemed to be studying Ivan. Disquieting.

THOMAS FOUND Jonathan Cotrell practicing archery in the training yard after breakfast. A practice Thomas often joined when he was at the castle, but not today.

Jonathan must have noticed as much, for his quick eyes dipped to Thomas's clothes for an instant—a finer vest and fuller sleeves than usual. "Ah, dressed for noble guests, I see. At least you're not daft enough to wear a doublet in the summer heat like Lord Dermont."

"Mm. Leave the bow and walk with me." Too awkward to ask what Thomas needed to among so many men.

They left the training yard and stopped by the well in the bailey, more from habit than need, though Jonathan reached for the dipper. "What did Duke Tristelle have to say about you being shot at?"

"He wanted the details—doesn't like it any more than anyone else." Thomas perched on the stone wall of the well, facing the barracks. "He, uh, told me not to ride alone."

Jonathan finished his drink and let the dipper swing from its chain. "That makes good sense, after all."

"Aye. Well, I'm usually with a company—with Captain D'Jorge, if not with the duke or duchess. But the duke told me to choose a squire." Thomas rubbed the nape of his neck. "This all seems really odd, but..." He met Jonathan's eyes. "Would you like to be my squire?"

Jonathan grinned. "Certain, I would, but why is it so odd?"

"You're my friend and, well, a squire is a servant, and I cannot think of you that way. Besides that, I don't know what to do with a squire. I never even saw a squire until I rode with the king. He has one, but I'm no king!"

"Don't the other Lavaycians employ squires?"

"Aye. Captain Hurth does. He picks a new one every year, and the former one is given charge of some men-at-arms. That seems more like military training. Sir Layton has a squire, but he tends horses and camp affairs. Yet, Duke Tristelle has no squire at all."

"Oh, as to the duke, he has two, but they have higher ranks, so they're not called squires." When Thomas only raised his eyebrows, Jonathan said, "Sir James and my father."

'Twas true that the duke was rarely far from one or the other —Sir James within the castle, and Captain Cotrell outside of it.

"There's naught to worry over," Jonathan said. "The duke gives them orders a dozen times a day, but you know they call one another friend and will do so to their dying day."

"This is true."

"And indeed, 'tis well for me." Jonathan came as near to glowering as his temperament allowed. "That stupid tradition forbidding a young man to serve under his father means I don't get to scout and hunt, which is what I grew up learning. When I'm under Captain Wellinstine, I'm stuck either on the wall here or in the new watch tower down by the sea. Captain D'Jorge has me stand watch beyond the workers. 'Tis dreadful tedious."

"You'll still have to keep watch when you're with me," Thomas teased with his smile. "That is the point."

"Aye, but moving about. With your long vision and my keen ears, the two of us should be safe enough." Jonathan glanced around. "I should find Captain Wellinstine and tell him of my new position. Ah!" His grin turned impish. "I believe squires may carry information, so I'll perform my first duty. Lady Sareen is looking down from the mansion's parapet."

What... Before Thomas could think of a response, Jonathan was striding away. Thomas stood and headed toward the mansion. It would not do to look up immediately—as though they had been speaking of her—but after several steps, he swept his gaze across the mansion roof. Aye, there she was. He checked his pace enough to incline head and shoulders to her, and she nodded to him. Was that adequate reason for him to join her? Whether it was or not, he crossed the terrace courtyard, entered the mansion, then climbed a tower's spiral staircase to the roof.

Stepping from the dim tower back into sunlight, he shaded his eyes for a quick look across the raised beds of vegetables, herbs, and flowers. Only Lady Sareen stood in view, but a loud rattle over the stone roof told him they were not alone.

"Sir Thomas, look!" Robin called over the clatter. "I can make my horse go myself now."

Thomas turned. Robin perched in the saddle of his wheeled steed, his chubby legs reaching the stone just enough for him to propel the toy forward. And of course, he was running while looking sideways.

"Eyes ahead, Robin," Thomas called out.

The lad narrowly missed colliding with a bed of laceroots.

The nursery maid caught up to him. "I told you to look where you are going."

"I was!"

Thomas crossed the stone paved roof and squatted beside him. "Ah, but remember, young hunter, when your horse runs, keep looking over his head. Only quick glances to the side, then straight over the head again." Thomas demonstrated. "Now, show me where you look and how quick you can glance aside and back."

Robin leaned over the withers like he was racing and showed off his steely gaze.

"Aye, you've got it."

"Push me, Sir Thomas. Really fast!"

"Not just now," Thomas said, turning the toy horse around to face an enclosure beneath an awning at the north end of the roof. "Off to your stable."

"But then—"

"Come along, Master Robin." The nursery maid's firm voice clinched the matter.

"Aye, Miss Evie," Robin said, sounding much put upon.

Thomas watched him set off, then turned toward Lady Sareen, who held one hand over her mouth and clutched her belly with the other arm. Thomas grinned and went to join her.

"Isn't Robin a little young for hunting lessons?" she asked, her dimples showing, and her voice all squeaky from laughing.

Not a proper sound, but it made him chuckle. "That wasn't the best advice for hunting. It might work for keeping him alive until he can reach the stirrups of his first pony."

"He is such a handful." Lady Sareen strolled toward a welcoming arrangement of table and chairs under a canopy. "'Tis a good thing that Duchess Tristelle has a brother so much younger than she. Robin's antics don't seem so outrageous to her."

Thomas walked at her side. "Last time she visited, Lady Fairiette said Robin was just like all of her sons and grandsons."

"I suppose after ten children, including Duke Tristelle, she holds unquestionable expertise." Lady Sareen spread her skirt and settled on one of the wooden chairs. "Robin is so much like his father. All that black hair and brown eyes, though not so deeply tan."

Not particularly tan, just skin a shade darker. Only that and a touch of accent in their speech set those of Moorelin apart from the Lavaycians born in the six southern duchies. Strange how that mattered to some. Even to the People of the Woods, who dwelled on land that was now part of Tristelle Duchy. Now Thomas had been silent too long, and sitting down across from Lady Sareen was not reason enough.

She tilted her head. "What are you thinking of?"

"Family likeness and whether that matters."

"Ah." Her expression changed, and he realized how his words could be misinterpreted. "Family. Birthrights. Inherited traits," she murmured. "Some days, I wonder whether we think too much or too little of such things."

"What do you think really matters about a person?" Thomas asked.

She blinked like she was surprised, then puckered her eyebrows. "I suppose who they are on the inside. Unfortunate though—the most important thing is also the most hidden."

"Not entirely. It flows out."

"In what we say, you mean?"

Now he frowned. "Sometimes. Maybe not always. Even when people speak true, 'tis not always understood. Then, there are tongues that move much but say little." Her smile seemed to laugh with hidden mischief, and he couldn't help but return it. "That's why I like to see some actions with those words. Preferably many days' worth of actions."

"Ah, indeed. For instance, you've never told me you have a fondness for Robin, but I am now certain 'tis so."

He grinned and told her of one of Robin's escapades, which led to an exchange of stories. Thus, they were laughing when Duke Tristelle and Lord Dermont came from one of the twin towers.

Lord Dermont's brow creased, and he scanned the rooftop as he approached. When his gaze reached the northern children's area, his brow cleared. Likely, he had seen the nursery maid. Perhaps then, he only objected to them being alone together, rather than objecting to Thomas himself.

"Your mare seems to approve of the castle's farrier," Lord Dermont told his sister. "She is trotting with a smooth gait today."

"Good. Then—"

"Papa, watch."

The rattling pony bore down on them again. By the time Robin's prowess had been suitably admired, Fullsham arrived with lemonade and ale.

He set his tray on the table, then handed folded documents to the duke and Thomas. "Letters from Purthellia."

Thomas didn't want to be bothered with such now, but the courier would need to know whether he should wait for a reply. The duke had already opened the first of his letters, which bore a royal seal, so Thomas perused his, while their guests waited in polite silence. More of the same from the lawyer. He doubted the matter of Navayn Manor would ever be resolved. He laid the letter aside and took a mug of ale Fullsham had poured.

Duke Tristelle finished reading. To Fullsham, he said, "I'll send a reply with the courier," then he turned to Thomas. "King Gairith mentioned there has been progress regarding Navayn Manor."

Thomas tapped his letter. "So this says. A point has been settled. Doubtless, the Duke of Maerton will raise another."

Lord Dermont shifted the chair he'd sat in. "Do you care so little for a landed inheritance?"

"I care if it is indeed mine, but I learned that it belonged to me in the same moment Duke Maerton swore it did not."

"My father," Dermont said, "told us of Duke Maerton's rant and that you never spoke a word."

"Why should I speak when the king had already done so? I will not wrangle in words with Duke Maerton, nor let my spirits mount and plunge with every letter. If Navayn Manor is mine, I will simply take possession when the court renders its final decision."

"Do you believe it is yours?" Lord Dermont asked.

Thomas hid a sigh. Why must everyone try to force him to take a stance? Duke Tristelle still stood with letter in hand, watching Thomas as though his words mattered considerably. "When I read my great grandmother's will, 'twas obvious that she bequeathed her estate to her son, Lord Thomas Kaituer. I am his only surviving descendant, which none contest." That was fraught with so many other meanings—a debate Thomas dreaded to hear. He had to turn this. "Those clear written words are contradicted by a great many other written words. The strangest part is..." Thomas switched to a quizzical tone. "The Duchess and Duke of Tristelle, *and I*, try to get the People of the Woods to write their agreements so they will be clear and... uncontested."

That drew a dry laugh from the duke. "We shall strive to keep their documents far briefer than those a lawyer would pen."

"No matter the length," Lady Sareen said, "I suspect it is *people* who make words contend, and not the words themselves."

"Astute," Thomas murmured, smiling at her.

ASTUTE? Now, that was a compliment no one uttered to Sareen at formal parties, nor on a fashionable promenade, nor during any other entertainment of the nobility. How did one even reply to it? A quick smile sufficed, for Duke Tristelle spoke, excusing himself.

As he strode away, Sareen took a sip of her lemonade, and her brother asked, "What is this talk I hear of someone shooting an arrow at you?"

Sareen choked and nearly sprayed lemonade across the table. "What?" she squeaked.

"Worry not, my lady," Sir Thomas said. "He missed."

How could he jest? Her giggle went all twisted. "Well, aye, but...'tis awful!"

"Is it? I was rather glad he missed."

Sareen slapped the table, splaying her fingers, but her brother's laughter kept her from blurting out the obvious. She settled herself by taking the drink she had intended.

"They say you don't know who shot it," Der said. "Or are you simply not telling the masses?"

Thomas snorted. "I have told the masses nothing, and you see how quietly the news is kept. The archer did not reveal himself."

"*I* didn't know of it," Sareen said. "When, where, and *why?*"

"Four days ago, now. I was at the border of Maerton Duchy for the traveling market. I had heard that the remains of Kaituer Castle are common ground, so I rode over to see it."

"Why the interest in that ruin?" Der asked.

Thomas looked at him for a second. "Have you seen where your grandfather was born?"

With an awkward twist to his lips, Der said, "Well...I grew up there." Perhaps he realized that could sound insulting, for he hurried on. "I see your point, but...that may not be the best place for you to visit."

"That is now apparent, but I'm curious. If you had ancestors buried there, would you be allowed to visit their graves?"

"I...suppose so."

"There is no *suppose* about it," Sareen said. "Graveyards are free to all." She leaned forward. "Whose grave would you like to visit?"

"'Twould seem fitting to pay respect to my great grandmother who penned that will. Also, the People of the Woods all have relations who lost their lives in the fall of the castle or in the village fire that preceded it. Occasionally, one of them asks me of that land."

A land he could not safely visit. Where he supposedly owned an estate. A quivery feeling moved through Sareen. Could he occupy Navayn Manor if someone was trying to kill him? Who? Her stomach went all queasy. She could not know, yet she dreaded finding out. That she even suspected...the man she considered marrying. Sareen pressed a hand to her belly.

TRISTAN FOUND Beth finishing a late breakfast in the sitting room between their bedchambers. The soft yellow walls enhanced the sunshine flooding in through the open window, along with distant sounds of castle life. "How fare you this morn, my love?" He raised the hand she extended to him and pressed a kiss to the back of her fingers.

"Wondrously refreshed. I cannot remember the last time I slept so late." He smiled and sat across from her as she spoke. "Had I realized that would happen, I would have bidden Marla awaken me an hour later than usual instead of telling her not to wake me."

"Then I'm glad you did not realize."

"But I am being such a dreadful hostess to Sareen."

"As though she would ever be disturbed by something so trivial. She is on the roof, at the moment, with Thomas and her brother. Ah, Robin is too. So you see, we are making do, somehow."

She laughed at his teasing tone. "I keep pondering how to keep Sareen safe from Lord Ivan."

"A definitive *nay* would be best, preferably conveyed through her father."

"Unfortunately, her mother is pushing for a definitive *aye*, so maybe I'm really protecting her from the duchess. Here is my plan. We could offer to take her down to the sea and stay for some days. Her brother, too, if he wishes to linger. We can take Robin, which he will consider a high treat with both mama and papa on hand. At the same time, we can give Sareen several days to relax and build up some determination for that all-important *nay*. What think you?"

"Lord Dermont intends to leave tomorrow. He mentioned an obligation." Tristan half closed his eyes, considering the plans that would be needed. "Since delay seems to suit your strategy, I could go to Fountain Isle first to see if I can persuade the Lady Havella to join our party."

"Perfect." Beth shifted forward as if to rise, but he laid his hand atop hers.

"Alas," Tristan said melodramatically, "not quite everything is perfect."

She let out a wry laugh and flopped back. "What is it this time?"

"First, there is a letter from the king. A matter we agree on, but certain, I must confer with my lady wife, the royal duchess." She smirked, and he said, "And then, there is a more troubling matter in Tower Woods."

Her brows dipped. "I have just come from there!"

"Aye, and you mentioned that you could not get enough information. It turns out that Thomas had some, though he arrived after your decision was rendered. He didn't want to tell you in the company of others, lest he seem to criticize you."

Beth sighed. "What does he know?"

Tristan related the details, and her shoulders drooped.

When he finished, she said, "Things seemed to go so well at first. Everyone greeted me wreathed in smiles. Now, they are... respectful. And it seems I have harmed a widow, who could not afford to be harmed. Yet if we waver in our decisions, they will always be doubted. What are we to do?"

"One thing is certain, if that neighbor tries this ploy again, the outcome will *not* fall in his favor."

"Indeed not, but 'tis Widow Marideth who concerns me. We must ensure that she has enough for her family, without appearing to grant special favors."

"Thomas can check on her when he rides that area. He has a quiet way of dealing with the People of the Woods."

"There is no denying that! What else has gone wrong?"

Tristan chuckled. "That is all for today, my sweet wife." He stood and offered his hand to help her rise. A perfect excuse to draw her into a gentle embrace. She lingered there for treasured moments. When she straightened, he said, "Let us go put your devious plan into action."

CHAPTER 7

Duke Maerton climbed into his carriage, his knees violently objecting as always. A servant closed the door, so he didn't have to hide his grimace as he dropped onto the thickly padded seat. With a jerk, the carriage set out across the bailey of his castle. The clatter of horses' hooves on the paving stones beneath the gatehouse changed to solid thuds when they reached the hard-packed road.

Maerton settled into the sway of the carriage, rubbing his poor knees. Hours he'd spent, formulating how to phrase the unspeakable, but he *still* hadn't figured out what he was going to say to his brother. He'd constructed a few explanations, but that apology... If Sathe disdained it, would there be any way to utter the most difficult words?

He braced himself as the carriage followed the turn of the main road where a lane continued straight into the woods. The lane was the shorter route, but it dwindled to a bridle path and forded a stream, besides. He and Sathe used to ride it when they were young men, either to hunt or to visit their widowed mother while she lived at Navayn Manor—the dower house in those days. After her death, he'd let Sathe live in the manor, which had pleased his brother at first. Not so much, later on. Foolish to have let things sour between him and Sathe.

A rut in the road jolted Maerton. Just as well. He needed something to distract him from this nostalgia. It made him feel older than his knees did. He gazed out the window at the groomed woods where he used to hunt. A doe raised her head to watch him pass as her fawns continued to graze. Only a crumbling stone pillar marked the border between his estate and the smaller woodland attached to Navayn Manor. Other markers traced the border through the woodland, but they hadn't been maintained. He'd viewed all this land as his, and his steward and gamekeeper managed it as a whole.

The land to his left had long been farmed, the crops also contributing to his income, along with the extra fee he charged these stubborn folk of Navayn Estate. The carriage slowed when they reached the roadside hedge that skirted the manor's demesne. A short wall supported wrought iron gates, through which they turned. The drive forked into a loop as they neared the manor. A structure designed with a mingling of stone and wood. Not imposing like the mansion of Maerton Castle. Instead, the A-line angles of the elegant manor house hinted at the look of a cozy cottage.

Just as well that it had a fair aspect to recommend it, for the front garden had been seeded with grass, and the fountain in the loop of the rutted drive no longer flowed. He had never considered appearances here, but now that he must pass it to another, he didn't relish being deemed a negligent landowner.

The carriage halted, and his servant opened the door, then braced himself in a wide stance. Maerton gripped his shoulder for support as he climbed out.

Shallow steps led to a wooden door set within a peaked stone arch. 'Twas opened from within, and beyond it, Sathe crossed the entrance hall.

He bowed for the formal greeting. "Welcome, my lord duke."

"Greetings, brother. How was your trip to Othair?"

Sathe lifted an eyebrow but only said, "Pleasurable," as he turned toward the salon. "Please join me for refreshment."

'Twas the finest room, meant for entertaining guests. Now Maerton saw it with fresh eyes. How long had it been since he'd visited here? Lowering himself into a chair of ancient style, he nodded toward the draperies. "Have they always been that shade of…I don't even know what to call that color."

Sathe pursed his lips, considering. "They must have been the green of Maerton colors at one time. It seems that dye fades to a rather swampy hue. No hangings have been changed since I took possession, so they are all quite dismal."

"I'd wager these were here when we visited our grandmother. Back when we were lads and you still called me *Viad*."

"Much to your displeasure, I believe."

Maerton snorted. "Our father's too, for a different reason. He so wearied of me endlessly correcting you, that he forbade me to do so again. Of course, he was correct that you would eventually learn to pronounce Naviad. Forgive me for a lad's impatience. The problem, no doubt, of the dozen years that separate us."

The aged houseman who had opened the door to Duke Maerton returned with a tea tray, which he set upon the table. "The tea has just been set to steep, my lord," he said in the overloud voice of the nigh deaf.

Sathe nodded and gestured toward the door. The man shuffled out, and Sathe asked, "What brings you to see me?"

That was a little too direct. "Oh, affairs of the estate. There is always something, is there not? I don't recall your man being that deaf."

"He has grown worse the past year. He and his wife really ought to be pensioned, so I will remind you that he is *your* man. There is no excess in the allowance you give me to cover their pension."

"Aye, naturally I shall cover it." Maerton took shortbread from the tray on the table. Meager fare. "I daresay the time draws near to consider changes. Are you fond of this manor, Sathe?"

He shrugged. "'Tis familiar. Not much beyond that, for 'twas always clear that it is not mine. Your steward makes the decisions without inquiring my opinion. Now, 'tis debated whether it is even *yours*—much less mine."

"True. Yet another point has been set aside. Our father once told me that the family claim to the estate is weak. A relative of the late Lady Anne Navayn once tried to advance a claim, which was countered because the late Lord Thomas was rumored to have sired a son. That relative gave up, but the king will not. Thus, it is only a matter of time."

"I see."

"If the house were vacant, I would give it up now." Maerton fixed an earnest gaze on Sathe. "But it is my brother's home. You may think me unfeeling at times. We have not always agreed on matters. But indeed, we have kinder memories too. I was thinking, on the drive here, how we used to hunt together in the woods." He achieved a chuckle in his throat. "When you were no longer such a wee lad yourself."

Sathe smiled faintly. It did not reach his eyes. "Pleasant days."

"Things were…" Maerton licked his lips. "…awkwardly left, though I didn't perceive the problem at the time. Youth, I suppose, and later…" He shook his head. "If only one could predict all outcomes."

"You've lost me, my lord."

"Please, brother, call me Naviad. 'Tis not often that we are alone together. In public, I would not dishonor you by omitting your title, but as one grows older, the things which truly matter mean more, not less."

"Is there some outcome—Naviad—that I should be concerned about?"

How strangely foreign his own name sounded. "The manor, certainly. Our father's will left me responsible for your living. If you want me to keep throwing more bait to the lawyers, I can retain the estate for your use a while longer. Or if you prefer, I will settle an allowance on you that would enable you to choose a different house elsewhere."

Sathe blinked at him, an exaggerated motion, since his eyebrows were so high.

"I wonder if the tea is ready," Maerton said.

Sathe shifted forward in his chair and removed the strainer from the pot, then poured two cups. "What, precisely, do you mean by *enable me to choose a different house?*"

"That is up to you. Perhaps you would wish to lease a house for a season until you have decided. Your allowance would cover the added expense. If you wish to own a house that is not beyond my means, I would purchase it with the deed in your name. Naturally, then your living allowance would be smaller." Maerton sipped his tea, though Sathe had yet to pick up his cup.

"You would buy me a house?"

Sathe's incredulous tone bit. Maerton's own fault. "Aye." He fortified himself with a deep breath. "This is what I meant about things being awkwardly left. My will is much the same as our father's, but...I have come to realize what a great disservice that will be to you when I pass on. I fear that Ivan does not value family obligations as he should. Thus, I will provide for you now. If you prefer to only lease, then I will leave you a monetary legacy that is in your full control. My will, I shall soon change. A fact that I prefer you do not mention to anyone."

Sathe finally picked up his cup and saucer. His chair creaked as he shifted back and took a slow drink.

Maerton longed to know what thoughts revolved as Sathe stared at nothing. Why did his eyebrows twitch? Maerton waited —a difficult endeavor.

Finally, Sathe looked to him. "I'll offer my thanks for your consideration, brother, and my apologies for misjudging you."

Maerton nodded, for his lips refused to part. He swallowed and raised his gaze from the threadbare carpet. "I cannot but accept your apology, for the fault is mine." Another breath. Damnation, this was hard. "I fear that I greatly erred in...making it so difficult for you to wed." Brittle silence. He couldn't look directly at Sathe, though he knew his brother's eyes were fixed on him. He had tied the money so that Sathe could never support a wife. The silence undid him. He met Sathe's gaze. "Do you want me to say *impossible* to wed?"

Sathe leaned toward him. "Naviad, is something else wrong?"

Curses, he still had no words for this. Maerton took a sip of tea. "I don't know. I worry but can never be sure. I simply regret so much, yet many of those things—I could not have known in advance. If I had married a different wife...if I had fathered more children...if I had allowed you to court a wife and perhaps beget heirs... But we cannot change the past. I cannot see taking another wife at my age. You, at least, still have time to marry, since I will not cling to my folly."

Sathe apparently felt the need to busy himself with tea and shortbread too. At last, he said, "You must tell me what has happened. You cannot walk in here, offer to buy me a house, apologize for the first time in your life, tell me to find a wife and sire children—and still not reveal what is wrong!"

Maerton chuckled despite how ghastly this all was. Sathe hadn't used that demanding tone with him in thirty years. It prompted the cocksure tone of his own youth. "Actually, I can."

"I'm not having it. Tell me."

"Ah, Sathe, I truly cannot, for there is never any proof."

"Did Ivan kill his mother?"

Maerton shrugged. "I did not witness her death. There was no evidence. The years passed with no other suspicions, and I allowed myself to believe all was well." Could he go on? He risked so much, but he desperately needed Sathe forewarned.

"What changed?" Sathe asked. "Did you discover some proof?" His pitch dropped. "Good Lord, has Ivan killed someone else?"

"I just learned…that…he probably did, shortly after his mother's death."

"Whom?"

"An old woman named Hettie died of apoplexy. No one thought it odd at the time, but Ivan recently implied he had something to do with it. He believed that she heard his mother's last words to him, and that she had been talking with Princess Ellabeth."

"I see," Sathe murmured. "I gather, you are trying to get things in order before you… What *are* you planning to do?"

Maerton set his cup on the table, for it was all he could do to keep it from rattling in the saucer. Sathe reached for the pot, but Maerton waved aside more tea. "The worst part of all this is that I cannot actually do anything. No evidence has materialized. If I repeat his words, Ivan will claim he never said them. Nor can you repeat what I have told you."

Sathe scowled and made a crude sound in his throat.

"Sorry to burden you with this, but you were rather insistent."

Sathe quirked the corner of his mouth. He squirmed a bit. "There is a tremendous risk when a murderer escapes detection, that he will murder again. If he did not balk at killing his mother, do you think he will balk at killing you?"

"Please remember—I do not know what happened on that staircase, save that they exchanged heated words. Ivan needs me, and he knows it. Though he has never wasted affection on anyone else—he does have some for me. We share a bond."

Sathe stared at him. "Why have you told me these things?"

"I believe Ivan is stable now. It grieves me to say this, but I do not know if that will always be true." Maerton drew a breath and tried to sound vigorous. "'Tis a weight off my chest, to get those words out. Many thanks for your time and your ear, brother." From the disturbed look on Sathe's face, he was rushing this, but he wanted no more questions. "Let us think to the future. Shall I fight to keep this manor for you, or should we three of the House of Maerton magnanimously let it go?"

"Let it go, but—"

"I daresay you'll have a lot of bother over this business." Maerton braced his hands on the chair arms and stood. "Best set aside what is yours from what might be deemed the Navayn inheritance—before any lawyers take it into their heads to do it for you."

Sathe also rose. "I'll tend to it and find somewhere to lease short-term." He walked with Maerton to the hall. "Your steward has dragged his feet on repairs. Unless you want to be accused of wasting the house, you had best send him over."

"Show me the worst of it while my carriage is brought around."

This was soon done. No damage too grievously expensive, it seemed. He would have some of it repaired. He endured being called Naviad once more—how awkward—before Sathe walked him out to his carriage. They parted company on better terms than in many a year.

As the horses picked up the pace on the road, Maerton found himself shaking. A dreadful business, but he'd gotten through it. Sathe could have ripped through years of anger. Maerton had seen the skepticism on his face, but for whatever reason, Sathe hadn't given it tongue. A relief, that!

When his pulse settled, Maerton thought through the conversation again, looking for holes. His biggest fear was that Sathe might use this knowledge against him, but he saw no sign of it. Sathe never had been good at devious dealings. The longer he kept his mouth closed, the harder it would be to ever speak a word of this.

The time had come for Maerton's next step.

<h1 style="text-align:center">CHAPTER 8</h1>

Tristan rubbed the center of his forehead. At this rate, he would need the waters of Fountain Isle to ease his headache more than he needed to persuade the Lady Havella. Why had he let half the household contribute to this plan?

Beth spoke over two competing voices. "The duke has given ear to all, but certain, he cannot implement every suggestion." She gained silence and used it to soften her voice. "Our thanks to all of you for sharing your thoughts. You may return to your own matters."

Those of lower status drifted away, leaving only a half-dozen standing around the circular table in the mansion's marble hall.

"My lady wife, I thank you a hundred times over." He kissed her fingers, enjoying the twinkle in her eye. "And I thank you, Lady Sareen, for I believe you are the only person who did *not* ask for some special provision."

"Oh, I'm only here for the entertainment. I particularly enjoyed the part about the entire venture revolving around Robin's naptime."

"Tosh!" the duchess said as the men chuckled. "When he droops, he may come into the carriage with me. Just tell me what time we are to set out, and I will ensure that Robin's maids do not pack his every belonging." She and Sareen departed, ascending one of the curved staircases that rose from the hall.

Tristan's gaze followed her. She climbed with graceful strength, one hand sliding carelessly along the black marble balustrade. He returned his attention to those remaining—Cotrell, Wellinstine, James, and Thomas. "Now, we can get this finished. I set out for Fountain Isle at first light with Captain Cotrell, Chilton, and Frith." Tristan looked around. "Did he… ah." His courier had lingered by the door rather than departing and now stepped nearer as Tristan continued. "The buggy will follow us over the ridge—and assuming I am persuasive enough—we will bring the Lady Havella back with us. Captain Wellinstine and Sir Thomas, you will depart at mid-morning, escorting the ladies and children along Vixicat Road. Hopefully, my party catches up with yours before you stop to rest at the pool."

"Two carriages or one?" Wellinstine asked.

"Two." 'Twould slow them, but with the duchess, Lady Sareen, Mistress Wellinstine, maids, and two small lads—not to mention luggage—Tristan could see no way around it. "Sir Thomas, I'm sure Robin will ask to ride. Will you take him up before you?"

He inclined his head with a subtle smile. "Until he droops, my lord."

"Captain Wellinstine," Tristan said, "you may choose men for the escort."

The captain looked to Thomas. "I assume you will have Jonathan Cotrell with you. Any objection to him carrying my son?"

"Far better that," Thomas said, "than having young Edward insist on riding his pony to the sea."

"No ponies," Wellinstine half growled. "With Marla and Adonna on horseback, a few riding horses on leads, the escort, and ultimately your party, my lord, this cavalcade will stretch half the distance to the sea."

"A slight exaggeration," Tristan said, chuckling. He glanced to Frith. "You may depart for the castle once the parties join."

"I'd rather continue with you, my lord duke." When Tristan widened his eyes, Frith murmured, "If I may, please."

"I thought you disliked staying by the seaside."

Frith's lips moved like he searched for words. "Perhaps...if I grow accustomed to the waves, they will not keep me awake."

"As you wish. Sir James, see to the food. We may need little, but my lady wife and the lads will never survive the trek without sustenance. Also—ah, you know how to see them off on time."

"All shall be done, my lord."

Tristan thought for a moment. "This all seems remarkably easy now. What am I forgetting?"

"Only naptime," Cotrell said, a grin lifting his chestnut beard.

Tristan shook his head. "That is all, then."

THANKFULLY, the weather held clear at dawn. Tristan set out with his captain, physician, and courier, up the well-traveled road that wound through wooded hills and over the ridge, then down to Fountain Isle. A far easier trip through the forest than in the early years. As they followed the snaking road down the north side of the ridge, he was relieved to find no sign of a crowd among the row of visitors' cottages, which followed the shore of the River Thane. The road straightened when they reached the grassland, and the horses covered the ground swiftly.

They left their horses in the corral downstream from the cottages, then crossed the arched, stone bridge to the isle. The guard, Torrence, opened the gate before they reached it, for he'd known Tristan many years.

"Is the Lady Havella tending to anyone at this moment?" Tristan asked.

"Nay, my lord duke." Torrence's gaze traveled their party, no doubt searching for someone in need of healing. His wife, Carlie, stepped from their cottage, wiping floury hands on a towel.

"We are in good health," Tristan said, "though my men would like to wait among the outer pools while I speak with the Lady Havella."

"She saw you coming and invites you in, my lord."

Tristan left his companions, then strode through the outer cave and passage into the cavernous reception chamber. Amidst the incongruous furnishings of carpets, lounges, and many mirrors, he bowed over the Lady Havella's hand.

"Always a delight to see you, Duke Tristelle."

"And you, my lady."

She inquired whether he'd brought anyone in need of healing, then dropped her formality and settled on one of the lounges in her echoey reception chamber. "I'll not hold my curiosity, Tristan. You have some plan in mind, do you not?"

That drew a wry chuckle from him as he sat down across from her. For all he'd known her since his fifteenth year, still she surprised him. "How do you know of my plans?"

"I was talking with Carlie at her cottage and witnessed your approach. So early in the day, and that empty buggy you brought... 'Tis not how you travel to Moorelin. You must be breaking your journey to somewhere else, but there simply *is* nowhere else."

"Ah, mundane knowledge. You have ruined the hint of magic."

She snorted in a most unladylike fashion. "I have quite enough of that nonsense, what with my fair visage and my elegant...*cave*." She ended on a sinister tone, making him laugh again, then she drew her shimmery white hair over one shoulder and began braiding. "You must tell me what brings you. Is it a long tale? Shall I make tea?"

"Not quite that long, my lady. Do you recall what I told you about Vixicat Lair, and how we suspected that it held waters like your fountains?"

"Aye, for Captain Cotrell noticed their smell at the beasts' lair, and only such waters could permit a crossed beast—vixicats—to survive."

"Exactly. Ever since the cave collapsed, water has seeped down the slope from Vixicat Lair toward the sea. At first, it just kept the hillside damp and prone to mudslides. Now, it has reached bedrock and found a channel. The stream fills a warm pool before continuing to the sea. Captain Cotrell's sensitive nose once again catches the scent that he finds only at Fountain Isle."

"So…the water has found a way out." Her twining fingers reached the end of her braid. "These waters that can mend or distort." She drew a ribbon from the sleeve of her lavender gown and tied the braid. "What do you intend to do with them?"

"Understand them first."

"Even I don't understand how they work. Only that they do."

"But you know the differences in their power." He gestured toward the deeper tunnel from whence distant gurgling issued. "Some fountains can heal quickly but can also harm." He turned his hand toward the exit. "In the outer pools, we may bathe without ill effect, yet skin heals in them and sore muscles ease. The waters that flowed through the lair allowed vixicats to breed and grow enormous. I *cannot* allow that to happen again. I must know what I am dealing with."

"If the pool is outside, the water's power is likely diminished."

"I'm aware of that possibility, but I must *know*." He perceived no understanding in her cloud-blue eyes. "The buggy is for you."

"For me?" Her eyes rounded. "For me? What are you thinking of, Tristan? I cannot leave!"

He had seen her merry, lonely, compassionate, determined… but never had he seen her calm shatter like this. He stood to draw nearer. "Let me say first that it would be a brief visit." He sat beside her on the lounge and took her hand in his. "I know that I ask much of you, but I'm not sure of the full extent. Will you tell me?"

"The sun! It burns me—blinds me!"

"I've seen your gloves and broad hats...how you always seek the shade in your garden. Veils can be let down on all sides of the buggy, so the sun cannot reach you. At the pool, we will stretch an awning. Sir James has already ordered it strapped to the carriage that will soon carry my family to the pool first, and then, to the sea."

"'Twould be pleasant, of course, to see Beth and Robin, but what if someone comes here for healing and I am absent? 'Tis sometimes urgent. You know this!"

"Indeed, and I knew you would not leave your post vacant. Perhaps you saw that my physician came in my party. Chilton has agreed to stay while you are gone. He does not know the waters, but he would do all he could to keep any sick or injured alive until you return."

She rocked side-to-side. "'Tis normal to you—this traveling here and there. But I...I have not left the isle since the days of my natural youth. Centuries, I have lived here sustained by the waters. I...I just..."

The only thing still about her was the hand that he gently held. "I know. This is the part that worried me most. Must you drink from the fountain each day? Could you spend one night away, and remain well?"

"Um, just one?"

"For certain, just one. If you cannot do even that, I could rush you to the pool for a hurried check, then rush you back again. But I find two faults with this plan."

"What are they?"

"'Twill work only if everything goes well. If anything goes wrong, we will travel the woods in darkness."

"Didn't you get rid of all those wolves?"

"All? Nay, my lady, that would be folly. We killed the oversized ones, and the packs are smaller. But you guess correctly—they favor night hunting, so I favor day traveling."

Something like a humph escaped her. "What is the other fault?"

He smiled gently. "You would miss so much in all that hurry. This isle is idyllic, but you know only plains and river. Beyond the ridge, are hills and vales. Trees far more varied than the few here on the riverbank. Rock walls and columns rise between them like a fairytale world. Instead of a river, there are myriad streams and then a beach and vast ocean. Would you not like to glimpse the sea at least once? To watch the crimson sun burnish the waves?"

Her restlessness had ceased as he spoke. "Oh, you tempt me." She stood and walked, trailing her fingers along the backs of chairs. "You should have asked me first, though. Not sent others ahead, whom I would not want to disappoint."

"Ah, I'll admit to enticing but not to pressuring you. Lady Sareen is visiting, and Beth entertains her with a trip to the sea. They will stay some days at the inn of Seaside Village, where you may also sleep in comfort."

She passed through shadow and light as she paced, for morning rays entered through gaps in the cavern's ceiling and bounced between plentiful mirrors. "It sounds thrilling—but frightening too. I suppose I can manage for two days, but what if something goes wrong the second day?"

"We will have time to resolve it before darkness falls."

"I don't know how to prepare for travel. What to take."

"A change of clothes. Perhaps a linen robe that you use in the fountains. Comb, brush, whatever you use each morn and night. Shall we ask Carlie to pack your things? 'Twould give you time to talk with Chilton, should you wish to give him instruction. Then, we'll set out."

"You want me to leave at once?"

"Soon. Indeed, you are so unsettled that I will not torment you with a longer wait."

She compressed her lips. "I suppose you think I'm daft."

"Nay, my lady, but I am now convinced that you need a change of scene more than I realized." He grinned at her. "Please say you will come."

"Oh...aye, then."

'Twas well that Tristan was determined, for the lady tried his patience. He dreaded that someone would arrive in need of her skills, for Lady Havella would not deny them. He had brought Frith to carry word if this occurred, but they were spared that delay. At last, the Lady Havella climbed awkwardly into the veiled buggy, the driver slapped the reins on the horse's back, and Tristan, Cotrell, and Frith set out with her across the wide swath of grassland. When they crested the ridge, Tristan did not even pause, for fear that she would look down upon her isle and ask to return at once.

No sooner did they begin the descent into woodland, than her voice called from behind him. "Duke Tristelle."

He shifted in the saddle, drawing Dauntless aside until he could ride beside her.

"Will you show me where you fought the vixicats?" she asked, drawing the veil back.

"Well timed. 'Twas here." He swung his arm in an arc to the side. "It looks rather different now, for we've felled trees and leveled ground where possible, so we could enclose these paddocks. If you look back, you'll see the travelers' cottage. Likely, we will stop there tomorrow."

She stared all around, her lips parted, as they proceeded at a walk into the thicker woods. "So this is the Wilde." She sounded awed. In the forest's shade, she tied back the thin curtains and asked the first of many questions. Flora, fauna, rocks, and soil. Nothing she saw escaped her interest. Not unlike Robin once his queries began. Tristan hid a smile and answered them all.

CHAPTER 9

At one time, Thomas would have marveled at such an
entourage as set out from Tristelle Castle. They numbered
more than a score. Two carriages for women folk. The men rode,
as did Lady Sareen and her maid. Thomas and Jonathan carried
the children for now. Captain Wellinstine led with his lieutenant,
and watchmen encircled the cavalcade, though they rarely had
much to do, now that the Wilde was tamed.

The captain had ordered that the children's escorts ride
behind him, where Lady Sareen also rode. A pleasant
coincidence, that Thomas could ride at her side. If only Robin
would allow him to enjoy it. Thomas guided his horse with his
legs and left the reins slack, which Robin took advantage of,
much to the horse's confusion.

"Nay, Robin!" Thomas said, recovering the reins. "I guide the
horse. You do not."

"I want to make him go."

"You may hold this end of the reins." They passed the
orchard and turned with the road to begin the long descent
westward toward the sea. "Reins are not for slapping the horse."

Robin bounced on the saddle. "I want to go faster."

"Then you had best settle yourself, or I will put you in the carriage before we round the first hill." Thomas spoke just firmly enough to gain a moment to converse with Lady Sareen. "How oft did you visit the sea before Tristelle Duchy was formed?"

"Rarely," she said. "Selta Castle could hardly be farther from the harbor. When my parents took me with them on their visits to Portlen Duchy, we usually went no farther than the castle. The beach here—"

"Sir Thomas, I don't have anything to do," Robin declared.

"Apologize to Lady Sareen for interrupting her."

"I beg your pardon." Robin barely paused. "But I still don't have anything to do."

"Oh, listen," she said. "Do you hear that rat-a-tat-tat? 'Tis a woodpecker. Can you see it? Look for a black and white bird on a tree trunk."

They exchanged another pair of sentences before Robin pointed and shouted, "There! I see it. Ehwood, do you see?" He twisted so sharp around to his friend, riding behind with Jonathan, that only Thomas's grip kept him from falling. "It flew away!"

"Imagine that," Sareen murmured.

"I hear another one," young Edward shouted, sending Robin into more contortions to find it.

"Jonathan," Thomas said over his shoulder, "ride alongside me." Now, perhaps he could—

"Why do they peck the trees, Sir Thomas?"

"To find bugs to eat."

"Why are there bugs in the tree trunk?"

"Look, Robin," Jonathan said. "Those squirrels are playing chase-me in the branches."

This was much the way of it. Snatches of conversation between endless questions. Jonathan did his best to entertain both lads, but eventually he resorted to pointing out a landmark and forbidding the lads to speak until they passed it. Not a bad plan. Alas, they passed each bent tree or contorted pillar all too soon.

"Sir Thomas, may I hold your bow?" Robin asked.

"You may not. I see a fox. Can you spy it?"

Blessed silence.

"There!" Robin whispered loudly as he pointed. "Atop that boulder. Shoot an arrow, quick."

"We are not hunting."

"But you can still kill it."

"Nay. We need no food, and the fox is causing no harm, so we'll let it be."

"Why?"

"If we kill all the foxes, there will soon be too many rabbits, and they will eat every green thing."

"I hope they eat the spinach and kale."

Lady Sareen let out a peal of laughter. Her dangling black curls jiggled like springs.

At least she was enjoying herself. They stopped for a necessary break, and Thomas found a curved stick and some weaver's grass. He hurriedly twisted the grass into string and fashioned a bow. When Jonathan returned from the bushes with both lads, Robin delighted in his new toy, while Edward gazed longingly at it.

Robin suddenly stopped his pretend shooting and stared round-eyed at his silent friend. "Sir Thomas, will you make another bow for Ehwood?"

"Not just now, lads," Captain Wellinstine said. "'Tis time to mount up."

Fortunately, Sareen's maid, Adonna, already had a handful of grass and a stick. "Cheer up. I'll try making one for you as we ride."

Moving again with the smooth gait of the Moorelin-bred horses, they followed the road around hillsides and through valleys. A circuitous route, but pleasantly shaded, and all the sweeter with Lady Sareen. Jonathan told a story, making it up as he went and letting the lads name all the characters. Excellent squire, to occupy them so Thomas could talk. Not entirely successful, for Sareen kept giggling at the ridiculous flights of the tale. She looked so much happier than the day he'd helped her on the plain.

They lunched on picnic fare, and the lads assured their mothers they were not tired.

"A little farther, then," the duchess said and returned to her carriage.

Robin soon forgot to ask questions. A couple times, he sagged forward over Thomas's arm, then straightened with a jerk.

"Captain," Thomas said, "we need a halt."

Wellinstine looked back, then signaled the halt.

Thomas turned his horse toward the carriage, and Robin blurted out, "I'm not tired."

Certain, this was a moment for a soft, steady voice. "'Tis time to ride in the carriage."

"My bow!" Robin's squeak edged higher. "Where is my bow?"

He must have dropped it. "Sometimes bows are lost or broken," Thomas said. "That is why we make new ones."

Though it seemed to take heroic effort, Robin sniffed and gulped back a sob. They'd reached the first carriage now, the door already open, and the duchess reached out for her son. Thomas passed the lad to her, while Jonathan delivered Edward to his mother in the second carriage.

"You are so good at handling him," Lady Sareen said, when Thomas returned to her side. "I didn't realize you had been around children."

He grinned. "I haven't much. Truth be told, I just mimic Duke Tristelle. He always uses that slow smooth tone when Robin teeters on the edge." Exactly why she tilted her head and smiled like that, he didn't know. But he liked it.

They continued on for more than an hour, then reached the pool below Vixicat Lair. Time for a long rest. Captain Wellinstine stared along the empty road behind them. "Quiet, everyone. Jonathan, have a listen for the duke's party."

Voices stilled, though horses could never be hushed completely.

Jonathan sat on his mount, intent. After a moment, he said, "Some horses are approaching beyond the last rise. Shouldn't be long."

The duchess climbed down from her carriage. "That's a relief."

From within it, Robin whimpered, "Is Papa coming?"

"In a bit, dear," she said. "Just lie down until he gets here."

The typical bustle began. Tying horses out of the way, stretching an awning, and arranging things for a comfortable rest.

Certain, the duke saw them when he crested the rise, for he drew ahead of Cotrell, shortening the minutes until he dismounted at his wife's side. She was stretching her back beside the carriage, and he asked, "Have you just now arrived?"

"Aye." She sounded worn. Suzanna appeared in the doorway of the carriage, Robin in her arms, all tear-stained and half asleep.

"Was it a hard trip?" Tristan asked his wife, reaching up to take Robin.

"The last part, aye. Robin just drifted off ten minutes ago, and now, he'll be weepy. Come, Sareen, let us greet the Lady Havella."

The duke turned away from the I-told-you-so look on the maid's face. "Robin, did you have a good ride with Sir Thomas?"

His squeaky reply was difficult to decipher, so Thomas said, "I believe he did."

After strolling into the shade on the far side of the pool, Duke Tristelle reached a conveniently placed log and sat down. He settled Robin on his lap, drawing him near his chest as he spoke too softly for Thomas to hear.

The duchess chatted with the Lady Havella. The long, loose sleeves of her gown fluttered with every movement. Gloves and a broad-brimmed hat further protected her from direct sun. They of Moorelin, who tanned so readily, didn't seem to understand, but Thomas had felt the sun's burn when working out on the plain years ago. It had to be worse for Lady Havella, with skin so fair.

The duchess often glanced across the pool at her husband. When the duke mimed sleep for an instant, she nodded, then began discussing the hot spring and its pool. Likely, the duke could hear it all. Captains Cotrell and Wellinstine answered Lady Havella's questions, and Cotrell helped her climb to where the spring burst forth from fissured rock. She tasted the water, then climbed down again.

The Lady Havella cast aside her shoes, hitched up her skirt, and waded into the pool. Not the sort of thing Lavaycian ladies did. Thomas glanced at Lady Sareen. Ah, that longing look on her face.

"'Tis between the heat of my two mildest pools," Lady Havella said. "'Twill harm no one to bathe in this." She nodded toward some short stumps around the pool that had been stripped of bark and smoothed. "Surely, some have already eased tired feet here. Did they notice any differences afterward?"

"Only that our feet rejoiced," Wellinstine said.

She uttered her tinkling laugh. "Doubtless."

"Animals come to drink," Cotrell said. "That is what worries us the most. Whether rodents or bears, we never want to see another crossed animal."

"Indeed not! At its source within the sealed cave, this water could have caused that. Out here, in sunlight and cool air, I very much doubt it."

"What of making an ordinary animal larger or stronger if it drinks every day?" Beth asked. "We know that used to happen, but we don't know where they actually drank."

"Could they get into the cave?"

"When the vixicat hunted, they could have," Captain Cotrell said.

"That is most likely where they found strong enough waters."

Lady Havella waded toward a stump. "I heard this pool is newly formed. Are there others?"

"Nay," Wellinstine said, "unless they flowed and dried up before we possessed this valley."

"Then the oversized animals must have drunk near the source." Lady Havella perched on a stump and swept an amused glance around. "You all look like you're longing to wade in. Why don't you?"

"Oh, indeed!" Lady Sareen put maximum drama into those words.

Thomas guided her to a well-placed stump so she could remove her dainty boots, then he pulled his off too. She gathered up the long skirt of her riding habit over one arm and placed her other hand in the crook of his arm as though 'twas the most natural thing in the world to promenade barefoot in a pool.

Some of the escort joined them. Mistress Wellinstine watched from a carriage, probably beside her own napping son. A few watchmen kept their eyes to the woods. Beth settled away from the pool, but told her maid, Marla, to enjoy it. Lady Sareen's maid, Adonna, watched from a slight distance, talking with Frith. 'Twas a restful scene. One that Thomas would gladly repeat...so long as Lady Sareen were present.

After a time, the duke carried Robin, utterly limp, to the carriage, and Suzanna took up her post again. He joined his wife, slipping an arm around her back.

"Could you hear us talk?" she asked.

"Aye."

"The pool seems safe enough to use regularly."

"It does, but the animals may still be problematic." The duke looked to Captain Wellinstine. "What do the night watchmen report, since you bade them leave torches burning?"

"Animals do come aplenty to drink. Predators know and linger near. A pair of wolves came last night for a drink and a meal."

"It won't be long until there are more," Cotrell said. He

rested a foot on a flat rock and crossed his arms on his knee. "We need a plan to deal with too many beasts."

"There is a spa," Tristan said, "in the mountains of Cayallrae."

"With healing waters?" Lady Havella asked.

"I have not heard that, but they are pleasant enough to draw visitors. Several pools are enclosed in high fences—some, even roofed. If animals cannot reach the waters, they will not congregate here."

Wellinstine's gaze rested on Tristan, and his smile slowly spread.

THAT EVENING, the sea calmed. Pebbles tumbled across the sand in the crystal-clear water that swept forward and back. Thomas walked with Lady Sareen along the beach. Sand oozed between their toes, only to suck away with the next retreating wave. She called her borrowed clothes bathing dress—a skirt covering her knees and something else beneath it, which he had only glimpsed when a wave betrayed her. Thomas had simply laid his vest aside and rolled up his trousers. Soaked now, the legs would dry stiff and salty.

Servants lit the oil torches anchored in rock along the sloped pathway to the inn. Some lingered, leaning against boulders and enjoying the view, while still on hand should they be summoned.

Sareen paused by the cliff that bounded the south end of the beach. "The low sun makes the undercut look welcoming instead of ominous."

"Light has that way about it," Thomas replied.

She turned as though to walk back, but dawdled, kicking at sand lifting in a gentle wave. Halfway up the beach, the duchess and Lady Havella sat on wooden chairs above the wave line, with Duke Tristelle standing behind them. "'Tis so peaceful here." Sareen swept her gaze around everyone. "Even servants, who so rarely get a moment to themselves, can relax. There isn't a soul who doesn't love the sea."

"Ah." Thomas angled his head toward a couple. "Do you see Frith, the blond man talking with Adonna? He detests the beating waves. I suspect something other than the sea draws him. Or I should say some*one*."

Sareen raised her brows and looked closer, then turned abruptly to the sunset. "He seems familiar. Who is he?"

"Duke Tristelle's courier. He came with him from Moorelin when the duke was still called Lord Petram and first set out to hold the Castle in the Wilde."

"I must have seen him bring letters to my parents." She tapped her toes into ripples that barely reached them. "The sun is so lovely, turning the waves to gold."

They stood quietly together. Her hand rested on his arm as the sun reddened and sank. A hulking rock in the sea grew black, and the sand island extending from it emerged as the tide departed. Waves no longer lapped their feet, and drying skin tickled. With the new moon approaching, not even a crescent provided them light.

"'Twill be quite dark once the sun hides," Thomas warned.

"I care not. I wish to see the last glimmer."

Thomas glanced around. Jonathan had acquired a torch and waited near the pathway, watching him. Thomas picked a spot he could reach without stumbling over rocks. He pointed to it, and Jonathan advanced to take that position. Already, it seemed easier to direct a servant than Thomas would ever have expected.

He turned back to enjoy the last sunlight and Sareen's blissful sigh. She swayed with the susurration of the waves as stars peeked out. Distant voices indicated movement elsewhere on the beach. Just how dark was dark enough to make this moment improper? Thomas felt strangely moved that she lingered, trusting him though the twilight hid them.

She sighed again. "I suppose we had best get back."

"Aye, my lady." He turned and led her toward Jonathan's torch. Another bobbed nearer, and he glimpsed Adonna and Frith in its light.

When they reached Jonathan, Sareen said, "I, uh, left my sandals on a rock."

On a rock. Among scores of them. "Do you...happen to know which rock?"

"Nay." By the dip in her voice, she recognized the dilemma. "'Twas high up the beach, though. Likely we can find them in the morning."

"Lead on, Jonathan, and try for sand," Thomas said. "My boots are to the right of the pathway torches."

Sareen was soon squeaking with every other step as the sand grew sparser over bedrock. Thomas wrapped an arm around her waist to support her and spare her feet. More catastrophe than help, for the torch cast shadows to-and-fro, hiding as many stones as it revealed. Thomas tripped and only saved himself from falling on top of her by stiff-arming a boulder. "I'm sorry. Did I hurt you?"

"Ugh. 'Tis nothing."

He got her upright again. "Are you sure?"

Frith had stridden off and returned with Thomas's boots. "Put these on, then we'll support the lady between us."

How foolish he'd been not to let someone properly shod assist her. He could have harmed her. In silence, he and Frith gave enough support for Sareen to make it over the rough part and onto the pathway, where steps led up the hillside. She grasped the railing to climb. Far better than his worthless support.

CHAPTER 10

Beth strolled along the inn's corridor from Sareen's bedchamber to her own. A servant left it with Tristan's boots in his hand.

Marla, waiting in the hallway, dropped a slight curtsy. "I have laid out your night things, my lady. Would you like anything else?"

"Nay, that is all for today. Thank you." The one inconvenience of this abode was the awkwardness of one another's personal servants in the shared bedchamber. Beth stepped within and found Tristan by the basin, rubbing his neck with a cloth. His loosened shirt revealed that the bronzy tan of his face and hands was not much darker than the rest of him.

He smiled at her, then nodded toward the small round table. "I ordered you some of the cool mint tea they make here."

Ah, her rugged-looking husband with his endearing ways. She sank onto the chair and picked up the pitcher. "You are so sweet to me. And don't tell me that all you did was order tea." The muslin curtains billowed into the room on a breeze from the sea as she poured. The two candles on the washstand whiffed out, but the oil flames burned steady within their glass chimneys. She took a long draught of the delicately flavored tea and leaned back with a sigh.

Tristan cast the towel over the washstand rack and sat in the other chair. "Tired, love?"

"Not too. I dozed in the carriage. Children don't know what they are missing."

He grinned. "How fare our guests?"

"Sareen is...puzzling me."

"Oh?"

"She told me dozens of things that she and Thomas spoke of —and she is absurdly embarrassed over losing her sandals on the beach."

He left a pause. "Why?"

Beth flipped her hand outward. "I've no idea, but there can be no denying that she doesn't want to appear foolish in Thomas's eyes."

"Interesting." Tristan stretched that word aplenty before asking, "Is the Lady Havella content with her lodging?"

"Oh, Tristan, *everything* is new to her today. She is like a child filled with wonder, though much wiser. I made sure she is in a rear bedchamber, and hopefully, she'll hear the stream more than the waves. I fear she'll never sleep, otherwise. But your talk of the spa today... Do you think of building one at the pool?"

"Not exactly. Rather, I am curious what Captain Wellinstine may suggest." Tristan angled his head. "Or seek to build."

"Why would you expect *him* to build it on *our* land?"

"I don't. And that is the point, my dear one. We've spoken but lightly over the last few years of establishing noble houses within Tristelle Duchy. I think the time draws near."

"But...but..."

He caught her splayed hand and slid his fingers gently between hers. With a smile equally gentle, he said, "Not right in this moment, you understand. I simply wish to start the thought, which we can decide later. Just take note of a few things. Our duchy sprawls over more land than any other, yet we govern without the aid of nobles."

"Our population is still the fewest of all."

"True, yet it grows quickly." He began to massage her hand. "Perhaps more challenging, is the mixture of peoples we deal with. The eastern villagers have customs similar to those of Verenlia. At first, our castle was entirely populated from Moorelin, and we brought our customs. Some Lavaycians—mostly of Selta and Fennish—have joined us in the castle's village. Though they tend toward views more open than their cousins back home, their customs are Lavaycian. Several families from Portlen have now relocated to our fishing village by the sea, so we have a different mix there. And then we have the People of the Woods. Who *still* surprise me."

The worst of it was, they surprised her too. Greatly. "Indeed. I had no idea they would cling so to the southern lands—where they have never set foot—when there is land to the north they can easily acquire." A pity to end the massage, but she withdrew her hand and began loosening the ribbons that held her braids coiled around her head. "What has any of this to do with a spa?"

"Those waters will bring more people to our valley. Even our little inlet from the sea draws more folk than I ever expected."

"You of Moorelin," she teased, "think fish only come from rivers."

"'Tis not the fisherman who concern me, nor the merchant ships that require deep waters farther out. 'Tis those small sailing vessels that come with other merchandise, which they are all too willing to cover with a single net-load of fish."

"Smugglers!" She curled her lip. "The bane that destroyed the House of Kaituer."

"Aye. Sir Thomas's opinions on the matter make you sound lenient. But I must point out that it was Captain Wellinstine who rid us of our first would-be smugglers and has kept any others from our shores."

She snickered. "Those stocks he erected with the words

Smugglers' Quarters mounted above them seem to get the message across...even to the illiterate."

"True, but it takes more than that. The men-at-arms under him maintain a firm watch, which I credit to their captain. Wellinstine knows the villagers now, and he can tell when something is off."

"He should, for how often he is down here."

"While his wife and son are at the castle," Tristan said. "He has spoken of building a home for them at the village, but I asked him to wait. If he lives like a villager, he will be viewed as a villager. I will not lower his authority, which is currently tied to our castle. I would rather raise it. A title and estate would give him and his lady standing of their own, still backed by the Duke and Duchess of Tristelle. Then, we would always have a couple who understand the local folk and are able to govern those who live from the sea's bounty. They would also be able to ensure that the duchy's new hot spring is managed appropriately."

Tristan pulled his chair nearer to her and began untwining one of the dusky braids she had released. "All of this is for another day," he said. "Enjoy your visit with Sareen, and we can decide this afterward."

Beth worked her way up the braid in her hand. "You've thought much of this, I see. Have you ideas for the other reaches of our duchy?"

"Not yet. Though it is a long ride to the eastern villages, I still believe one born of the House of Petram is best suited to deal near the Verenlian border."

"My parents will doubtless agree with you in that!" She smiled at the memory of the day the king and queen formally honored her beloved Tristan. 'Twas not that she was biased. He truly deserved those honors for negotiating an advantageous border with their troublesome neighbor. Fine, she was biased, but he'd still handled the whole affair brilliantly. She let out a happy sigh. "What of Tower Woods? Do you ponder setting up a noble house in that land? I swear, 'tis wilder than the Wilde!"

Creases appeared beside his nose. "My thoughts twist as much as their winding trails. It doesn't help that the People of the Woods along Selta's border see everything different than those along Maerton's border."

"Ah, Tristan, most days I'm sure you are getting Sir Thomas ready to take on some sort of role there. Other days, I wonder if you will always keep him nigh, for I think you love him like a little brother."

He quirked the corners of his mouth. "I won't deny that, but I would never tie a brother to my home. I'd rather help him find his own home. I thought that might be in Tower Woods. But though the western portion will always be loyal to him, those of the eastern strip keep muttering about how their kin do things in Selta Duchy."

She smirked and ran her fingers through her long, waving tresses. "'Tis a good thing that Duke Selta is my uncle."

"Mm." Tristan gathered up a lock of her hair, winding it through his fingers. "Enough of lords and dukes, and of peoples and lands. I would rather fall asleep thinking only of my sweet wife."

He kissed her hair and then her fingers. Which proved to be a means to draw her to her feet...then snug against his chest. Comfortably familiar motions, though he accommodated her firm belly now. His arms...a haven so warm and safe. His lips moved down her neck, and *safe* yielded to the tingles that coursed through her. Tomorrow, he must leave again, but tonight they could simply *be*. What was it like for husbands and wives to spend every day together?

CHAPTER 11

'Twas late afternoon when Duke Maerton's carriage reached the cobbled streets of Maerton Castle Village. Almost home. Strange that reaching a destination once held inherent satisfaction. Why? Just more of the same. His own dullness disturbed him. Granted, much worried him of late, but he'd made provisions. His current strategy gained him the king's favor. A welcome change after the setbacks of previous years. A pity that it was hard to enjoy.

He shook his head as though that could fling away his discontent. 'Twas a bad mood, nothing more. Probably the result of talking through the points of his new will. His lawyer was laden with knowledge, but his emotionless, straightforward speech grew tedious. At least his lack of imagination might prevent suspicion. Did he believe Maerton's explanation for going to his office in Purthellia, rather than summoning him? 'Twas true, Maerton had met with the king, but that had never made him visit one whom he could summon. If the lawyer found the new provisions curious, he did not say so. He seemed to take the phrase *possible future instability* in stride and recommended a dual-will approach. That spared Maerton some heartrending in

96

the moment. May he never be called upon to sign that alternate will.

None of these dismal thoughts made home any more desirable. Less, in fact. They were nigh the inn now, and Maerton pulled the check-string to alert the driver to stop. The carriage drew aside from the road and entered into the inn's foreyard. How long had it been since he'd shared a pint in the taproom? A common habit in his younger days, all but forgotten now.

Maerton's servant jumped down from his place beside the coachmen and opened the door. "My lord duke...?"

"I'll stop for a pint."

Surprise crossed the servant's face, but he took his position to support the duke as Maerton climbed down. The workday was nearing its end, so several folk strolled toward the inn. For an awkward moment, Maerton did not recognize even one of them. Then, as he strode toward the steps, he spied an elder man on one of the benches beneath the inn's porch roof. Unpleasant to realize they were much the same age. Perhaps the sun-etched wrinkles made the fellow look older than his years. Maerton climbed the stairs to the porch, where his acquaintance stood up with the aid of a crutch. One leg ended above the ankle where his trouser was sewn shut. Ah, he'd forgotten, the fellow had lost that foot some years back.

"Good day, Everett," Maerton said. "Seems an age since I've seen you."

Everett performed a credible bow on his strong leg. "Good day, my lord duke. It has and all."

"Come in and have a pint with me."

Beyond the main door, a massive fireplace stood with an empty grate, its gray stones climbing to the peaked ceiling. Dining tables to the right and taproom to the left, just like always. The man at the taps seemed vaguely familiar. Fair-haired with a brown beard. Too young to be the proprietor, whom he resembled. Had the innkeeper's son become a man?

He bowed from behind the short bar of polished wood and murmured, "My lord duke."

Maerton said, "Two pints of ale." Every head turned to him, and a few chairs scraped, so he motioned with his palm down, lest the patrons rise to bow. That much formality always tied tongues. He acknowledged their inclined torsos with a simple nod. He and Everett settled at an empty table as the tap man whispered to a maid, then reached for mugs. A scent took Maerton back to the days when he'd chatted easily with townsfolk. Pipe smoke. It must permeate the walls from decades of that evening custom. Indeed, the plaster above the wainscoting had a smoky tint. Maerton glanced around the patrons. They avoided staring but didn't turn away either. He felt far more conspicuous than in his young days. "How fares your family, Everett?"

"Well enough. They're all wed now, except young Neil. That strapping lad can handle anything I cannot, which isn't much, now that I'm accustomed."

Maerton answered with interest, and Everett went on to speak of his eldest, which suited Maerton well, for other patrons seemed to realize they should continue their own conversations.

The innkeeper emerged from the doorway beyond the taps, picked up the mugs that had just been filled, and delivered them with a bow to the duke. He, at least, was easy to recognize, though his own blond and brown mane was now dulled.

Maerton nodded toward an empty chair. "Good to see you."

"Been awhile," he said, sitting down. "What brings you in, my lord duke?"

"Nothing...except suddenly realizing how long it *has* been. Time gets away from one."

That got a few comments about age and started conversation rolling. Maerton managed to recognize a few faces by accounting for sags and wrinkles. One lone man with a rim of gray hair around his bald head puzzled Maerton. He could see no face, for the man seemed intent on the mug he clutched. The only time he released it was when he rubbed a coin between restless fingers. The maid leaned near, tilting her ear, then returned with another mug.

Talk meandered on. Nothing of substance. As Maerton finished his ale, he nodded toward the immobile hunched man and softly asked, "Who is that?"

The innkeeper followed his nod, then turned back. "An odd soul. Passed through, he has, a few times this summer. Buys a bottle of wine when he's at high tide, or a mug of porter when he's down to copper. He's usually in and out, quick like. Took a couple tries to get a name from him. Drossin, but m'wife calls him Old Rosy Nose."

Maerton tucked that curious tidbit away and left silver on the table. Had it been worth his while to stop? Doubtful. Better to spend time bestowing favor among the nobles of his duchy than the common folk.

WHEN THE DUKE'S footsteps faded, Drossin took a long pull of his porter. He hadn't been caught. He took another pull, trying to soothe his hammering heart, and allowed only his eyes to turn to the window. The duke climbed into the waiting carriage and drove off toward Maerton Castle.

He would just wait until talk was in full swing. That didn't take long, for everyone had to comment on the duke stopping in. Didn't seem they liked him much. Drossin slipped away before they got far into their griping. He hurried behind buildings and into the strip of woods that bordered the churchyard. This hid him until he reached the horse he'd tied among bushes in the true forest.

He leaned against the horse's shoulder until he caught his breath. That was close. The master hadn't mentioned the duke in his warning not to be seen nigh the castle, but certain, that included him. How was Drossin to know the high and mighty duke would come into the taproom? At least he'd kept his head down. Likely the master would skin him alive if he found out.

It wasn't his fault. Days, he would wait in hiding before the master came with wine and coin. And likely just tell him to wait again. What sort of service was that? Watching here and there, but only once catching sight of that Kaituer spawn. Waiting and waiting through gnats and rain and often having to fetch his own drink, though he wasn't supposed to be seen. Well, he'd gotten away, after all.

The horse turned his head and nudged him. The one good thing he'd gotten from the master. Horses never minded if you needed a drink. 'Twas only the stablemasters who caused him trouble. Turning him out of a job so he had to work for a master who wouldn't give his name and paid him to sit hiding in the woods. Trouble, for sure, but that's all life was—trouble.

Drossin tightened the saddle girth and mounted. Best get back to the latest meeting place and settle in to wait again.

MAERTON SET his empty teacup on the low table and leaned back in the corner of the salon sofa. The tea had failed to settle his stomach. Foolish to have drunk common ale. The tick of the hall clock reached him in the silence. 'Twould strike the hour for dinner any minute, and still Ivan had made no appearance.

Beyond the salon's archway, the mansion's hall door opened... muted words...then hurried footsteps. One pair running up the staircase, the other approaching.

Soon his steward bowed before him. "Pray pardon my absence at your arrival, my lord duke. I was seeing to the repairs at Navayn Manor."

"So I was told. How is the work progressing?"

"Well enough. The broken roof tiles have been replaced. I found more rot when we removed surface wood in that area, but such is usually the way of it. The damage does not extend too far, and we have adequate lumber on hand." He glanced over his shoulder toward the archway to the hall and lowered his voice. "Has an occupancy date been set?"

"Not exactly. Why?"

"One of the carpenters asked why I hurried them. I brushed it off with wanting the work done before Lord Maerton returns, but I could see that he doubted me."

"The formal announcement will be made at court within a week," Maerton said. "Keep it quiet until then. Occupancy will likely occur within a week or two more." His steward nodded, and Maerton asked, "Do you know where Lord Ivan is?"

"He returned with me, when word was brought that you had arrived home."

"Returned with you?"

"Aye." The steward's nostrils pinched. "He, uh, often inspects the work at Navayn Manor."

Maerton raised his brows, to see what more the steward might say.

"He startled a scream from the housekeeper today when he was on one of the back staircases for no reason. Loud enough for her husband to hear, which made him complain that Lord Ivan was in the cellar recently and took a couple bottles of wine when he left. Not truly a problem, since you pay for the wine, but the old man doesn't want to be blamed for theft."

Disturbing. At one time, Maerton had worried that Ivan imbibed too much, but as he'd matured, Ivan had curtailed that indulgence. Disastrous if it was recurring. To the steward, he said, "I have no interest in counting bottles of wine. Is there anything of more significance I should know of?"

"The gamekeeper reports that there are too many deer," the steward said. "He also mentioned an oddity to me yesterday. He has found a few trampled places in the woods with stripped bushes."

"How is that odd when there are too many deer?"

"If deer caused this particular sort of trampling, they have learned to bury their dung and sweep away hoofprints." The clock began to strike, and the steward bowed. "I will leave you to enjoy your dinner, my lord duke."

He exited toward the hall, and Maerton left through the opposite door toward the small dining room. Ivan's tardiness annoyed, but by the time Maerton sat at the head of the table, his son entered. Not in riding attire. Some of his brown locks were slightly disarranged within his pomaded hair. He must have changed in considerable haste.

Ivan bowed to him. "Welcome home, Father. How unfortunate that I was away when you arrived."

"No matter." As the servant placed the first course before him, Maerton prompted Ivan to talk. All inconsequential subjects...no mention of Navayn Manor, but much talk of hunting and such. Maerton was relieved to see that Ivan sipped his dinner wine slowly and the glass was not refilled until the servants removed the final dishes.

"Early for hunting," Maerton said, once they were alone. "Though I'm told there are plenty of deer."

"Aye. Newton Eberle and I took two within an hour of setting out, this morn."

"Newton? Isn't he the lad?"

Ivan laughed. "He snaps that he is nigh twenty every time someone calls him *lad*. Apparently, 'tis a nuisance being the youngest. I have found that he—much appreciates—being treated as a man. Are you going to lift the common hunting restrictions this year?"

"Likely. Speaking of the woods, have you seen anyone lingering about?"

Ivan blinked his oddly set eyes. "Lingering? What mean you?"

"Apparently, someone has been covering the signs of his stay on our land."

"A poacher perhaps? What does he look like?"

"I don't know that he has been seen, nor that he has taken deer."

Ivan shrugged. "Then perhaps he—like everyone else—hopes for open hunting and is looking for a well-traveled deer trail. Certain, 'tis nothing to worry us."

Likely true. "How are things at Navayn Manor?" Maerton asked.

"Fine, I should suppose. Didn't the steward report satisfactorily?"

"He did. What takes you there?"

Ivan shrugged. "'Tis still ours. Why shouldn't I go there? I ride all of our estate."

"Riding the estate raises no eyebrows. Taking wine from neighboring cellars attracts attention."

"That cantankerous old man! As though we do not stock that cellar for my uncle."

"Stop pretending to be obtuse. Why would you need to take wine from the manor?"

"'Twas simply convenient when I was on my way to meet Newton one day." Ivan shoved his chair back to angle it toward his father. "Why must we bore on about this trivia when you have come from the king? What had he to say of your proposal?"

Hm. Being friendly with the noble families was no bad thing. "The king is pleased. Indeed, he hasn't spoken so favorably to me in many years. He will summon Sir Thomas to the royal court and send letters of a special audience to the dukes. Likely, some will come to see what that is about. 'Tis an opportunity for you to be seen at a favorable time—to show a welcoming demeanor to our new neighbor."

Ivan smiled. "If Lady Sareen goes with the Duke and Duchess of Selta, you could invite them to stay at Maerton Castle."

CHAPTER 12

Abell clanged high above the beach. Only one strike. Thomas shaded his eyes and looked up to the watch tower, which had been built atop the cliff over the sea inlet. The ring of windows still gaped, for the glazing had yet to arrive. The sloped roof above them supported a bell chamber.

"No pattern of repeat...what does that signify?" Lady Sareen asked.

"Nothing of concern. A single ring only means that the watchman desires attention from below." He grinned at the sight of Duke Tristelle holding Robin in the window.

Ever since the duke had returned from escorting Lady Havella home, the lad had begged to go up the tower. His high-pitched voice was unintelligible at this distance, but he waved both hands over his head.

"Normally, the watchman would use a signal banner to show his need," Thomas said, waving in return. "In this case...I'd say Robin wants to be noticed."

Lady Sareen also waved. "What?" she sounded aghast. "Is there no signal banner for *look at me?*"

Duchess Tristelle peered up from the shade of a large

"

umbrella and waved her fan. "Oh, that lad. He had better not start clanging the bell every two minutes."

"Not to worry," Mistress Wellinstine said. "My husband went up with them. He has strictly charged that Edward may only ring the bell on his birthday or if an adult has ordered the ringing. I cannot imagine the duke contradicting him, for false alarms breed confusion."

"Ah, that explains it," Sareen said. "I couldn't help but notice Edward was ready and waiting when the priest requested that the bell be rung for the rest day gathering."

"Edward never misses that opportunity when we are by the sea," his mother said with an amused smile.

"'Tis no marvel," Sareen replied. "Such fun, all the children had that day."

Two fishing boats drew near, their bowmen leaning forward to watch the shifting sands amidst shouts of *port*, *starboard*, *steady on*, or *hold*. Then, fishermen leapt into the shallows and dragged their boats as far up the beach as the waves would assist. The offloading began.

Sareen wrinkled her nose, and Thomas took the opportunity to ask, "Would you care to walk with me to the south cliff, my lady?"

"Always." She rested a hand on his offered arm, her borrowed skirt spreading like new leaves unfurling in spring. "You have excellent timing. You never fail me when the boats come ashore."

"Do you think I haven't noticed your opinion of the fine scent of fish?"

She laughed. "Nay, I do not think that at all. Or is it perhaps your opinion too?"

His shoulders shook. "Alas, my nose and tongue are not as impressed with the sea as my ears and eyes are."

"Too true."

They stepped over the many rivulets that the valley stream

etched across the beach. The flow seemed to pick new courses every time the tide went out.

"What are your favorite things of Selta Duchy?" he asked, then savored the lilt of her voice as she described her joys. Extensive gardens beyond the castle walls...riding on the bridle paths...midsummer night, when the castle was brilliantly lit with lanterns and torches, and everyone from the least to the greatest danced all night. 'Twas gentle joy to listen to her. He angled his steps toward her favorite bench near a jutting boulder.

"What of you?" she asked, gathering her skirt to sit. The duchess called it a walking skirt, but on Sareen, it nigh brushed the sand. "What do you love most and least in Tower Woods?"

"'Tis a shame to say it, but they are one and the same. The rising mist at dawn is more beautiful than an ocean sunset, but the damp nights are aggravating."

"Rising mist? I don't much care for cloudy days."

"'Tis not clouds that I mean. When the day is fair, sunlight slants between the trunks and lights up the mist as it drifts. As a lad, I would climb into a broad maple every morn and watch the mist float up from the land to the tower tree spires, then vanish away."

Her smile was half wonder. "I wish I could see it."

"Come with us when next we ride south."

Before she could answer, a voice called out, "Letters." Frith had returned from a ride to the castle. He stood on the lowest landing of the pathway stairs, waving a handful of paper overhead. He looked all around, then apparently satisfied that he had been heard, tucked the letters back into the satchel he carried over one shoulder and descended to the rock-strewn sand.

Sareen stood, her brow showing a crease of trouble. "I suppose we should see what has come."

Thomas offered his arm to Sareen again and spotted the duke and Captain Wellinstine on the cliff ledge that had been widened into a walkway down from the tower. Each kept a firm grip on his son, for the cedar slat railing was not yet completed all the way to the top.

Frith gave letters to the duchess, then turned to Thomas and Sareen as they reached him. He handed a letter bearing the royal seal to Thomas. "I have no letters for you, Lady Sareen, but I bring you word from the watch tower of Tristelle Castle. A carriage and riders approach along Queen's Road, with the colors of Selta. Likely, they will reach the castle by this eve."

She murmured thanks, but her voice sounded dull.

The duchess was already reading a letter that also bore the royal seal. An ordinary occurrence for her, since she was also a princess of Lavaycia. Not ordinary at all for Thomas. Despite the king's and queen's favor, he was, after all, just a commoner.

He broke the seal and read his letter, then read the short summons again. *Pertaining to Navayn Manor,* it said. He refolded the letter while his stomach did strange things. The manor he refused to think about, because it was his but not his. Summoned to an audience...did that mean something was about to happen? To make it truly his? Or to confirm that it never would be? Which did he want? He tried to figure it out as the duke reached them and perused the letter the duchess handed to him.

Thomas took a few steps away and looked out to the sea. In truth, he dreaded both outcomes. Hard enough to prepare oneself for bad news. How did one prepare for contradictory forms of bad news? Separate them? Absorb each on its own merit?

He imagined hearing the words. His great-grandmother's will set aside. If so, they would dishonor the late Lady Navayn. That would anger him for her sake. For his own sake... Finally, he acknowledged that he would feel...robbed...devastated. So strange for an estate that he refused to consider his own. He smirked. Apparently, he had been fooling himself on that point.

What if they declared him undisputed owner of Navayn Manor? Hair raised on his arms. *What* would he do with an estate? He swallowed hard. He'd best get this under control, or he'd be a tongue-tied fool in an audience before the king and queen. What ailed him that warranted a tight chest and all these tingles? How could owning an estate unhinge him so? Worse than having an arrow shot at him! Oh, curse upon curse, would he live in that friendless duchy as a hunted man? He let that simmer for a moment. Oddly enough, that was not as intimidating as finding himself responsible for an estate.

Words behind him penetrated...discussion of whether to leave for the castle after lunch or tomorrow morn. Footsteps crunched the sand, stopping beside him.

Jonathan asked, "Do you have any particular orders for me?"

"We shall ride with the duke and duchess. Prepare to set out."

THE RIDE UP to the castle was always slower than the descent, but at least the party was smaller. The Wellinstines remained behind, Sir James and Frith had ridden ahead, and Robin started the journey in the single carriage with the duchess and Lady Sareen. Nor did they pause at the hot spring, for the duke and duchess wanted dinner at the castle, even if it must be a late meal. The only pauses would be short necessary stops.

The ride allowed plenty of time for Thomas to mull over unanswerable questions.

A few hours into the journey, Duke Tristelle said, "Ride ahead with me, Sir Thomas." Glancing back a few yards to where Captain Cotrell rode with his son Jonathan, the duke said, "Give us space," then quickened the pace of his fine black stallion.

Thomas matched his speed and awaited his words.

"You barely open your lips," the duke said. "Do you dwell on the summons to the royal audience?"

"Aye, wondering what it means."

"Your days of avoiding the subject of Navayn Manor are over. What think you of it?"

"First, I am guessing that something has been…or will be…decided." Thomas angled a questioning look at the duke, always wondering whether he guessed such matters aright.

"Likely." The duke shifted his legs to slow his horse and maintain the distance from their party.

Thomas could no longer hear the father and son's conversation behind them. A relief to have private words with the duke. "I am so torn over the manor. I admit, 'twould seem unjust if they tell me it is not mine. And yet, I know not what to do with a house…especially one I have never seen. What do I know of managing an estate? If there are servants, would they stay? If they do, would they resent me and remain loyal to the Maertons? How would I even know? And if they must be told what to do, how would I know what orders to give them? If I must hire new workers, I would be even more lost."

"Valid concerns."

Thomas rode a few paces in silence. "In truth…if you asked me whether I wanted a fine house, I would say *certain*. But if you asked me whether I want to live in Maerton Duchy, I would say *never*!"

"Mm. What if I asked you whether you wanted to live in the land of your ancestors?"

Thomas looked sideways at him, as a surge spread through his chest. The indescribable feeling that came in moments like this. "That is more certain than the offer of a fine house. But I…I don't know if…if it is what I believe it to be. The land is, of course, but then…it really isn't about the land. It seems to me that 'tis the people who matter. My ancestors were driven out, along with everyone who may have supported them." He huffed. "And criminals."

"I wouldn't worry about the criminal contingent anymore. There will always be a few of that ilk, but the king was thorough, and we have maintained order since then." The duke seemed to ponder, a slight divot forming between his brows. "Those who were driven out may not be the only ones who could think favorably of the House of Navayn."

"The House of Navayn doesn't really exist anymore."

The duke raised his eyebrows. "Do you exist?"

"Well, aye, but my name is Kaituer."

"Mm. The Kaituer who feels in his heart that it would be unjust if he were denied Navayn Manor." The duke shook his head.

Thomas rubbed the back of his neck. "I know." He half-groaned the words. "The restored exile. The one who is shot at if he sets foot at the ruins of Kaituer Castle—while the king seeks to restore the inheritance that does not bear his name."

The duke nudged his horse closer and clapped a hand on Thomas's shoulder. Dauntless uttered a threatening neigh, startling Thomas's mount into angling away.

Thomas smirked. "No wonder the stablemaster says Dauntless ranks himself higher than the duke."

The duke admonished his horse. "You are an arrogant creature!" He reined him back to his place on the road. When the horses settled into their gaits, he asked, "Are you concerned for your life if you dwell at Navayn Manor?"

"The thought does occur. 'Tis pleasant to ride with Jonathan, though, and I will have little cause to be alone. In truth, I worry more over managing an estate."

"As though you have not a single friend to ask for advice."

Thomas grinned. "I know. A considerable ride, though...not to mention the need to *find* you, and possibly Sir James as well."

"I hope to ease travel in future," the duke said, "but that is for another day. Many things are yet unknown. Even whether you are about to receive your inheritance. 'Tis too early to make plans, but not too early to view possibilities in another way." Thomas met the duke's gaze, as he said, "Think back to your youth and compare the lad Tom from Tower Woods to Sir

Thomas of Tristelle Duchy. Are you not more capable of taking on an estate today than five years ago?"

"Well, aye, but still far from knowing all that I should."

"Perceiving where you lack knowledge nearly always causes you to gain it. You had never possessed a single coin in Tower Woods. Now, you manage what you earn. You do my bidding without oversight among the People of the Woods. After I bade you take on a squire, you have not hesitated to give him orders. I suspect that your early years cause you some needless self-doubt, but you *do* step up to whatever challenge is presented. You are more capable than you realize."

Thomas's shoulders eased. "Your encouragement...I don't know how you do it. 'Tis as though I go from the ground to the top of the highest tower tree in a moment."

"I am only successful because you value my opinion highly."

What exactly did that mean? "Did you have someone to encourage you when you were young?"

"Aye—my father."

"If only I could keep you with me for all the times when I flop back to the ground."

"You don't need me every moment," the duke said. "A drawback of being the ninth child was losing my father quite early. My eldest brother filled the gap some, but no person can always be on hand when you need him."

"I wish I possessed your steadiness."

A puff of air escaped the duke's lips. "If only you knew how frustrated I am by the contradictory needs in my scattered duchy."

Thomas blinked at both his tone and words. Before he could think of a response, the duke continued.

"I had too much loss when I was nigh your age, and a priest suggested I read the holy book. Which only made me angry, because it tells so often of how much we can overcome, and I felt only defeat. But then I read one of the passages about how much our holy Father loves us. I knew that already, but I *truly* saw it that night. Understood that it meant He loves *me*. The following words extolled His greatness, and I grasped that too. The next time I read about overcoming challenges, I knew the one speaking to me—and *I valued His opinion*. That was the first time my confidence soared like an eagle, *far* above a tower tree. Much higher than my natural father could lift me. Not every day that followed has been easy, but I know now to angle my wings into the wind of *God's* opinion and rise back up."

Thomas rode such a wind himself. Not unfamiliar—for he, too, read the holy book—but 'twas still new somehow. "That… that part about valuing God's opinion. I've never thought of it thus."

The duke drew a breath as if to answer, but Captain Cotrell shouted, "My lord, we need a halt."

Turning Dauntless, the duke rode back down the slope to the carriage. Thomas dismounted, for they had covered a good distance without a break.

A moment later, Jonathan rode nigh and also dismounted. "We'll take some minutes here and rest the horses." He found a tree with a low branch and tied his mount. "We've not had time to talk, what with leaving so hurried, and I am fair bursting with curiosity. What is this summons from the king about?"

Thomas told him briefly of the contested will that might give him Navayn Manor. "I don't know what this audience will yield, but it could be the final decision, one way or another. Regardless, we must attend. Duke Tristelle says we'll rest tomorrow at the castle, then ride south through Tower Woods—maybe tend to things for a couple days—then on to Fraetinloch Palace in Purthellia. I don't suppose you've seen the capital city of Lavaycia yet, have you?"

"Nay," Jonathan said with a dismissive gesture. "This Navayn Manor—where exactly is it?"

"In Maerton Duchy. I've never seen it, but I understand the estate's woodland borders the demesne of Maerton Castle."

Jonathan whistled. "You're telling me, we would be living right next to the people who want you dead?"

Thomas crimped the corners of his mouth. "I never learned who shot that arrow, but—'tis true, living nigh to someone who is after my blood isn't the most pleasant thought."

"Our blood. And you've less to worry over than I have."

Thomas stilled in surprise. "Aye, we're in it together, but what mean you? Do you think I wouldn't defend you with as much loyalty as you would defend me?"

"With loyalty, aye. With skill, nay. If we fight at a distance, we are safe enough, for even my father cannot match your aim with a bow. But if we face a near fight, you'll likely watch me die. Certain, they would come two against us. 'Twill be up to me to defeat them both, since you'll not lift a sword."

"Well...I... Jonathan, you know how I feel about swords."

"I've heard the words. Swords are only for killing men, you say—but 'twas an arrow from your bow that killed that assassin and saved the king's life. So, your words make no sense to me. You could at least defend me with a sword, even if you didn't kill our assailants. But they won't wait for you to nock an arrow."

"At close quarters, I can defend with any staff or cudgel."

"Prove it." Jonathan drew his sword, and Thomas glanced around for a stout branch. Jonathan stepped near and growled, "Too late—you're already dead."

He'd leveled his sword, inches away, but Thomas said, "Not so. They would have to dash from cover. I would have a moment to react."

"Every friend who arrives at the castle has a sword belted on. You know not who your enemy is. Anyone who shot an arrow from hiding would also pretend friendship." Jonathan stepped back. "But let's try this dash from cover. Get you ten feet distant."

Thomas ran between trees and grabbed a fallen branch he had spied. Jonathan charged for him, teeth gritted. The branch was thick but light—rotten. Thomas realized his mistake at once. A swing and chop. Jonathan's sword severed the branch.

He lunged forward, sword poised. "You are dead again."

Thomas spun away behind a trunk. He couldn't stop, for Jonathan followed. He used some moves he'd learned ages ago, but unknown ground made them risky. He threw the next branch between Jonathan's legs and snapped a live branch into his face, but Thomas could not gain enough distance to set an arrow to the bow he wore over his shoulder. He grabbed a heavier branch and parried a few strikes of the sword.

"I could have taken your hand on that one," Jonathan said, "so that would soon be a kill." Blade and wood continued to swing. Jonathan dodged an uppercut and shortened Thomas's branch. "You're thrice dead. How many more do you want?"

Thomas kept on, for he had learned staff fighting in Tower Woods, and Jonathan trained in a yard. Thomas defended successfully several times, then a sapling fouled one of his swings.

Jonathan grabbed a branch, too, tripped him with it, and stabbed the dirt as Thomas rolled away, hampered by the bow and quiver he wore. "I missed you on purpose. You are dead again."

A shout of "Hold!" from downhill ended it. "You're frightening Robin," the duke said.

Indeed, a wail shrieked behind his words.

"Uh-oh." Jonathan sheathed his sword and offered his hand. "We'd best walk down as friends."

Thomas stood, cleared the anger from his face, and gripped Jonathan's shoulder as he turned to walk with him. Charming. Everyone was watching, including the ladies. Even from this distance, Lady Sareen's eyes looked like saucers around a teacup. Doubtless, he was covered in dirt and leaves. "All is well, Robin," Thomas said, loudly. "We were just sparring for fun." Between unmoving lips, he whispered, "I could strangle you."

"Sorry," Jonathan whispered between closed teeth.

His sincere tone changed nothing. Their audience had doubtless heard every time Jonathan claimed a killing blow. Thomas's spirits plunged from the treetops to the dirt. His friend had proven his point, but to little purpose. Swordsmanship took years to learn, and Thomas had none.

Lady Sareen's gaze had narrowed and pinned Jonathan with accusation. "My brothers do not spar like that—with steel against sticks."

"Blame him not," Thomas said. "I bear no sword in honor of my grandfather's oath to never take up arms against the House of Fraetinloch. He broke his sword that day, and no Kaituer has carried one since."

The tilt of her head and twitch of her brow showed confusion. "But you have sworn allegiance to the king."

The common response. 'Twas why he rarely offered this explanation. "So, too, had Lord Thomas." And yet his grandfather had been hunted afterwards. Thomas knew how that felt.

"'Tis true," the duchess said. "Written in a letter, still stored in the royal archive. Such a curious tradition, it has created." She smiled at Sareen in the way they shared. "And don't we have our own views on tradition?"

Lady Sareen returned the smile, which doubtless meant something between them. The women turned their attention to feeding fruit, cheese, and bread to sleepy-eyed Robin.

Thomas slipped behind the carriage, where Jonathan swept dirt from his back and hair while promising to never make such a scene again.

"I said I forgive you," Thomas muttered. "Cease reminding me."

The duke soon called for everyone to mount, which instantly prompted Robin to ask, "May I ride with you, Papa?" There was nothing like food to restore the lad's joy.

Thomas couldn't prevent a grin as Duke Tristelle smiled on his son and replied, "Aye, Robin." The duke mounted Dauntless, then reached down to take Robin as Captain Cotrell lifted him. The captain mounted last, and the duke said, "Sir Thomas, take the lead."

Surprising. Thomas took a quick check that everyone was ready, motioned Jonathan to his side, then set out. "Keep an ear to those behind," he said, "and glance back now and then."

"Aye, sir."

Why had the duke given him the lead? Possibly because he carried his son, but the more Thomas thought on it, the more certain he became that the duke was hinting at what Thomas was capable of. Hinting at the future.

Then, Robin's voice reached him, clear in the woodland's calm. "I know, Papa, but it scared me because I just dreamed someone was chasing Sir Thomas, and the bad man was gonna hurt him. I don't want *anyone* to hurt Sir Thomas."

CHAPTER 13

Sareen descended from Duchess Tristelle's carriage, but all her thoughts were on the carriage from Selta. It stood nigh the stable, on the far side of Tristelle Castle's bailey. The horses must have been led off somewhere. Likely, her mother was in the mansion. A sweet mother when she was content. Guilt wormed through Sareen, for her hasty departure...for dreading the imminent meeting with her mother...for not wanting to go home. Why didn't she? 'Twas a good home, filled with happy memories. Mostly. And *mostly* was enough, after all.

She followed Duchess Tristelle up the terrace steps to the half-moon courtyard that spread along the mansion's frontage. If only she could borrow some of her dear cousin's confidence. A small crowd gathered—their party and the household servants who greeted them. Her brother strolled from the arched double doors.

"Dermont!" She extended a hand to him. "I didn't expect *you* to welcome me here."

He clasped her fingertips briefly. "Neither did Sir James, who arrived a few minutes after I did."

Sareen looked at the doors again. "Where is Mother?"

"At home." He burst out laughing, so, doubtless, her face

betrayed her relief. "Come within. The sooner everyone gets settled, the sooner we can eat."

She accompanied him but said, "I'm settled enough, and we are not changing for dinner." They crossed the entry portion of the hall, and she drew him toward the elegant indigo seating framed by the twin staircases and gallery. "Why the carriage, if Mother did not come?"

"She was going to—carrying on about the scandal and all."

"Is it bad?"

Dermont shrugged. "There was some local chatter about how you left. Father made little of it, but Mother made much. Until she wore out his patience, anyway. I wish you could have heard him, because it was all I could do not to laugh aloud."

Dermont mimicked their father when his speech grew measured with irritation. "He declared, 'Our daughter is visiting her cousin, the royal Duchess of Tristelle.' Then, he ran through every description and title for her that he could call to mind. 'The daughter of my sister, the queen. A princess of Lavaycia. Second heir of the House of Fraetinloch. Our daughter's dear friend since childhood. What scandal do you speak of?' It must have taken Mother a full minute to mutter, 'Well, that is true, of course, but she shouldn't have left that way.' To which, he said, 'She is of age and may come and go as she pleases.'"

Sareen wiggled her shoulders and exhaled an ecstatic, *ooo*.

"Then, Mother spent a day on, 'We'll see how she likes getting along without her gowns.' I don't recognize the one you're wearing, by the way."

"My 'dear friend since childhood,'" Sareen quoted, "lent it to me. How can she think Beth wouldn't take care of me?"

"Apparently, she doesn't, for the next day, she ordered your travel trunks packed. She was going to come, too, but Father must have talked her out of it. She begged me to come so you would have a proper escort." He dramatically gripped an imaginary sword hilt. "For your dangerous journeys."

"Truly? Did she say that?"

"'Course not, silly. But the fuss is ridiculous, all the same."

The duke came to greet Dermont, and before much longer, they were all sitting down to a late dinner, with much talk of the seaside, the upcoming trip through Tower Woods, and the reason for it. Her brother had left Selta Castle before notice of the royal audience arrived there, so he was surprised, but said little of the news. That subject made Sir Thomas silent, too, but he spoke more freely now than when she had first come.

As the duchess was yawning over her dessert, Lord Dermont looked to Sareen. "Dear though you are, my sister, I refuse to journey tomorrow. The next day, our hosts set out, and I shall escort you wherever you like. What is your pleasure?"

"Certain, I shall be at court for the audience." She tapped the tablecloth. "If I go home first...nay, our parents won't know that I wish to travel with them and may set out before we arrive." She divided a requesting look between the head and foot of the table. "May I trespass on your welcome a little longer and travel with you through Tower Woods?"

"You may," the duke said. "Not that I would deny your right to travel a public road. I am planning a slow journey to tend a couple matters. It may grow tedious for you, but you can always proceed ahead of us."

THE NEXT MORN, Beth drooped over her plate of toast. Likely, her guests had already broken their fast in the dining room. A pity that the sunny sitting room between her and Tristan's bedchambers did nothing to lift her spirits. His approaching footsteps did, though.

She managed a tired smile, as he entered and said, "Good morn, my love." He sat in the other chair beside the table, studying her face. "I was going to ask if you slept well, but I think I already know the answer."

"I tossed and turned all night, and I swear I was awake every time the hour struck."

"'Tis well we are home again, with no pressing matters on hand."

"Tristan, I have guests."

"Sareen loves you too dearly to make demands when you need rest. Besides, they are going into the village to shop before we set out tomorrow." He compressed his lips for a second. "I know you'll say you don't want to coddle yourself, but, my dear one, will you at least consider staying home? The trip will be slow and tiresome. Not the sort of journey Robin could endure. He would be happier to stay home if you were here. And most important of all—you could relax."

Beth cradled her teacup. "I hate to admit it, but I was wondering if I should stay." Tristan looked pleasantly surprised, so she smirked at him before taking another sip. "I would so like to attend the audience for Thomas's sake. And for Sareen, too, since Lord Ivan will probably attend. I ought to talk with Duchess Selta, and I haven't seen my parents in months."

"All fine desires, but none more important than your rest and health."

"What a surprise that you would say so."

"Nay, you are not surprised, for you know how much I love you." He took her free hand, doubtless to kiss her fingers, then paused. "What is this? Breadcrumbs?"

"And butter." She wiped her fingertips on his chin.

"You fairy imp!"

She laughed and tossed him her napkin. She hadn't buttered her toast, but she wouldn't tell him that. "Wait until you hear what else I have come around to."

"What?"

"Well...you know I didn't like your idea at first, but...I think it would be wise to have a lord and lady we can trust down by the sea. You may tell the king and queen what we are thinking of.

'Tis our right to grant the land and title, but 'tis also better not to surprise them."

"I shall," he said, and she loved the warmth in his smiling brown eyes. "We will decide what land to grant when I return."

THOMAS LED the small party under the gatehouse, then took the left turn that curved around into the village. The group had expanded after Lady Sareen said at breakfast that she needed some things. Her maid, Adonna, walked with them, clutching a small leather purse. Likely the first time she had been paid a wage. Frith had announced that he needed tooth powder when he saw who was setting out. Doubtless, pure coincidence. Naturally, Jonathan shadowed them and Lord Dermont came, too, belting on his sword when they set out. Why did he need a sword in Castle Village? A habit, perhaps, but that made Thomas ponder Jonathan's words again.

Though this was not a market day, one street was lined with two-story, wooden structures. Homes above and shops below, most with displays open to passers-by. Lord Dermont escorted his sister as they strolled past the wares for sale, but when the talkative proprietor of a watch shop distracted him, Thomas promptly offered Lady Sareen his arm.

He waited patiently while she helped Adonna with her first purchase, then he pointed out a sign with a black and yellow bumblebee. "We must stop at this next shop."

"A honey shop?"

"That, too, but they have the finest lotions in the duchy."

His words reached the young proprietress, and she stepped forward. Thick braids the color of raspberry honey were double-coiled around her head. "Ah, Sir Thomas, you are kind, but I will not deny 'tis true."

Merry as she had always been. "Good morn, Mistress Nellian," Thomas said. "Have you persuaded your husband to

scent all his candles yet?" He winked to the young man at the
back of the shop, who shook his head.

"A few," Nellian said, with a pretended arch look. Jonathan
slipped into the shop, and she paused to give him a quick
sideways hug.

"G'morn, Nellie. Did you save me a honey roll?"

"'Tis awful the way they starve you at the castle. You know
where they are." She flicked a hand over her shoulder, then
smiled at her startled customers. "He is my brother, you see.
What sort of lotions are you looking for?"

By the time Lady Sareen and Adonna had made their
purchases, Lord Dermont leaned against the corner of the shop
with faint surprise lifting his brow. A look that recurred as
Thomas led the group on and the lady and her maid enjoyed
many a chat with the villagers.

When Thomas ended a deeper talk with some old friends,
Lord Dermont asked, "Do you know everyone in the village?"
with an odd hint of disapproval in his voice.

"Nay, it grows too fast. That particular couple, I've known all
my life."

"From Tower Woods, then?"

"Aye."

"Have many of them come to live here?"

Thomas shook his head. "Few. They prefer the village within
Tower Woods, though 'tis not near so profitable."

"Along the south road toward Maerton Duchy?" Lord
Dermont asked.

"Aye."

"What of those farther east? Which village do they prefer?"

"I believe none have moved to either village." Where did his
questions lead? There was occasional griping in the east, though
Thomas did not understand what flowed beneath the surface
complaints.

The women rejoined them, Adonna having acquired a large
woven bag for traveling. They made immediate use of it to carry

their purchases. Lord Dermont hung back a few steps, and Thomas was again able to escort Lady Sareen as they strolled back to the castle.

～

A KNOCK on her bedchamber door stopped Sareen's packing. She glanced at Adonna, who was still folding a garment. "Answer the door."

"Oh." The lass went to open it. She still needed instructions for every little thing.

Lord Dermont strolled into the room, looked at Adonna, and tipped his head toward the corridor.

"Wait outside," Sareen said.

Once the door closed, Dermont smirked. "Mother said Adonna was no maid, and you would hate having her wait on you."

"She doesn't wish to be a maid, but she tries her best, and I do not hate it at all."

"Oh, calm down. Your servants are your own concern."

"Indeed, that is true. What did you want?"

"You are making a much bigger mistake with one who is not your servant. 'Tis not well done of you."

"I know not what you mean."

"Mm. You should. Sir Thomas should, as well, but he grew up as a peasant, and then learned the customs of Moorelin, which are loose. He may not understand, and 'tis unkind of you to lead him on."

"Lead him on? What are you talking about?"

Dermont compressed his lips. "Sareen! He talks to you like he talks to no one else. And you saunter along at his side, chatting and laughing like nothing has ever amused you before. But he is still a commoner."

Sareen lifted her chin. "There is a great deal more to Sir Thomas than you realize."

"All the more reason not to give him false hope. No matter how much our father dislikes the future Duke of Maerton, he will never permit you to wed a commoner."

"Sir Thomas has said nothing of that nature." She spun away from her brother before she even finished the sentence, for she was nigh stunned with realizations. She gripped her hands at her waist, keeping her shoulders rigid as she spoke over one of them. "And besides, he may well have an inheritance one day."

"Duke Maerton will never give up one inch of land," Dermont said. "Much less will Ivan when he becomes duke. He would never let a Kaituer live in Maerton Duchy. If Sir Thomas tries to possess that manor, he will lead a horrible life. So, too, will whatever wife he takes and any heirs she bears him."

Sareen swallowed hard.

Dermont stepped around her and lightly gripped her shoulders, his face serious and voice soft. "I care for you, Sareen. I don't want your life ruined. It may be that I read Sir Thomas wrong, so I will say nothing to him. Just don't let him think you have tender feelings for him."

Her brother left, and Adonna returned, but Sareen stared out the window at the valley descending to the sea. She must not let her flush be seen, for those words *horrible life* clanged through her mind. If anyone could make them come true, 'twas Ivan.

CHAPTER 14

When they set out early the next morn, Thomas rode on Duke Tristelle's right, Lord Dermont on his left. Disappointing that Lady Sareen had decided to journey across the plain in her carriage. Once they reached Tower Woods, she would ride again, for the roads among the enormous trees were mostly rough cart tracks. According to the duchess, the only road suited to a carriage had so many twists, turns, dips, and rises, that such a journey was more tiring than riding.

While they rested at the inn where the plain met the woods, Thomas overheard Lord Dermont talking with his sister.

"I can understand if you prefer to be out of that carriage, but let us continue along the most direct road," he said. "The duke tells me we'll reach the central village before nightfall, and you may sleep in a bed."

Thomas couldn't catch her answer. In truth, he shouldn't be trying to, so he went out to the horses. Would the party split? He had hoped to enjoy Lady Sareen's company a few more days. Not that he had any right to claim it. He wished he could tell her not to marry Lord Ivan—another thing he had no right to do. He grew hot every time he thought about her with Ivan, though. Did he dare breach etiquette and warn her anyway? Would it help her if he did? Probably not. More likely to make her never talk to him again. Why must everything lead to an impasse?

He rubbed his sore wrist—the reminder of his ineptitude. Better stop before someone noticed. He took a few minutes to stroke his horse's favorite spot above the nose, then retightened his saddle cinch as the others exited the inn. Lady Sareen preceded her brother, head up and firm tread warning that she was ready for battle. Absolutely endearing in one so petite.

Lord Dermont said, "Don't blame me when you find out what sleeping in the woods is really like."

"I shan't," she declared with cold dignity, and mounted her horse.

More than a dozen set out in their party, plus extra horses loaded with camp supplies. They followed the track along the perimeter for a while, then turned in among the tower trees. The misty air in permanent shade provided a welcome respite from the midday sun.

The horses of Selta took little comfort from it. No surprise, since horses mistrusted the unknown. The duke redeployed the riders to shield the skittish creatures on both sides with horses accustomed to this woodland. Thomas took the opportunity to ride beside Lady Sareen, and Jonathan rode on her other side. They ambled along the track, speaking softly to soothe the nervous horses.

Lady Sareen kept forgetting her mare's worries, staring instead at the massive trunks and distant treetops. "They are amazing!" she whispered.

"Have you never seen them?"

"I have, but always from the edge of the woods. One simply cannot perceive the truth of this landscape from outside. All these vast piled roots, and the shift of the land."

Behind her, Adonna sounded even more stunned.

Thomas soaked it up. The awe that Tower Woods inspired was normal to him, but he always delighted in the enraptured wonder of visitors. Fortunately, he and Jonathan maintained watch, for a disturbed owl suddenly took flight across their path. Lady Sareen's mare reared with a shrill neigh. Thomas pressed a strong hand behind her back as Jonathan grabbed the mare's bridle.

Their intervention was unnecessary, perhaps, for Sareen was a good enough rider to swiftly adjust and maintain her seat, though she sounded breathless. "Even the owls are enormous!"

"Not really," Thomas said. "They only appear so because we rarely get to see them in flight."

Sareen hunched like she had a turtle's neck and peered around. She drew a breath and straightened, then glanced at the front riders, who had stopped and were watching. She directed a firm look to her brother and said, "I'm perfectly fine. Let us ride on."

'Twas not the only delay, but when the afternoon was well advanced, they reached the clearing that the duke aimed for. Duke Tristelle gave the order to make camp, then motioned Thomas aside. "Do you know a good route to Widow Marideth's holding?"

"Aye, my lord." Thomas pointed. "There is a path beyond that stand of ferns."

"How long will it take to reach her cottage?"

"A quarter hour."

The duke looked westward and scowled. "Is it not hard enough to judge time in these woods without the sun hiding too?"

"We have time enough to get there and back," Thomas said.

"Then, I want you to go now."

Thomas's brows shot up. "Just me?"

"You and Jonathan. Bid him wait at the edge of her cleared land. I am hoping that the widow will speak freely if you come alone." He tilted his head. "Why are you massaging your forearm? Are you injured?"

"Nay, sir." Thomas looked aside. "I, uh...in private, I had

Jonathan show me some defensive sword work. To see how badly I would fumble."

"Ah!" The duke's broad lips stretched. "How did that go?"

Thomas grimaced. "My squire tells me that my upper arm strength is adequate, but I have no cunning in my wrist."

"That is to be expected. A skillful wrist can only be gained with practice."

"Speak not of it, please. I still feel 'tis ...unwise...dishonorable for me to take up a sword." Thomas caught sight of Jonathan approaching their horses. "I'd best stop him from unsaddling." He and the duke took a few steps toward their camp, and Thomas said, "By the way, 'twill rain tonight."

The duke looked up. "How do you know?"

"The north breeze has picked up, and clouds are lowering early."

Thomas told Jonathan their task, then grabbed some dried meat from the camp provisions as workers started hoisting a firepit covering. Back in the saddle, Thomas found the path that led to the widow's holding. So narrow, they had to ride it single file and duck under branches often.

When they arrived, the widow was working in her field. She must have cut the first harvest and left it to dry. Yesterday, perhaps, before it clouded over. Now, the weather threatened to ruin it. She nodded to Thomas, bent again to gather another armful of grain, then hurried to the three-sided shed.

Thomas said to Jonathan, "Tie the horses away from field and garden." He unstrapped the meat he'd bound to his saddle and went to intercept the widow as she returned from the shed. "Good eve, Marideth. I've come to see how you fare and brought you some dried meat."

She barely glanced at it. "I thank ye, Sir Thomas. Be so kind as to put it on the table." She pointed toward the one-room cottage and hastened back to the field.

Certain, she had no time to spare. Thomas crossed the porch and took the food inside, where the oldest child—perhaps six or seven summers—watched the two youngest. He gave them a friendly smile and hurried out.

Jonathan stepped near. "Shouldn't I help instead of staying away?"

"Aye. Start at the far side and copy what she does." Thomas gathered grain near the widow and matched her pace in silence. Within the shed, he found that she'd propped the stocks in tilted drying racks. Her late husband must have built them for just this need. More racks waited outside. By the scraped dirt, she must have dragged another in after filling the one against the back wall. From then on, Thomas and Jonathan carried an empty rack inside whenever the previous one was filled.

Marideth's frantic breath had eased since they arrived. Finally, she spoke to Thomas as he bent beside her among the mounds and dips of her field. "I think we'll get it all in now, afore the rain comes."

"Aye, we'll finish in time," he assured her.

They lifted their armloads and turned to the shed, as Marideth said, "That stinking thief cut it this morn. I did *not* ask him to. Cut it all at once, he did, so it would be harder for me to gather it in. 'Twasn't even sunny, and now that the clouds are lowering, it cannot dry in the field as it should."

Her incensed voice had gone wavery, so Thomas held his tongue.

She swung her armload into the rack with practiced grace and dragged the back of her hand across her cheek. "He's trying to force me, and I've got no one to turn to." She fair snarled those words as she stomped away.

Thomas stacked his load, then caught up to her in the field. "Warten will not get away with anything more. The duchess didn't know what he had done before, but when I discovered who had gotten half your new field, I told the duke. They will never let him have even one stock of this grain."

She sniffed. "Ye don't understand. That's not what he's after."

She took off with another load to the shed, and Thomas followed.

They carried the next load in silence. Thomas managed to get a look at her face, though she avoided his gaze. Fighting tears, it seemed, though she looked more furious than sad. As they strode back to the field, Thomas asked, "What is he after, then?"

At first, he thought she might not answer. Her voice was husky when she did. "Our entire holding. And...me."

"What?" Thomas dropped the load he was gathering and gripped her arm.

She let her sheaf slip to the ground. "He came courting not long after my husband died. I said nay. He kept helping me—like he was proving himself and hinting that I needed him. When he asked again, I still said nay, 'cause he's a weasel. That's when he claimed half my field. But he's still not givin' up." She stomped a foot. "And why would he, when he always wins. He tried to ruin this grain, sure as the rain comes down. Then, me an' my little-uns will starve if I don't marry him." The tears broke through, and she covered her face with her hands. "Probably will, anyway, 'cause I can hardly feed them, as it is."

"We will not let that happen."

She made a high-pitched snort. "Ye came just in time today, but...but every day I barely make it through, and my back aches fierce. I've tried my best to go it alone, but I'll never keep it up until my children are old enough to help." She pushed back the wisps of hair that stuck to her wet cheeks. "I've got no time for crying." She grabbed up an armload again and stomped away.

They worked on while Thomas pondered. As they flipped loads into the next rack, he asked, "Do you know young Rodder? He's hung on to his parent's holding after they passed."

"Oh, sure. We helped him a bit before my husband died. I just can't no more."

"Of course not. But what if he could come here and help you with the heavy work? When I saw him a few weeks ago, his clothes could have used some patching and he was right lonely. If you traded light work for his heavy work, it would ease your load, and Warten would have no excuse to push unwanted help on you."

"Call him Weasel Warten, if you must keep speaking that foul name." She walked back to the field, slower now, her brow knit. "Help from Rodder might work out. He's a diligent, humble lad. Fair grown when I saw him at the spring fest." She gathered stalks of grain. "Hard to ask him, though. Take me an hour to get to his holding with my children, and another hour to get back. I'll have to shift all this grain tomorrow if I want it to dry, and I hardly dare leave it, with that weasel coming here so often."

"I'll ride over to ask Rodder tomorrow, then bring you word. Perhaps even bring him with me if he agrees to trade work with you."

She licked her lips and swallowed. "You're...you're a true friend, Sir Thomas. I don't know how to thank ye enough."

"Then don't waste time on it, because we still have to get the rest of this grain into the shed, and my squire and I need to ride a bit before the light fades."

"Ye two can spend the night here."

"I thank you, but nay. Duke Tristelle is camped at the clearing, and I must return." Thomas walked off with another load before she could answer. Fortunately, Jonathan had been hustling, and they had little left. Thomas moved faster now, for he found it best to be absent after he helped the womenfolk of Tower Woods. The unmarried ones had a tendency to cling.

As soon as the last armful was in the shed, he and Jonathan strode off to their horses. Certain, it had taken longer than expected, and Jonathan heard a whistle from Captain Cotrell. Thomas had long ago taught them the codes he'd grown up with, for it was only good sense to make use of their acute hearing. Jonathan whistled back that they were returning, so no one would set out to find them.

Thomas brushed chaff from his clothes as they rode, lest he look all dirty. The way his stomach was rumbling, he'd probably sound crass, anyway. Scant light remained when they reached the camp. Everyone else had eaten, but still lounged around the firepit under sloped canvases. Meat waited beside the coals, with some bread, cheese, and ale.

Thomas and Jonathan took their portions as the duke asked, "What kept you so long?"

"Grain, of all things." Thomas took a long drink and set the mug down by the stump he settled on. "Or should I say, the absent scoundrel Warten, whom I now long to thrash."

Captain Cotrell threw some wood on the fire. "Sounds like this tale could take a while."

Thomas bit meat from the bone. It must have been served that way, and he wished he had been here to see Lady Sareen eating from a bone. Firelight revealed how rounded her eyes were. She'd wrapped her skirt snug around her ankles and wore a shawl over her head. Was she cold or avoiding bugs? Something else, perhaps, for her gaze kept darting high into the darkness. He swallowed his latest mouthful and began a slow telling as he ate. Not near so lengthy as the captain predicted.

"'Tis not a bad idea," the duke said, "to get her some help, but that lad also has a hard time on his own."

"He has succeeded for two years and is stronger for it. Besides," Thomas said, "he worries too much. Might help him if he looks after someone else."

"Does he still have that strange dwarf horse?" the duke asked.

Thomas grinned. "Aye. It shuffles along, but still carries a load or pulls a plow." Why was Lord Dermont staring so? Thomas drank the rest of his ale to avoid his gaze.

Duke Tristelle must have seen it too, for he asked, "What think you, Lord Dermont?"

"Oh, nothing, really. Just...I'm not surprised Sir Thomas knows the People of the Woods, but...do you know them all?"

The duke angled his head. "Nay, but I know the widows and

orphans. 'Tis the obligation of those who follow the holy book, is it not?"

"Well...aye, but 'tis everyone's duty to their own neighbors. Don't the People of the Woods show each other kindness?"

"They do," the duke said, "but they are so scattered, 'tis difficult. When a scoundrel takes advantage, that becomes my duty."

CHAPTER 15

'Twas a dim morn. Thomas finished the last of his bacon beside the fire as Lady Sareen emerged from her tent.

She tugged at a sleeve as though it stuck damply to her skin. "Oh, heavens!" she said, looking around at the dense whiteness that enveloped the camp.

A grin accented Thomas's words. "That's one way to describe it. Although, this cloud got lost and came down to us."

Adonna sidled past the wet tent flap with a bundle of clothing in her arms. She, too, gazed about with disbelief. "I... was hoping to hang these to dry somewhere."

Thomas washed his hands in the bucket of warm water on a stump. "Wait an hour. The cloud will lift."

Lady Sareen shivered. "Is this what you meant about the mist lifting in the sunlight?"

"Nay, my lady. Come sit by the fire." Her brother was smirking at her, so Thomas added, "Think of it this way. You can now claim with perfect sincerity that you have walked around inside a cloud."

"That is true," she said, keeping her chin up.

The cook poured a fresh mug of coffee, and Thomas handed it to Sareen when she sat down. That won him her smile, but she still looked uncomfortable. Lord Dermont suddenly bestirred himself to wrap a cloak around her, nudging Thomas out of the way.

Abrupt, but Thomas had plenty to do and had best be off to visit Rodder.

THOMAS'S SUGGESTION found instant favor with Rodder. He tied his blanket around a jumble of clothes and got himself onto the extra horse that Thomas and Jonathan had brought. The saddle and reining were unfamiliar to him, so Jonathan led the horse, and they made decent time along the muddy path back to the widow's holding. Sunlight widened holes in the shifting clouds. 'Twould soon be fair.

Jonathan frowned as they neared. "Do you hear that, Sir Thomas? Someone's shouting."

"Can you tell who, or what's being said?"

Jonathan's expression grew intent. "Nay. The loud one has a voice I don't recognize." After a moment, he added. "The duke is there. Curses, that loud-mouth speaks of making the widow his wife!"

Thomas touched a heel to his horse's side and sped toward the holding. He burst into the open, fairly seething. The widow stood in her doorway, with children peering around her. A large leather pack was upended between the porch and ground. Two goats were yoked to a stake, so they must have been walked here. Warten, on his knees, faced the duke, who spoke with clipped words. He never made anyone kneel. What had happened? Captain Cotrell, a step behind Warten, lifted a hand to stop Thomas.

After halting his horse, Thomas dismounted, and one of the duke's men took his reins.

Thomas had caught the gist of the duke's words now. He needn't have worried. Widow Marideth's expression eased him further, but he skirted around, stepped up onto the side of her porch, and whispered, "Did he harm you?"

She shook her head quick, as if enjoying the scene too much to spare Thomas a glance.

The duke moved on from the charge of lying to trespassing. "You cut another's grain without her permission. Had it not been for the chance arrival of extra hands, the grain would now be lying sodden in the field. For this, you owe half of your current crop, which you will cut, dry, and bind. If it is not stored in yon shed when I return, you will forfeit your entire crop. I now doubt your word on all matters presented to both the duchess and myself. I shall hold court at Tower Woods Village a day past the full moon. Present yourself for a hearing, or I will have you fetched in bonds. Now, take your pack and do not trespass here again."

Warten got to his feet, scowling at the small crowd who witnessed his disgrace. He shoved tumbled belongings back into his pack, hefted it unto his shoulder, then grasped the stake that held the goats.

The duke's voice ground low. "Leave the goats."

"They are mine!" Warten declared.

"No more," the duke said. "They are forfeit in payment for today's lie and slander. Be off."

His scowl deepened, but he took a step away. Captain Cotrell growled something at him, and Warten halted to bow. "My lord duke," Warten grumbled. Then, he hastened past the far end of the field and up a path.

The agitation began to settle, though there was a fair amount that needed arranging. At last, Thomas rode with the duke's party back to their camp, where Lady Sareen waited with her brother and servants. She wanted to know everything, and though the duke kept it short, she seemed to take great delight in the outcome—for the aid of a lowly woman, whom she had never met.

Endearing that she cared for someone experiencing

difficulties. Or…was it because the widow had been saved from an unwanted marriage? Thomas silently chided himself. Could he never stop thinking of Lady Sareen's future husband? A thought escaped from the impossible hopes that he sequestered. What of Navayn Manor? Would it make a difference in his standing? Nay, he must stop this! He didn't know if he would gain it. Even if he did, she was a lady, and he would always be common.

~

"'TIS DAWN'S FIRST LIGHT, my lady."

Sareen moaned, hoping the words were dream. Nay, Adonna was pushing her shoulder and insisting that it was morning despite the inn's dark bedchamber. Well, she had asked to be awakened, and this was probably her only chance. Sareen sat up on the side of the bed.

Unlikely that she would have gotten dressed in time if Adonna hadn't helped her, but the tiny inn still lay wrapped in silence as they crept down the stairs by the light of a candle.

Adonna fumbled with the latch, then pulled the door open. Indeed, faint light glowed outside. They snuffed the candle, stepped onto the porch, and softly closed the door.

Sareen led the way. She had chosen a spot when they'd arrived at the inn yesterday. The building was too small to hold them all, so most of their entourage was camped beyond the stable behind it. Beside the camp, she had spied a long bench fastened between two trees. 'Twould be the perfect vantage point, in the woods yet close enough to her own party to remain safe.

She and Adonna skirted the inn and stable, then felt their way over hard-packed ground. Though the tops of the tower trees glowed through the mist, 'twas harder to see the path than she'd expected. At least the woodland was silent. That must mean there were no bears, right? She tried to rely on Thomas's promise from when they had entered Tower Woods. That the black bears here were nothing like the big brown bears of the Wilde. That they were afraid of people and would not come near. 'Twas much easier to be brave when a dozen men surrounded her, carrying bows, not to mention various spears and swords.

"I think I see it," Adonna whispered, pointing.

They reached the bench. Adonna moved around to stare between trees, but Sareen sat. Aye, this would be perfect. The ground sloped down to disappear in the mist, which now glowed brighter in the distance. Dark pillars striped the haze. The nearest foliage shifted like spidery fingers behind a sheer curtain. Sareen raised her shawl higher up her neck and pulled it close. In truth, her shivers were not entirely from cold. Odd how a hint of fear doubled her excitement. Already, the mist was thinning. Would it rise like Thomas had described?

"Someone's coming," Adonna said.

Sareen heard the footsteps, too, a steady tread through vegetation. Would someone ruin her one chance? Who? A tall form half-hidden in mist—light hair. Sareen eased out a breath as his face became clear, a hint of surprise in his eyes, which slid from Adonna to her.

"Good morn, Sir Thomas," she whispered, hoping he would also speak softly.

He did so, bowing. "Good morn, Lady Sareen."

"I...I saw this bench yesterday and thought it might be the perfect place to...to watch for the mist to rise."

"Indeed, 'twas built here for that very reason."

She glanced to her side. "The bench is plenty long enough for you to watch with me." She turned to the eastern glow, trying to hide how forward she felt. "Is this the sort of weather that you meant?"

"Every morn is different, but there is a good chance of it."

She no longer looked at him, but the change in his voice revealed that he drew near. The bench shifted slightly as he sat.

This was a very odd time of day—and place—to be sitting beside...a man. Even with a maid present. Adonna stood off to one side, gazing steadily east. Present, but somehow separate from them. Sareen tried to think of something to say. Futile. Apparently true for Sir Thomas, as well. She turned just her eyes toward his profile.

He was watching the sunrise. Which both of them had come for, after all.

The golden rays were sliding down the treetops now. There was not so much mist as before, though she hadn't noticed it leaving. Still plenty down the hill, like froth in a bowl. It really did have a magical feel. Every instant, another branch seemed to form in a shifting ray. Misty trunks displayed hard outlines as sunlight cut past them and yet another shroud was suddenly gone. Birds twittered, and faint sounds whisked through the underbrush. She sought the rising wisps that she so much wanted to see, but found none among the branches. Disappointing, but lovely, just the same. Ah, there! Vapor stood above the whiteness down the slope.

She gasped and pointed. "Look! They are like...like ghosts. So still, not moving at all."

"Look longer." A smile lifted his gentle voice. "Though still, they change."

'Twas true. The strands faded, and new shapes thickened, only to vanish. She pointed again. "That one is like a lazy cat's tail." She glanced at him to see if he found the one she meant, but his gray eyes were fixed on her...in morning's brilliant light. She had not thought this through! "I must look a fright." She smoothed a hand over escaping curls toward the single braid at her nape. "I hurried so to get out here in time."

"All I see is a lady savoring the dawn with me...and your delight is more beautiful than the loveliest styling of your hair."

She could hardly breathe. No one paid compliments like this, and she couldn't think of a witty reply. That day on the mansion's roof came to mind, and she stuttered, "I...I suppose...'tis like seeing what's inside a person." Did that even make sense?

Though he nodded with a faint smile, he said nothing.

She'd sounded so daft. She must explain, somehow, even though her thoughts darted about. "Like how much effort you went to for that widow and...and that lad too."

"I have been in want and difficulty. Things are well for me now because of another's kindness, so..." His brows dipped, and his voice altered. "So...naturally...I seek to aid those in trouble. Or on the verge of trouble. Like..." He looked even more uncertain. "The idea that she might be forced into a marriage she would hate...perhaps with a man who would neglect or mistreat her children...it just seemed that I must do something."

Did he intend the double meaning that she perceived? Certain, he spoke of the widow, but was he also referring to her and Lord Ivan? How would Ivan treat children? That question sickened her. Her heart pounded so, she grew lightheaded, making Thomas's whisper all the harder to catch.

"I wish that I..." He drew another breath. "'Tis not my place, but...please, Sareen, don't—"

He whipped his head around in the same instant that she heard footsteps.

Her brother! He paused and looked between the three of them. Thomas sat with his back straight now, and he faced east, but Sareen had been leaning toward him. Which Der probably saw. Time for a recovery. "Ah, Der. What a pity you didn't come earlier." She pointed downhill. "See where that thin sheet of mist is? 'Twas thick, and forms were rising up out of it in dawn's light. The sunrise was enchanting!"

It took him too many seconds to answer. "Doubtless. Could you not have asked *me* for an escort?"

What...oh, no. "If you are thinking that I asked Sir Thomas for an escort, 'tis no such thing. I wanted to come alone...that is...with just Adonna, in case I should chance to meet anyone. Which happened, as you see."

"You're telling me that *you* came out in the dark woods with no protection?"

She stood and lifted her chin. "Have I not just said so?"

Adonna turned toward the path, her speech as casual as her stroll. "Indeed, though there was faint light when we set out. If ladies were not so hedged in, I daresay you would know that my Lady Sareen is braver than you think." Adonna had passed Der, and thus was spared the annoyed look he cast at her back.

"If you will excuse me," Sareen said with great dignity, "now that the sun has risen, I must prepare for the day."

THOMAS TOOK care to curb his expression, for he wanted to cheer Lady Sareen, which would enrage her brother. That would also have an amusing side. Better to calm him, though, for Lavaycian nobles were touchy. When Lord Dermont quit glowering after the departing women, Thomas gestured to the far end of the bench. Welcoming but indirect enough that he could leave if he wished.

After a considering look at Thomas, Lord Dermont straddled the bench. "How convenient that you chose today to enjoy the sunrise."

"I watch the dawning of every fair day."

"Unlike my sister, who has never noticed a dawn in her life. I wonder what brought her out this morn."

So tiresome. "When we were visiting the sea, I happened to mention the beautiful sunrises in Tower Woods. So now, if you wish to think ill of either your sister or me, you can use our passing remarks to claim that one or both of us planned to meet here. But the truth remains that I neither planned it nor expected it."

Lord Dermont's lips compressed in a twitchy manner. "You could have left when you discovered her here."

Thomas shrugged. "I *could* have, but I don't see why I *should* have." He swung a leg over the bench to face Lord Dermont. "I have escorted her both in your presence and your absence. Certain, I would never dishonor Lady Sareen, and I think you know that. As for her safety in the twilight…the risk is low, but I agree with you that she should have an escort. How can you think I would abandon her?"

Lord Dermont's lips no longer compressed, but his face remained inscrutable through the long moment that their gazes held. At last, he said, "My sister tells me I do not know you. Likely, she is right. Think not that I find any fault in your honor." His brows rose as he drew a deep breath. "But that actually makes me worry more." Lord Dermont stood and licked his lips. "I do not know how—or if—I should say this, so I will ask your pardon in advance if I misconstrue or seem to insult. 'Tis only fair that you know. My father will never let Sareen marry below her station." He bowed as he finished the sentence, then turned and departed without chance to observe Thomas's reaction.

Thomas clenched his teeth till they hurt. Breaths whooshed in and out his nose, loud in the silence. Not until they slowed, could he acknowledge that Lord Dermont did him a kindness in his swift exit. Though Thomas still wanted to hit him.

Unfair. Lord Dermont spoke only truth, which he did not create. A truth that Thomas already knew. Never would he have been spurred so far down this path if it wasn't Ivan who pursued her. Thomas's fists clenched on his knees. Anyone but him. He endured a powerful wave that swept through him. Rage? Dread? Was there even a word for this?

As the worst of it passed, a whisper spoke through him. *Anyone but Ivan?* That question seemed to echo until another replaced it. *Who?*

Anyone!

Imagine the face of the man you would happily see her wed.

No such face existed. Could he have no peace? In the silence of his mind, he shouted back at the voice—at God. *Then, let her find someone I know not.* He swallowed the knot in his throat. *And let her be happy with him, since I cannot wed her.* How odd. It didn't seem that God was bothered by his angry yell, but he did seem displeased over those last few words. Almost as though Thomas had lied. 'Twas true, though—he was a commoner.

I am King of kings, and I call you noble.

Thomas recognized the similarity to a passage in the holy book. 'Twas about character, not class, but it lifted his spirits in a way. Rather like what Duke Tristelle had described. In truth, Thomas was comfortable with his own worth—when he didn't have someone telling him he was dust aspiring to wed a star. He rubbed the back of his neck. Too bad this moment of inspiration would mean nothing to Duke Selta. Why did it so often seem that the world and the holy book didn't match?

CHAPTER 16

The party from Selta took their leave with friendly formality that acknowledged no undercurrents between them and Thomas. Doubtless, 'twas for the best.

Thomas focused on the matters at hand. Indeed, Duke Tristelle kept him closely involved as they traveled to Berry Hill, and then to another holding where a tower tree had fallen and caused considerable damage. Their circuitous route eventually brought them to Purthellia a day before the royal audience.

They entered the city from the northwest, so the ride between buildings was comparatively short. Here, they accommodated the Lavaycian custom of wearing doublets year-round. Thomas was all too aware of his sweat-soaked shirt and longed to exchange the doublet with his sensible vest.

Being in Duke Tristelle's party provided luxuries within Fraetinloch Palace that Thomas would never receive on his own. Amusing that his bedchamber was likely better than what most lords were granted. Buckets of hot water were brought up for a bath within half an hour of his arrival, and a lad was assigned to lead Jonathan through the back hallways and stairs of the vast palace. A good thing, because a simple task here seemed to involve a ten-minute walk both coming and going.

No matter to Thomas, however. His trunk was already in his chamber, since it had arrived with Lady Sareen's carriage. He bathed and dressed slowly, for he had nothing to do until dinner. Duke Tristelle was meeting with the king and queen, an event that did not include Thomas.

Granted, he could go mingle with the arriving nobility. At least four of the duchies were represented by their duke and duchess. Numerous other lords and ladies had also arrived. Doubtless, they were politely chattering in some ornate salon. The last thing he wanted to participate in. If they were speculating about the audience, he didn't want to hear it. If they asked what he knew of it, he didn't want to say. Or worse, if they knew what he didn't and tried to detect his hopes…intolerable! Fidgeting about in his chamber grew so tiresome, he grabbed the iron poker from beside the carved fireplace and maneuvered it to strengthen his wrist.

At a tap on the door, he replaced the poker and said, "Enter."

Jonathan came in with Thomas's travel things. "I had to go all the way to the stable to get your bow and quiver, but no one could tell me what became of your saddle packs." He raised them as he spoke. "I finally discovered that they'd been carried up to Duke Tristelle's chamber. I miss Sir James."

Thomas chuckled, for indeed, such would never happen in Tristelle Castle. "With all the guests in this sprawling palace, I suppose it is no wonder."

Jonathan straightened from setting things aside. "Do you know what *is* a wonder?"

"Do tell."

"No one here knows what the audience is about."

Strange—gossip being what it was. "There must be some who know."

"Not among the servants. They were all trying to get information from *me*."

"I hope they all failed," Thomas said.

"Certain. I'm just glad I had a reason to keep moving. 'Twas easier to avoid questions on the way back, now that everyone is dressing for dinner."

An event that Thomas could not avoid, though he went down to it no earlier than necessary. The company took places around the queen's long table, where candlelight glimmered over crystal and porcelain. Here, Thomas only needed to talk with the lady on either side of him. On his left, the lady, whose name he could not recall, mostly ignored him, but on his right, Duchess Prushane made pleasant conversation. He enjoyed the dinner more than he'd expected, despite the fact that Lady Sareen was seated many places away on the same side as he. Thomas couldn't even see her. Probably just as well, for if she were seated opposite, he would have to avoid looking at her too frequently.

He endured more small talk afterward in the grand salon. Like everyone else, Thomas bowed to King Gairith and Queen Ellianne, who sat among their guests, yet always separated by status. His turn came earlier than most, for he accompanied Duke Tristelle at that moment. They exchanged a few words about their journey through Tower Woods, then made way for the next guests.

As soon as Thomas parted from Duke Tristelle, the hum of conversation buzzed around him, while excluding him. How long must he linger? Sir Layton talked with him for some time, pleasant since it was just the two of them.

The Duke and Duchess of Selta acknowledged him. Better yet, Lady Sareen and Lord Dermont spent several minutes chatting with him. Her gown tonight was pearlescent, daintily embroidered with scarlet silk. Some of her hair was intricately twisted high, but a fall of black curls descended over her left shoulder. He must not stare. He must ease out of the conversation after the correct amount of time had passed.

Thomas never was sure how to judge that, but was spared the decision, for Duke Prushane drew him into conversation. Odd, but interesting. The duke's unremarkable appearance, short stature, and receding hairline masked his considerable intellect. How their conversation wove through topics to the subject of land husbandry, Thomas didn't know. At least he wasn't required to say much. Then nearby, someone remarked about Duke Maerton's absence.

Duchess Prushane answered in her musical voice. "Doubtless, he will make a grand entrance at tomorrow's audience."

Thomas failed to hear what Duke Prushane had just asked. He recollected himself. "I beg your pardon. You were saying...?"

The duke's thin lips stretched slightly as he looked up at Thomas. "Doubtless, too much. I was forgetting that you've ridden Tower Woods for days and are likely wishing for your rest more than conversation. But you must visit us at Prushane Castle. All this talk will mean more when you have seen the land I speak of."

Thomas hid his surprise with a bow. "'Twould be a great pleasure, sir."

He escaped the crowd then, and ascended the grand staircase to his chamber. Amazing. He'd been invited to large parties before, but never to stay at any of Lavaycia's southern castles!

He just wanted it to be over. Thomas turned to face the oval mirror and buttoned his doublet. 'Twas dark brown, accented only with a bit of white where the split collar revealed his shirt. 'Twould not be nearly as flashy as what most of the men wore, but when Thomas tried to don their styles, he felt foolish.

Besides, brown set off his blond hair, and he was in a mood to shout his Kaituer heritage. 'Twould serve Maerton right! The heirloom dagger hilt showing above his belt, which he now fastened, was embellished with sapphires and bore the stylized *K* of his disinherited noble house. So, too, did the ring he wore, once his grandfather's signet, that of a younger son.

Jonathan smoothed the back fabric under Thomas's belt and finished looking him over. "'Tis all right and proper."

Another pair of footsteps passed his chamber door. He wished he could arrive last, but probably not wise since he had been summoned. "I'd best be getting down, then." Soon, he would know.

Thomas paused at the throne room's open entrance, and the doorman announced, "Sir Thomas Kaituer."

Precious little notice was given him as he stepped within. This chamber cast all others in the shade. The ceiling was painted like a sky with hints of faces peering down from the edges of clouds. The carvings that framed it mimicked clouds until they merged into the foliage-topped pillars, which descended to bases of rugged stone. Floor tiles radiated from the pillars in a muted two-toned pattern, lost beneath the noble feet that trod upon them. Velvet-covered chairs and sofas stood in groups at the sides of the room. Green predominated, and gilt accented each corner, carving, frame, and sconce. But nowhere did the colors of the House of Fraetinloch shimmer as they did behind the twin thrones. On a background of iridescent, emerald green, enormous wings spread, their tips nearly reaching the side walls. How the gold had been crafted to mimic glimmering feathers mystified Thomas. Between the wings, King Gairith and Queen Ellianne sat upon their matched thrones. Impossible to see the queen without thinking of Duchess Tristelle, who so resembled her mother.

Recent years made protocol easier for Thomas than in his first visit to the throne room. He approached at the proper pace and bowed low before royalty. "My honored lieges, King Gairith and Queen Ellianne."

They granted him majestic smiles and benign greetings, then invited him to linger near the dais where Duke Tristelle already waited, representing the royal Duchess of Tristelle. The throne room was filling, some coming to bow before royalty, while those who had already done so exchanged spritely talk. Faces always seemed to blur when there were so many of them, but Thomas found Duke Maerton's portly form, and then Lord Ivan and Lord Sathe Maerton near him. A limited number of servants lined the back wall. A lawyer and scribe waited on the opposite side of the thrones. Thomas's mouth grew dry.

Duke Maerton drew near the dais, seemingly to converse with the king, but his voice carried. His thanks to the king for the audience merged into reminiscence of Navayn Manor, of visits to his brother, mother, and grandmother in that home, and then on to Prince Maerton dwelling there when he became the royal Duke of Maerton.

What a great deal of time he took to reassert what he had always claimed. And apparently was going to keep claiming. Thomas kept trying to avoid locking his jaw. Had it really been necessary to summon him for *this?*

"And yet," Duke Maerton said, "despite my family's long ownership, we now waste years in arguing a claim which I fear can never be settled. The estate's income pays legal fees rather than benefitting either family who lays claim to it. Setting aside our familial sentiment, the manor itself is small compared to the holdings of the House of Maerton. I, my brother, and my son concur that it grows petty to argue any longer in the courts." His voice, already clear to the silent gathering, took on greater formality. "Thus, I, Duke of Maerton, agree this day to release ownership of Navayn Manor and its demesne to Sir Thomas, the heir of Lady Anne Navayn."

Thomas nigh reeled from the shock. Had he heard correctly? The king responded, and then the queen, thanking the Maertons for withdrawing their claim. Then, it *was* his.

It came time for Thomas to utter the words he had planned for this turn of events. He bowed to Duke Maerton. "I thank you, my lord duke, for bringing complete and final clarity to my ownership of Navayn Manor."

The duke blinked, then uttered magnanimous words, which hinted that the manor had been a gift from him.

Thomas held his tongue. The duke could think what he liked, but in his heart, Thomas thanked his great-grandmother.

Words ebbed and flowed—the king addressing the lawyer and scribe, fresh chatter among the nobles who shifted with their conversations. A random split in the crowd allowed Thomas to catch sight of Captain and Jonathan Cotrell. Their expressions warmed his heart. They stood nigh the door, so Thomas chanced to notice more people coming into the room. Who were they?

Several of the gathered nobles felicitated Thomas, but as he began to move away from the thrones, Duke Tristelle touched his arm and murmured, "Stay here."

Why? The Maertons now conversed on the far side of the throne room. What remained to be done? Royal aids busied themselves, and a couple from among the newcomers by the entrance were escorted forward. Certain, Thomas had never seen them, but by the look on Duke Maerton's face, he knew them. And was not pleased.

The couple offered their deepest bow and curtsy, and the queen said, "We thank you for responding to our invitation."

As though anyone rejected a royal invitation. Perhaps she had said it to keep them out of trouble with Duke Maerton.

"Sir Thomas," the king said.

He stepped nigh and bowed. "Sire."

The king nodded to a herald, who lifted a parchment and read. "While he was Duke of Kaituer, Liam Kaituer wed Lady Anne Navayn, who bore Lord Thomas, their only child. In exile, Lord Thomas sired Nathan Kaituer, who sired Thomas Kaituer, his only surviving child. This day, Sir Thomas Kaituer is recognized as the sole heir of Lady Anne Navayn. The Navayn estate is hereby transferred to Sir Thomas Kaituer."

Thomas waited out the over-worded formality. Why was this couple staring at him, and what was he supposed to do now?

Fortunately, the queen addressed him. "Sir Thomas, are you aware of Lady Anne Navayn's cousins?"

"Only that...some cousins existed, madam."

"Indeed," she said. "Their offspring are now far removed from you, but a few still bear the name Navayn. 'Tis my pleasure to introduce the most senior of your distant cousins." She gestured to the couple. "Master Vincent Navayn and his wife, Mistress Crella Navayn."

He had...family? They bowed and curtsied to him, stammering out a greeting, which he acknowledged. They seemed as dumbfounded as he felt. What could he say? "'Tis a pleasant surprise to meet you. Do you...reside on the Navayn estate?"

Master Navayn recovered. "Our farm is just beyond the, uh, beyond *your* demesne. 'Tis the largest of the farms of the old estate. Also, I am the reeve of Navayn Village."

"Ah. I look forward to inviting you to the manor in the near future." Conversations were beginning to buzz again, much to Thomas's relief, for anything he said would likely be criticized. He asked about children, thereby including the mistress.

She turned out to be a direct sort of woman. "Pray pardon my ignorance, but how are we to address you?"

Had she not heard all those repetitions? "As Sir Thomas."

She tilted her head. What was he missing? Could he not possess his inheritance for five minutes without fumbling?

Though some had lost interest in him, the queen apparently had not. "In this," she said, "you can see that Sir Thomas is not presumptuous."

The Navayn couple seemed to feel this ended their moment before royalty and, stepping backward, murmured their thanks again.

The queen gestured for them to move aside rather than back. "'Tis our pleasure that you linger through the audience."

What now? Others stood near the entrance, but no motion was made to bring any forward. Thomas looked to Duke Tristelle, but his calm expression said little. The creases beside his eyes...he must know something.

The herald's voice boomed again. "All rise, for the crown shall speak."

All this pomp. Only a couple elder women were seated, anyway, for everyone seemed to expect something. A firm tread approached, giving Thomas time to step next to Duke Tristelle and whisper, "Does everyone but me know what's going on?"

The duke's lips twitched. "Very few."

Men-at-arms carried a long, narrow chest between them and set it beside the king's throne. Captain Hurth dismissed them with a gesture and stood tall beside the chest.

"For those who may not know," the king said, "on the day that the House of Kaituer fell, King Carleeton took possession of the contents of a chamber which held certain heirlooms and parchments. Many of them, he gave to Prince Maerton, but some, he stored in the royal archive. Lady Navayn's final will, for instance, and the symbols of the noble House of Navayn. We have chosen to hold them in trust until such time as the Navayn estate was restored to its rightful owner." He nodded to the captain, who bent to open the chest.

In the breathy silence, Duke Maerton closed his parted lips and set his face. At his side, Lord Ivan scowled.

The king said, "Sir Thomas Kaituer, approach the throne."

He set his shoulders and obeyed as the captain placed items in the king's hands. Coiled fabric, the king gave to the queen, but the pouch, he emptied onto his palm. The queen took her husband's hand, and together, they stood.

Thomas knelt on one knee.

The queen let a sash unroll—amber divided by a trace of green and bordered with brown. The king held up a gold ring. "The signet and sash of the House of Navayn. With these symbols, we acknowledge the current holder of the perpetual title. Sir Thomas Kaituer, Lord of Navayn."

CHAPTER 17

Thomas could not think. The queen was draping the sash over one of his shoulders. The aged fabric brushed his hand as he drew his arm through. She stepped back, and the king extended the ring. Thomas's hand seemed frozen before his chest, his gaze locked on the bulky gold. How could he take the ring of a lord? The king slid the signet onto Thomas's middle finger. Still, he could not move, nor open his clenched throat.

"The sword," King Gairith said.

The captain lifted an embellished scabbard from the chest, and with a bow, laid it across his forearm, presenting the hilt to the king. The blade hissed from the scabbard as the king drew it.

He raised it with the words, "The sword of Navayn," then rested the blade on his hand and presented it to Thomas. "Your sword, Lord Navayn."

Thomas extended his hands, palms up. Cool steel touched one—the hilt, ornamented with polished lynxstone, rested in the other. A ceremonial sword, but the marked blade had been used. A sword with purpose. Thomas swallowed and gathered words. "As Sir Thomas, I swore my allegiance to you. Now..." He nearly choked but had to get the title out. "As Lord Navayn, I swear my allegiance to the House of Fraetinloch, to the king and queen of Lavaycia."

"We accept your oath. You may rise."

Thomas closed his fingers over the hilt and stood as the king and queen returned to their thrones. Captain Hurth drew nigh and presented the scabbard to Thomas with a bow. Thomas sheathed the sword, relieved that the tip did not quiver. He took two steps back from the dais, for dukes approached from the sides—Tristelle and Maerton. How sweet to hear a beloved voice first.

"On behalf of the royal Duchess of Tristelle and myself, we acknowledge you, Sir Thomas Kaituer, as Lord Navayn."

"I thank you, my lord duke."

Then, Maerton's voice, falsely pleasant. "A happy day for us. Not only shall I have a new neighbor, but also a new lord in my duchy. I wait only for your oath."

An oath—to Maerton? Entailing what?

The king spoke, sparing Thomas the need. "The time for that is past. Had you wanted his oath, you could have had it any time since his exile was lifted. But you chose another path. His oath is already given to the House of Fraetinloch, and I will not allow it to be weakened by a dual oath. There are other matters to make clear—which shall be written forthwith—but for now, understand this. Lord Navayn holds his estate in his own right and owes no service or rents to the House of Maerton."

The duke's expression remained calm. "Of course. The—"

"I also noticed," the king said, "that you mentioned the demesne of Navayn Manor but not the estate." The king glanced to his common subjects at the side and far end of the throne room. "To the reeve and other tenants of Navayn estate, whom we are pleased to host this day, duties once owed to Duke Maerton are now owed to Lord Navayn."

"Ah, clarity," Duke Maerton said. "Always advisable. Thank you for mentioning it, sire."

Other nobles drew nigh to exchange courtesies with Thomas.

He heard his new title again and again. All these bows, with the awkward addition of a sword in hand. Slowly, he moved toward the back wall and caught Jonathan's eye.

His squire hastened near and bowed. "Lord Navayn."

Thomas glanced around to be sure he wasn't heard, then murmured, "That sounds even stranger from your lips."

"I've been wanting to say one thing." Jonathan leaned near his ear and emphatically whispered, "Rah!"

Thomas burst out laughing. He squelched it to shaking shoulders as quick as he could. "Many thanks. For now, tend this sword for me."

"I am honored, my lord." Jonathan relieved him of it and touched the hilt. "What is this?"

"Lynxstone," Thomas said.

Lord Sathe Maerton had drawn near and said, "Often called lynxeye, when polished. 'Tis the gemstone of the House of Navayn, matching the amber and brown of the sash."

Jonathan slipped away as Thomas turned. "Ah. I've seen lynxstone in Tower Woods. Is it also found in Maerton Duchy?"

"Aye, within your demesne, in fact. When you come to take possession, I would be happy to ride the land with you and show you about."

"An offer I gladly accept. Truth be told, you are the one person I suspect may be harmed by how this has all fallen out."

"Think not of it. The house has always been a temporary abode, and my brother's steward has managed the land. As it happens, I gain more than I lose in the matter." He cleared his throat. "You must wonder about the manor. 'Tis among the older homes of the region, but well architected. The original furnishings are rather dated, and the hangings are in need of replacement. Nonetheless, I think you will find it comfortable enough to occupy at once and—"

"Certain, he will," Lord Ivan said, approaching with Lady Sareen. "I'm sure its quaint charm will be just the thing for him."

Lady Sareen gave her hand to Thomas and curtsied to his

bow. "I am so happy for you, Lord Navayn. You are the most patient of all peers to wait so long for what is yours."

"I thank you, Lady Sareen."

"I'm sure the wait was easier for him," Lord Ivan said, "having been a woodsman lord for so long."

Sareen's brows rose. "Doubtless, you meant woodland, for indeed, he is respected in Tower Woods and all of Tristelle Duchy."

"Ah, by the People of the Woods. Quite understandable." Lord Ivan gave an ironic half-bow. "I now greet you as neighbor, for our land shares a border. Do please ask when you have questions, for I'm sure they will be many. I'll even confess that I find the changes in protocol awkward. Doubtless, more so for you."

"Worry not over making a mistake," Thomas said. "Since we share the same title, I shall set you at ease by copying the depth of your bows."

"Just such a nuance is what I mean. Your bow should be lower, for I will be duke."

"On that day, it shall be lower." Thomas turned back to Lord Maerton. "You were saying, sir?"

He watched his nephew oddly but turned back to Thomas. "Where were we? 'Twould be convenient to know when you plan to arrive, for the steward wants some minor repairs completed before that date."

Others drew near. Lady Sareen moved from Ivan's side to her father's, and Duke Maerton's presence quieted his heir.

Strangely enough, Duke Selta joined the discussion of plans, addressing Thomas. "We've decided to journey with Duke Tristelle's party as far as the main road through Tower Woods. He tells me he returns home from there. Would you care to continue west with us, Lord Navayn? We travel as far as Kaituer Castle."

"Indeed? For what purpose?" Duke Maerton asked.

"All this talk of ancestors—Lady Anne Navayn and such—has

reminded the queen and me that we have an ancestor buried there. I told her I would visit the grave."

Duke Maerton raised his brows. "Do you? 'Tis not a frequented place, but I shall send someone to scythe the grass."

Duke Prushane claimed Thomas's attention, exchanged pleasantries, and then moved on.

Master Navayn had been watching and stepped into the gap. "If it pleases you, Lord Navayn, I should be happy to introduce my kin, who are also your tenants."

Thomas greeted them much as he did the People of the Woods, giving careful attention to the introductions. Names, he must remember. He turned from the last one and chanced to overhear his own name repeated in conversation. But not his name. Lord Thomas Navayn.

His jaw tightened. 'Twas not addressed to him. Best to ignore it until his ire passed. Until he formulated a proper way to correct the usage.

One of the king's pages approached. "His majesty requests your attendance, Lord Navayn."

Thomas turned, surprised to see the king's back passing through a side door. He followed the page into an elegant salon behind the thrones, where the king settled into a large chair that seemed to offer more relaxed comfort than the throne. The page closed the door, leaving Thomas with the king and Duke Tristelle, who stood to one side.

King Gairith watched Thomas with a slight curve to his firm mouth. "What think you of your title, Lord Navayn?"

He swallowed. "In truth, sire, I am too stunned to know what I think."

"A far better answer than the polite compliments lately showered upon you. What think you of the reactions of your peers?"

Peers. How many more oddities awaited him? "Most were polite, as you say. 'Tis better than impolite." Not all had approached him, of course. As for sincerity...no profit in doubting.

"And what of the Maerton clan? Remember that I like direct answers."

"Duke Maerton shows nothing, and Lord Ivan mocks. Much like always. Lord Sathe Maerton speaks like an ordinary man."

"Ordinary," the king said. "An apt description of Lord Maerton when he is not trying to implement his brother's twisted directives. The duke will not wish to anger me and is likely to grant you common courtesy. Perhaps his heir will, too... if it suits him. Should they ever seek to exploit some fault in you, 'tis wisest to tell me of it."

Thomas had heard of their ways, but probably shouldn't say that. He bowed in acknowledgement.

"'Tis unfortunate that your estate is situated near a clan you cannot trust. Duke Prushane, however, is an excellent landholder and is willing to advise you. 'Tis known that you have the patronage of Duke Tristelle, but in Maerton Duchy, 'twould be wise to let the favor of other dukes be seen."

"Never would I disdain their favor, sire, but 'tis not my nature to court it. Even if I knew how."

"Duke Selta is riding with you as far as Kaituer Castle, is he not? A simple invitation to Navayn Manor will give him reason to continue with you." The king studied Thomas a moment. "You need not wonder at this. I have heard of the arrow that nigh struck you. In giving you land and title, which you did not seek, I have placed you in some degree of danger. A danger that I plan to end, but first I must understand it fully. Thus, a subtle defense is best. The queen and I have admitted Dukes Selta and Prushane to our confidence. We also have the means to watch and learn from a distance. Be neither careless nor overtly cautious. Tell no one what we have spoken of. Doubtless, you will have plenty to occupy your time. The granting of estate and title is only a beginning. 'Tis up to you to solidify your position."

Thomas inclined his head.

After a short pause, Duke Tristelle said, "A task you are well capable of."

"Thank you, my lord duke," Thomas murmured.

Another brief silence, then the king said, "Master Wissent will be updating the genealogies to determine near-relation marriages. 'Tis unlikely that he will find any of concern, so you may find yourself...sought after."

"Pardon?"

"By ladies."

A wave of heat washed over Thomas. "Surely not! Uh, sire."

The king chuckled. "I am glad that you are disinterested. Do not court any woman."

Thomas closed his lips. What shock would come next?

King Gairith watched him. "Would you have preferred to be untroubled with an estate?"

"Nay, sire. Please do not think me ungrateful."

"Do you dislike the title?"

"Though it sits oddly now, I appreciate that too."

"Mm. What troubles you, then?"

He couldn't say the worst of it. "Uh...my name is Thomas Kaituer, yet I heard...must I change it?"

"'Tis not required, though Navayn could be added."

"I prefer my name as my father gave it to me."

"Then it is so. Nonetheless, in presenting you with the Navayn sword, I have released you from the Kaituer vow."

Thomas's face must have betrayed him, for the king said, "Worry not. I have men-at-arms enough, and I will not call you to battle when I need you at Navayn Manor. But neither will I have you fumbling with a sword worthy of honor. Thus, my sword master expects you each morn until you depart Fraetinloch Palace."

"As you wish." Thomas steeled himself for the next surprise.

"That is all."

Relief sent a tingle down Thomas's back. He made a proper exit to the corridor.

Duke Tristelle followed him and briefly clasped his shoulder. "Come. Let us walk where we may breathe." The duke knew each turn to take, leading toward the back of the palace. The privileged access of a son-in-law. No need to speak in these corridors where they might be overheard. The duke opened a simple, arched door and led him through it.

Thomas halted and stared around the enclosed garden. "I had no idea this was here."

"'Tis a private, family garden. We should be alone." Duke Tristelle strolled along a flagstone path, then pointed. "Unless the little princess, Shellisse, remembers her doll." It sat propped between broad, variegated leaves, dressed in demure white muslin with colored ribbons inexpertly tied in its hair. The duke retrieved it and laid it upon a bench as they walked past.

"How long have you known the king planned this?" Thomas asked.

"Since yesterday."

"I still cannot grasp it. Why would he suddenly decide to ennoble me?"

"I doubt 'tis sudden. The signs were small, but he has always shown interest in you. Asked, for instance, whether you read the Lavaycian histories he gifted to my library. When you were not present, he often wanted to hear of your involvement in Tower Woods. He is a king and thinks to the future. And indeed, 'twould have been cruel to drop an estate and title upon you when you were barely grown and half-educated."

"True." Thomas followed the path around a bed of burgundy foliage. White flowers nodded above the leaves in a square of sunlight that made it past the four-story walls. "I have never even understood why he raised the matter of the will and Navayn Manor."

"Could be the desire to check Maerton's grasping tendencies. Could be innate pursuit of justice, for he knew the truth of its ownership. Could be other reasons yet unstated. I did hear him say he needs you at Navayn Manor. Perhaps some concerns of the common folk go unmet, which you will soon learn of."

"He had no need to ennoble me for that."

"I think you are missing the point. You have always been noble."

"You've called me noble before, but I thought you meant…in character."

"Both are true."

"Not by birth," Thomas said. "The House of Kaituer was stripped of nobility."

"The House of Navayn was not."

"But none of us held a title."

"Because you were in exile. A title is granted in ceremony, such as today. 'Twas wise of you to swear fealty again with your new title. Most lords are vassals of their duke or duchess. You are among the elite lords sworn directly to the king. Did you realize that?"

Thomas shook his head. "My mind devises no schemes of rank. Especially in *that* moment. 'Twas simply in my heart to swear allegiance."

"Interesting point," the duke murmured.

"What?"

"Schemes are of the mind, and wisdom is of the heart." He seemed to ponder, then said, "But regardless of all that—you *were* born noble."

Why did he not understand? "We were common!" Too loud. "You have seen the little holding where we lived. There is a proper cottage now, but we lived in a hovel before the king came to Tower Woods. A floor of dirt, beds of ferns and grass. How can you call that anything but common?"

Duke Tristelle stopped and turned to face him. "You were noble but *believed* you were common. And yet, Thomas, you lead. 'Tis in your character. Because of you, your mother and stepfather now dwell in safety. You find solutions. You pursue justice. You aid the impoverished. Shake off the lie you were taught and admit that you are noble."

The duke's words reached deep—resonated within—and shrieked discord with all else. "'Tis as though I'm not who I am." Thomas grimaced and shook his head. "I mean, *I* know who I am, but...others won't let me be that. When I was honored as Sir Thomas—by the king and queen, no less—the nobles still disdained me. This time, the king honors me with the title of lord, but the duke in my own duchy will always mock me. Nor will he be the only one. The nobles have always considered me unfit for their daughters." His breath sounded huffy. "For a few minutes, one hope made my new title seem precious. Perhaps I could have a wife and family. Then, the king himself forbade it."

"Ah." The duke's brow puckered. "That did surprise me when he forbade you to court a woman, though it sounds temporary to me."

Thomas crimped his lips. "If it is temporary for too long, it will become permanent."

"Mm. This brings back memories of my own courtship."

"What did you do?"

"I remembered that we serve a God of hope, so I asked him to bring her back to me. And then I asked him a hundred times for patience. At least you have a greater command of that virtue than I do."

"So you have said before, but I feel none today."

The duke chuckled. "As for the rest—what others think or say or do—know this. Whenever you pursue a worthy purpose, someone will *always* stand in your way. Ignore what has no power to stop you. Overcome *real* obstacles. Certain, my advice is neither pleasant nor easy, but you have only two choices. Live true to your destiny or live in regret."

CHAPTER 18

Duke Maerton departed the palace as soon as the audience ended, taking his son with him. Best to get Ivan out of company, since he wouldn't still his mocking tongue.

The carriage clattered through the cobbled streets of Purthellia, then left them for dirt roads through the surrounding fields and into Maerton Duchy.

The duke barely listened to his son's complaints, so laced with contempt for Thomas Kaituer. The sway of the carriage triggered his accustomed process of thinking through all that had occurred, searching out unseen problems or opportunities. Much easier when the carriage held no griping son.

"Why didn't you tell me?" Ivan demanded.

"Tell you what?"

"Have I not said enough to make that clear?"

"Far more than enough, but little to the point," Maerton said. "What should I have told you?"

"That the Kaituer would gain a title. So *knowing* as you claim to be, why did you not foresee *that*?"

"The greater question is why *you* did not foresee it. That possibility existed ever since his lineage was confirmed. All the more likely, when he saved the king's life. I had hoped the king would limit his advancement to the courtesy title of *sir*, but 'twas always clear that Thomas Kaituer had a right to the title of Lord Navayn."

At last, silence in the carriage. Except for Ivan's quivery breaths. At least he seemed to be smoothing them. The duke resumed his own considerations, only to be interrupted again.

"Your attempt to keep control of the rents also failed."

"I made no such attempt. Lady Navayn's will, which you kept pretending to misunderstand, clearly bequeathed the entire estate. I only left some vagueness, which *might* have been useful against a naïve lord. A slim chance, worth only minor effort. Learn from this. 'Twas far better to give it up gracefully than to let others accuse us of retaining what we gave." Maerton steadied himself as the carriage headed down a bank toward a stream and bridge. "Likewise, it would be well for you to stop raging when you have no valid complaint."

Ivan cast him a daggered look but kept his lips closed.

They rattled over the bridge planks as Maerton said, "You have obtained what you first proposed—releasing Navayn Manor to Thomas Kaituer. Yet you rage over success. What did you hope to gain?"

"Not to call him lord or exchange equal bows."

"Such bows look the same whether you respect or despise the recipient. They cost you nothing but may hide your thoughts at a crucial juncture. Unless, of course, your mockery gives it all away. But you have not answered. What did you hope to gain?"

"To keep him near, of course."

Near? Maerton's stomach tightened. He cast about for other possibilities than the first one that occurred. Perhaps to keep a Kaituer out of Tower Woods, where he held much favor among the People of the Woods. Somewhat problematic, but not enough reason. Perhaps to separate him from Tristelle patronage. Even less important. Maerton swallowed and asked, "Why do you want him near?"

Ivan turned from the window and regarded him. "Ah, you can

more easily pretend you do not know if I do not state the obvious. But it matters not. Indeed, I thank you for your counsel, Father, for the irritation caused me to forget the most important point. I have gained the desired result and have plenty of time. His title will not matter in the end. I shall perfect my bow and use of that title." He narrowed his eyes thoughtfully, leaning back as the carriage ascended a long slope. "I think a gift is in order for our new neighbor. Something innocuous, that he would value. What should it be, Father? A pity, I suppose, that the Kaituer jewels were reset for the use of Maerton ladies. Perhaps we can present him with a stone from Kaituer Castle. Make a little ceremony of it when he visits the graves."

"You will do nothing so ill-judged."

Ivan chuckled. "Something else, then. But we *are* going there, aren't we?"

"Certain. Dukes Selta and Tristelle have access to the royal ears like no one else. I'll not have them in Maerton Duchy without my presence. Even in the wasteland."

"I hope Duke Selta brings his family. If Lady Sareen is with him, we must invite them to stay at Maerton Castle." Ivan talked on, weaving back to the mundane...hunting...some trivia about the seaward cliffs. Calm now.

But Maerton remembered what Ivan had not answered.

CHAPTER 19

Thomas rode with Lord Dermont behind Dukes Tristelle and Selta. The ride was neither as dusty nor as hot as it could have been, for it had rained in the night. Grain stood tall in the fields that flanked the road. Forest remained wherever the lay of the land was not conducive to farming. They passed a few estates, and Lord Dermont pointed them out to Thomas. He could see but little of the manor houses. Stone structures beyond lawns with spreading trees. Would his new home look similar?

Lord Dermont seemed determined upon cheerful friendliness. Did he feel awkward over their conversation in Tower Woods? Thomas tried not to think of that or even of Lady Sareen, who bore Duchess Selta company in the carriage behind them. At least she was present, though it gave scant comfort. Lord Dermont pointed out another estate and spoke of the family. Nothing to be seen but a high hedge.

"Am I boring you?" Lord Dermont asked.

"Not in the least." Thomas turned his head to meet his eyes. "Forgive me for conversing so little. 'Tis only because I am trying to remember the road and land along with everything you tell me."

"Have you not ridden this road before?"

"Nay. When coming from Tower Woods to Purthellia, we approach along the north side of the River Vale."

"I don't envy you trying to grasp so much at once. But you'll have a reprieve soon." Lord Dermont pointed to where the road entered woodland—the ordinary sort, dwarfed by the tower trees beyond. "'Tis only about a mile from the forest's edge until we reach the new road north through Tower Woods."

New compared to the roads of Maerton, though it had seen a few years of travel now. Much like all the roads of Tristelle Duchy, not yet worn down between banks like here. This was a different land in so many subtle ways.

They reached the T junction, where the new road branched from the old. Here, the woods had been cleared somewhat, allowing space for travelers and horses to rest. A few structures had been built, one ready to become an ale house the instant travelers arrived. With sudden bustle, workday furnishings were shoved aside in the front room and replaced with trestles and boards. Even so, many sat outside, for this was a large cavalcade. Two households—and the Duchess of Selta did not travel light.

Unimaginably odd, Thomas also had a carriage with two horses. A gift from Duke Tristelle. At the moment, it held his travel trunk and a rather remarkable collection of household supplies.

Duke Tristelle greeted the proprietor, whom he'd met when traveling this way before. "Has the king's herald reached you yet and read the title decree of Lord Navayn?"

"Aye, my lord duke."

Thomas stepped to his side for the introduction. He completed this one much like all the others, also introducing Jonathan Cotrell as his squire whenever he met commoners. Best to be well known here now, and he was going to need all the help he could get in remembering everyone.

Thomas sat at the head table on Duke Tristelle's right. This was going to be the last time for...he knew not how many days. Bittersweet. They ate plain fare, then walked outside together, moving a little apart from those who were preparing to resume travel.

"I don't much care for today's parting," the duke said.

"Nor I. It seems as though...we part ways." Thomas cleared his throat, for it had tightened. "Not entirely, of course."

"True. A two-day journey between us. 'Twould be wisest for you to remain at your estate until you've built knowledge and trust with your new servants and tenants. I shall come eventually to visit, and I daresay my duchess will be anxious to set out, as well. In the meantime, I'll send Captain D'Jorge to see how you fare. He may be of use to you if the buildings are not what they should be."

"He will be most welcome." Thomas licked his lips. Why were the most important words always the hardest? "My lord..." He raised his eyes to the man to whom he owed so much and saw his feelings mirrored.

The duke grasped his shoulder. "You are like a young brother to me, Thomas, so when we are not in company, use my name, *Tristan,* as I use *Thomas.* In days to come, we will visit like family, and Tristelle Castle will always be another home for you."

Though his lips fought to frame the words *my lord,* Thomas said, "Tristan..." Such an odd feeling, but the duke smiled. Thomas shook his head. "There are so many things...your words, deeds, advice, trust...so much you have done for me, and I would like to thank you for each, but I cannot even seem to say one of them. So just...thank you!" He clasped Tristan's shoulder, returning the pressure of his grip.

"You are most welcome. It has been my joy to do so."

They turned, then, toward the dividing parties. Jonathan was talking with his father...perhaps a leave-taking as well. Thomas remembered one of the more mundane things he had wanted to say. "I daresay the news of my title will spread through Tower Woods as if tongues are wings."

"Doubtless. I'll ensure reading of the decree in Tower Woods Village on my way through."

"It seems disrespectful for my mother and stepfather to hear it by rumor rather than from me, but I must go south. Will you detour from the main road to tell them for me?"

"Certain."

"Also..." Thomas puckered his brow. "I've not had time to think much on it, but if any of the People of the Woods seem inclined to seek work with..." He smirked. "...this new Lord Navayn fellow, perhaps they could come along with Captain D'Jorge." He rubbed the back of his neck and huffed. "I don't even know how many I need or what tasks...ugh."

"Probably some to tend the demesne fields, at a minimum. Worry not. D'Jorge is good at such. I'll tell him to bring a few, and he can fetch more later, after you've judged your need. All these details will come together in the end." They reached the horses, and the duke took Dauntless's reins. "Fare you well, Thomas."

"Fare you well, my lor—Tristan."

The duke's broad smile stretched, then he mounted.

Thomas strode to his own horse, where Jonathan met him. Better yet, one of Duke Selta's grooms—How many did he have? —led Lady Sareen's mare to her. Thomas unhooked the bow he'd left on his saddle, slipped it over his shoulder, and situated it aside the Navayn sword. His sword. This was the first day he had worn it while riding. Awkward like everything else, but he would get used to it. Dreadful if the need arose to draw it after only a few days of training. The sword master had mostly taught him some ways to use his strength and agility to advantage and cautioned against trying anything fancy until he had much more practice. Thomas mounted, hoping he *never* had to draw that sword against a true opponent.

They rode westward, and Lord Dermont spoke of the best approaches to Tower Woods. The tower trees so contorted the rocky land that it was best to know pathways if one wanted to enter. This area, Lord Dermont knew well, for he'd commanded men here when King Gairith took Tower Woods from Duke Maerton's control.

The farther they rode, the more Thomas's thoughts harked back to that arrow. This was not the route he had taken on that ominous day, but he soon recognized the changing landscape. 'Twas rockier here, and little was cultivated.

The road began a long rise through sparse trees, and in the distance, Thomas glimpsed the one remaining tower parapet of Kaituer Castle. Where he had nearly been killed.

Some minutes later, Lady Sareen shaded her eyes and said, "I think I can make out a structure."

"Likely the tower," Duke Selta said. "One is mostly intact—or was when I saw it years ago."

"I hope we will be alone," Lady Sareen said. "That is, without Duke Maerton's people hovering about."

Thomas smiled gently at her. "I hate to disappoint, but there is a carriage nigh the castle ruins."

She squinted and shaded her eyes again. "Where? I can't see it."

"You will soon. Off to the left."

"Oh, your long vision. I so often wonder what that is like."

"Much like yours, I imagine, just farther." Realizing how soft his voice had grown, Thomas set his focus ahead.

Hints of abandoned farms appeared. Rows of stones and bushes, which may have divided fields. A barren pathway branched to the right. Perhaps a lane, once. Even the road they traveled had grown rough and weedy, long unkept. It seemed it would continue straight but ended in tall grasses a few yards after two cart tracks split to either side.

Here, Lord Ivan met them, mounted on a tan horse with a mane like ripened wheat. A beautiful animal, albeit rather nervous. "Greetings, my esteemed friends," he called out as they approached.

"Good day, Lord Ivan," the duke said.

He spread an arm toward the south cart track. "My father would like to welcome you, and we have cleared space for you to rest not far from the graveyard." He turned with the words and led them on to where his father waited in the shade of a broad tree, likely old enough to have witnessed the fall of the House of Kaituer.

Ample space had been cleared, and coachmen halted their jolting equipages. Duke Selta helped his wife step down from her carriage, and greetings ensued. Throughout the courtesies, Thomas surveyed the land. Grass had been cut around the taller monuments in the graveyard, which lay south of the castle ruins. The forked tracks must flank the site of the burned village.

At his side, Jonathan studied the environs too, as did the groom that had helped Lady Sareen. Or perhaps he had some other position, for he did not tend horses now.

The Maertons offered cool water to quench the travelers' thirsts. Likely a stream had flowed here for centuries, caring nothing for the rages of men or the ravages of time.

"We discovered," Duke Maerton said to Thomas, "where the Kaituer graves lie. Come, I will show you." He clasped an ebony-topped walking stick and trod a cleared path. A well-dressed servant followed him, and other men stood off beyond the graves, their tools at rest. All in workday clothes, though some garments looked poorer than others.

Lord Ivan must have seen the direction of Thomas's gaze, for he said, "We summoned locals to help clear such a large area. They seemed strangely reluctant to scythe the Kaituer graves for your visit."

Not worth answering. A long row of tall monuments paralleled the bare foundation of the castle wall. Each plot was bordered with a rectangle of stones, their lines now awry. The finely-dressed party seemed out of place, parading past desolate crumbling headstones, then stopping before the final three.

"Liam Kaituer," Duke Maerton said, pointing to the center one. "His first wife on the left, and his second, Lady Anne Navayn, on the right."

'Twas the latter site that Thomas looked to first. Gray stone, carved with the name *Anne Navayn Kaituer*. He let wordless thanks to her whisper in his heart, for he knew that his grandfather would have been a different man without her rearing. Insects buzzed in the taller grass. Birds flitted overhead. Movement caught Thomas's eye, and his gaze flicked above the graveyard. A falcon caught its prey in midair. No cause for his pulse to quicken as it did.

Thomas lowered his eyes to his great-grandfather's grave. "I didn't expect to find the last duke's grave, much less a fine marker."

"Doubtless, the marker was set in advance." Duke Maerton said it like that was something everyone knew.

It did look like it had been chiseled by the same hand that fashioned the second duchess's marker. "Is it known whether he was actually buried here?"

"So it seems," the Maerton servant said, taking a step nearer. "A few locals still live near who remember the, uh, siege."

Duke Maerton gestured to the servant without looking at him and murmured, "My steward, Lord Navayn."

Was it possible that Thomas could find his questionable guide here? "If any are nigh, I would speak with them."

The steward set off toward the workers. Thomas scanned their faces. The ruddy-nosed guide was not among them. Nonetheless, the steward returned with one of them, a scythe propped over the man's shoulder.

Many lines etched his weathered face, though he bore himself upright. He bowed and said, "My lords and ladies." When he straightened, he stared at Thomas. "Aye, ye 'ave the look of Lord Thomas. Are ye the new lord?"

"I am Thomas Kaituer, Lord of Navayn. How old were you when you last saw my grandfather?"

"Just old enough to trot along holding my mama's skirt. She carried her baskets through the castle gate each morn."

Thomas pointed to the grave. "Were you old enough to remember whether Duke Kaituer was buried here?"

He shrugged. "My mama said he was."

"Do you know what became of the bodies of his three older sons?"

"Oh, aye. My mama *hated* them. Said they were thrown together into a single grave. 'Twas dug in the walkway behind the duke's and first duchess's grave, so folk would walk on it." He pointed to rocky dirt. "That spot there, for sure. They covered the grave with the wall's broken stone, for the miscreants threw a lady from the wall."

Ivan uttered a faint snort as though amused. "Do you walk it often, then?"

The man glared at him. "'Tis folly to walk on graves." He turned back to Thomas. "Mayhap the good duchess will rest now."

"Do you remember her?"

"Nay, but my mama spoke kind words of her. Some say she walks at night, moaning for her lost son. Others say that the moans rise from the village—from the bones and ashes never buried."

"Where?" Lady Sareen murmured, looking over her shoulder.

"Yon." The man pointed toward the desolate land between the ruined keep and where the road ended. "The east gate was there, and ye can still see the cobbles that ran under the big gatehouse. The village stretched beyond, along the road."

"Do you happen to know where the Harnon family graves are?" Thomas asked.

The man scratched the back of his head. "Don't know that name."

"Who were they?" Duchess Selta asked.

"My grandmother's family."

"Ah, your common ancestors," Ivan said. "We had best look among the farthest graves, then."

"Among the nearer," Thomas said. "They were well-off and educated. The duke considered Lady Esther a suitable bride for his son."

Their party began walking along the graves, searching for Harnon and the name of the ancestor the Seltas sought. The local man tromped off to his friends, then returned with some of them.

Soon, Lady Sareen said, "Here is one that says Harnon. Ah, several of them."

"If you'll just step back, my lady," the eldest local said, then he swung his scythe, as did a younger man.

Duchess Selta found the grave she sought and called her family nigh. The better dressed of the workers set to clearing it, though the locals stayed with Thomas.

He read given names he didn't recognize, but mostly studied the dates—all before the fall of the castle. A headstone—one of a pair—bore a woman's name but no date.

A worker with a rake swept away the cut grass, revealing no outline of stones. "None rest here," he said. "Whoever 'twas meant for must 'ave burned in the village."

Somehow the unused grave struck Thomas as sadder than the filled ones. "Lord Thomas's wife, Lady Esther, had a grandmother Harnon who died in the fire. Her body would have been in her house." He looked around the faces that watched him. "Were no remains gathered and decently buried?"

A disgruntled voice said, "'Twas certain the king's and prince's men cared naught for burying the dead."

Another said, "From all I hear, they did na' care about the living either."

Someone else whispered *hush* and looked sideways to where the Maertons attended the Selta family.

"Grievous, hungry days, those were," the eldest local said. "Folk searched for food, not the dead."

Thomas looked to the grassy village site. "I've heard how hard it was for those who fled into Tower Woods, but I know little of those who stayed nigh the castle." Near their unburied beloved ones. Like Lady Esther's grandmother. So long, it had been—was there any chance that her bones could be found?

He strode up the slope. Entangling grass caught at his boots. Easier to walk the wall's stripped foundation.

Footsteps followed him. Jonathan's among them, certain, for his squire would not leave him alone here. Thomas trod the foundation, crossed the cobblestones that the local had mentioned, and continued on. Esther's house must have been on the north side of the village. He left the castle ruins and followed the north cart track.

Jonathan came alongside him. "What are you looking for?"

"The Harnon house where Lady Esther once lived. 'Twas of stone at the edge of the village. It collapsed with her grandmother inside."

A small crowd of locals followed him. One of them said, "Aye, there is a stone wall in the rubble just ahead."

They were able to get near enough to discern part of an outline—a couple feet high where stones remained intact. Thomas studied the remains. The others talked of what they knew of the ruins, and who else might know more—perhaps even be certain whether this was the Harnon house. Thomas stared at coarse grass among char and rock washed by decades of rain. Futile to think he could find remains. Yet, he offered silent respect to the ancestor who'd guided his grandmother's childhood.

After a moment, he turned to the locals. That servant of Selta hovered in the background too. Odd, but no matter. "I thank you for clearing graves and helping me find where one more may lie."

"'Tis well to honor one's dead," the eldest said. "If, uh, if we were to find out for certain where she lay, what would you want done?"

"I've not thought on it." He glanced over the barren expanse. "So many lie here, also worthy of burial."

"Aye, my father's in there, too…somewhere."

Others murmured of relatives they never knew…lost to the fire.

After a bit, the eldest said, "My mama took to the Eberles' after the fire, for there was no food here. When Lord Eberle tossed us all out, we came back. Not that it helped much, 'cause the new duke didn't care if we ate. I'd see folk staring out over the burnt village—it still smelled of fire back then—but I never saw anyone search for bodies. Too late, I suppose, and much too late now."

"'Twould seem that…" Thomas struggled for something worth saying. "That something could be done in memorial. Maybe ring the village with stones or such to mark it as a gravesite."

The elder snorted. "Folk started doing that between their days' toil. Shifting the fallen stone from the walls. Then, the new duke sent men to take it all away to build his new castle."

Thomas realized his mouth had dropped open and closed it. Lord Ivan was approaching the site from the far side. Would he cross the village remains? "Come," Thomas said, and strode along the cart track toward the castle ruins.

Another had noticed and said, "Let's make haste to the edge, afore he walks on our ancestors again."

"Does he come here often?" someone asked from behind.

"Not oft, but he rides about the land now and then, acting like a great man. Saw him a few weeks ago."

Another said, "I once saw him ride his horse right through the village. Likely on the road, but no one knows where folk died. Disgraceful!"

Ivan did tread along the edge of the village ruins, but Thomas caught his eye and nodded toward the castle, thus diverting him. By the time they met on hard-packed ground by the foundation, the locals were hastening past in tightlipped silence.

"Looking for more ancestors?" Ivan asked.

"Did you want me for some cause?"

"Duke Selta does," Ivan said. "Apparently, one of those gifts to the dead is planned and requires your presence."

What could he mean?

CHAPTER 20

Thomas returned with Ivan to the graveyard, rejoining the Selta family near the Kaituer graves. The gift proved to be a decorative monument cast in bronze and representing two lilies in a vase. Duke Selta presented it on behalf of his sister, the queen, and read a message from her, which included the words engraved on the monument.

In memory of
Lady Anne Navayn
Duchess of Kaituer
presented by
King Gairith and Queen Ellianne

In all the formal words spoken at the palace, none had included her title of duchess or the name of Kaituer. What did the Maertons think of this? Though he wanted to look at the father and son standing to one side, Thomas instead addressed words of thanks to Duke Selta as royal proxy. Duke Maerton murmured something about the king's magnanimous gift, and Lord Ivan said flatly, "Quite so." He strode off toward their carriage, and Duke Maerton made a more polite exit from the graveside.

Thomas watched them go, then turned back in time to catch Lady Sareen directing a pointed look to her mother. The raised brows and quirked lips seemed to say, *you see what I mean?*

"What a charming neighbor you'll have," Lord Dermont said.

Duke Selta regarded Thomas with a considering eye. "'Twould seem, Lord Navayn, that you are the least annoyed of any of us."

In truth, Ivan was behaving better than he had in the past, but Thomas only said, "His manners reflect on him, not on me."

Duke Selta's shoulders shook. As he moved aside, he motioned to a couple of his servants who held tools, though he spoke to Thomas. "They will set the base and see that all is properly affixed. Do you think of setting out at once, or of looking over the castle ruins?"

"Oh, do say you will look around," Lady Sareen said, "so that I may have an excuse to look too."

Thomas tamed his smile. "That was my intent, my lady, so I will gladly escort you."

Duchess Selta tsked. "Do go with them, Dermont, for I daresay it is too rugged for a lady."

Lord Dermont bowed and declared, "We will protect my delicate little sister, Mother."

"Oh, children!" she exclaimed good-naturedly. "Do not play too long in the castle, for we still have a journey ahead, and I fancy I heard thunder."

She began walking away, but Thomas hurried to take the opportunity he'd been seeking. "As to the journey..."

The duke and duchess looked at him, waiting.

He cleared his throat. "If you'd like to break it at Navayn Manor—and can excuse that I don't know what we'll find there—you are most welcome to, uh, stay with me."

"Our pleasure, thank you," the duke said.

The duchess waved her hand aside. "Oh, I daresay 'twill be

comfortable enough, and if not, we will call it an adventure." She strolled away toward the carriages in the shade, but Duke Selta accompanied them, soon drawing Thomas back.

Thomas readily complied, for that servant of Selta was behind him again. "Why does your servant follow me?"

"I told him to. Does it concern you that you will likely employ servants who have worked their whole lives for the Maertons?" The duke's voice was soft enough that it may not even reach his children, stepping onto the foundation ahead.

"The thought has occurred." 'Twas no less worrying that others thought of it too.

"Mm. I can vouch for this man, who has performed various tasks when I had additional needs. He understands the situation, and since the Maertons have never seen him—except today, nigh you—they will assume he was already in your employ. Should you choose to hire him."

Now Duke Selta was helping him? It seemed a little too good to be true, but aid would be hard to reject. And indeed, an advantage—if Thomas could overcome his suspicions of the well-wishers who had so recently disregarded him. "His name?" Thomas asked.

"Griven." They stopped atop the foundation, and the duke looked over the ruins. "I'll leave you to clamber over this jumble."

He left, and Griven waited a couple paces distant on the foundation. Jonathan eyed him. Best not let this look like an introduction. Thomas hopped down a foot to what must have been the bailey. "Come. We can talk of details later, but for now, Jonathan is my squire—the son of Captain Cotrell, of Duke Tristelle's household. Jonathan, this is Griven, now in my employ, though you may allow those of Maerton to assume he has been with us longer."

"Oh." Jonathan said without enthusiasm.

The two matched Thomas's slow pace, watching for uneven paving stones.

"Lest we contradict each other," Thomas said, "what work skills do you offer me, Griven?"

"I can do most anything, my lord. Tend your horse, repair furniture, weed your garden, carry messages. Perhaps you hired me in Purthellia after the king granted use of your title. You might need a man of many trades, willing to fetch and carry. The less we claim to know of each other, the less likely we'll trip up."

"True. Later for the rest, then." Thomas caught up to Lady Sareen, who kept looking over her shoulder at him.

"It has just occurred to me," she said, "that...well, wasn't it near here that an arrow was shot at you?"

"Aye, my lady, you needn't look so worried. Even if the coward were here, he would not shoot again with so many to witness and likely catch him." Thomas hoped that was true.

"Where did it happen?" Lord Dermont asked.

"At the keep." Thomas took them onward, with Lady Sareen between him and her brother. They skirted clumps of weeds and grass that filled every fracture in the bailey. Though Thomas chatted, he swiftly studied every gaping window in what remained of the keep's towers.

He stopped beside the wall the arrow had struck. All looked the same as he remembered.

"Is this the place?" Jonathan asked, eyeing the ruined keep as diligently as Thomas.

"Aye."

"Which direction did it come from," Griven asked.

Thomas considered...the blur...the ricochet. He pointed. "I think from that way."

"High or low?"

"Slightly above, but not by much. Now that I have time to look...the archer may not even have been in a tower."

Lady Sareen was staring, wide-eyed, at everything. Were they scaring her? "Would you like to go inside and get a look from the tower, my lady?"

She nodded, her sweet smile appearing. "Please."

Thomas took them up to the top chamber. Now that he had walked along the village and through the bailey on a clear day, he grasped the lay of castle, village, and forest. As much as he could judge from ruins and old stories, this must have been his grandfather's chamber.

Jonathan glanced into the circular room but stayed in the corridor that opened to the sky.

Thomas stepped back to him. "Where is Griven?"

"He clambered off to where the arrow had come from."

Thomas raised his brows and returned to his guests. Nay, not his guests, for this was Maerton land. Why did it feel like he was the host? Would he even feel like a host in Navayn Manor?

Lord Dermont's booted steps echoed as he circled the bare space. He ran his fingers over the chisel scars above the gaping fireplace. "They even scavenged the mantel."

Thomas looked down from the north window. Not much rubble...the stones likely removed rather than battered.

Lady Sareen joined him at the window. "I had hoped to view the village from above," she said. "Maybe discern streets and such, but I cannot see any of it."

He shook his head. "The keep wall wouldn't have permitted a window facing that direction."

"So sad...all those people dying in such a horrible way." She licked her lips. "So desolate here." Her lips still moved like she had more to say.

He waited.

"'Twas uncanny when that man spoke of the moaning at night. What could it be?"

Lord Dermont's grin was stretching. Before he could tease her, Thomas said, "Owls. There are at least a half dozen kinds in Tower Woods, which isn't far to a bird. Some of their hoots sound mournful."

Her breath eased out. "Ah, that explains it far better than he did." She narrowed her eyes at her brother's grin. "I did not say I thought it was ghosts!" A distant rumble merged with his laughter, and Sareen glanced outside. "Ugh! I was hoping Mother was wrong about thunder."

"She's not going to be happy," Lord Dermont said. "We'd best head down."

This, they did and found Griven on the stairs that had once led into the keep. A servant was heading their way and motioned for them to come as distant clouds rolled.

They headed across the bailey. "Jonathan," Thomas asked, "where is the storm?"

"East of us. Been moving south for the past hour. Likely miss the castle, or I would have told you."

The other three stared at him.

"His ears are as keen as my eyes," Thomas said.

"Long vision and sharp ears?" Griven asked, looking from one to the other.

"Aye," Thomas said.

"How I envy you both."

"You wouldn't envy me as much," Jonathan said, "if the storm were right overhead. That's the one time I want to find the innermost room of a castle."

"My mother too." Lady Sareen hurried along, gripping the bent arms of each gentleman. "Though exactly what she hears, I've never quite known, for she covers her ears before the sound reaches mine. Which direction are we heading next, Dermont?"

"East, southeast."

"Oh, dear!"

Duke Maerton's carriage was gone. Likewise, the workers. Grooms were busy with the horses.

Duke Selta stood beside his carriage, looking impatient. "Come, Sareen."

She hastened up the steps as Lord Dermont said, "Ride inside with them, Father. I know the way."

"Whatever you do," the duke said, "don't go to Maerton Castle. The duke invited us, and they took offense when I told him we are staying at Navayn Manor."

Thomas hooked his quiver with the bow on his saddle and donned his cloak. He kept the garment folded back, since rain was doubtful. The haste seemed strange. 'Twas only thunder, after all. Lord Dermont mounted and rode around the group attending the Seltas, reminding Thomas that he, too, had a carriage, which would be last upon the road. He assigned Griven to ride with it, lest a need arise.

A moment later, they set out, Thomas and Lord Dermont leading. The afternoon was well advanced, but they should be able to reach the manor by the dinner hour. Lord Dermont's talk ran more freely now, as he pointed out landmarks while they traveled and told of the last hunt he had joined on Duke Maerton's estate.

The road angled more southward. Clear sky to the west met the cloud line overhead. It seemed to trace the road. "How much farther?" Thomas asked.

"About a mile to Maerton Village." Lord Dermont raised his voice over rumbling thunder. "I don't know the road to Navayn Manor, so we'll stop at the inn to inquire the way. It shouldn't—"

Lightning cracked double. A shaft ahead, and another behind. Shrill neighs made Thomas turn back. A rearing horse nearly unseated its rider. One of the led horses was trying to bolt. The carriage horses fought the coachman, one of them seemingly out of his control. Someone grabbed its bridle, but it took a moment to stop its rearing and kicking.

When the chaos settled somewhat, Duke Selta's voice demanded, "Well? What is it?"

Lord Dermont rode to the opened window of the carriage. "One of the horses got his leg over the traces and kicked his mate." A high-pitched voice uttered something else, and Lord Dermont said, "We'll take care of it. All is well."

Jonathan came back from riding to the rear and reported nothing worse than fidgety horses. The grooms were sorting out traces, their voices calm and steady. Delay and then more delay, for the kicked horse limped. They traveled on at a walk, only to halt again at a limb lying across the road, its branches waving in the fitful wind.

"Now, what's to be done with *that?*" Lord Dermont snarled.

Rhetorical question, but Thomas rode nigh to check how the limb rested. "Have you ropes?" He pointed. "A horse or two can drag it off that way."

Lumpy, gray clouds extended above them, murmuring like grumbling old men. Servants hastened to clear the obstruction, doubtless thinking of the lowering sun and the light that darted among clouds. They were just gathering up their ropes when pattering swept the leafy forest.

"Here it comes," Thomas said, flipping his hood up and drawing his cloak around him.

Lord Dermont rejoined him, lifting his voice above the rain. "My father suggests we spend the night at the inn, rather than searching for the manor in the dark."

"Aye," Thomas said. They'd be soaked soon.

They set off again, soon passing some cottages. Then, the welcome sound of cobblestones under the horses' hooves. A large building with lanterns hanging below its porch roof materialized through the rain.

Thomas pointed and shouted, "Is that it?"

"Aye," Lord Dermont also shouted over the rain. "Ride ahead and tell the landlord we're coming and want rooms and dinner."

Thomas and Jonathan picked up their pace and arrived as the downpour began to ease. Thomas dismounted, passed his reins to Jonathan, and ran up the porch steps two at a time. Lights glowed from windows, hinting at cozy welcome.

He pushed the door open and stepped within. A taproom to his left and dining space to the right, with a stone fireplace between them. A casually pleasant room, not too crowded. Sudden silence descended.

A man of several decades straightened before him, his blond hair and brown beard well sprinkled with gray. Nothing cozy or welcoming about those narrowed eyes, nor his growling pitch. "Never did I think to see a Kaituer darken the door of my inn."

How did they recognize him so quickly? Thomas had no time for the disdain. "Nor did I think to see it. Please direct my squire to—"

"Now that you have, you may take yourself off."

Softly hurried footsteps pattered. Thomas kept his voice level. "Ladies will arrive shortly in need of dinner and beds. If you will—"

"*Ladies* stay at the castle. Don't know what sort of women would be traveling with you."

Heat darted through Thomas, quick as lightning. A matron emerged from a back room, gasped, and stared like all the patrons. Thomas let a single breath pass, then said, "Insult me, if you think it well, but do not insult the Duchess of Selta or Lady Sareen."

A younger man squeezed past the woman and stopped beside the innkeeper, whom he resembled. "Pray pardon my father... him not knowing...uh...who are you?"

"Lord Navayn."

This younger man managed a slight bow. "Ah! My father did not realize..."

"I did, and I don't care about titles comin' out of nowhere. We are loyal to Duke Maerton."

"Clearly," Thomas said. "Are you also loyal to the king?"

"Well...'course we're loyal to the king, but..."

"Then, accustom yourself to his decree. Will you provide dinner and beds, or not?"

The door behind Thomas opened as he spoke, and Lord Dermont demanded, "Has no one here an umbrella for the ladies? What is the delay?"

Someone scurried past, and the younger man hurried through a bow as he headed for the door. "At once, my lord. Pray pardon us for being caught in surprise."

Lord Dermont scanned the staring faces and narrowed his eyes toward the innkeeper. "Is there a problem?"

Thomas answered, wanting an end to it. Calm words were best. "'Tis only I, to whom he objects. Doubtless, they will make the ladies comfortable."

Thomas began to turn, but Lord Dermont held an unyielding pose, gaze fixed on the innkeeper. "Since you were surprised, allow me the pleasure of introducing Lord Navayn."

Footsteps crossed the threshold, and the innkeeper's gaze darted past Thomas, then he bowed and said, "My Lord Navayn."

CHAPTER 21

A lad hefted a can of hot water onto the washstand, then stepped back to the open doorway. He looked up at Thomas. "Will there be anythin' else, sir?" Certain, he was the youngest member of the establishment.

"Was it you who brushed mud from my cloak and boots?" Thomas asked.

His eyes rounded. "I did the best I could, sir."

"For which I thank you." Thomas smiled and held out a coin.

The lad brightened and clutched the coin. "Thank ye, sir." He backed into the corridor, and Thomas was about to shut the door, when an irate voice issued from the largest bedchamber. Whatever the demand had been, it sent an inn servant scurrying down the stairs. The lad looked up at Thomas and whispered, "I'm glad I got to wait on you instead of the duke."

Thomas nodded and closed the door. The shaving water was tepid, but he made do.

Jonathan returned from the stables as he finished. "Your coachman is unhappy with the feed for the horses and with Griven."

"Over what fault?"

"Being friendly in the morning, I gather." Jonathan began to stash yesterday's clothing into a pack. "Don't see the problem myself, for he helped brush down the horses last night, and if he can get on the good side of all these prickly folk, 'tis worth a little extra chatter." He straightened. "The weather is shaping up fine today. Do you need anything other than the usual?"

"Nay." Thomas selected the lightest of his doublets and drew it on over his shirt. "We'll set out after breaking our fast."

Thomas descended to the dining area and sat across from Lord Dermont at the linen-covered table. The meal was not as bounteous as Thomas was used to in Tristelle Castle. Best to assume that they had not enough on hand for so many guests.

Lady Sareen came down a few minutes after Thomas and sat beside him. "Mother had a disturbed night, but she and Father will be down shortly."

A young woman poured coffee for them. "I'm sorry to hear that," she said, setting the coffee pot on the table. With a curtsy, she introduced herself as the daughter-in-law of the innkeeper couple. Her husband—the man who had tried to smooth things last eve—waited on them as well after the duke and duchess came downstairs.

Thomas noted his blond hair. As fair as Thomas's, and even more distinct since his beard was brown. Fairly tall too. So, height and hair color alone were not what marked Thomas so clearly as a Kaituer. Granted, his nose was long, but he'd seen others just as long.

As they neared the end of the meal, the inn door swung open, and Lord Sathe Maerton strolled in. The bows that the inn servants swiftly offered him were notably lower than those Thomas received.

Lord Maerton nodded to them, then joined the Seltas and Thomas at the table. "Just coffee, please," he said when the young man placed a chair for him.

"Pray, pardon us," Thomas said, "for not arriving as planned at Navayn Manor yesterday."

"No matter," Lord Maerton said. "I heard you had a difficult journey." Thomas blinked, and Lord Maerton smiled thinly as he picked up his cup. "Word of unusual events travels quickly." He sipped his coffee. "For instance, the reading of the king's decree of Lord Navayn. That raised expectations for even more stirring events. Almost as though the exile himself returns, for you are so like your grandfather."

"So I have been told," Thomas said. "Yet few are old enough to remember him. I understand why you would think so, for I know a portrait of Lord Thomas hangs at Maerton Castle. As for the rest, I am certainly not the only man who is tall and blond. How is it I am so easily recognized?"

"For quite a number of years, Lord Thomas's portrait was periodically carried through towns between this castle and Tower Woods."

"Why?"

"Lest he return. A troubling thought to the first duke. He even declared it to be treason to give aid to Lord Thomas or to fail to report his whereabouts if he were seen."

"None of which pertains to Lord Navayn," Lady Sareen said.

"'Tis certain he cannot be arrested. Equally certain that the name of Kaituer was greatly besmirched in Maerton Duchy." Lord Maerton turned to Thomas. "This, I say not to dishonor you, but to inform you."

Thomas nodded, lips closed.

"To be frank, I believe you err in not changing your name to Thomas Navayn. I advise you to wear the colors of the House of Navayn."

"The dyed fabrics have been ordered, though not yet delivered."

"Matching colors often requires many attempts," Duchess Selta murmured.

Duke Selta folded his napkin and laid it on the table. "Then wear your sash. A little formal, perhaps, but arrival to take possession of your property is adequate reason."

Thomas glanced at the taproom, where his few servants and

Selta's plenteous ones had broken their fast. Most had finished and gone to their duties. Thomas stood. "Let us set out." He motioned Jonathan near as he strode to the steps. "Get my sash from the trunk." A portion of him balked at what seemed like show. Then he hid a smile. His biggest objection was that the sash tangled with his bow. "Hook my quiver and bow to my saddle."

"Aye, sir."

They soon set out. Even Duchess Selta chose to ride the short distance, so they did not linger for the carriages. They left the village by a different route than the one they'd traveled yesterday. It took them past the village church and castle, then through woods and fields. Lord Maerton named the roads they followed and crossed. He pointed out a couple of riding paths and a broken pillar that marked the Maerton and Navayn border within the woodland. Deer watched them ride by.

"The deer seem fearless to be so nigh the road," Thomas said. "Are they not hunted?"

"'Tis because the herd is too large. We usually hunt later in the year, but the duke has already opened common hunting on his land."

What exactly did that mean?

Duke Selta glanced at Thomas, then asked Lord Maerton, "What are the poaching laws in Maerton Duchy?"

"The same as in all the duchies."

Duke Selta's pitch dipped. "Tristelle Duchy is heavily wooded and lightly populated. They don't bother with poaching laws. Even I give certain exceptions. So I ask again, what is deemed poaching in Maerton Duchy?"

"Oh, I see." Lord Maerton turned to Thomas. "Deer may not be taken from an estate without permission, punishable by a fine of double the market price of a deer. By custom, common hunting of bucks is allowed after the rut, with a quarter-fee payable to the lord of the estate."

"What is a quarter-fee?" Thomas asked.

"Originally, a hind quarter of the deer, but it can also be paid in coin or field produce. Gamekeepers monitor the herd. If it is small for some cause, the duke—excuse me—the lord of the estate may not allow hunting that year. If it is too large, common hunting may be permitted early. Naturally, you may hunt on your own estate at any time."

"Does this mean that…if a farmer sees a deer eating his crop…'twould be considered poaching if he killed it?"

"Certain. Rarely is one arrow enough. The deer must be tracked, and there is no telling whose land it will fall upon."

"If I shoot a deer in my demesne, but it dies on Duke Maerton's land…then, what?"

"You owe him a quarter fee. Likewise, he owes you a quarter fee if the reverse is true. 'Tis more problematic here, for your common border in woodland is marked by neither road, stream, fence, nor hedge. Nor have the marker stones been maintained in several decades. My brother no longer hunts, but Lord Ivan takes great pleasure in the sport."

"He would!" Lady Sareen said.

"Please, dear," her mother murmured.

They paralleled a hedge, and Lord Maerton spread an arm to his left. "This is one of your tenant farms." He nodded right. "Beyond the hedge, is your demesne."

Poaching concerns gave way to wonder. Thomas was riding his *own* land. A quickening sensation coursed through him.

He wished he could see over the hedge. Widely separated trees spread beyond it. Then it joined with stone and wrought iron, which swept upward into a broad arch over the drive. They halted before the gate, and Thomas stared at the top. The letters of NAVAYN were wrought within the arch, as much a part of its structure as the latticework. The gates stood open, their end posts supported on flat stones set to either side of the drive. The grass—in need of trimming—lay over the gates' bottom rungs. "Can the gates not be closed?" Thomas asked.

Lord Maerton shrugged. "They can be, but for what purpose?

Three sides of your estate are unfenced. I have never been robbed, if that is what you are thinking of."

A castle, this was not. The others waited, spread to his sides in the road. Thomas nudged his horse and proceeded at a walk. Some trees flanked the rutted drive, but if they had ever arched it, too many were missing to create that effect. Thus, the manor stood fully revealed in morning sunshine.

A wide structure of two full floors and a partial third. Two thick beams of dark wood formed a central peak and angled all the way to the foundation, ending near the tower-like chimney structures at each end. Additional beams sloped between stone, always aligned with the primary angles. There was more wood in the second story than the first—a fine contrast to the beige stone—and what Thomas could see of the third story was mostly wood.

As he rode closer, the details grew plainer. The latticed windows were stone-encased on the first floor and wood-encased above. The top of each curved toward an arch, then peaked at the center. Somehow, the angles and curves gave the manor a relaxed symmetry not found in castles.

He stopped where the drive split into a loop. This was his?

The ladies of Selta stopped on either side of him. "'Tis utterly charming!" Sareen exclaimed. She looked to him with brows raised. "Do you like it?"

He smiled at her. "Very much so."

"A pleasing aspect," the duchess said. "I was a little worried it might be worse for its years, but that does not seem to be the case at all."

They rode along the curve of the loop, and Lord Maerton said, "My father used to say it was the best built of the duchy's old homes. 'Good bones,' to use his words. I will warn you before we go inside that it could use fresh garb."

Thomas dismounted at the wooden door, with decorative iron strapping, knocker, and latch. The near stonework was composed of irregular blocks but fitted so tightly that mortar barely showed. He rested a hand on the door enclosure, another peaked arch. Subtle stripes in shades of brown radiated like the markings of a lynx, and the stones had been dressed to make the most of the pattern. "This is lynxstone."

"Aye." Lord Maerton gestured to the window beside the door. "The stones not suited to polishing were used to frame all the first-floor windows. The finer stones are within." He stepped back and pointed to a window that stood open on the second floor. "That is the master's chamber, just right of the primary beam."

Master's chamber. Thomas set aside the feeling that he should wait to be invited in and opened the door.

The hall was much smaller than Tristelle Castle's but fit well with the structure. The front half was widest, and a fireplace angled across one corner. A staircase ascended through the narrower back hall and turned out of sight.

Ah, but that fireplace! The surround was semi-polished lynxstone, which brought out the golden glows streaking through rich browns. A mantelpiece above the shelf was carved from wood and featured a lynx with his face turned toward the door, as though he had just turned his head to see who entered. Thomas drew nearer to study it, as did Duke Selta.

After a moment, the duke murmured, "That is remarkable workmanship!"

"Indeed," Lord Maerton said. "I wish I had realized it was there. It has been covered for years with a portrait of Prince Maerton in his youth—one of the items removed, since it is not of the Navayn period." He managed a thin smile. "It also seemed to be in rather poor taste."

Thomas's lips twitched. "Are the rooms still furnished?" he asked, for the hall held only a plain settee and a halfmoon table against one wall.

"Aye, most of them. The salon is here." Lord Maerton led them through a side door. "An older style, you see, but serviceable."

The duchess stared at the draperies. "Oh, *dear!*"

Thomas glanced at the angled fireplace in the corner. "Does this share a chimney with the other?

"Three share a chimney here. 'Tis a common design in the manor. All the fireplaces have dampers, I assume to prevent cross flow." Lord Maerton gripped an iron handle protruding above the firebox and pulled. Iron scraped within. "This opens the damper, and pushing it in closes it." He suited action to words. "'Tis an unusual feature, but the house is less drafty than most. Make sure that all who work or dwell here know they *must* open the damper before lighting a fire, and do not close it until the fire is fully extinguished. Else, smoke will fill the room in moments."

Thomas had never heard of such a device. He worked the handle both directions, then met Jonathan's eyes to make sure he was attending.

"Speaking of chimneys," Lord Maerton said, "I suggest you have them cleaned before autumn. I did not use the entire house and cannot vouch for the chimneys on the south end." He motioned toward the opposite side of the hall.

"How many of the bedrooms are available for use?"

"All of them, really. Though not used, they are cleaned on rotation. You'll not find them in dust and cobwebs."

Thomas strolled around the central cluster of furniture. Bare hanging rods and less-faded rectangles showed where artwork had been removed. "Do any servants remain in the house?"

"Only an elderly couple resided here. They have been granted a pension cottage on my brother's estate. They are here at the moment to speak with you or your servants and to pass on the household keys. 'Twill be easier to converse with the housekeeper, since her husband is nigh deaf. The stablemaster remains on duty and wishes to speak with you. Shall we go through the rooms?"

"Please." That seemed to settle the question of whether Thomas would be plagued with servants of doubtful loyalties.

And raised the question of how he would provide for his guests. The Seltas and Jonathan followed him through all the first-floor rooms, and then on a briefer inspection of the bedchambers upstairs.

The only one Thomas looked at in detail was the master's chamber. A fireplace on one wall and the bed opposite, with plenty of space between. Furniture darkened with age. Dull plaster above wainscoting. More heavy draperies than needed—they even accented the room's corners. No personal effects sat on the dresser or washstand, but 'twas clearly an inhabited chamber. Partly burned candles stood in holders—kindling and split wood waited on the hearth grate. Perhaps cool nights bothered Lord Maerton.

Thomas crossed to the open window and looked down on the unkept lawn. A limb had fallen from a tree that looked to be half-dead, and some grass seemed matted to the ground. Small matters. A cart with a single horse stood in the drive's loop. A couple sat on the back of it, chatting with a sandy-haired man. Thomas glimpsed the roof of a coach beyond the hedge. Good, that was his coachman upon the box.

He returned to the corridor, where Lord Dermont gave him a wry look. "It appears that my mother and sister are assigning rooms. Do you have any preference in the matter?"

Thomas chuckled. "None at all. If you'll excuse me a moment."

He ran down the steps to the hall and found Griven, an elderly couple, and the village reeve, Master Navayn. Each offered a curtsy or bow.

"It gives me great pleasure to greet you here, Lord Navayn," the reeve said.

"I thank you."

"I pray you will pardon me for arriving before you could settle," Master Navayn said, "but I thought I should check on whether you brought servants or need to hire some on short notice."

"Ah." Could it be this easy?

"Also, my lord," Griven said, "your coach is here."

"Good." Thomas turned to the elderly couple and addressed the woman. "Are you the housekeeper?"

"Aye." Her voice was rough with age. She held out a bulky ring of keys to him, seeming in a hurry to be done with them.

He eyed the keys. "I shall speak with you shortly." He gestured to the settee. "Please sit for a moment." The couple gaped, but he didn't wait to see whether they would accept the courtesy. He turned to the reeve. "I *am* in need of servants. Are there any you can recommend?"

"Aye, my lord. I took the liberty of bringing a couple with me, who could start at once—on trial approval, of course—until you have time to meet folk hereabouts. Shall I fetch them in?"

"Please do."

'Twas the couple he had observed from above. They hadn't even finished their bow and curtsy, when the former housekeeper bounced up from the settee. "Eldred clan. Well then. They've cleaned and done odd jobs here, so I daresay they'll be good enough for you, my lord." She shoved the keys into the younger woman's hand and marched out the door, her husband shuffling after her.

The woman's jaw dropped, and she stood like a statue clutching keys. Griven closed the door, and Thomas burst out laughing. The others relaxed enough for uncertain chuckles, and without further ado, Thomas hired a houseman and housekeeper.

"Come," he said, then strolled outside to the carriage. His trunk sat on the flagstones between the drive and door. He pointed. "Take that to the master's bedchamber, then unload the carriage, which contains sundry items for a household."

He then met the sandy-haired stablemaster, named Santhorn, who claimed that his family had served the Navayns through many generations. His puckered brows drew up at the center. "They only continued on here," he explained, "for love of the horses, which Prince Maerton took as his own when he forced the Navayns out. If ye be willing, I should much appreciate staying on here as stablemaster."

Thomas nodded. "I shall visit the stables when I have time." He swept a hand to encompass Selta's squires, tied horses, and carriage. "For now, tend to all of these."

Movement commenced, and Thomas joined Jonathan and Master Navayn, who were talking. "Do you know Lord Maerton's stablemaster?" Jonathan asked the reeve.

"Oh, aye, all my life. A good man. His brother is the village farrier." He tugged the hem of his vest. "Please understand, my lord. We have all worked for the Maertons in one way or another. Due service was required at harvest and planting as Maerton's steward ordered."

"I assume you had no choice in the matter," Thomas said.

"Just the bitter choice to leave. We worked only upon the Navayn land, though, not the duke's estate." He shifted his stance. "Might you be riding into the village today?"

"I shall, when I set out again to ride around the estate."

The reeve took his leave then, and Thomas believed that he had things settled. A pleasant fallacy that lasted until he walked back inside. The Selta ladies were giving multiple instructions to his new housekeeper, who turned wide, questioning eyes upon him. The household supplies unloaded from the carriage cluttered the hall, and the pile was expanding. Where did all these things belong? Worse, the questions rivaled the chaos of crates, baskets, and sacks. Thomas made quick decisions with no idea whether they were sound.

Lord Maerton interrupted the next question. "I was under the impression that you wished to ride the estate. Am I mistaken?"

"Nay. I shall be with you in a moment."

At least two people began asking questions, but Duchess Selta spoke over them. "Quiet, please." She cast a firm look around her audience. "It appears to me, Lord Navayn, that your new housekeeper knows enough of the manor that we will be able to find places for all this...*if* we are simply left alone with a couple men to carry things for us. You gentlemen may resume your ride, and, Sareen, dear, you may go with them."

Aghast, Thomas stuttered, "M-my lady..." She raised her brows, and he tried again. "You are most kind, but you are my guest."

"A guest who brings her family to stay the moment of your arrival expects to make herself useful. Now, be off with you, so I may think for a moment."

Lady Sareen took Thomas's arm and turned him toward the door. "Worry not."

They went outside again, and the duke said, "She manages an entire castle. This will be as play to her and will entertain her better than riding your estate."

Lord Maerton was already striding along a side drive that led around the house. They followed him to the stable, mounted, and set out again.

"Where does Navayn Village lie?" Thomas asked Lord Maerton.

"South, along the road past your gates."

"Let us go that way first."

The quiet of the road between farms was just what Thomas needed. Gentle sounds calmed him—a shushing breeze through hedgerows, steady clopping of the horses, and cattle lowing. A distant dog barked, chasing a deer into the woods until a whistle recalled it. Lord Maerton occasionally pointed and named farm boundaries. Land. This, Thomas could take in more easily than a house. Jonathan rode on his other side, also listening attentively.

They reached a cluster of cottages smaller than Maerton Castle Village and proceeded to its center. A market, an alehouse, and a church wrapped around a green where the reeve stood upon some low structure addressing a group of folk around him. At Thomas's approach, his face lit in a smile. Everyone turned, and a cheer arose.

Never had Thomas expected this. It nearly undid him. The other riders halted as he approached at a walk, with Jonathan a length behind him. Thomas dismounted and handed his reins to Jonathan. Mistress Navayn greeted him with a curtsy and words of welcome. Thomas recognized a few faces from the royal audience and nodded to them. People ran from cottages to the green, and chatter mounted to a din. All the curtsies and bows kept him nodding this way and that. Someone ran from the churchyard, pulling a robe over his homespun clothes. A couple supported a bent woman between them as she hobbled toward the green.

By now, the reeve had stepped down from the stone bench he'd stood on—one of several around a well. A few children stood on the one nearest the aged woman, trying to see over their elders.

"Clear a path to let her through," Thomas said. "Children, give her the bench."

They hopped down, and the oldest lass swept dirt off the bench with a hand.

Mistress Navayn tilted her head up to whisper toward Thomas's ear. "She is past ninety years, but her mind is fair clear for her age."

He nodded, then spoke to those who supported her. "Let her sit here."

She heaved a rough sigh as they lowered her.

Thomas sat sideways on the bench, for he didn't think she could lift her head far.

She looked to the sash on his chest, then his eyes. "Pardon an old woman for no curtsy, Lord Navayn."

"Nay, Mother," he said, inclining his torso. "'Tis my place to bow to your years."

Wrinkles curved around her lips like parchment. "Oof, to think I should lay my gaze on Lady Anne's son."

Her escort cleared his throat. "Gamma, this is Lord Thomas's grandson."

"D'ye think I don't know that?" Still spry enough to tell off her young folk. She turned back to Thomas. "Lord Navayn, you are, but they tell me your name is Thomas. 'Twould make my sweet Lady Anne happy, it would." Her eyes fell to his sash again and grew watery. She reached a shaky hand to touch it against his chest. "My lady wore this."

"You knew her, then?"

"Aye. A kind soul. And strong." She gave him a decisive nod. "Strong kindness is the best sort. I'm tired, now, Chas. Take me home."

"Aye, Gamma." Her escort—Chas—lifted her like she weighed naught and carried her across the grass. The woman with him mouthed *thank you* as she dropped a curtsy, apparently too overcome to speak, then hurried after them.

Thomas became aware of approving stares, including one from the robed man who said, "That was right good of ye." He neither looked nor sounded like a priest. Thomas gave him a slight smile and stood.

"If I may ask, my lord," a man said, "the deer are a curst nuisance, and the duke wouldn't speak of hunting on the Navayn estate."

"Ah," Thomas said. "'Tis open for common hunting."

"And the fee, sir. Is it still a quarter and a half?"

Thomas frowned and flicked a glance toward Lord Maerton, still on his horse in the road, and then back to the reeve and this man. "Quarter and a half? What mean you?"

"'Tis what the duke has always required," the reeve said, apparently trying to hide a disgruntled tone.

"If I may state some ancient history," Lord Maerton said. "The first Duke of Maerton was displeased that those loyal to the House of Navayn would provide only service in the fields, but no men-at-arms. Nor would they give him their oaths. Thus, he added half to all fees. His descendants never lifted the burden."

Thomas drew a slow breath, for his jaw had clenched. To the

reeve, he said, "The fee is one quarter. Produce is welcome in its place, for as you see, I have guests and could use all manner of food." He extended a hand toward those who waited on horseback. "The Duke of Selta, his younger son, Lord Dermont, and his daughter, Lady Sareen."

The folk gave his guests dutiful bows and curtsies, then turned swiftly back to Thomas.

Someone said, "My lord, if I may ask…"

Thomas held up a hand and looked to the reeve. "Master Navayn, will there be dozens of questions now?"

He raised his brows apologetically. "Scores, my lord. It has been a very long time."

Thomas turned in a slow circle, speaking to them all. "Long, indeed. I request only a short time more, that I may answer you with clear understanding. I ask Master Navayn to gather your questions, so I may consider them. Then, we shall meet to settle the most pressing first, and to discuss others. Does that seem well to you?"

Several in the crowd murmured assurances that it was well. A voice rose above them. "Only tell us what day we may gather to give you our oaths."

That nigh undid him again. He swallowed. "The warmth of your welcome will never grow cold in my heart. We shall choose a day soon, and all will know it."

He managed to find a way through the crowd to his horse, unsure how to meet the gazes of his peers. Would they show mockery or praise for how he'd handled this? Then, he caught Lady Sareen's eyes. She was beaming. He didn't even bother to look at the other faces. Thomas mounted, swift and sure, and led them from the village.

CHAPTER 22

T he rest of their ride took them through the demesne.
Fields first, where the wheat was doing well—according to
Duke Selta. Thomas must remember what this looked like and
the time of year.

The lane that served the fields turned away, heading back
toward the manor, but Lord Maerton left it and slowed his horse
from a trot to a walk. Patches of tall grass waved amid scruffy
bushes. "If you hear someone refer to your wasteland, this is
what they mean."

"Why is it not cultivated?"

"Too rocky, as you will soon see. I believe it was once used as
goat pasture, but those creatures are a nuisance, not worth the
trouble to fence or protect."

Such nonsense. Goats provided clothing, milk, and meat to
the People of the Woods. Thomas kept his opinion to himself.
They continued on, crossing weathered ruts. The tracks spread
wide from a single point and led down to excavations. They rode
among straight cliffs of weathered, beige stone...clearly the
source for the manor's construction. One deposit bore a few
darker stripes, hinting at lynxstone.

Jonathan craned his neck. "There is a goat here somewhere."

"Perhaps a few gone wild." Lord Maerton continued on, keeping his horse to a walk, but Thomas followed Jonathan, who rode around the cavities, some carved out by miners and others natural.

The bleating now reached Thomas's ears, too, and they soon found its source. A ewe with a long black coat, and a kid of black and white. Were they trapped? The slope was too steep for a man, but not for a goat. Thomas watched the ewe struggle to reach a bit of grass, one hind leg held clear of the ground. "She's hurt."

From a short distance away, Lord Maerton drawled, "Are you interested in seeing your land, Lord Navayn?"

"Can you find this spot again?" Thomas asked Jonathan.

"I daresay."

They rejoined the others and rode up a long slope. Thomas spied the back wall of the manor in the distance. "Does the track lead straight to the manor?"

"More or less. Do you wish to return?"

"Nay, for I want to see the woods and where my border lies. Lead on." As Lord Maerton turned along the path of his choosing, Thomas said, "The goat was black and long-haired. Is that the type formerly grazed here?"

"I know not. Doubtless, a lynx will take it tonight."

"There cannot be many lynx, for they can take down a fawn or even a doe."

Lord Maerton raised his brows. "If you say so." He pointed out a distant line of poplars beyond the wasteland. "That is the western border of your land. The fields beyond them belong to the Maerton estate. Ahead, is the woodland that meets my brother's demesne."

They picked their way over rough terrain and soon entered the welcome shade. The narrow path widened enough to ride two abreast. Signs of deer stripping the vegetation were common, as Thomas expected. Lady Sareen and Lord Dermont spoke of riding here in days gone by.

Surprised, Thomas asked, "Do you hunt here every year?"

"The duke always hosts at least one hunting party," Lord Dermont said. "Mark me, he will have more this year, and we shall be invited."

"Ah, know that I would enjoy a visit from you whenever you are in the neighborhood." They acknowledged, and Thomas said to Lady Sareen, "You sound like you know the paths well. Do you also hunt?"

Lord Dermont snorted. "If you can call it that."

Lady Sareen drew the corners of her smile down. "My brother finds me too squeamish. Indeed, I do not kill anything, but I love to ride with the hunt. Besides, Duchess Tristelle and I oft visited Maerton Castle as children...before Duchess Maerton...uh...died." She looked wide-eyed at Lord Maerton's back, like she had blundered. He had drawn a little ahead as the others conversed and showed no indication of hearing—though he probably had. Lady Sareen cleared her throat. "We used to walk or ride on all the bridle paths. There are a great many, for the forest wraps around much of the castle."

"We can hunt while you are here, if you like," Thomas said.

Before anyone could answer, Lord Maerton stopped at a juncture of paths. He pointed into the brush. "Lord Navayn, this is one of the border markers."

A few stones stood atop one another with bits of crumbled mortar between, and others lay beside them, much overgrown. The plain, beige rock from Thomas's quarry, with a flat cleavage.

Lord Maerton pointed farther. "The line extends roughly that direction. Perhaps a trail once flanked the stones, but pathways change over the years, and several cross the line. I can show you all the markers that I know of."

This took much weaving about. It was past noon when they finally returned to the manor, and Thomas's stomach growled.

"I shall take my leave of you," Lord Maerton said, bowing from the saddle. "I trust you will find the estate to your liking. I will be at Maerton Castle for a day or two. Should any pressing questions arise, you may send me word. My brother asked me to extend his welcome to you. He will visit after you've had a few days to settle in."

Thomas bowed in return. "I thank you for your welcome and for taking time to guide me around the estate. Please tell Duke Maerton I look forward to his visit."

Thomas's chest expanded easier when the former occupant trotted off toward the road. The stablemaster had hastened to the drive, and he and Duke Selta's squire took charge of the horses. To Jonathan, Thomas said, "Find yourself a bite to eat, then take Griven and fetch the goats."

"Aye, my lord. Are you staying nigh the house this afternoon?"

Thomas grinned. "Worry not." Then, he steeled himself for whatever domestic disasters lay beyond the arched door and stepped inside. A pleasant surprise. The hall had been emptied of trunks, baskets, and crates. The only items remaining were a stack of linens on the settee and a box of candles from which many were missing.

Lady Sareen looked around with a satisfied air. "Did we not tell you as much?"

Before he could answer, the duchess strolled into the hall, looking cool and calm. "I trust you had a pleasant ride. A cold repast awaits you in the dining room. Though I must admit—I started without you."

Thomas smiled. "What? Could you not guess the exact time of our return?"

She gave him an arch look as she uttered a dainty huff.

He followed her through the salon into the dining room and found more food on the table than he'd expected. The housekeeper waited nigh the corner doorway that led toward the kitchen, and she curtsied as they entered. A chair, with arms and a high back, stood at one end of the table. Thomas took his seat at the head of the table, revealing none of the hesitancy he felt. His guests took places along the sides, leaving the matching chair opposite him empty. Would Sareen someday—nay, he must not think of that.

"I brought ham and cheese among my supplies," Thomas said, "but where did the rest of this come from?"

"Some is from your kitchen garden." The duchess held a thin carrot strip up, before taking a bite. "Enough is planted to feed a limited household. Also, one of the local farm wives brought a half-dozen loaves of bread. One was a gift and the rest...she *said* she was taking them to the market, but I think otherwise. I bought them all."

Thomas paused with a hand partway to his mug. "What do I owe you?"

"Don't be silly. But you must leave coin with your housekeeper, so she may purchase from vendors or go to market."

"Of course." He knew that. "I've simply not had time yet."

"True." Lady Sareen said. "So much bustle, and I really do think Lord Maerton could have found more patience."

The duchess wrinkled her short nose. "He also could have left a day's worth of food in the pantry and a candle or two."

The duke took a slice of ham. "Grant it as a courtesy that Lord Maerton left harvestable food in the garden. The will and transfer documents allowed him to take everything brought to the manor by Prince Maerton and his heirs."

"Indeed, all that we have found is old." The duchess tapped her plate, and Thomas noticed two chips on his, as she spoke. "We found some tarnished candleholders, a few rusty pots and pans, and some wooden kitchen things. 'Tis fortunate the kitchen's oil lamps are attached to the walls, or I daresay they'd be gone too. Not a drop of oil anywhere to replenish them."

Thomas looked to the housekeeper, who was filling the last mug. "You must keep a list of all that we need, so we may buy it in the market."

"I shall, sir. Lamp oil may be hard to get, but I can find a little in Navayn Village. Not salt, though."

"I brought some. Did you not find it?"

"A canister, aye. 'Tis enough for the kitchen, but we'll need much more for curing the meat, or it will go to waste. There is no salt on Navayn land, so we must buy it at Maerton Castle Village. 'Tis always costly, and everyone will be wanting extra for so many deer." A tiny shift lifted her voice. "Plus, there has always been the half-tax."

That sounded like a question. And what was a half-tax?

Lord Dermont lowered his fork to his plate. "Do you mean... does everything cost half as much more for you?"

"Oof, not everythin', sir! Just what we buy from beyond Navayn."

"Is that only from the Maerton Castle Village, or from every village?" Lord Dermont asked.

The housekeeper shrugged. "All of them within reach of a market journey. The Duke's got a collector in every market, and the lords are all sworn to him. 'Cept ours," she added with a proud lift of her chin.

"Father, is that legal?" Lady Sareen asked, her black eyebrows tilted in anger.

"It was...before Lord Navayn was granted title and possession. Now, it would be inappropriate to impose extra tax upon commoners sworn to another lord." His brow wrinkled with thought as he chewed and swallowed. "There is a lord in Selta Duchy who is sworn to the king rather than to the dukes of Selta. We trade freely, but he also has valuable goods from his land to trade. If I were so foolish as to place a burden on that trade, he could place the same burden on mine. Thus, all we would gain from one another is contention."

The duke looked to Thomas. "You have crops, wood, and meat —either wild or domestic if you buy stock. All of which are good to possess, but they can be found anywhere. A pity you have nothing like iron, copper, or even salt. I doubt Duke Maerton will attempt to tax you, for you are sworn to the king. He has lately put too much effort into winning the king's favor to risk it over a questionable tax." Creases deepened beside Duke Selta's nose. "*However*...he can set any price he wants on valuable commodities that he controls."

Food sat leaden in Thomas's belly. Living here was going to cost him. He already knew where those commodities lay. On Kaituer land, now owned by the Dukes of Maerton. Whether through tax or inflated price, Maerton's purse would fatten, simply because Thomas lived here. He had only wanted to take care of his own household. To speak for those of his estate if they had need of it. Not contend with a neighbor. Strange. He had just become wealthier than he ever imagined. Now he felt certain he would be poor before the autumn harvest. What to do about it?

That thought kept recurring, especially when he took a moment alone in his bedchamber. He laid aside his sash and glanced around. His trunk was here now, the bed had been made, and on a small table beside it, stood an ugly oil lamp. Was it made of tin? No wonder the hideous thing had been left behind. At least it held a wick and some oil. Dared he use it, or was he too poor?

Ridiculous! He had a fine house, albeit lacking provisions. All this land...with fields planted. Tenants who welcomed him. This was wealth. And a neighbor all too likely to steal it. Of course, he had not done so yet. If he did, Thomas could go to the king. He hated that thought. What sort of lord went whining to the king? Not the sort he wished to be.

Thomas left his chamber. A breeze wafted down the corridor, for all the windows had been opened and the bedchamber doors stood ajar. He strolled into one that no guest had claimed and looked out from the back of the house. A kitchen garden below, off to the left, only half planted. A lot of lawn. Winding flagstone paths. There must have been a pleasure garden once. The western reaches drew his eye, though he could not see details of the wasteland past scattered trees. So much seemed disused here. The stable was cared for, but some of the outbuildings looked to be in poor repair.

Thomas had best get down to that stable and actually converse with its master. He descended to the hall, then followed the side drive around the end of the house. Perhaps the duke—nay his steward—only bothered with easy income where he could demand labor from the tenants. That part still bothered Thomas, though he understood that labor was required in exchange for use of another's land. Not that Maerton had rightfully owned this land nor provided the normal services of a landowner. One thing was certain, Thomas was going to fulfill his share of the exchange better than the duke had.

Stablemaster Santhorn greeted Thomas like he had been waiting for him, and promptly showed off how he'd cared for Thomas's horse in a broad stall with fresh straw. "I brushed him down, my lord. He's, uh, not quite like any horse I've seen."

"He was bred in Moorelin...one of their famed riding horses capable of the smooth running-walk gait."

"Sure looks jerky with the way he bobs his head."

"Better his head than my body."

The stablemaster burst out laughing and slapped his thigh.

That was funny? Thomas rubbed his horse's neck and whispered, "Don't take it personal, lad."

When the stablemaster recovered, he took Thomas on a tour of the stable, delivered with far more love of his domain than Lord Maerton had shone for the house. "We have twenty-two stalls," he said with a broad sweep of his hand. Many more grand gestures were needed to point out the carriage shed, paddocks, and feed storage.

Thomas compressed his lips as he viewed the half-wall bins. "'Tis empty."

"Don't ye worry about that." Santhorn strode back between the stalls as he spoke. "The steward cleaned it out, but we have plenty of grass for the horses to graze over summer. We cut hay three times a year, and our oats are growing well." He pointed to an alcove beyond the first stall. "Lord Maerton used to keep his hunting gear there. He took it all with him, of course, but I told Griven he could put your things there."

Racks held the arrows Thomas had brought—probably not enough—as well as two spears, his longbow, and shorter hunting bows with their strings hanging loose.

Santhorn led the way through a split door. "This here is the tack room."

Clean, with the tack for Thomas's horses on one side, the Selta's tack on another, and many empty pegs. Also a wall covered with pegs and racks, which held one wooden rake. Thomas frowned.

"Noticed the tool rack, have ye?" Santhorn said.

"You have no tools?"

The stablemaster cleared his throat, glancing over his shoulder. One of the visiting grooms was brushing Lord Dermont's horse not far away. "If ye care to come along this way, my lord, I'll show ye some of the other buildings."

They went outside and passed the coachmen—sitting in the shade in deep discussion over the best carriage design—then reached a nondescript shed. "You needn't worry about my tools," the stablemaster said. He fumbled with some keys on his belt. "I saw what the steward was doing here, so I threw all my tools into the market cart, covered 'em with feed sacks, and drove it into the village to my brother's place. I never got on with the steward, and Lord Maerton long ago bade him stay out of the stable. He wouldn't know what had been there. I rode the horse back, 'cause that belonged to my lord." He shoved a fat key into the lock to release the heavy bolt, then pulled the broad door open. "This is the tool shed. The steward took every scrap of iron, he did. Plow, scythes, hoes, shovels, axes, saws...everythin'!"

Thomas stared at the few wooden implements lying on the dirt floor.

"Lord Maerton argued with him—managed to save the big old chains and hooks in the smokehouse, but the steward took the smaller ones, insisting they were newer. As if he were here when Prince Maerton stole the land. He didn't find the butchering blades. He gave up too easy because nothing's been butchered here in years. They were oiled and packed away a long time ago."

"Do you know where?"

"I think so. Just didn't want to go looking while any of Maerton's folk were about."

"I see. You should take a horse and bring that cart back. I don't want you or your brother accused of theft if anyone sees what is hidden there."

"Mm. Do you reckon the Selta folk can be trusted not to talk about me coming back with tools?"

"How are they to know that I didn't send you into the village to buy tools from anyone willing to sell them? Besides, I think we'll need that cart."

"Always have before." The stablemaster locked the shed. "Your squire took some sacks and rode off. Said he was fetching *goats!*" They began walking back toward the stable. "Wanted me to find a place for 'em."

"Aye."

"We don't keep goats here."

"We do now," Thomas said. "Put them in a stall and give them water and hay."

Santhorn grumbled. "Likely they'll bother the horses, my lord."

"Not at all. Just don't let them near a garden nor around any loose feed."

"If ye say so, but what d'ye want with 'em? They're good for nothin'."

"We shall see." Thomas turned toward the house, then stopped. "Oh, I almost forgot. You may stay on as my stablemaster."

That wiped away his ill-humor over goats. "Thank ye, my lord."

Thomas pondered as he walked back to the manor. Interesting that Lord Maerton had apparently saved a little iron for him. At least the stablemaster had saved more. Thomas grinned. Was that because he felt the tools were his own, or because they belonged to the Navayns? Maybe both, for these folk held loyalty for generations. Thomas left the drive and crossed a swath of lawn toward the kitchen garden. A low wall encircled it with plain wrought iron posts rising from the stones. He gripped one, looking over the garden. 'Twould be a shame to sacrifice such a sturdy fence. Could he find iron somewhere other than from Maerton? How long did it take to make tools? Was there even a blacksmith in Navayn Village?

He walked along the garden wall and spied riders approaching from beyond the farthest outbuilding. Jonathan and Griven, each holding a goat with only its head sticking out of a sack.

Thomas strolled back to the outbuildings to meet them. Before long, the lame goat and her kid were settled in a stall at the far end of the stable. Standing on three legs, she drank lustily from a bucket, then devoured hay.

The stablemaster seemed resigned. Or perhaps he couldn't refuse an injured animal. "Once she's full," he said, "I'll see if I can get a look at that leg she's holding up."

"Thank you," Thomas said, and the stablemaster blinked. He probably didn't get much thanks from his former master. Thomas motioned to Jonathan, who walked with him down the length of the stable.

After several paces, Jonathan asked, "What's troubling you?"

"That obvious? Duke Maerton's steward took every scrap of iron out of the tool shed."

Jonathan grunted. "That's not good news. Griven and I were talking about getting that dead tree cut up for firewood. I gather, that won't happen soon."

"Another problem I hadn't thought of. Wood for the kitchen

and more for winter. No ax or saw to cut it. Hay, oats, and wheat growing well, but no scythe."

"Is there nowhere to buy tools?"

"Maerton owns all the local iron. I suspect he would charge me a small fortune to buy back the tools he took from the estate."

Land full of wealth and no way to harvest it.

Was Thomas avoiding her?

Sareen shifted the candleholders she'd placed on the hall mantel toward the outer edges. 'Twould create a better effect on the relief carving. 'Twas tempting to light them now, but better to save them, for light still shone through the second-floor window over the staircase. Her fidgeting did nothing to alleviate the strange loneliness that crept out of hiding whenever she wasn't busy.

Thomas was only a few yards away—in the library with her father. Had been for hours before dinner, and now again afterward. She hadn't minded at first. Helping her mother get the house into running order had been fun. 'Twas a good thing that Sareen had brought Adonna instead of her normal maid. She had done whatever was asked. The duchess's maid had only deigned to clean the bedchambers that the Selta family would use. True, they had not been filled with cobwebs, but they had missed many spring cleanings.

As soon as her mother had decided they'd done enough for one day, Sareen could find nothing to distract herself from all the thoughts that plagued her. This house...so charming at its core, and yet somehow forgotten. Stripped of the signs of being lived in. Never refreshed in decades. She could do so much with it, but it wasn't hers. She shouldn't want it.

Except she did. Senseless, for 'twas nothing like the nebulous ducal castle she'd long expected. This could only mean that the draw was not the house, but the man who owned it. A man who still ranked beneath her—according to some. Tainted by his years of impoverished exile and the name he retained. What did her father think of all that? How could she ask him when she didn't know what Thomas thought?

'Twas certain what the estate folk thought, though. They pronounced *Lord Navayn* at least with pride, if not outright joy. Quite a number of them had arrived with small gifts of welcome, and with food to sell or questions of what might be needed. The housekeeper arranged for daily deliveries of milk, butter, and eggs, and circulated a request for hens and chicks. Likely, the farming folk also came in hopes of seeing the new lord. An unrealized desire.

For her too. Couldn't Thomas spare her even a few minutes? Nay, Lord Navayn. She must stop thinking of him by his given name, or she'd call him Sir Thomas in public.

In truth, she shouldn't be thinking of him at all. She sighed and went to the back hall door under the staircase landing. The ceiling was so low that when Thomas first saw it, he'd reached up and touched it before walking beneath. Ugh—Thomas again!

Sareen went outside and stood for a few minutes on the broad swath of flagstones, so tightly laid that few weeds grew between them. 'Twould be a pleasant spot for an outdoor table and chairs. A tree with an arching canopy gave it afternoon shade. The sun had sunk below it now, but so late in the day, it wasn't too harsh. What would it be like to sit out here in the evening with Thomas? Nay! Lord Navayn. Except, his title made him seem distant. Nothing like all their treasured walks by the sea.

Frustrated and restless, she began walking one of the flagstone paths that twisted and looped through lawn. Doubtless, gardens had flourished here once. What other purpose for these paths? 'Twas a shame the gardens had been transformed into lawn, but that could be rectified. With tools. She silently condemned Duke Maerton. Thomas had looked careworn all through dinner and said little. Tools could be bought, of course, but not peace. And she would not easily forgive Duke Maerton for stealing Thomas's peace.

Maybe hers, as well. She tried planning flower beds. Not nearly as effective at settling her heart as the sight of Thomas walking out the hall door. He met her gaze and smiled, then walked straight across the grass, not following the paths as she had.

"Ah, here you are." He took her hand, then seemed unsure what to do with it for a second. He recovered and tucked it into the crook of his arm. "Did you come out to enjoy the sunset?"

"Not really. I'm planning your future gardens."

He laughed. "Someone other than me needs to. At least that one task can wait."

"Does it seem there are too many that cannot wait?"

"Myriad. Some, I expected, for Duke Tristelle advised me. Others, I've never thought of in my life. No sooner do I understand a new need, then I realize I don't know how to fill it."

"Like getting things, you mean?"

"Worse. Like that salt, for instance. Of course, I know meat is salted, but I've never thought of ordering it. Suddenly, I realized I must. But I don't know where to order it from, and I loathe going to Maerton Castle Village for it. Even if I find a source...I have no idea how much I need."

"Ah. One figures it. Start with how many people must be fed through the winter. Then, consider what sorts of animals must be butchered and stored to feed them, and additional animals you may butcher to sell. Multiply that by the pounds of salt needed for the number of animals of each type. Then, add it all up."

"Have you done such calculations?"

"Of course. With my mother, that is. We do it every year for Selta Castle. And for my father's men-at-arms too. We'll figure it out for you tomorrow."

He shook his head. "I cannot imagine how I would have gotten through this day—and likely the week to come—without the aid of your family. You have all done so much."

They reached the middle of the curving path farthest from the manor, which would now take them back. Thomas paused and faced westward. The sun filtered through distant trees and reddened his blond hair.

What did he think of? She had to laugh at herself, for he covered a prodigious yawn. Sleep, most likely.

"Forgive me," he said, beginning to walk again. "I fear I'm poor company. I cannot remember having such an exhausting day in my life...though I spent half of it sitting indoors."

"What were you and my father discussing forever in the library?"

"Looking through the estate books. Lord Maerton mentioned them when he showed us the library."

"So, he did. Was it dull work?"

"Nay. Mostly, I discovered what I need to go back over. When we found something important...or puzzling...we discussed it. I even found the oaths of fealty that, uh, my forebears documented...and how they did the ceremonies."

"*That* is good to know! It wouldn't do for you to be ignorant of what your people may recall or have heard tell of."

"Quite so. I see, now, why they are in a hurry to give me their oaths—that they actually *need* a lord or lady. I'm going to plan the ceremony for the next rest day."

"That will be perf—" His sudden tension halted her. What

did he stare at? She followed his gaze, but could see nothing. Did his long vision catch something beyond her sight? He shifted position between her and the woodland, then scanned the whole line of the shadowy forest.

Jonathan must have been lingering nearby, for he appeared beside them. "What is it?"

"Nothing now," Thomas said. "I saw the back of a horse trotting into the woods." He seemed to recollect Sareen's presence. "'Twill be dark soon. Shall we go in, my lady?"

"Aye, my lord."

Jonathan fell back, following as Thomas led her straight across the grass.

Sareen had forgotten that attempt on his life. Obviously, he and Jonathan had not. How could she have been so careless as to keep him wandering outside in the dusk!

They reached the manor, and Thomas stepped inside with her, then paused in the open doorway. "Jonathan, where are you going?"

"To check the woods before the sun sets."

"Not alone."

"Fine. I'll take Griven."

Thomas closed the door and walked with her into the front hall. Someone had lit the mantel candles. Thomas looked at her, and his brow lowered. "My lady, what is amiss?"

Why did her face always have to betray her? "Whoever was out there...do you think they could have...might have meant to... kill you?"

His expression calmed. "Worry not. I saw only a horse... leaving. There could have been any number of reasons why someone was there. And you may have noticed...no arrow was shot. At that range, 'twould be most unlikely to hit anyone near the house."

"I suppose that's why you—and your squire—showed no concern."

Thomas chuckled, looking a little sheepish. "You must excuse Jonathan, for he saw me switch sides to shield you. As for me...I was surprised. Protecting you...'twould be any gentleman's instinct." His voice changed halfway through that sentence. Like he had meant to say something else and caught himself. His gaze left hers, searched, then landed on the relief carving above the fireplace. "Ah, 'tis fair glowing in the candlelight."

Sareen stared at it, too, enjoying the effect. "The lynx almost looks alive with the light dancing over it."

The cat stood with its forefeet on a log and its head turned, revealing the beauty of both its body and face. The artist had achieved stripes, perhaps through the angle of his knife. Polished lynxeye had even been perfectly crafted and embedded within the wood to form its golden eyes.

"'Tis so calmly regal," Sareen said. "Like nothing could ever disturb its poise."

Thomas's tone grew deeply thoughtful. "'Tis one advantage, I suppose, of being carved in wood."

Sareen laughed so hard she splayed her fingers over her mouth to cover it. "That is *not* what I meant."

He ended his silent chuckle, smiling down at her. "I know, but I'm rather fond of the sound of your laughter."

Footsteps struck the upper portion of the staircase, and Adonna descended to the landing. "My lady, your mother was looking for you a few minutes ago."

They must have heard Sareen's laugh, and now she couldn't linger. "I shall come up." She spread her skirt and curtsied. "I wish you good eve, my lord."

Thomas bowed. "Sleep well, my lady."

THOMAS WATCHED her gracefully ascend the staircase. Footsteps overhead...doors closing. Quiet settled on the hall. Such a day, this had been! He considered the lynx. Symbol of the House of

Navayn. A pity he could not hold his poise like a statue. Or maybe not. Perfect poise wasn't living. Neither was being skittish over a chance rider in his woods.

Thomas climbed the stairs to his bedchamber. 'Twas dark, and he didn't know where his tinderbox was. That never would have bothered him in the woods. The things he took for granted in a house! He groped to find a candle, carried it to the lamp at the top of the staircase, then returned to light his oil lamp and another candle.

He shed his doublet. Where was Jonathan? The sun had set. He hoped his squire wasn't foolish enough to prowl the woods in darkness. Likewise, 'twould be foolish for Thomas to go searching alone, especially when he had no idea what direction Jonathan had taken.

Still, he couldn't ready for bed when he didn't know whether his friend was safe.

Thomas picked up his sword from where it was propped in the corner and drew it from the scabbard. He could at least practice the motions he'd learned. The chamber was spacious enough. He twisted and wove the blade through the air, the grooves of the polished hilt now familiar in his grip. His non-countered swings and fluid footwork eased his muscles as much as they worked them. Restful exercise for his mind, as well.

What was that thumping? Too faint to place. Thomas opened his bedchamber door to listen, but the sound had stopped. A moment later, footsteps ascended the stairs. Jonathan reached the corridor, bearing the pitcher missing from Thomas's washstand and scowling. Thomas sheathed his sword, then closed the door after his squire entered.

Jonathan poured a little water into the basin. "I hope you don't mind tepid water. Can't imagine why someone didn't bring it up, since I was out. Nor why they saw fit to lock the kitchen door, when I had yet to come for your water!"

Thomas hid his grin. Jonathan seemed to have as many expectations as he did. "Give them time to find the way of things." Thomas tossed his shirt aside and wrung out a cloth in the water as Jonathan drew curtains over the open window. "Leave a gap for air. What did you and Griven discover?"

"Nothing," Jonathan grumped, "for Griven was nowhere to be found! In the end, the stablemaster and I checked every building, but he carried a lantern, which just made me feel like a target. By the time we finished that worthless search, there was no point in checking the woods."

Thomas considered this as he washed. "There may not have been a point in checking, anyway. The best hunting is at dawn and dusk, so we should expect people in the woods."

"I suppose, though the local common folk will be hunting on foot, not on horseback."

"True, but 'tis no crime to ride the woods. We also need to be more careful how we react, for we worried Lady Sareen."

That altered Jonathan's frown to concern. "Pray pardon me. Is she...?"

"Worry not over the lady. But do look for Griven in the morn."

"Aye, sir." Jonathan handed Thomas a dry towel. "The, uh, stablemaster asked me if I'm a lad, since I go by my given name. I explained, of course, but... It seems as bad here to go by Jonathan as it was to be called *young Cotrell* in Tristelle Duchy."

Thomas had known him far too long to not understand. The endless diminutive, since his father probably had a few decades to live. "'Tis far less likely to cause confusion here if you simply go by Cotrell. Certain, your father will come when the Tristelles visit, but you can always go by Squire Cotrell if there is confusion."

Jonathan nodded. "Except to you, of course. I'm not making much of it—just for new folk I meet."

Thomas yawned. "Do you have a place to sleep?"

"Across the hall. The houseman tells me enough beds were made on this floor to accommodate servants. He said all the third-floor furniture is stacked in a mess because of repairs."

"Take one of the candles. I need nothing else."

Thomas crawled between the sheets as soon as the door closed behind Jonathan. Name changes. No one else seemed to mind them. Why did it bother him so much? Should he change his? Try to move beyond the past? Beyond Kaituer? All the life that hummed through him rebelled at that thought.

CHAPTER 24

Thomas found Griven in the kitchen garden the next morning, frowning at whatever Jonathan was saying to him. Weeds lay in a pile by his feet.

Griven shifted his gaze to Thomas as he stepped through the door from the kitchen hall. "Indeed, my lord, I'm sorry I wasn't nigh when you needed me. I thought the day's work was done."

"It was," Thomas said calmly. "Where were you?"

"I just went for a walk in the woods, sir." He rubbed his short beard with the back of his fingers, looking worried. "I like to know the lay of the land and to just be alone for a bit."

Feelings Thomas knew well. "I find no fault in that. Do you oft stay out after the sun sets?"

He glanced aside like he was embarrassed. "Not so far off that I couldn't be found, though I do find night peaceful. In truth, I got turned around in the dusk and couldn't get my bearings. When I started tripping in the dark, I decided to sleep where I was. Sunrise gave me sufficient light and direction to get back easy enough." He gestured toward the patch he'd been weeding. "Just thought I'd make myself useful here before breakfast."

"Did you see anyone in the woods?"

"Nay, sir. Wish I had spotted whoever you saw. What did he look like?"

Thomas shook his head. "I can't say...only caught a glimpse of a brown horse departing."

"Breakfast is served, my lord," a woman's voice said behind Thomas.

He walked through the kitchen hall—a utilitarian space. A simple wash basin stood beside the door. A board held the morning deliveries of a bucket of milk and a basket of eggs, both half-depleted. Herbs hung in bundles from a stretch of twine, scenting the air. He strode past the long servants' table and turned through the broad opening that gave access to both the kitchen and central corridor of the house.

Thomas passed his library and crossed the main hall, savoring the fact that it already felt normal to walk through all this house—as his. By the time he entered the dining room along with Lady Sareen and Lord Dermont, the housekeeper had set a platter beside his plate and was pouring coffee. He took his place at the head of the table. What was this food rolled together? Sausage wrapped in fried egg and wrapped again in pan bread nearly as delicate as a handkerchief. And tasty.

The duke and duchess joined them, and when appetites were sated, the duchess asked, "What are your plans for today, Lord Navayn?"

"To the village first. I must meet with the reeve and priest about the oath ceremony, and I wouldn't mind a stroll through the market. 'Twas rushed yesterday."

"I've a fancy to see the market too," the duchess said. "Sareen, dear, will you come with me?"

"Of course, Mother." Lady Sareen turned to Thomas. "What of this afternoon?"

"I shall ride the forest and wasteland a little slower than yesterday. If we see a deer, I wouldn't mind bringing it home."

"If!" Lord Dermont said. "In that case, I'll bring my bow and squire."

Delays interrupted their departure. First, the houseman and housekeeper, with whom Thomas had barely had time to speak. Their concerns settled, Thomas sent Jonathan to fetch the horses and went to his bedchamber for his quiver and wrist guard. From the window, he glimpsed movement and looked closer. A rider approached along the drive, the horse's golden mane flowing with its easy lope. Lord Ivan. A carriage had just turned from the road onto the drive. Duke Maerton, already?

Thomas descended to the hall to greet his guests. Jonathan had returned from the stable and opened the door at Lord Ivan's knock.

He entered with a courteous welcome and bow. No sooner had he finished it, than his gaze locked on the lynx above the fireplace. His upper lip lifted. "Ugh! What a ghastly sight when one is accustomed to seeing the prince's portrait. I do hope you don't mind that my uncle brought our family art to the castle."

"Not at all," Thomas said. "I could not miss what I had never seen."

"I daresay you'll find something to replace it." He nodded toward the mantelpiece. "I can see why the first Duke of Maerton covered that when he lived here."

"Aye, for a lynx symbolizes the House of Navayn."

"A double reason to cover it, then," Lord Ivan said.

The carriage had stopped beyond the door, which Jonathan held open for the next arrival. A servant opened the carriage door, but no one stepped out.

Thomas raised his brows. "The duke is not with you?"

"Nay, he will come in a day or two, but I wanted to bring you a gift of welcome. 'Twas hard to know what would be most suitable at first, but then I realized you would have no art for your walls. I fancy I have hit on the perfect gift for your little manor." The servant had withdrawn a flat object draped with a cloth from the carriage, and Lord Ivan motioned him to enter. "Bring it in and hold it up for Lord Navayn."

Accustomed to Lord Ivan's contempt, Thomas prepared himself for something insulting.

The servant braced the object as if he were a human easel, and Lord Ivan drew the cloth from it and dropped it on the floor. "An ancestral portrait. Your grandfather, Thomas Kaituer."

Thomas blinked. Indeed, no gift could have pleased him more! The likeness he had so long heard of. A youthful though serious face. Gray eyes and blond hair, just like his. The long nose and shape of the face...'twas uncanny how strong the resemblance was. But the brass plate on the bottom of the frame! Now, *that* was more like Lord Ivan's usual style, but doubtless it was placed there long before Ivan was born.

Offering a slight bow, Thomas said, "I thank you, Lord Ivan. 'Tis indeed the perfect gift."

Lord Ivan smiled broader—a most uncharacteristic expression. "I am so glad it pleases you." He glanced around. "Ah, here is an empty hook. An ideal spot for it." He motioned the servant to the side wall, near the door. "Hang it here." Ivan assisted in anchoring it, then stepped back to admire. "The effect is all I hoped for. And who can say...perhaps it may even still those mysterious footsteps where none could be walking. Have you heard them yet?"

"Nay," Thomas said. "Think not that I am credulous."

"Ah, like my uncle, then, who also refused to acknowledge them. But I gather from your woodsman appearance that you have plans for the day. I'll not keep you."

Ivan took himself off, and Jonathan closed the door again, saying with a scoff, "I swear, he has never seen a woodsman if he thinks you look like one."

Thomas only laughed.

Duke Selta and Lord Dermont entered the hall from the central corridor, for they'd been in the library. The door had stood open, so 'twas no surprise that they had heard the exchange.

Lord Dermont grinned. "'Tis the vest and snug sleeves. The look of Moorelin, in fact."

"I doubt he cares much about the accuracy of his insults," Thomas said.

Duke Selta stared at the portrait, the corners of his mouth drawn down. "Doubtless, he is hoping for a little ignorance on your part. 'Tis said that the portrait once hung nigh the door in this hall, and I see the inscribed brass is still on it."

"As did I." Thomas pulled the halfmoon table away from the wall. "Bring it here, Jonathan."

The table was wide enough to support the frame, though the corners stuck out over the edges. Thomas read the inscription again. *Thomas Kaituer—Condemned to Death*. Not him, of course. Or did Ivan mean it that way?

Thomas inspected the brass plate. Just a simple rectangle, rounded like it had been formed along a cylinder rather than fit to the curve of this expertly carved frame. Two brass nails held it in place. Thomas tried to wiggle it. Snug, but it gave a little. He pulled his hunting knife from his belt and slid the tip under the plate beside a nail. Slowly...gently...he lifted alternating sides until he could grip it between fingertips and pull it free. The nails popped and bounced on the canvas. Thomas raised his brows at another brass plate he'd exposed, a smaller oval embedded within the wood.

Lord Thomas Navayn Kaituer

Hmm. He'd never heard that Navayn was part of his grandfather's name. Nor seen it recorded as such. Not even in Lady Anne's will. With the title of *lord* included, this would have been written after her death. That meant the last duke of Kaituer had added the name.

The ladies were descending the staircase. Thomas looked up at the sudden quickening of Lady Sareen's footsteps, her gaze fixed on the painting.

Exclamations rolled together...his likeness to the portrait... Ivan's crassness for leaving the condemning plate attached.

Thomas paid little heed, for his thoughts shot down a dozen paths, of days gone by and days yet to come.

Lord Dermont was saying something about filling the nail holes…that they would hardly show.

"Nay," Thomas said. "I'll leave them empty."

"Why?"

"Because empty nail holes declare that condemnation is removed."

Blank stares for an instant, then Sareen smiled. "Ah! From the holy book."

It pleased him inordinately that she was the first to perceive his meaning. He smiled at her, picked up the portrait, and carried it into the salon. Empty hanging rods gave him plenty of options for placement. "Where shall I hang it?"

Lady Sareen had followed him. "Hmm." She pointed. "There, by the door to the dining room."

'Twas a prominent spot she'd chosen, and that pleased him too.

As he hooked it, she said, "I think the light from those candles on the angled mantel will illuminate it well. This evening, we can check."

That didn't matter to him, but for the first time, the candleholders caught his attention. Carved stone, about eight inches tall, polished to a luster. Lynxeye. Sword hilt…mantel… candle holders…how many things could be fashioned from this stone?

"'Twill be fine, I'm sure," the duchess said. "Shouldn't we be setting out?"

Thomas remembered his plans—already delayed. "I had thought to be finished with my business before you reached the market."

"Worry not." The duchess waved her hand in a flitting gesture. "I have far more time to spare than you have."

～

229

THE REEVE WAS NOWHERE in sight when Thomas reached the village. He farmed, of course. He could not hang about the village on the chance that his lord may stop there. The priest, however, was sitting on a bench on the sloped lawn beside the church, surrounded by a dozen or so children of varied ages. Some of them leaned over, apparently writing. One child sat beside him, reading aloud from the book they held between them. Thomas paused, not wanting to interrupt what must be lessons.

The priest said, "Well done," to the lass. Her gaze caught on Thomas as she stood, then she blushed and curtsied, drawing the priest's attention to him. "Ah, forgive me," he said. "I did not see you there."

Thomas drew nearer, acknowledging the priest and his students, all of whom had risen, and with wide eyes, offered bows or curtsies with varied degrees of skill. Endearing children.

"We'll be done for the day now," the priest said to his charges. "Put your things away inside, and then be off to your parents."

They gathered up an odd collection of pale slates, bark, and charcoal sticks. Only the oldest one held rough parchment, ink, and quill. Then, off they ran, pounding up the steps to the church.

The priest carried the only book, walking slowly until the gaggle of children came pelting out of the church again and scattered. "I was wondering if you would stop by. Wondering, too, if you would know about the portraits. Never got a chance to introduce myself yesterday. Name's Simmon."

"'Tis a pleasure to meet you, Priest Simmon."

"Well, I'm not really a priest, though. *Do* you know about the portraits?"

"Uh, what portraits do you speak of?"

"I thought as much." They climbed the stone steps to a door shaped much like the peaked arches of the manor. Inside, Simmon placed the book on a narrow table holding the school things. The back two sets of pews faced each other, and Simmon spread his hands to the space. "The village school when the weather is not so fine as today. But the portraits…I'll warrant, I have you curious now," he said with a humorous lift of his curly eyebrows. Indeed, all of his brown hair was the curliest Thomas had ever seen.

"That, you do." Thomas walked beside him down the aisle between pews. Colored light scattered across the stone floor, for the window arches held wedges of stained glass. The lower rectangles allowed more light to penetrate through clear glass, bordered by grape leaves twining on amber backgrounds.

"The story goes," Simmon said, "that a cousin of Lady Anne Navayn—a lady much revered here—this cousin lived in Navayn Manor after the lady wed Duke Kaituer. When he saw which way the king's wrath would blow, he brought the Navayn portraits from the manor and hid them in the church. They've been here ever since."

They neared the altar table, which was draped in an embroidered cloth and flanked by wooden enclosures. One gave access to the raised pulpit. Simmon turned past the front pew toward the other enclosure. At first glance, its carved panels appeared decorative—until Simmon tugged on one and swung it open as a door.

Faint light revealed a lowly bucket and broom in the corner and a table with folded linens, candles, two wine bottles, and a matching tray and chalice. The pattern in the chalice…was that what it looked like? Thomas picked it up and turned to see it in better light. Lynxeye again, polished to a silky luster. A fine specimen with much of the amber hue. A lovely treasure, but this small room held no portraits.

Simmon fidgeted with the wall opposite the door, then half of it shifted back and he slid it aside, the wood scraping in some sort of track. "Here they are. I can't deny, the secret stash made me fair burst, wanting to see it. I brought them all out…" He arched his eyebrows again. "To clean them, you understand."

Thomas grinned. "Of course."

Frames stuck up from a crate. Simmon lifted the front one. "The rest can wait, but this one, you'll want to see. Lady Anne herself." He carried it out and stood it on the front pew.

Thomas looked in silence. A young, gentle-eyed lady with hair between blond and brown and delicate lips that hinted at a smile. He must say something, for Simmon was watching him. "For the last few weeks...it seems that I stumble across treasures everywhere I look."

The priest nodded sagely. "I think it reveals much that these are the treasures her cousin rescued and hid. Not coin or jewels —the family. And the other Navayns kept the secret too. They didn't tell me about the portraits until I started doing the holy book readings on the rest days. I suppose they figured I would find them sooner or later, what with me taking on the priest duties. 'Course, I'd been here for a while then. I never heard a word about them when my sister and I first came."

"You're not from the village, then? Did the church send you here?"

He snorted. "More like they *drove* us here. Well, more rightly, they drove us *away* from our birth village. We settled here because there was no priest. Never thought *I'd* be taking on priest duties. Couldn't stand that sort. It wasn't till later, I found out they're all different, just like ordinary folk. An old priest used to come through on the full moon rest day. A kind soul, he was, who never said foul nonsense about my mother or sister."

"What mean you?"

"My sister's legs aren't right. Short and bowed. She was born that way, and the priest of our old village said it was a judgement on our mother...that she must be harboring wickedness in her heart. Made my mother's last years awful, he did. And when my sister was old enough to take the holy bread and wine, the priest wouldn't serve her because he said she was born of wickedness."

Simmon shook his head. "Use to make me rile up somethin' fierce. The traveling priest here finally got me to understand that only forgiveness would bring me peace. And besides that, he served my sister just like he served everyone else. Folk are kinder here than in my old village, and they made no fuss over her funny walk. They buy her wares, and I was able to find enough work so we could get along. In time, I started reading the holy book and found out it says a whole lot of things I never heard as a lad. Some folk think I get too taken up with it, but…" He slapped a hand to his brow. "Oh, here I am rattling on. Folk say I do that too. But what I meant to tell you is that when the traveling priest died, the village folk asked me to do the readings, and it just fit. So now, we live in the priest cottage, and I built a workshop for my sister."

"Ah! An unjust judgement is something I can understand. As well as the joy of being freed from it." Thomas picked up the portrait. "I'll just leave this in its place until I can take them all."

"They'll be waiting for you."

They slid the false wall into place again and were just stepping from the enclosure, when the church door opened and the reeve started down the aisle.

"Ah, happy chance that brings you," Thomas said.

"No chance about it. I'd told the local lads to fetch me if you came into the village." He glanced to Simmon. "Did you show him the portraits?"

"Aye, Master Navayn. 'Tis as we thought. He'd never heard of them."

"A pleasant surprise," Thomas said, "but another matter brought me here. Yesterday, I found the records of past ceremonies for the oaths of fealty. 'Twas always done on rest days after the morning service. I propose we do the same on the next rest day. What say you?"

Master Navayn's smile grew wider with each word. "I say, the whole village will rejoice. I will spread the word to every family."

Thomas nodded and turned to Simmon. "The priest opens the ceremony with a prayer and closes it with a blessing. If both of you will visit Navayn Manor tomorrow, I will show you the records I found."

Simmon shuffled his feet. "Right kind of you to offer me that honor, but as I said, I am not a priest."

The reeve swung his head side to side. "Thought we'd settled that nonsense! Duke Maerton would never grant us a priest, miserly heathen that he is, so God sent you to us. A priest's heart, he gave you, so a priest you are!"

"Aye, calm down, my friend. I've come to terms with it, but certain, I must be truthful with Lord Navayn." He turned to Thomas. "Just so you know, I've never been recognized by the church."

"If Duke Maerton would have had anything to do with appointing a priest here," Thomas said, "I am *glad* you came by a higher commission. Quite likely, that was also the case with the traveling priests who served in Tower Woods during my childhood. I have but one question. Does this mean that you are paid no wage?"

"Nay, though the village folk bring us meat, now and then. The rest, we take care of with our own labor."

"And you teach the children too?"

"'Tis not much. Just letters and sums. I can spare them a couple hours each morn."

Thomas shook his head. "I'll not have you go unpaid. Just grant me patience, for there is much to be done. I will see you both tomorrow morn at Navayn Manor."

"Aye, my lord," they said in unison.

The three of them walked the aisle toward the door. "By the way," Thomas said, "Lord Ivan is trying to convince me the manor is haunted. Nonsense, of course, but do the local folk tell such stories?"

Both priest and reeve made derogatory sounds. Master Navayn said, "Never heard even a whisper of ghosts. If anything were haunted, 'twould be Maerton Castle. Lord Ivan is a strange creature. 'Tis a great relief to us that you were restored to this land, Lord Navayn, *before* the current duke passes on."

They left the church together, and as they descended the steps, Simmon said, "My sister was sad she didn't get to see you yesterday. 'Tis hard for her to get out much." He pointed to a cottage with a newer structure beside it. "If you would be so kind as to stop over, I would be most grateful."

"Aye, though it must be brief, for others wait on me."

"Quite, quite." A moment later, Simmon ushered him into the workshop and introduced him to Sallie.

At first glance, Thomas saw nothing strange, for she sat on a low bench behind a potter's wheel. Then, she stood…and grew no taller than she had been while seated. She bowed instead of curtsying. "'Tis a right honor that you visit, my lord."

Thomas took in the low shelves, all filled with wares. Finished pieces on one side, both earthenware and wooden. On the other side, sat tubs of clay and water. Fresh pieces stood drying on racks. "You are skillful," he said, taking a closer look at the finished work.

"I thank you, sir." A smile softened her voice.

"Did you carve these wooden pieces too?"

"Aye. We always say that if wood needed a mallet or saw, my brother made it. If it is turned on a wheel, I made it."

"How do you shape wood on a wheel?"

"My papa made a fitting for the wheel to hold the block, and he got me some special blades. Took some practice to get the feel of wood, but now 'tis as natural to me as clay."

Thomas picked up a vase. "This is stone!"

"Aye, soapstone. 'Tis hard to get, though."

"Could you fashion lynxstone?"

"Ooo! I don't know, sir. I only have one tool that might be hard enough." She licked her lips. "I'd love to try, but it takes practice to learn how a new medium likes to be handled. I'd hate to ruin a precious stone."

"Some are better than others. I will give you a lesser stone to practice on."

"Oh, I thank you, sir! You are most kind."

He smiled. "It may well work to our mutual advantage."

With that, Thomas left them, his steps lighter. If the stone could be worked, it could be sold. And that could bring in much needed coin. He found Jonathan waiting for him in the street. "Do you have any idea where the ladies are?"

"Aye, this way. I've been shifting back and forth, trying to keep both them and you in view."

Thomas walked at his side toward the market. "How well you envision my needs." Ahead of them, Griven carried a large basket across the road toward their market cart, and the housekeeper bargained with a vendor.

"I've never seen a fellow like Griven," Jonathan said. "In between fetching loads, he slides into conversation with complete strangers and parts from them like they're long-time friends."

In this, Thomas found no common ground as he had this morning. What was it like to have such ease with all people? Like Lady Sareen there, chatting with a villager. Her, at least, he could easily join, and he asked the villager where pastries could be found in the market. Thus, he hosted his guests to a light repast in the shade of the alehouse porch, where the proprietor carried out a small table and four chairs. He served ale to Thomas and Lord Dermont, and the proprietress offered the ladies a drink she called fruited waters. Fresh strawberries and mint leaves floated in the pink-hued water.

Thomas suspected that Duchess Selta found the village outing uncomfortably rustic, but she kept a smile in place until they finished, then climbed into her carriage to return to the manor. The rest of them strolled to their horses, tied alongside a livestock pen at the outskirts of the market, and set off to explore.

CHAPTER 25

Duke Maerton read the short reply he had received from Duke Selta. A polite refusal of his invitation to dinner. He was not surprised, but...Ivan. How would he react?

He had insisted on the invitation this morn. An unusual irritant while they shared tea in Ivan's study. The one time of day when Ivan kept his sarcastic tongue in check...when it was possible to envision a tolerable future. Besides, Ivan made tea better than anyone else, and the ingredient he'd found to ease arthritic complaints did seem to be helping.

Maerton laid the note beside the book he'd been reading and heaved himself from the armchair. Less pain than usual in his troublesome knees. He walked to the hall where a page was assigned to wait, so the duke need not climb unnecessary steps. He was about to send the lad to fetch Ivan, when an empty space on the wall captured Maerton's attention.

He blinked at it. "Where is the portrait of Thomas Kaituer?"

The lad, proper in gray vest and white shirt, bowed stiffly. "Lord Ivan took it, my lord duke."

"Took it where?"

"Um...he had it put in the carriage with a cloth over it, sir."

"Has he returned?"

"I think not, sir. At least, not through the hall."

Ivan's voice spoke from above. "True in part, but I have returned." He descended the steps in leisurely fashion. "Did you want me, Father?"

The duke pointed at the empty space. "Where did you take the portrait?"

More footsteps neared from above, and Sathe started down the staircase as Ivan answered. "To the one person who would value it." Ivan looked pleased with himself. "I fancy I hit on the perfect gift to welcome the younger version of Thomas Kaituer. Since we had removed all the Maerton portraits, the manor walls are lamentably bare." When Ivan reached the duke, he turned enough to include his uncle in the conversation. "Worse, there is a ghastly snarling lynx above the fireplace where Prince Maerton's likeness used to greet visitors."

"Would you speak plain?" Maerton demanded.

Sathe reached them. "He refers to a mantelpiece. The first duke must not have appreciated the Navayn symbol and covered it with his own likeness. A pity, in a way, for it is a remarkably fine relief carving of a lynx—though *not* snarling."

"An impression, of course," Ivan said. "Or perhaps it shifts. I've heard stories of things moving on their own in that manor."

"Complete and utter nonsense," Sathe said flatly.

Ivan laughed.

Maerton was not amused. "Do not spread absurdities. Come." Best to get him out of the hearing of servants. Ivan and Sathe followed the duke to his library. When the door was closed, Maerton asked, "With what words did you present the portrait?"

"Nothing untoward, Father. I used all proper curtesy, and Lord Navayn accepted it with genuine pleasure."

"Who else was present?"

"None but he." Ivan shrugged. "A servant with the look of Moorelin, but he would know nothing."

"What of the inscription? Was it still attached?"

"Certain, Father. You have not had it removed in all these years, so I honored your desire to leave it intact."

Maerton closed his eyes, taking a slow breath. "What did he say of it?"

"Not a word." Ivan looked more pleased than ever. "There was an empty hook nigh the hall door, so I hung it for him. It seemed a fitting location."

"Did you have to be so obvious?" Maerton demanded. "Now, I must apologize when I visit."

"You need not. He showed no understanding."

"You err in thinking him naïve," Sathe said. "He has more understanding than you realize."

Ivan assumed his fixed smile. "Thank you for your opinion, Uncle. Will you be staying much longer with us?"

"Nay. In fact, I came downstairs to discover whether I should stay for dinner. Are the Seltas joining us, brother?"

"Duke Selta sent his regrets." Maerton watched Ivan's non-reaction, fully aware that Sathe watched it too.

After a few seconds, Sathe replied, "Then, I shall depart after the noon meal."

He left the room, and Maerton sank into his favorite chair as Ivan strolled to the window. "I daresay, you are disappointed, Ivan, but it was too much to expect of them. Odd indeed, to accept an invitation to dinner *here* when they are guests of Lord Navayn and he was not invited. Try to appreciate these nuances of propriety."

Ivan strolled back from the window. "I do understand, Father. There is only one thing that would have made them accept, despite the conventions. But they did not, and that is the answer I needed."

"What is this?"

"I thought I would have more time, but I don't. Lady Sareen pays much attention to Lord Navayn."

"She is visiting *with her family*."

"I noticed. And also notice that the family is *not* visiting here."

"They will come for the hunting parties. I'm sure the queen arranged their current visit in order to settle Lord Navayn. Certain, he has no knowledge of how to lord an estate. It will not look well for the king if Lord Navayn immediately fails, so do not build too much upon their visit."

Lord Ivan stared at him without expression.

"Well?" Maerton said.

"I have eyes and ears. My own and others. Lady Sareen favors him. I saw it at court and again at the ruins. She even revealed it at the inn near our very gates. Last night, they walked the garden paths alone at dusk." A trace of contempt swept his face. "So daft to follow paths around gardens that do not exist." His bland look returned. "She rides with him whenever he goes out. And if the queen arranged for their visit—regardless of her purpose— that also lends a certain approval."

"I still say you are building too much upon it. They will come for the hunting and stay with us. Lord Navayn, living so close, will have no reason to stay at the castle. You will have plenty of opportunity to spend time with Lady Sareen when he is not present."

A second passed, and Ivan produced his calm smile. "True, I shall. How are your knees, Father?"

"They are better, thank you."

"I am so glad." Ivan departed with those words.

DROSSIN WAITED IN THE THICKET. Things hadn't been so bad lately, though his head ached. The master had come regular this past week or two, bringing him a pouch of food and a bottle of wine every day. Little, but enough. Not sending him hither and thither, but letting him stay in a cave. It had room enough for the horse too.

He could get along like this. Easy. No coin, but food and wine and a roof over his head—that was good enough pay for sleeping till the sun was high. Besides, staying out of sight suited him just fine. He had enough places where no one could see him and only the master knew.

He heard the hooves but stayed low, awaiting the smooth voice. Couldn't be too careful, for the master warned him to avoid hunters. They didn't come this far, though.

The hooves stopped. "Dross."

He hated the shortened name, but wine was wine. He stood and emerged. Lately, the master had just exchanged the full leather pouch for his empty one, so Drossin held it out. The master just looked at him from the one eye that wasn't covered by the drooped brim of his cocked hat. His mouth was straight as ever. Drossin drew the pouch back and hooked his thumbs in his belt to hide his shakes.

"'Tis time you earned all this food and wine," the master drawled. "I have a task for you tonight. Quite a simple one."

"What, sir?"

"You shall light a fire for me. Precisely where I tell you. The wood is dry and laid ready. You need only provide the spark and slip away."

"I'll not be settin' things afire. That'd make me as foul as the Kaituers."

The master uttered a joyless laugh. "The wood is on a hearth beneath a chimney. 'Tis for a wager and a jest on one who speaks his disdain of ghosts. No harm shall come of it."

That didn't sound so bad.

The master lifted the pouch from his saddle. "Will you do it, or shall I leave with this?"

"Aye." They exchanged pouches, and Drossin felt how light the new one was. He flipped it open and drew out the bottle. "This only has a few swallows in it."

"When you have finished tonight's task, I'll bring you a full bottle."

He might have known. "Where d'ye want this fire?"

CHAPTER 26

Thomas's party rode swiftly past the fields. No deer spoiled them at the moment—probably because a lad walked the edge, with a long staff in hand. Thomas turned from the fields and traversed the wasteland, traveling farther west than Lord Maerton had led them.

"Why are we wandering in this waste?" Lord Dermont asked. "The deer will favor the woods."

"Because the only reason to call this land such, is that Duke Maerton, or perhaps his steward, let it go to waste. I've seen three goats already."

"Are we here to rescue goats?" Lord Dermont sounded so incensed that Thomas laughed.

"Nay. To get a feel for the size of the herd. For every one that climbs up to look at us, there are more grazing below."

"Goat is not a fine meat," Lord Dermont said. "Do they provide a challenging hunt?"

Having hunted to survive, Thomas was still mystified by the nobles' love of sport hunting, but he refrained from comment. "I don't want to hunt them. Goats are easily tamed, and their wool has value, assuming I can get enough of them. Clearly, they can survive on this scruffy land, so all I would need is a few goatherds."

"I cannot imagine where you will find goatherds."

So obvious.

When Thomas failed to answer, Lady Sareen narrowed her eyes at him. "Do *you* know where to find them?"

"The People of the Woods know how to handle goats."

"But why would they come here?" Lord Dermont asked.

"Do you really believe I am the only one among them to remember my heritage? They know where they came from—that their grandparents lived in villages or farmed in this duchy. Some of them have grown to love Tower Woods, but 'tis not an easy place to scratch out a living. Others still long for what their families lost in this land."

"For five years," Lord Dermont said, "they've had no need to fear arrest or execution. Have *any* of them actually come out of Tower Woods to live within Maerton Duchy?"

"Nay, they would not live under Maerton rule."

Sareen's gentle smile sweetened her voice. "Ah, but they would live under Navayn rule."

"I believe so." He longed to show his pleasure in her understanding, but far too often the king's prohibition whispered in the back of his mind. Thomas drew a little ahead on one of the forsaken tracks and led the others down into the quarry. His guests followed, and the two squires and Griven trailed along.

As they spread out on bare ground, Jonathan rode near Thomas. "What are you looking for, my lord?"

"Lynxstone. Look for stripes running through the rock." Here and there, they spied the faint pattern. In a place where it was more prevalent, Thomas dismounted and picked up a rock that had fallen nigh the base of a low cliff. 'Twas a foot or more in each dimension. This should do. He hefted it. "Griven."

The man rode near, the only one without a bow and quiver. "Sir?"

"Carry this back to the manor."

He took it from Thomas and rested it on his saddle and legs. "Aye, my lord." He shifted it around. "Perhaps when we have eaten, I could pack it."

"If that is a hint, 'tis well timed," Jonathan said. "I have heard at least three stomach rumbles."

Lord Dermont snorted. "Can a man have no privacy?"

They laughed and found a shady spot to spread out the lunch Thomas had requested from the housekeeper. The ground cloth would provide no comfort in a quarry, but Thomas folded it into a pad for the boulder Sareen chose to sit on.

'Twas not the most pleasant place to linger, and they soon prepared to mount. Griven put the rock into an empty food pack and lashed it to his saddle with the ground cloth beneath it. When Thomas gave him leave to return to the manor, Griven said, "I need not, my lord. 'Tis secure enough that I can stay with you."

Thomas shrugged and permitted. An extra hand would be useful if they took a deer. In truth, he was more interested in learning the land and its trails than he was in hunting. They explored at a walk, Lady Sareen often telling him which trails led where. In late afternoon, they spotted a yearling buck. 'Twas too easy to pass up. It stared at them, munching on leaves as the men drew their bows and shot together. Three arrows struck true, so they didn't even have to track it.

The servants dismounted to get their kill ready to carry, and Lord Dermont said, "That arrow you shot...I only saw it for a second. What was it tipped with?"

"Flint."

"Why not iron? I've seen Duke Tristelle use it."

"I buy arrows from the People of the Woods. They have little to sell, so 'tis a means to encourage their use of coins."

"'Tis kind of you," Lady Sareen said, nudging her horse farther from the deer.

Ah, the part of hunting she didn't care for. Thomas rode a

few paces down a trail and conversed with her while they waited. Soon, the deer was tied to one of the horses and they continued on. Leaving the woods, they began crossing the unkept lawn toward the manor house.

What was this coming along his drive? Two rough-market carts from Tower Woods, and leading them, a tall man straight in the saddle, his brown hair tied back.

"'Tis Captain D'Jorge!" Thomas turned quick to Lady Sareen. "Will you pardon me if I ride ahead?"

"I shall not. This is my first chance to canter all day."

She got a start on him, but he caught up and, together, they rode to meet his friend at the manor's door.

Thomas dismounted and clasped shoulders with D'Jorge. "How did you get here so soon?"

"Soon? How far do you think it is? Duke Tristelle met me on the south side of Tower Woods. Which is also the easiest place to find those who hanker for civilization. Come and meet those who dared to cross Maerton's land."

The first cart had stopped, and folk climbed stiffly down.

Thomas greeted them and was soon introducing them to his bemused houseman and housekeeper.

A worried look lay behind Mistress Eldred's kind smile as she looked over the folk unloading their belongings. "My lord, I don't know where we shall put all these folk, nor how we shall feed them."

Five couples, an elderly woman, and a few children didn't seem like so many to Thomas. "They of the Woods know how to make do," he assured the housekeeper. Those who overheard nodded, and Thomas lifted his voice above the chatter. "Who among you can help cook, and better yet, brought a pot or pan to cook in?" To the immediate offers, he said, "For today, please go with Mistress Eldred, who will direct you. Also, there is a deer to be butchered. Master Eldred will show you where that can be done. I fancy, some of you know my squire, who is called Cotrell here." He pointed to Santhorn, who approached along the side drive. "This is my stablemaster, Santhorn. These four may direct you and answer questions. Tomorrow, we will talk of... of all that must be arranged. Ah, by chance, did any of you bring tools?"

No harvest tools, but they found an ax, a saw, and a spade among them. Better than nothing. Thomas stepped from amidst the crowd. "Captain D'Jorge, I have some cottages, long untended. Will you inspect them with me?"

"Certain."

"What are you grinning at?

"You, Lord Navayn, whose words I distinctly recall. At first hearing of this estate, you told me you wouldn't know how to manage."

Thomas returned the grin. "That seems like a long time ago. But indeed, there is so much to be done here that I am wildly glad you have all arrived."

That got some smiles from the new folk who still lingered near.

Captain D'Jorge said, "The only thing you have forgotten is to take a deep breath."

Thomas pressed a hand to his head. "Ugh. I never offered refreshment to anyone. Jonathan, at least draw from the kitchen well and take water around."

"I can help with that," a young lad offered.

"Then, come with me," Jonathan said. "The rest of you, come along too. I will show you about, and we will at least find roofs that don't leak for your first night."

They headed in the direction of the kitchen hall, most of them staring open-mouthed at the manor house. Doubtless, it seemed huge to them.

"Let us go in," Thomas said. D'Jorge had just bowed to Lady Sareen and Lord Dermont, and they followed him through the arched door.

D'Jorge scanned the hall, top to bottom. "I like what I'm seeing. Is it in sound condition?"

"The house and the stables are." Thomas gestured to the salon. "Come rest for a bit before I drag you around the outbuildings."

D'Jorge made his bow to the Duke and Duchess of Selta.

The duchess had prepared for their return and poured from a pitcher into glasses, mint leaves swirling in the water. "The infusion is raspberry and mint." She nodded toward a divided serving dish mounded with an assortment of berries and plums. "Please enjoy some fruit with it."

Apparently, she had not totally disdained the refreshment at the ale house. Lady Sareen filled one of the porcelain bowls with fruit and took it to her father, while the rest served themselves. Conversation flowed as it did when anyone came from a distance and news could be exchanged. Soon, it turned to D'Jorge's questions about the estate, and he shook his head over the absence of tools.

"That seems less than honest, for some tools must have been here when the Maertons took possession. But I suppose nothing would come of bickering over it. I'll inform Duke Tristelle of your need."

Thomas nodded, tight-lipped. Tools were expensive from any source, and he would need so many at once. And though he was glad of all who had arrived, he would have to feed them and pay them. Would his limited coin last until harvest?

THE TOUR of buildings with D'Jorge overwhelmed Thomas. As they turned to walk back to the manor, he said, "I don't know how I'm going to remember even half of this or figure all that I need in supplies."

D'Jorge looked sideways at him. "I'll not leave tomorrow until I've written a full list of needs, organized by building, and the order to tackle the work. And another list for me of what I think we should bring from Tower Woods. How many more workers can you draw from your own estate?"

"None, I suspect, until the harvest is done. Those with a moment to spare guard their fields or mine from the, uh, oversized rodents we call deer. And if they aren't doing that, they should be hunting. Speaking of which, I need more arrows."

They went in to eat dinner, where Thomas met the only servant his housekeeper had been able to hire from the village—a lass named Trenda, who carried dishes from the kitchen to be served in the dining room...and only dropped one. She stared at the steaming beans and gasped three high-pitched breaths, as if a flood of tears was on the way.

"Fret not," Thomas said. "Just clean it up and continue on."

When Mistress Eldred and Trenda carried the remains away, Sareen said, "I see you favor a quiet household."

He spread butter on half a roll. "One as calm as your name, my lady. Green beans are *not* my biggest concern."

The challenges rolling around his mind made him glad that D'Jorge had plenty to talk of. Just remembering so many tasks seemed beyond possibility. He'd best adopt D'Jorge's method and get things written down. Everything from fixing boundary markers, to delivering a rock to Sallie, and collecting the portraits, fought for attention with the critical matters of understanding his land and providing for—and directing—his people. And he'd forgotten to check on the goats in the stable. Thus, when the party dispersed for the evening, he took parchment and ink to his bedchamber.

Jonathan brought him water to wash with, then pulled the window partially closed and drew the curtains to a narrow slit. "This room has an odd smell."

"What mean you?" Thomas asked, unbuttoning his vest.

"I can't describe it...so faint."

Thomas sat in the armchair and held out a leg for Jonathan to pull the boot off. "This house is hundreds of years old. Plenty of time to acquire an odd scent or two. I admit I'm glad I don't have the sensitive nose that you and your father do. Does it annoy?"

Jonathan pulled the boot off. "Nay. Why should it?"

"To be inundated with smells...'tis not as though you can stop breathing if a smell is foul. Aren't they overwhelming?"

"I don't care to be nigh rotting dung, but no one cares for that." He tugged on the other boot. "I'm not sure what smells are like for others, but maybe they aren't that much stronger for me. I do notice all the nuances, though. But either way, I'm used to it."

He set the boots outside the door, then walked around the chamber, sniffing. "Might be that the curtains absorbed something."

"Decades of something!"

Jonathan held one close to his nose. "There's a whiff of it in here. Maybe by the fireplace too." He pulled the iron handle to open the damper and sniffed again. "I just cannot place it." He closed the damper and asked, "Have you need of anything else?"

"Nay. Just quiet to end this day." Jonathan left, and Thomas went to the narrow table against one wall. Setting a candle on his left, he began his list. It seemed that the more notes he jotted down, the more things he remembered. The night stilled as footsteps and the closing of doors subsided to a minimum.

If only his mind would still as well. He capped the ink and stood. Would he be able to gain from the wasteland as he hoped? The remaining lynxstone...perhaps it had been left because it was inferior. Certain, it looked nothing like the polished lynxeye. He picked up his sword and studied the ornate hilt. So finely crafted. Should he seek out a jeweler in—

A bloodcurdling scream pierced the night.

Thomas jumped, then wrenched his door open and sprinted down the corridor. The shriek still emanated from a distant door, as others were jerked open. Without pause for thought, he flung open the door to Sareen's chamber.

The lady's scream paused only for breath and pierced his ears again.

Why? What threatened?

Sareen cowered against the wall with a pillow over her head, and Adonna swung a blanket through the air. A bat darted away from her flailing.

Thomas choked down the laughter that surged toward his throat. "Adonna, stay back. And for pity's sake, quiet your mistress."

"What is going on?" the duke demanded.

"Stay in the corridor," Thomas said, motioning them back with his left hand. He could not use the sword he held if they crowded into the chamber. He pulled the scabbard off and tossed it aside as he watched the bat flit about. For the second time, it swept under the bed canopy and darted around the tied curtains.

The instant it turned away from him, he swung. The sword hissed, and the bat dropped. Ugh. He'd severed a wing, and the creature flopped on the carpet. A quick stab with the sword tip put it out of its misery. And stained the carpet. Eh, 'twas faded anyway.

Sareen uttered a shuddering sound of revulsion, clutching the pillow to her chest.

Thomas looked around. "Was there just the one?"

"Aye, my lord," Adonna said. "But it came from the fireplace." She was made of sterner stuff than her mistress, but her finger shook as she pointed.

The hearth was bare. Was the damper not closed? Indeed, the iron handle protruded. Nor could he shove it in. "The damper is stuck open—probably rusted."

All the Seltas stood in the room now. The duchess exclaimed over the bat carcass, and Jonathan hovered in the doorway.

Thomas turned from the fireplace, and Lady Sareen nigh threw herself upon his chest. "Oh, thank you!"

"Sareen! Calm yourself," the duke ordered, while the duchess poured a glass of water from the pitcher on the washstand.

Thomas's chest ached with the effort it took to stifle his laugh. He patted Sareen's shoulder. "'Twas nothing, my lady."

She disengaged from Thomas but blinked like she was about to cry.

"Most unpleasant," her mother said, handing her the glass of water. "But it is only the size of a mouse, after all."

Sareen took a drink, then said, "You wouldn't say that if it had nigh tangled in your hair."

"They don't, though, my dear. Trust me, there were plenty of bats on my father's estate, and I used to be fond of night walks. For all they careen about, they never collide with anything. One learns to ignore them."

"I'm not staying in a room with bats. Not even a dead one."

"Jonathan," Thomas said, sheathing his sword, "get that mess out of here, would you?"

He removed the tiny carcass, as the duchess tried to soothe her daughter and Adonna shoved a pillow into the chimney.

"I don't care," Lady Sareen said, her black curls jiggling. "I will not be able to sleep a wink in this room."

Lord Dermont said with his brotherly smirk, "Perhaps your hero will stand watch with the mighty Navayn sword. Provided his ancestors don't rise in outrage over it being used to kill a *bat*."

"Nay, they would only rise to honor me," Thomas said, "for I have killed a dragon and rescued a damsel in distress."

Sareen uttered a watery giggle. Much better than the tears that had been threatening.

The duchess laid a towel over the bloodstain. "Indeed, and now that the dread creature has met its fate, we can go to bed."

The pillow fell onto the hearth with a soft *foof*.

Sareen made a shuddery sound in her throat. "I am not sleeping in this room!"

"You need not," Thomas said. "I will switch with you. Just let me get a few things from my chamber, and you may take your belongings there."

The men left her chamber, and Thomas closed the door on the ladies within. Then, he braced his back against the corridor wall and shook with silent laughter.

Captain D'Jorge had emerged, too, though Thomas was sure he'd only stayed to discover the farce. Lord Dermont gave him a dramatic account, but at least had the grace to move away from the door and keep his voice low. The duke ended up chuckling over it too, but said, "Let us not be in the corridor laughing when she emerges."

The exchange was soon accomplished. Alone again, this time in a guest chamber, Thomas sat down to add to his list. Chimney cleaning, damper inspection and repair, and carpet replacement. Several other items occurred, and he wrote on until the well-spring of needs dried up. For today.

Thomas let his gaze wander the chamber. He smiled fondly at his sword propped in the corner. Who would have thought! His chest shook again. Unfortunately, he was more awake than ever. A few feminine belongings had been left behind in the hurried switch. He was in Sareen's chamber. She had embraced him in her chaotic moment. Silly though the uproar had been... it revealed much. And fired the ache in his chest to a fever's heat. Why—why had the king forbidden him to court anyone? How long would he have to wait? Could he go to the king and ask him? How did one phrase such a thing?

He should undress and go to bed. But what if another bat got through the gapped window of the master chamber, where Sareen lay? Absurd! Yet, the most he could make himself do was to snuff the candle and stretch out on the bed fully dressed. And invent persuasive arguments for the king. And rise to pace the moonlit chamber.

〜

SAREEN HAD FLOPPED into the armchair in the master bedchamber. Her trembles must have been the only thing that had held her upright, for now she felt like...what? One of those wet tents in Tower Woods, collapsing when the stakes were pulled.

Had Thomas noticed that her gown's ties had been loosened? And she threw herself at him. How uncouth! Heat suffused her. And yet... He'd wrapped one arm around her, while holding his sword safely away. He'd made light of the whole debacle without mocking. In fact, deflected Der's teasing to himself. Why didn't a brother know when something wasn't funny? How did Thomas know? 'Twas he who made things comfortable for her.

"Come, my lady," Adonna said. "Won't you undress now?"

Sareen peeled off the gown, which held far too much of her perspiration, and slipped her nightgown over her head. She eyed the curtain slit. "Do you suppose a bat could get through there?"

"Oh, surely not," Adonna said, but she frowned at it. "Bats really don't like to be around people. The other one just got confused in the chimney."

Not convincing, but it was too hot to close the window. As Sareen crawled into the bed, Adonna snuffed candles. Only the oil lamp beside the bed still burned, soot streaking its glass chimney. "I'll take care of this one," Sareen said. "Is there still a light in the corridor so you can find your way?"

"Aye, a lamp burns low nigh the top of the stairs. Sleep well, my lady." Adonna departed, pulling the door softly shut.

What was that brushing sound at the window? So little wind tonight. Was it enough to move a curtain? This was ridiculous! How many nights of her life had Sareen slept with a window open and never thought of bats? Still, she couldn't make herself snuff the oil lamp's small flame. It troubled her eyes when she closed them. She could neither sleep with it nor without it. She untied one bed curtain and pulled it between the lamp and her pillow. Much better. Now, if she could just stop thinking about Thomas!

CHAPTER 27

Drossin stared at the back of Navayn Manor—dark against the hazy sky. No light at any window. The air was heavy, but not so cloudy that it hid the light of the nearly full moon. He crossed the open space and found the cellar door, just as the master had said. He inserted the bent iron pin the master had given him into the old lock. Some jiggling was all it took. The door opened on silent hinges. The master had promised that too.

Drossin stepped within, careful to keep his boots quiet on the stone floor. He drew his tinderbox from the pouch on his belt and took out the flint and candle stub. With a single strike, he lit the wick, then quickly closed the door. Even a tiny light could draw attention. He put his tinderbox away, looking around.

A flight of stairs led down, but he was to follow the corridor along the short side of the house. He crept along it, then turned the corner. There—the stairs he was to climb. His candle flame flickered over the steep steps. Aye, the master knew an awful lot about this house. So sure, he was, about wood being laid ready on a certain hearth. Mindful of his instructions, Drossin climbed in silence, shielding his flame even though there should be a curtain at the top blocking the light.

His sweaty palms made the candle slick. He was a fool to have agreed to this. What if he woke whoever slept here? What if they chanced to be awake already? What if the curtain was open, and his light alerted them? Even if it wasn't, he must open it to finish the job. Candlelight would show against the ceiling and wall.

His hand shook so hard, he feared the candle might go out. At least the curtain was where the master had said. 'Twas so long that a fair amount of it heaped on the floor. He nudged the thick fabric aside.

Curses! The room was lit!

He dropped the curtain and almost snuffed his candle. Except...maybe it wouldn't show as much in the room's glow. Not a sound did he hear. He waited several minutes, but no one moved. Perhaps someone fell asleep with a light burning.

Drossin got his nerves settled down. Squatting low, he pressed a cheek to the wall and opened a finger-width gap in the curtain. An oil lamp burned on a table beside the big bed. He couldn't see anyone upon it, but he heard slow, steady breathing, Relief made him sag against the wall.

His luck was in, for a change. Stay low, stay quiet, all would be well. Drossin slid the heaped fabric forward to make a gap, then crawled into the room. There was the stone of the hearth, meeting the wood floor. A little farther, and he reached the firebox with split logs piled in the grate. Wood shavings and sticks underneath, just like the master said.

Still no movement on the bed. He was so close. He extended a hand, the candle trembling beneath the grate. A shaving caught. Flame edged along it to a twig, which doubled the flame, then passed it on.

Enough. Drossin turned back to the gap. The candle went out in his haste. *Silent! Stay Silent!* He scuttled past the curtain and hastened down the steps. With a hand on the wall, he followed the black corridor to the door and got out. He flopped against the door, closing it. A quick glance to either side. Still clear. He fled. The fire would brighten and crackle—awakening whoever slept there. Drossin must be in the woods and on his horse before anyone raised a cry.

THOMAS STARED out the window over the back lawn. Hazy moonlight silvered the dewy grass. The flagstone paths twined like dark script. A few trees formed pools of shadow.

A door banged. Outside, but off to the right. Odd. The outbuildings were all to the left and stretched back from the house. He swung the window wider and leaned out.

For a moment, he saw nothing unusual, then a man ran from the cover of the house, angling for the woods. Too dark to see clearly, but moonlight revealed a bald head, and his gait was less than spry.

Which door had banged? Why did someone flee from the house? A crawling sensation made him open his door to check the dim corridor.

It smelled of smoke.

In the light of the night lamp, smoke crept along the floor—coming from the crack below a door. The master's chamber!

Thomas shouted, "Fire!" He sprinted down the corridor and burst through the door.

Smoke clogged the air. It poured from the hearth, where a blazing fire crackled and threw sparks.

Coughing, Thomas darted to the bed. "Sareen!"

She didn't move. He flung the coverlet aside and shook her. Nothing. Trying not to breathe the fouled air, he slid one arm under her shoulders and the other under her legs, limp as rags.

Bare footsteps thumped. Voices called in the corridor. Thomas lifted Sareen and turned. Jonathan was coughing beside the fireplace. Iron scraped as he pulled the damper handle.

Thomas made for the door. Behind him, water splashed, and the fire hissed.

A deep voice demanded, "Get out!" D'Jorge stood at the door.

Thomas staggered past him. Coughing. Eyes stinging. He wasn't going to make it through the corridor. But he had to!

The duke, with an arm around his wife, ran down the stairs ahead of him. A door slammed behind him. Someone gripped his arm and partially supported Sareen's torso, running with him to the stairs. A gasping cough followed them. D'Jorge shouted orders. At least the air wasn't foul out here. Somehow, Thomas got down the stairs and out the front door.

'Twas Dermont who supported him...helped him cross the drive, then eased Sareen onto the grass as Thomas's knees buckled. Thomas let himself fall sideways and rolled onto his back. He pressed his hands to his eyes, drawing moist air into his lungs. Something dragged his mind down. He fought it, forcing his eyes open.

Next to him, Jonathan coughed and swayed on hands and knees. He was nigh gone too.

Thomas moaned and rolled, forcing himself up. Only by bracing both arms against the ground, could he keep himself from collapsing again.

The duchess knelt beside Sareen, patting her cheek and pleading, "Sareen, dear, wake up. Wake up, Sareen!"

That raspy breath—was it Sareen's? "Is she breathing?" Thomas asked.

"Aye, but she won't wake up." The duchess's voice broke.

The duke held his wife's shoulders. "She will, my dear. She just needs a few minutes."

The broader scene crept into Thomas's awareness. Lanterns glowed, adding to the moonlight. A plume of smoke drifted above the open window of the master's chamber. It spread from a diminishing base. Another plume rose from a chimney. So, Jonathan had gotten the damper open. But why was a fire burning?

The servants, in their night clothes, clustered in groups.

More folk came running from the outbuildings. Captain D'Jorge—looking absurd with long legs protruding from his nightshirt—stared at those on the ground. Sareen lay unconscious. Jonathan sat with his arms around his knees, maybe needing as much support as Thomas did. Something felt...off.

"Did everyone get out?" Thomas asked D'Jorge.

"All are accounted for. Do you feel all right?"

Thomas scrunched his eyes, drew a deep breath, and opened them. "Not really, but better than I was." He found that deeper breaths helped, so he drew a few more. "Jonathan, breathe deep."

Jonathan released his legs and leaned back, drawing more air. Before long, he muttered, "That smell. 'Twas in the smoke."

Sareen finally stirred, and her family urged her to draw deep breaths. In a wheezy voice, she whimpered, "What happened?"

The duchess patted her cheek. "A fire, dear, but don't talk yet."

Sareen coughed so hard, she probably didn't even hear that.

Adonna stood near, wringing her hands. When the coughing fit eased, Adonna asked, "My lady, why did you light your fire?"

"I didn't." More coughing.

Griven stood by, holding one of the lanterns. "We need to check the manor. Make sure the fire is out and get all the windows open."

"Aye, the master's chamber first," D'Jorge said. "The rest of you, wait out here until we come back."

"I'm going with you," Jonathan said. He heaved himself to his feet. His first couple steps were uneven, but they steadied, and D'Jorge kept an eye on him.

The three men went inside, and a moment later, the arched window of Thomas's chamber filled with light. Arms swung the casements to their widest, and the curtains were fully opened. Smoke no longer issued from it. The men lingered briefly, then the arch went dark, and they returned, bearing a couple blankets, which they gave to the duchess and lady. Jonathan held Thomas's boots and sword.

"The fire was mostly out," D'Jorge said, "but we doused it again. It didn't spread beyond the hearth. We snuffed the lamp, left all else as it was, and closed the door. I had thrown a blanket against the door crack when we first fled the house, and I've put it back."

Thomas nodded, pulling on his boots. "That room must be left as is until I say otherwise." He shifted to stand.

D'Jorge stepped near and offered a hand, then steadied him. "Do you feel better?"

"I can make do now." He took his sword belt from Jonathan and buckled it. What a crowd had gathered. Everyone on the estate seemed to be on the front lawn. Thomas spoke louder. "Start opening—" He coughed. Loud was a mistake.

D'Jorge took over the talking. "Open all the windows and pray for a breeze. Bring blankets and pillows downstairs. We'll finish the night there."

Lord Dermont patted his mother's shoulder. "I'm going to open and check the salon. Then, I'll come back for you and Sareen."

Much coming and going ensued. Lord Dermont carried his sister inside and laid her on a sofa in the salon. Thomas followed, declined the other sofa, and sat in a chair where he could see Sareen's dear face. She had nearly died...because they'd switched rooms.

Coughing spasms forced her to lie on her side, for they racked her so, allowing her only a moment to rest between each. All of his guests gathered in the salon, as well as Jonathan and Griven. Servants darted in and out with the items they fetched, mostly at the orders of the Seltas. Lord Dermont pulled trousers over his nightshirt, then belted on his sword.

These swords... So, Thomas wasn't the only one who thought the details didn't make sense.

Thomas stood. "Jonathan." He walked into the dining room, and Jonathan followed.

So did D'Jorge and Griven, who closed the door.

Thomas frowned, mostly at Griven. "You're all named Jonathan, then?"

"Pardon, my lord," Griven said, "but I need a word with you."

"He saw your chamber just as we did," Jonathan said. "Those extra curtains...for looks, I'd thought, but when we went up to check, one was twisted askew. I found a staircase behind it!"

"To where?"

"Down. We didn't follow it—yet."

"We should leave it for an inspector," Griven said. "In case there are footprints or any other sign."

"I heard a door slam." Thomas coughed. "A minute later, someone ran from beyond the north end of the house, angling a little west toward the woods. So, there must be a way into this house, and I want it locked. Immediately! Lady Sareen almost died."

"*But*," D'Jorge growled, "whoever did this would have been after you. Jonathan says the wood was already laid in the grate. Had been so on the day you arrived."

"Indeed." Thomas frowned. "No other fireplace has wood laid, but it made sense because Lord Maerton had used that bedchamber."

"You were first to enter the room," Griven said. "What did you notice?"

"Only Lady Sareen, of course. She did not wake. So limp that she was hard to lift, and I was sure I would drop her in the corridor."

D'Jorge's lips were tense. "Both you and Jonathan were staggering like drunkards when you came out. 'Tis why I closed the door and blocked the crack. You two nearly swooned, and Lady Sareen was out for too long. That fire was blazing hard and fast. It should have awakened her. And Jonathan talks of odd scents. All considered, this was a vile deed at best. Maybe attempted murder."

"There's no denying it looks bad, my lord," Griven said. "Please permit me to ride to the king at once. An inspector must be called, and...well, I don't mean to speak slanderous, but I don't want one of Maerton's inspectors prowling over the evidence before the king's inspector arrives."

There was good sense in that. "I permit."

Griven's frown eased. "I'll hurry, my lord. Can I persuade you to leave all exactly as it is? Even keep everyone off the lawn and out of the woodland—if you can do it without raising suspicion."

"We can set everyone to work on cottages. 'Tis likely to rain soon, anyway, which gives us good reason to stay within." Thomas rubbed his brow. His head ached. "The reeve and priest are coming to meet with me tomorrow morn. Er, *this* morn. Doubtless, there will be soot streaked above my window, and they will see it."

"Can you bid them keep it quiet?" Griven asked.

"I can, but it won't work. Farmers bring milk and eggs in the morn. Likely, other vendors will arrive, too, for they know I have a house full of guests who need to eat."

"A score of people know at least part of what happened," D'Jorge said. "There is no way to keep this quiet."

Thomas shook his head. "Let us simply state what is broadly known. That a fire was lit, and the damper was not open."

Griven uttered a dissatisfied grunt. "Well, I'll slip away as soon as I can get dressed." He was one of the few men who hadn't yet found a pair of trousers to pull on, so his legs, bare beneath his nightshirt, were likely uncomfortable. "Uh, my lord, if you don't mind me asking, why are you in your day clothes?"

Odd question. However, Thomas probably did stand out, being the only one who didn't look ridiculous. "Too restless to go to bed, what with all the fuss over a bat and a hundred worries on my mind." His insides scrunched hard as a rock. If he had slept, Sareen would be dead.

THE MORNING CAME TOO SOON. Grit filled Thomas's eyes, and sleeping on the library floor, with only a carpet and folded blanket beneath him, had been anything but comfortable. He sat up. "How did I get so soft? Have I not slept on the ground, times out of mind?"

Jonathan groaned. "I'd welcome a little soft, right now." He shoved himself upright and walked to a window where a crack of light snuck between curtains, then jerked them open. "The sun's been up an hour."

Footsteps above them revealed that the household was awake. Thomas moved from the floor to a chair. "I'd better get presentable before the reeve and priest come. And awake. See if any coffee is brewed."

Jonathan opened the door into the corridor that branched from the entrance hall. A lass from Tower Woods was waiting there to carry word when they awoke. In moments, they had a basin and pitcher of hot water, coffee, and breakfast.

D'Jorge wandered in. Thomas offered to send for another plate, but he said, "Nay, I've eaten." He pulled a chair closer to the table desk where Thomas and Jonathan sat. "Your housekeeper has decided that the rooms on the third floor must be readied, so I checked them over. Recent repairs appear solid, and nothing has leaked. I daresay, they will have that level swept and furniture placed quickly, for those whom I brought are determined to make everything right."

The People of the Woods were Thomas's folk, after all. In the midst of disaster, they would do everything possible for him.

D'Jorge continued. "The smoke smell is not unbearable on most of the second floor. We can sleep on the opposite end from your chamber, at least. Your houseman told me about a cellar door, and I think that must be the one you heard. He said it has been locked the whole time he has worked here—not long, of course. I touched nothing, but I walked along the back of the house to take a look. 'Tis unlocked."

"I'm not leaving it that way overnight," Thomas said.

D'Jorge grunted. "'Twill need a better lock than it has. I daresay, we can rig some way to lock it from within, but I didn't want to walk through. Apparently, there are stairs to the cellar, both at the door and at the kitchen end. The houseman says it contains a wood room, empty wine racks, and some root vegetables he carried down yesterday."

Thomas scraped together his last bite of eggs. "'Tis possible the inspector can reach us today, so we will wait a while."

"Mm. I'm not leaving today as I'd planned. Do you want me to manage cottage repairs once the work on the third floor is finished?"

"I would much appreciate it." Thomas had a feeling that he looked boyish, but oh, he was glad to have a friend both knowledgeable and loyal. All three of them stood. "Come, Jonathan. Let's get presentable."

They went upstairs. Fortunately, they'd carried his trunk to his temporary bedchamber before the fire, so he was able to don fresh clothes after he shaved. A doublet today, since he wasn't riding and the rain had cooled the air. He was buttoning it when a knock struck the door. "Enter."

Duke Selta walked in. "How fare you, this morn?"

"I am well. How is Lady Sareen?"

"Between coughing fits, she insists that she is getting better." As if on cue, a cough sounded down the corridor. "I am told a few of her clothes are here, and I came to request that her maid be allowed to fetch them."

"Of course."

The duke motioned to someone in the corridor. Adonna entered, offered a quick curtsy, then hurried to the wardrobe. Thomas moved to the two armchairs and gestured for the duke to sit.

"My lady wife is talking of Fountain Isle," the duke said,

settling into the chair, "and my daughter insists that is not necessary."

"Ah."

The duke leaned back. "I shall wait a few hours to decide. Our possible departure creates a bit of a quandary. The oaths of fealty...they should be witnessed either by a duke or by three lords."

Thomas nodded. Another disappointment. "I had hoped that you and your family would attend, but I cannot deny Lady Sareen the healing she may need."

"If she does need to depart before the ceremony, I shall send Lord Dermont to escort his sister and mother, and I will stay here until the ceremony is completed. Or perhaps until Duke Prushane arrives, for I know he plans to come soon."

Yet again, the duke acted in Thomas's interests ahead of his own. 'Twas almost stunning after a lifetime of disdain. "Your kindness...I deeply appreciate it."

The duke murmured a courteous response, watching Adonna pick up a shawl from a chair back and add it to the gowns over her arm, then grab a stray glove and a pair of shoes. She left with her load, somehow managing to close the door too.

"Have you thought more of what happened last night?" the duke asked.

"I have. Several aspects concern me."

"I noticed the narrow table set to block the entrance to the master's bedchamber."

"We have decided to leave it as is for today. Doubtless, it reeks of smoke." Thomas licked his lips. "'Twas Griven who suggested it and also asked to ride to Purthellia to request an inspector from the king."

"Ah, wise."

"Who, exactly, is Griven?"

"Why do you ask?"

"He is not merely an unskilled commoner in need of work."

The duke took a moment to answer. "Your question places me in a difficult position, for the king bade me tell no one."

Not what Thomas wanted to hear. "Would it help if I agree to maintain the secret?"

"That will have to do, I suppose. He is an inspector from Selta. The king wanted a skilled observer on hand, should anything suspicious occur. That fire…if it was attempted murder, I am shocked that it happened so soon."

Thomas frowned. That was a valid point. As he pondered, knuckles rapped on the door again. "Enter."

Master Eldred opened it. "My lord, the priest and the reeve are here to see you."

Thomas went down to the hall where they waited and invited them into the library. A quick glance reassured him that all sign of last night's use of the room had been cleared.

The instant Thomas closed the door, the reeve blurted out, "'Tis all over both villages that your bedchamber caught fire last night. Or perhaps Lady Sareen's. I cannot make sense of the rumors."

"The fire was on a hearth. The chimney has a damper, which was closed. Odd, but we shall discover more precisely what happened."

They both stared at him with round eyes until Master Navayn spoke. "'Tis said that no one lit the fire. 'Tis also said that Lord Ivan hints of ghosts at the manor and of things mysteriously moving."

"Nothing of that sort has happened here." Thomas walked to a bookcase that held small chests. "And that is a statement you may repeat to any who would spread such false tales."

The priest nodded. "I've been reminding folk that no servant at the manor ever mentioned anything amiss."

Thomas carried a chest to the desk. The reeve was fidgeting with the hem of his vest. Best to know why. Thomas asked, "Does something disturb you, Master Navayn?"

"Well, not disturb, exactly. Just, uh...well, we heard that a great many strangers arrived here."

"I wouldn't call it a great many. Five couples from Tower Woods."

"Oh. Uh..."

"Nor do I consider them strangers. You must know that I grew up as one of the People of the Woods. I have also assisted Duke Tristelle in his dealings among them."

"I suppose, but it makes folk wonder."

"About what?"

"Whether you..." Words suddenly flooded from him. "That you may not care so much for the folk already here who have stood loyal to the House of Navayn—even while there was neither lord nor lady—and have never sworn to the Maertons, though it made things harder for us than for any others in the duchy. And some speak of how we were ready to give you our oaths the day you came, and instead you bring strangers to serve you."

Thomas held his tongue, though anger rose. Would the People of the Woods find no welcome here, either?

Master Navayn rolled the hem of his vest tighter. "I mean no disrespect, my lord."

The priest apparently felt he should help. "Indeed, no one is disrespectful. 'Tis just that hardships make folk susceptible to worries."

In the silence of his heart, Thomas uttered simple words. *Help me*. Then, he answered with a calm he did not feel. "You know hardship and rejection. So do I. So do the People of the Woods. Doubtless, they hope that after generations of being denied any place in the land of their ancestors, they will at last be accepted. Not by the Maertons, but at least on my estate, for they have been my friends my entire life and they trust me. If I were so fickle as to cast them aside now, why would you trust me to remain loyal to you?"

After a brief silence, the reeve said, "Those are sound words to think on."

Thomas debated going a little further. The opportunity existed. "It seems that they of Navayn estate want me to accept them. Those who *seek* acceptance should be willing to *give* it. 'Twould bring joy to this little land tucked within Maerton Duchy. Rejection would bring grief and make us no different than our disdainful neighbors."

The priest uttered a low laugh behind closed lips. "And here, I was wondering what would make a fitting sermon on this special rest day."

Thomas blinked. His point was fit for a sermon?

The priest raised his curly brows. "You read the holy book, do you not?"

"Oh. I suppose there is a passage along those lines." Thomas opened the chest and withdrew papers. "Please sit down," he said as he settled into his own chair. "By the way, there is considerable work needed within the manor's demesne, beyond what the local folk could accomplish, so no one here will lose any work they once had. Also, I currently have servants from Tristelle, Selta, and Purthellia. Perhaps from other duchies in the future. 'Twould displease me if they were treated poorly."

"I understand, my lord," Master Navayn said.

"Then, let us read through the oaths that our ancestors used."

CHAPTER 28

An hour later, Thomas said good day to his guests. In the stillness of the hall, he pondered how their complaints had worked out. They had seemed petty to him, for the People of the Woods had faced greater hardships. So easily, his anger could have soured his new friendships. What had turned it? Acknowledging the hardships faced here? Certain, these folk knew only their side of the matter. How could it have been otherwise?

He let gratitude swell within. At times, he was simply amazed how something could work out well in the middle of disasters.

Then, a coughing spasm reached his ears.

Ah, Sareen! Injured—because of him. His comfort twisted into agony. He needed more help now than he had in the library.

The sound quieted, and he walked into the salon, where Lady Sareen was just standing up from the sofa, and the duchess was saying, "...so please be reasonable."

Chin high, Lady Sareen spoke with steady calm. "There is nothing unreasonable about fresh air. I am going outside."

Oh, how he adored her! "May I escort you, my lady?"

"Indeed, and with my thanks." She rested a hand on his bent

arm as her mother flopped back in her chair with an exaggerated sigh.

Thomas led Sareen through the front hall door and paused on the flagstones that met the drive.

She looked over the grassy teardrop shape within its loop. "I wonder if that fountain can be made to work. Either way, there should be flowers around it."

"Perhaps in the spring."

She smiled up at him. "I know. Dozens of other things must be done first."

He returned her smile. "Where would you like to walk?"

"To see any of those dozens of things."

They turned and strolled along the side drive. "I keep forgetting," Thomas said, "that I now own two goats and should see how they fare."

Her coughing interrupted whatever she had started to say. "Pray, pardon me. I fear it shall be quite tiresome for you to listen to all this hacking."

"Think not of that. 'Tis natural for your lungs to clear themselves."

"Do you think…that fresh air is wise?"

"Aye."

She must have caught the surprise in his voice, for she said, "Oh, certain, you would." She coughed. "The least exertion makes it worse."

"I'm no physician, but I suspect that coughing is actually good, so long as it does not rack you constantly."

She grunted. "I daresay, you would already be at your destination if you didn't need to walk so slow with me."

"Perhaps, but getting there would be far less pleasurable."

His words won a smile that deepened her dimples.

The stablemaster approached. "Do you need anything, my lord?"

"Just coming to check on the goats."

"Ah, I've put them in the elderbird pen." He turned to lead the way.

"Do you keep elderbirds?"

"Not oft, but if we get a chance to catch some, we'll clip their feathers and feed them until the housekeeper asks for meat."

Thomas spotted the penned goats. The ewe bent her head to a pile of grass, all four feet on the ground, while the kid frolicked around her. "What was wrong with her?"

"Had a wicked shard of flint stuck between the pads of her hoof," Santhorn said. "I cannot figure how she got it in there, and she didn't much like me when I held her down and pulled it out. Once I'd fed and watered her and brushed some briars from her coat, she decided I might be tolerable."

"It doesn't usually take long to tame them," Thomas said.

Someone within the stable called out "Santhorn?" and Thomas nodded dismissal. He and Sareen walked to the pen, and he rested an arm on the top rail. The ewe grew flustered and took her kid to the far side, revealing one white hind quarter contrasting with her black fur.

"Odd coloring," Thomas said. "More of a long silky coat, not wooly like the goats in Tower Woods."

"Black is a hard color to obtain with dye," Sareen said. "A natural black fiber may be worth more."

She surprised him again, but only for an instant. The nobles never spoke of such things at their parties, but of course, someone managed everything behind the scenes of their showy salons and fancy foods.

"Why are you looking at me so?" she asked.

"I'm just wondering about all the things I don't know about you."

"Hundreds and hundre—" She turned away to cough. This one did not last long. She sighed and rubbed her belly. "Poor muscles. I keep hoping I can work enough of this out that my mother will stop insisting on dashing off to Fountain Isle."

"I...I would rest easier if I knew that you came to no harm from last night's fire."

She touched his arm. "'Twas not your fault. We are not the sort to run away when you need us."

"Your father told me he would stay to witness the oaths."

"I would enjoy the ceremony too." She turned her brown eyes to him...so earnest.

"As I would enjoy having you there." He looked down, then back up. "But I cannot endure the thought that you might come to harm—and worse—because of me."

Her black brows wrinkled at the center. "No one is trying to harm *me*. 'Tis *you* I fear for."

How was he supposed to say this? "If I am at risk, then you may be too."

"That doesn't make any sense at all."

"Uh...shortly after the king granted my title, he summoned me to a private meeting." He paused, and she nodded. "The king bade me to...court no woman."

"Oh. Uh..."

"'Twas a curt statement," Thomas said. "I assume temporary, but I had no chance to ask why. The fire...it seems like an attempt on my life. Which is extraordinarily brazen. Even your father said as much. Perhaps this is the reason the king forbade courtship. If..." Thomas drew a deep breath. "If someone believed that I might be likely to marry soon...if they suspected I might marry you...then, I think we are both in danger. And for that reason, as well as for your health, I think you should go to Fountain Isle."

"Oh...I see." She cleared her throat, perhaps staving off an imminent cough. "That will spare me danger, but not you."

"Perhaps not entirely, but it does remove the need for haste if, indeed, someone does prefer me dead without an heir."

"So, you want me to leave."

"I think it *wise* for you to leave, but I do not *want* you to go. I shall miss you dreadfully!"

Her mouth did odd things. Was it chasing smiles or tears? "I shall miss you too."

273

CHAPTER 29

Duke Maerton swallowed the last of his coffee when Ivan finally made an appearance in the breakfast parlor.

He pulled out a chair and dropped into it. "I should inform you, Father, that we have a guest."

"Do we?"

"Newton Eberle is in the blue guest chamber. His head is likely splitting, for his steps wove so erratically last night that I couldn't let him ride home on his own."

"Have you seen him this morn?"

"Nay."

"Does any member of the staff know he is here?"

"The night porter does."

Who was probably sound asleep. Maerton turned to the servant who waited near the door. "Inform the housekeeper to send a footman upstairs with hot water and an invitation to breakfast." When the door closed behind the man, Maerton said, "A host has a duty to see that his guests are tended to."

Ivan bit into a slice of toasted bread and wrinkled his nose. He touched one of the boiled eggs, then complained, "Everything is cold."

"That happens when you come down late. How is *your* head?"

"Fine. I sipped the wine, though I poured generously for my guest."

"Where were you?"

"The inn. I also played my cards generously, which wasn't easy, for Newton is less than shrewd at cards. Thus, my friend slowly won all night and could not be persuaded to end the game until the wee hours of the morn." He sneered. "The tap man is a bit of a fool. As though I should care that he wanted his bed."

The door opened again, and the servant returned with hot toast and eggs. Maerton could not demand an explanation—yet. He waited as Ivan ate in silence. Another interruption—this time, a servant with the information that Lord Eberle had arrived and wanted a word with him.

Likely searching for his son. "Show him in here," Maerton said. After acknowledging Lord Eberle's bow, he said, "Won't you sit down and share a cup of coffee with us?"

Lord Eberle looked impatient, but he strode around the table and took a seat opposite Ivan, whom he glared at. "I learned, this morn, that Newton never returned home last night. They tell me at the inn that he left with you. Where is he?"

"In a guest chamber upstairs," Ivan said. "Doubtless, he will soon come down to break his fast."

The servant set a cup beside Lord Eberle and poured coffee into it. As he set the pot on the table, Maerton dismissed him with a gesture.

Ivan passed cream and sugar to their guest. "'Tis unfortunate that you worried. He was enjoying such a winning streak at cards, that I suspect the time slipped from his mind. Indeed, he was so, uh, tired when we finally ended the game—and rain was falling too. How could I send him off alone all the way to Eberle Manor when I have room to spare here?"

Lord Eberle stirred cream into his coffee. His brow remained low, but he took a sip and leaned back. "Have you heard of the fire at Navayn Manor?"

"What?" Maerton demanded.

"The talk is all over the village."

"A fire in the rain?" Ivan said. "Probably just overblown rumors."

Lord Eberle continued to sip his coffee. "No mention was made of rain, so it must have occurred earlier in the night. Apparently, it was confined to one bedchamber and was swiftly extinguished, for they went back inside afterward."

"I trust no one was hurt?" Ivan murmured with a hint of question.

"Lady Sareen was unconscious for some time. As best—"

"Lady Sareen?" Ivan demanded, his poise vanishing.

Lord Eberle resumed his interrupted words. "As best I can piece together, Lord Navayn and her brother carried her outside and she regained her senses on the lawn."

"What was she doing in his chambe—" Ivan clamped his mouth shut.

"Really, Lord Ivan," Eberle snapped. "The conclusions you jump to! And of the lady you favor, no less. Two men carried her out, and any man in the house would have gone to the rescue of any lady."

"Indeed, that is so," Maerton said. "Can you tell us how the fire started?"

"No one seems to know. Some say it was in the fireplace, but who would start a fire after yesterday's heat? So I doubt that is true." Eberle drained the rest of his coffee and stood. "I'll not disturb you any longer. If you could show me to the chamber my son is using, we'll be on our way."

"Of course," Maerton said, and went to the hall with his guest. From there, he sent the page to escort Lord Eberle upstairs and then carry word to the stables to fetch their horses. His guests tended, he returned to the breakfast parlor.

Ivan still sat rigid, his mouth an ugly line.

Maerton rested his hands on the back of the head chair. "What is all this? Why do you dishonor Lady Sareen?"

"I had heard of the fire," Ivan said, "but far less. Only that it burned in the master's bedchamber." He closed his eyes and cleared his face. Voice calm again, he said, "Indeed, I never meant to dishonor her. Shock and fear for the lady I am courting made my words random. Father...I am still greatly worried about her. They know you plan to visit, anyway. Will you go today and learn more?"

"I shall."

DUKE MAERTON MADE the short journey that afternoon. By then, he had learned the gist of the rumors from select servants who kept him informed. Most disturbing!

As his carriage made the turn onto the manor's drive, he eyed the darkened stone above the master's chamber window. 'Twas obvious to anyone who knew the house which room had caught fire. And many did know it. Workmen from the Maerton estate had made the recent repairs, so 'twas reasonable that Ivan had a source for his information.

Maerton averted his gaze, wishing he need not think along these lines. He spotted Thomas Kaituer striding from the stables toward the manor. A robust young man. In the days of his own youth, Maerton would never have believed this possible. Any of it. Lord Navayn even out-ranked Lord Eberle, who had talked so boldly at his table this morn.

The carriage rounded the loop and halted. Lord Navayn waited outside for the duke to descend, then greeted him with the bow due his rank and the words, "Welcome to Navayn Manor, my lord duke."

"Thank you, Lord Navayn, and welcome to Maerton Duchy. How do you find your estate?"

"Pleasing, and in particular, the welcome from my distant family and tenants is most heart-warming." As he spoke, Lord Navayn opened the hall door and ushered his guest inside.

Maerton paused to study the arresting mantelpiece. Certain,

Sathe's description was more accurate than Ivan's. "Ah, the lynx I have heard of. It does warrant my brother's praise." He'd already caught sight of a frame from the corner of his eye, fortunately not where Ivan said he'd hung it. 'Twas above the halfmoon table on the side wall instead. Only now, did he turn to it, then twitched in surprise. "What is this?"

"A portrait of Lady Anne Navayn. It seemed fitting to give it prominence in the hall since I would not be standing here without her. I even wonder whether the village would have survived, had her influence not been strong."

Maerton dragged his eyes from the face and stared at Lord Navayn. "I have ne'er seen it before."

"I suppose not. It has been stored in safety since Prince Maerton acquired this manor."

"How fortunate for you."

"Indeed. Will you come in and sit down?" Lord Navayn said, turning toward the salon.

The movement gave Maerton a chance to scan the hall, but the portrait of the first Thomas Kaituer was not here. Ah, in the salon, which they entered. "Your grandfather's portrait looks well there." Maerton took a moment to look closer. "I didn't realize it had another nameplate beneath that rather objectionable one."

"'Twas a pleasing discovery," Lord Navayn said.

All these courteous remarks were getting him nowhere. Maerton took a seat on a sofa, while his host sat in one of the chairs. "I must admit, I would likely have visited tomorrow, had I not heard disturbing rumors. Was there indeed a fire here last night?"

"There was."

Such an uncommunicative young man. "I saw the smoke stain outside. If I am not mistaken, that was the very bedchamber my brother used."

Lord Navayn nodded. "As did I."

"You seem to have taken no harm from the fire."

"The only harm was smoke, for the fire remained upon the hearth."

"Did my brother not tell you about the dampers?"

"He did."

This was ridiculous. "Lord Navayn, the rumors in the village contradict strangely. Pray pardon what may seem like idle curiosity, for I am quite worried. Will you tell me plainly what happened?"

"Last eve, we had an unfortunate visitor." Lord Navayn paused, and Maerton hoped his face did not pale. "A bat." Lord Navayn's lips twitched. "In Lady Sareen's bedchamber." He coughed. "As you may imagine, it rather upset her, so I switched chambers with her. Thus, she was asleep in the master's chamber when the fire started."

"How dreadful!"

"Quite so. I was unable to sleep. In the dead of night, I heard an outer door bang and went to the corridor. Smoke was spreading from the chamber where Lady Sareen slept. I shouted the alarm and found her unconscious in bed. My squire opened the damper and doused the fire, while her brother and I carried the lady out."

"Please tell me...is she well?"

"She regained consciousness after several minutes outside, but still coughs a great deal. The spasms are disturbing enough that she has left for Fountain Isle with her mother and brother."

Maerton fought to catch his breath, then realized he was opening and closing his mouth. "How long did it take her to awaken?"

"Too long, but I cannot guess the minutes, for both my squire and I were also nigh swooning. We must have inhaled far less than she, even though I'm certain the fire had not been burning for long. It seems that one coincidence saved my life, and another saved hers."

Maerton shook his head. Dreadful! A servant woman brought in a tea tray—a welcome interruption—and handed him a cup. He took it mechanically and sipped. The door closed behind the woman. He needed to say something. What? Could any words undo this harm? Shift suspicion. He must at least appear to help. How? Help unravel the mystery, perhaps. Maerton took another swallow of tea and asked, "Did my brother give you a detailed tour of the manor?"

"Only the commonly used rooms of the first and second floors. Since then, I have seen the third floor and cellar, and also discovered there is a hidden corridor and staircase to the master's chamber."

"There is another back stair on the kitchen end too," Maerton said. "I believe they are used for bringing wood to the upper floors."

"I daresay."

Maerton shook his head. "I cannot conceive how such a calamity could have happened." He rubbed a hand across his eyebrows. "Frankly, I had thought to find that some misuse of the dampers—unusual devices—had caused a smoky room. Not learn that someone had nearly died! Dear Sareen...I've known her since she could walk...countless times, the children have run playing in my own home...'tis just shocking!"

"I imagine so," Lord Navayn said soothingly. "I don't believe she is in immediate danger, and doubtless, the waters of Fountain Isle will heal whatever damage may have been done."

"They are a great comfort in this moment."

"Won't you take a little bread?" Lord Navayn stood and refilled Maerton's cup. "My overworked housekeeper has no time yet for sweet delicacies, but her herbed butter is delicious."

"Thank you. I often prefer savory to sweet." Maerton took one of the buttered rounds, welcoming the change of subject. "I trust you are settling in comfortably, though certain, that will take time."

"Well enough. I am blessed with many friends."

"Good, good." Maerton achieved a humorous twist of his lips. "Meat, at least, will be plentiful. No doubt, the deer have come to your attention. When the leaves turn, I will host hunting parties, as is my custom, and you are welcome to ride with us."

"Thank you. Since our forested land is adjoined, 'twould be hard to separate the hunt. I assume we can work out some sharing of the meat."

"Easily, with much to spare." Maerton wove through a few innocuous subjects, then took his leave.

Back in the privacy of his carriage, Maerton pondered what he'd been told. Gaps in the story began to bother him. Had Lord Navayn omitted parts? Perhaps he didn't know all. Or perhaps he didn't trust Maerton. No matter the reason, there was too much room for suspicion.

He must get the truth from Ivan. Which he dreaded.

His son must have been watching for his return. As Maerton entered the hall, Ivan came down the staircase with a polite greeting on his lips. He turned for the library, and Ivan accompanied him, heading for the chairs by the fireplace. The duke went to the desk instead and lowered himself into the chair behind it.

Ivan watched him through narrowed eyes and came to sit on the other side of the desk. "What did you learn, Father?"

"Apparently, a bat got into Lady Sareen's bedchamber last eve, causing Lord Navayn to switch bedchambers with her. 'Twas she who slept in the master's chamber when…the fire was started."

Ivan's oddly set eyes widened. He looked appalled. "Is she…is she…"

"She is troubled by coughing spasms."

Ivan rubbed a hand over his mouth. The end of his deep breath trembled a bit.

Maerton kept his voice so low, he nigh whispered. "Had Lord Navayn not discovered the fire—by random chance—the bride you hope for would now be dead." Oh, the look on his son's face! "Ivan, what have you done?"

"I never meant her any harm," Ivan hissed.

Maerton propped his elbows on his desk and braced his forehead against his clasped hands. His stomach roiled.

After a moment, Ivan's harsh breathing quieted. "Doubtless, the manor smells of smoke and continues to trouble Lady Sareen. You could invite the Seltas to stay here, so that she may recover."

Was that the best Ivan could come up with? "She has already left to seek healing at Fountain Isle."

"Oh." Ivan stared past his father. "Then, some good *has* come from it."

"Good?"

"She will recover at Fountain Isle, so no harm is done. She is no longer staying with that Kaituer, and quite likely, the event has given her a dread of his manor. Definitely good."

"Ivan, what was in that fire, and how did it start?"

Already, he looked smug again. "What mean you, Father?"

"Don't try that ignorance with me again. Lord Navayn is certain the fire had only recently started. Yet the lady was unconscious for some time. Navayn and his squire both entered the room, and they almost swooned in the time it took to open the damper and carry her out."

"Indeed? That is good to know. 'Twas a little troubling that I could only test the mixture on an old dog."

Maerton's breath halted, then he demanded, "Where is that evidence?"

"Worry not. 'Tis burned. As is all the evidence in Navayn Manor. Really, Father, I think you should have more faith in me. If my hand had not been rushed, that fire would not have been lit until some autumn night. The effect would have been slower from a vented chimney. In the morn, the Kaituer would likely have been found to have died in his sleep. Or if I were unlucky, he might have recovered, but either way, the evidence burns in the fire."

Maerton swallowed bile. "Ivan! You cannot kill people. You will end on the gallows!"

"Nay, Father. What you mean is that I cannot be caught. I shall make very sure that I am not. I know it is often better to... uh, sway people. But not all can be swayed, so 'tis less trouble to remove them." Ivan leaned back as though he looked at the high shelves of the bookcase behind Maerton. "'Tis unfortunate that I cannot again use such a promising method...at least for many years." He knit his brows. "You said the Kaituer believed the fire had not burned for long. Why?"

'Twas a dream. A nightmare. But Maerton must continue it until he knew all. He drew a slow breath, for he must get through this. "How would I know? Who started it for you?"

"A worthless tool who will never be missed. He is no concern. Are you well, Father? You look a little pale."

"'Tis because I fear for you, my son, that you have overlooked some detail and will be caught. Who is this tool?"

"A stranger and a drunkard...one easily led. A bit of dross in human flesh. He is well hidden away, where none can find him."

Dross in human flesh...too odd a reference to be overlooked. Of course, Ivan didn't know that his father had heard the name of Drossin. Best he remain ignorant. "You created an alibi for yourself last night. Rather obvious."

"Not so. I have an alibi every night that I am here. I simply let my absence from Navayn Manor be seen before anyone knew of the fire. Thus, I will not be called upon to give an alibi."

Maerton dredged words up from the void within him. "I'm glad to see you've thought of everything."

Ivan produced his joyless smile. "And I am glad to see you have stopped pretending that you don't know."

Maerton curled his lips too. "Ah, but I am going to keep

pretending. Nothing could be worse than an accidental slip of the tongue."

"True. Thank you for bringing me information and for setting my mind at rest about Lady Sareen."

"Speaking of the Seltas, I mentioned our customary hunting parties to Lord Navayn and invited him to ride with our hunt. He himself suggested that we would ride both his land and ours together."

Ivan smiled broader. "When will you send the invitations?"

"At the normal time, and not one day before. There is no need for haste, Ivan."

"Quite so." Ivan stood and left the room with a lively step.

The door closed. Maerton jumped at the sharp snap as though it were the bang of the guard tower door.

His face sagged, the weight opening his jaw. He propped his elbows again. Only that kept him from collapsing onto his desk. His head fell forward...eyes pressing into the heels of his hands.

His son. Once his hope. Now his despair.

Long, he sat. A pit opened within him. Was this what others felt when someone died? Was this why they moaned so? Nay, their grief could be nothing like his. He would have to betray his own son to death. And live with the shame and grief for years to come.

A great shuddering swept through him. He could not give way. He straightened and clenched his fists on the desk as his stomach burned. He had overcome calamity before. He would do so again. He just needed time.

He licked his lips and swallowed. Time to think. Time to plan. If nothing else, time to accustom himself to the inevitable. Was that the purpose of mourning? Oh, curse upon curse, he must do this while pretending all was well!

His stomach burned hotter, and he rocked. Fists opening and clenching. He would have to sit in Ivan's study, drinking tea— knowing that he would betray him. When the time was right. How long?

He must contact his lawyer. Send for the alternate will they held in keeping. How long would these documents and formalities take? He must wait it out, for the truth could not be revealed until all was finalized. If Ivan were declared mad and not hanged...Maerton shuddered.

He tried again to calm himself. He must. Must hold his demeanor through all these days.

CHAPTER 30

From the salon, Thomas heard a carriage rattle along the drive. Losing his battle with impatience, he strode into the hall and flung the door open as sweating horses swept around the loop and halted before him.

Griven jumped down from the carriage and folded the step down. An older, though spry man descended as Griven bowed to Thomas. "Lord Navayn, this is Inspector Curlow. He is the crown's *chief* inspector."

Curlow bowed. "It affords me pleasure to make your acquaintance, Lord Navayn."

"I am pleased to welcome you."

The coachman set the horses in motion, and the inspector spun. "My trunk and satchel, if you please." More demand than request.

The coachman spoke angrily over his shoulder. "I'll be walking 'em one turn before I unload anything."

The houseman stepped forward and said in a soothing tone, "We'll see to your things, sir."

"Come in," Thomas said, "for the light is fading fast, and I want you to look around the cellar door before we lock it up."

"You've not touched it yet, then?"

"We have not, though we long to. I'll not have the manor open overnight."

"Quite, quite. Griven here has told me all that he knew. I will study that door and the stairs first." He bowed to Duke Selta, responded to the introduction of Captain D'Jorge, then looked pointedly toward the housekeeper, who had stopped where the back corridor from kitchen to dining room passed through the hall. She held a pitcher in both hands, and her brow puckered.

Thomas said, "This is my housekeeper, Mistress Eldred. 'Tis her husband who is seeing to your things. This is Inspector Curlow."

"Pleased to meet you," she said hurriedly. "I was about to announce dinner, my lord."

Curlow lowered his iron-gray brows. "If you could show me the door and stairs first, my lord."

Already torn between courtesy to the duke and the need to secure his house, Thomas gave in to the demand. To the housekeeper, he said, "Serve in a quarter-hour," then turned to the duke. "Pray, forgive the delay, my lord duke."

"Tend your business. I shall survive."

Thomas took the inspector through the back hall door to the corner of the house where the cellar door was located. Griven and D'Jorge followed, and Jonathan arrived with a lantern, which he lit and had ready by the time Curlow entered the dark corridor.

The inspector led the way slowly, raising and lowering the lantern, and occasionally touching the floor or a step. He asked many questions but did not comment on the answers. In the master's chamber, he finally gave words to an observation as his eyes traced something on the floor. "If a ghost lit this fire, it dribbled much wax along its route."

Thomas now spotted the drips too. The inspector touched a candle on the mantel and said, "Not the same."

Jonathan wiped a finger through a drip, smelled it, and said, "Tallow."

The inspector gave him a thin smile. "What do the mantel candles smell of?"

"Beeswax."

Curlow asked several questions about the smoke, which D'Jorge mostly answered. Until this moment, Thomas hadn't realized that the smoke had flowed oddly—some low and some higher. Curlow stared at the black logs on the hearth. "Not much burned. I can inspect those later, for I'm as hungry as anyone. If you are willing to include your squire at the dinner table, we could go down now and spare your housekeeper distress over her neglected meal."

"By all means," Thomas said.

Curlow requested that all courses be served together, so the servants could be dismissed. Dinner table conversation became a recounting of every detail of the event. Curlow seemed quite interested in Jonathan's acute sense of smell and took him off to the wood room in the cellar after the meal ended.

Thomas didn't see his squire again until he brought hot water up to his bedchamber. D'Jorge still lounged in one of the chamber's armchairs, talking with Thomas in the cooling breeze from the window.

"Has that Curlow fellow kept you all this while?" D'Jorge asked Jonathan.

"Not quite. He went off to Maerton's Castle Village an hour ago. I was just settling things among the newcomers afterward. Did you get a lock rigged on the cellar door?"

"Of sorts. It can only be opened from within now. Good enough until we can replace that decaying door and get a smith on hand to fashion a new lock."

"What of the wood room?" Thomas asked. "What scents did you notice?"

"Only wood. Not the unusual scent in the master's chamber. I mean, the scent it had before the fire. Curlow dragged me through every nook of this house, but I didn't smell anything unusual."

D'Jorge made a rumbling sound in his throat. "Very mysterious, but I suppose we should be glad you couldn't find any more of it." He stood. "I'll leave in the morning, then. The sooner I am gone, the sooner I can be back with materials and tools." He looked down at Thomas. "Stay alive, please."

Thomas grinned. "That is one of my many plans."

MAERTON LEFT the daily gathering of his chief servants. Ivan often sauntered in to listen, but not this morn. A relief. It had been hard enough seeing him at breakfast...and pretending all was normal. Strange. Ivan claimed Maerton had been pretending ever since the duchess's death. This did not seem like the same thing at all.

He climbed the steps, leaning his weight on the banister. Why did it feel so different now? Perhaps because he'd been unable to prevent the earlier deaths. There had been no point in damaging his own house when that would help no one. This time, he knew what was coming. And worse, he'd seen how little Ivan cared that Sareen was injured by his hasty, failed attempt. Her survival mattered, but her pain was nothing to him.

Maerton reached the top step and walked on until he opened the door to Ivan's study.

Ivan lounged in a chair, apparently inspecting the juncture of ceiling and wall. He turned a welcoming smile to his father. "Ah, time for the morn's tea. Always a pleasure."

"Quite so." Maerton settled in his accustomed chair as Ivan went to the tea shelves and selected two tins, one containing the mixture that eased painful knees. A moment when the pleasing side of Ivan came through. A touch of kindness. Available to his father, but for others...only when that suited his ends.

Ivan glanced up from measuring tea. "Why so silent, Father? Had the servants nothing to say, this morn?"

"Only one thing of interest. The king has sent Inspector

Curlow to investigate the fire at Navayn Manor." Maerton watched his son's face as he poured water from the pot on the brazier. Not a twitch.

"How convenient," Ivan said.

"Is it?"

Ivan carried the tray with two cups and a steeping pot to the tea table and set it between them. "Indeed, it is. Since no evidence will incriminate me—quite the reverse, in fact—the inspector's futile mission will confirm my innocence."

"His arrival also confirms suspicion in high places, which is not to our advantage when I am trying to regain favor."

"That will fade away like steam from cooling tea."

"Why heat steam that does not serve us?" Maerton said. "Lord Navayn's estate is small. It need never concern us."

"I am surprised, Father, that you do not know what both the first and second dukes of Maerton knew. Any living Kaituer is a threat to the House of Maerton."

"Nonsense. *Our* house is established. The House of Kaituer does not exist. The House of Navayn cannot aspire to hold a duchy."

"The House of Navayn," Ivan said, sneering, "did not seem to exist a few weeks ago either. One must also note that the Lord of Navayn does not relinquish his despised name of Kaituer."

"The very way you pronounce his name, shows passion rather than logic."

"Only in your hearing, Father. In addition to logic, his foul name gives me a second reason to be rid of him, and his arrogant pursuit of Lady Sareen gives me a third."

Ivan lifted the strained leaves from his father's cup and then the others from the steeping pot. Working with tea always seemed to calm him, as though it were an art that took his mind to a gentler place. He glanced at Maerton before he began to pour into his own cup. "Forgive me if I have troubled you, Father. I will be careful. Nothing need worry you."

Maerton sipped the brew. "This all brings your mother's

death to my mind. Those were awful months. 'Tis the possibility of your haste that worries me."

"Ah, I see now." Ivan leaned back with his own cup of tea. "I have taken your warning to heart. You are quite right that I have no need to hurry. Nor will there be evidence of any crime in Thomas Kaituer's demise."

"A dead body is evidence of a crime."

Ivan laughed. "*That* is true, but it will have nothing to do with me."

THOMAS WATCHED D'JORGE DEPART. The empty market carts followed him, a driver from Tower Woods upon the seat of each.

Duke Selta strolled from the manor to Thomas's side, shading his eyes as he looked toward the cart making the turn onto the road. "I was surprised yesterday, when the drivers refused to return home without Captain D'Jorge's escort."

"Not I," Thomas said. "They were mistreated by Maerton's men far too long to trust him now. I often wonder if they of Maerton realize that their name is as much besmirched among certain peoples as the name of Kaituer is among others."

"And I wonder if they realize that it does not bother you at all when they disparage the name of Kaituer."

Thomas laughed. He snatched a glance at the duke's face as he tried to stifle it, for he was never quite sure of Duke Selta's intent.

The duke allowed a slight smile. "Aye, you may laugh."

Apparently, Thomas was not good at hiding his thoughts. Eh, maybe he didn't want to be. At least not always.

"Your plans for the day?" the duke asked.

"The most critical is to make sure all is ready for the oath ceremony tomorrow. Beyond that, I shall tend to things at the manor, and I indulge the fantasy that I may be able to sit down with a book for half an hour."

"Miracles do occasionally occur." The duke strolled beside Thomas as they turned toward the stable. "What has become of the inspector?"

"He asked for the favor of a servant—Griven, of course—to guide him in the woods."

"Ah."

The day, though busy, gave Thomas a hint that some future day his life here might feel natural. Duke Selta bore him company at times and only gave advice when Thomas asked it of him. After visiting the village, Thomas stopped at the farm nearest his own drive. Perhaps he could visit one each day, until he had a better feel for the land. Thus, he found himself inspecting a herd of cattle that a few dogs had been sent to collect.

"What do ye think of them, my lord?" the farmer asked, as a frisky young cow dog licked Thomas's hand.

"It looks like a fine herd." With a grin, Thomas added, "both of us understanding that all I know of cattle is that the ones with udders are cows."

With a monotone laugh, the farmer said, "I never could abide those who pretend to be knowing ones." He parted from Thomas on the best of terms.

His frisky dog followed Thomas and Jonathan home and had to be returned on a leash. Twice.

The dog came back again in time to bark at two simultaneous arrivals—the duke of Prushane with a small following on horseback, and Inspector Curlow on foot.

"I didn't realize you had a dog," Curlow said. "Did he bark at the stranger leaving your grounds last night?"

"I *don't* own a dog," Thomas said, looking at the creature who now sat panting before him, clearly expecting praise for his efforts. "Though, I know of one who is trying to make me look like a liar and a thief."

Jonathan grinned. "Do you want me to take him back again?"

Thomas tilted his head toward a distant figure striding

through his gates. "I believe that is our neighbor coming to collect him."

Duke Prushane began asking questions, so Thomas had to explain the fire and the inspector's presence. When the farmer showed reluctance to draw too near, Thomas moved a few steps from his guests and asked, "Does this wayward dog know herding commands?"

"He does now," the farmer said, "for he runs the herd with his dam and sire. Better than his littermates did when I sold them, so I'm hoping I can sell him after all, even though he's undersized. Then, he'll quit bothering you."

"Or I could buy him—provided you will let a couple of my people come and watch how you herd with him."

"Oh, aye." After agreeing to a price, the farmer held out a hand for the coins that Thomas counted from the purse on his belt. "Send those folk over tomorrow about the time the sun starts ducking behind your roof. Er...I suppose, you cannot tell that from here. I'll send my lass to fetch 'em when 'tis time to gather the herd."

"Has the dog a name?"

"First, he was Littl'un. Then, Wander."

Thomas shook his head. "I'll not bid him wander whenever we call him."

The farmer laughed in his flat way. "Ask my lass, 'cause she's fond of naming the beasts. Good eve, my lord."

Thomas scratched the dog's ears, which he could just reach without bending. The dog's coat was more black than white, with a bushy tail of russet. "Let us hope you can herd goats as well as cows, my nameless friend."

The dog cocked his russet-edged ears and wagged his entire backside.

The stablemaster had come to collect the horses, and Thomas said to him, "Find a spot for the dog to sleep out of the weather and see that he gets some meat scraps tonight." To his guests, he said, "Shall we go in," then led them into the mansion's hall.

Duke Prushane strolled around the front hall. "A pleasant entry, Lord Navayn. Allow me to introduce my steward, Master Jacksen, and his son, Gregory Jacksen."

That explained their resemblance, though the elder was gray-haired. They made their bows to Thomas. Apparently, the introduction granted them permission to ask much about the estate.

"I have ridden the cropland, but not measured it," Thomas replied to yet another question from Master Jacksen. A variation on his oft repeated answer of, "I know not." Fortunately, the younger Jacksen asked less. Instead, he scrutinized the hall's structure, while tapping an index finger against his neat brown beard.

The houseman paused in the midst of helping Duke Prushane's squire carry in the second of his cumbersome leather travel bags. "Pardon me, gentlemen," he said, "but I daresay you'd like to know that dinner is in about a quarter-hour."

That got everyone up the stairs, where it seemed a much simpler matter to offer bedchambers than it had been upon Thomas's arrival. Dinner was equally smooth, even without Duchess Selta directing the housekeeper. Conversation with his two ducal guests flowed with talk of estates and the plans for the oath ceremony.

"I am glad, indeed, that I arrived before the ceremony," Duke Prushane said, offering his calm smile. "Certain, Duke Selta's witness is adequate, but another will not hurt."

"I, too, am pleased," Thomas said. "I heard from the village reeve that news has spread, and a couple of the southern lords of Maerton may attend. 'Tis the rest day custom here to share a noon meal on the village green. 'Tis likely there shall be archery and such."

Duke Prushane raised his brows toward his receding gray hairline. "You must attend that."

"Certain, I shall!" Perhaps his voice revealed how much he looked forward to it. "You are welcome to bring your bows and take part."

"I will have you know," Duke Selta said, good-naturedly, "that I can still bring down a deer. Which you shall see when we come for the hunt."

After dinner, they toured the house and nearest outbuildings.

Here, the farmer's lass came boldly up to Thomas, carrying a tattered piece of burlap. "Good eve, my lords," she said, bobbing a curtsy. She couldn't be more than ten or eleven. The dog frisked joyfully and grabbed the cloth. "Sit." When he obeyed, she said to Thomas, "I came to bring his bed, so he'll stay the night with you. And also to tell you his name. 'Tis Nander."

Thomas maintained gravity suitable to her serious demeanor. "I thank you. May I ask how his name came to be Nander?"

"He answers to Wander without fail, so it should not change too much. He wandered to *Navayn*, so now he is Nander."

"Ah, it fits him perfectly."

The goat bleated from the nearby pen, attracting the lass's attention. "Does Nander like the goats?"

"As far as I can tell, Nander likes everything."

She laughed. "He still thinks like a pup." She swirled an arm overhead and commanded, "Circle."

Nander took off in a quick circuit of the group of men. The lass cast her eyes to the dimming sky. "Silly dog!" She dropped the cloth and took off running around the pen, the dog racing beside her as she said, "Nander, circle." She made only one circuit but sent him around a few more times. "There. He will do, now, sir." She patted the blanket, and the dog came. "Sit, Nander. Good dog. Stay here." She turned without further ado and walked off home.

Thomas subdued his urge to laugh, and the dog whined, watching her go. Best distract him. Thomas bent to rub his ears back. "Remember me? You couldn't stay away and all that."

The stablemaster had drawn near and said, "Just now saw her

as she left. Hope she didn't bother you. She's a saucy one, but her heart must be pure, for the creatures love her."

"That, I can believe. This particular creature, she has named Nander, and that is his bed. Find him a place where he cannot run off to his former home."

When the stablemaster was out of hearing, Master Jacksen said, "Saucy or not, I'd have her nigh animals all her growing days."

"My steward," Duke Prushane said, "believes in finding the gifts of a person before giving them work."

"Sound guidance," Thomas said. "'Tis too dark to see more today." They followed the side drive back toward the front entrance. A white shape sailed from the master's chamber window and fluttered to the ground.

"What now is happening?" Duke Selta exclaimed.

Thomas smirked. "Not a ghost, merely a sheet. I bade them toss all the linens and draperies from the room. They smell so smoky I don't even want them carried through the house. They're too old to save, anyway."

Another sheet followed it, spreading and twisting until it landed upon the heap below.

Duke Prushane said that he would retire early, so they climbed the hall stairs to the second floor and divided toward their various chambers.

The houseman exited the master's chamber, carrying a ladder. Thomas backed to the wall to let him pass. The housekeeper also stepped from that room, closed the door, and waved a hand before her face. "Phew!"

"Mistress Eldred, the sun sets. Surely you need not work more this day."

"True enough, but I wanted all that mess out so the room can air two nights and a day before we scrub it."

"Have you sat down once since the old housekeeper shoved those keys into your hand?"

"Oh, I drop off my feet when I can, but I'll not deny these

have been the busiest few days of my life." She cleared her throat. "'Tis our custom in the village to eat a cold breakfast on the rest days."

Thomas perceived the faint question in her voice. "A familiar custom to me, too, and all I expect in the dining room tomorrow morn. Just provide hot water from the kitchen, break your own fast, and enjoy all the festivities through the afternoon. Even dinner can be simple tomorrow evening."

She heaved a happy sigh and curtsied. "I do so look forward to this rest day. Good eve, my lord."

Thomas lit a night candle, which sat beside the oil lamp, and carried it past the master's chamber into the room beyond. It still held a bare bedframe, draperies, and worn carpet, but all other furniture had been removed. Only today, Thomas had realized that it was the mistress's chamber. The drapery in one corner of the master's chamber covered a short passage to this one. A corresponding heavy velvet of faded pink concealed this end. Doubtless, the widowed Maerton ladies had slept here and furnished the chamber to their tastes. Which explained its current emptiness.

He walked to the latticed window and fingered the fancy-trimmed, white curtain tied back in folds. Dainty stitching edged the scallops and the tiny hole within each curve. It tugged at childhood memory.

Footsteps approached, and Duke Selta paused in the doorway. "Do I intrude?"

"Nay, you are welcome."

"I know your thoughtful look by now. What do you dwell upon in this dainty chamber?"

Thomas uttered a wry laugh. "Dowagers and...my mother. She had a gown trimmed something like this." He flicked the curtain's edge. "Though, I've not seen it since before my father died." These were not memories he wanted to share. "What brings you to find me?"

"I wanted to tell you that I will leave tomorrow, after the

oath ceremony and noon meal. 'Tis likely to be hectic with no time for more than a simple farewell."

"Ah, true." Thomas licked his lips. "Then, I shall offer my thanks now, for your journey, time, and company. Your family has made these first days pleasant and far easier than they would have been were I alone."

"It has been our pleasure to welcome you in this way, Lord Navayn. You will do well here, for you grasp needs quickly and you ease naturally into the flow of your people."

Thomas inclined his head. "Will you travel to meet your ladies at Fountain Isle?"

"That is my plan."

"Would you be so kind as to send me word of how Lady Sareen fares?"

"Of course." The duke let silence linger, not hurrying away.

How Thomas wished he could ask...but he could not. "It disturbs me greatly that she was harmed here."

"'Twas not your fault in any way."

"I know, but...she was in danger in my house. Which should never be. I hope that...in some future day...we will have answers and peace, so she need never fear my home. So she could be comfortable here."

"I share your hope. Good eve."

Thomas bowed. "Good eve, my lord duke."

His footsteps receded, and a door closed. Alone...in the silent, empty mistress's chamber. Had the duke understood what Thomas really wanted to ask? How could he, with hints so vague?

CHAPTER 31

The special day arrived.

Seemingly trivial events rolled like waves of destiny through Thomas. Like descending the staircase before the portrait of his great grandmother, wearing the sash she had worn. Or finding his horse decked with his colors—an amber saddlecloth with a brown border...old but carefully preserved, doubtless the stablemaster's doing. Amber ribbons hung from the reins, a single green in their midst. Then, riding into the village at the head of his party, and a cheer rising as he halted at the green—who would have thought any of this possible?

He walked down the aisle of the church and sat on the front pew, attended by two dukes also wearing their house sashes. If only Duke Tristelle—Tristan—were here too. Still, Thomas's throat kept closing with emotion. How could this be happening to him?

During the sermon, he smiled as Simmon proclaimed a different version of what Thomas had said in his library. Then, the priest read a passage Thomas never would have thought applied to him. *He lifts the poor from the ash heap and seats them with nobles.* He recognized the story it came from, but only now did he see how it mirrored bits of his life. In truth, it fit all the offspring of those who'd fled the burned village.

Outside, upon a platform stretched across the stone benches of the green, he listened to the reading of the fealty oath, which the villagers repeated in unison. He somberly read his oath to them and pressed his signet into wax upon the parchment before their eyes. The dukes impressed their seals in witness. Lords and ladies gave verbal confirmation. The People of the Woods looked on, wide-eyed, perhaps pondering whether they would someday give the same oath.

The priest began his closing prayer. A moment for Thomas to settle his amazement while Simmon blessed the land and people of Navayn, invoking everything from bountiful crops to health and safety. Then, the priest stretched it further, including the entire duchy as he prayed for peace and serenity. Serenity. Pressure built in Thomas's chest, for that word struck him as Sareen's name. As though the priest had asked for Sareen, a request confirmed by the people—and especially by Thomas—as they closed the prayer with the words, "So be it."

Then, the solemn atmosphere burst into cheering and feasting and games. In archery, Thomas demonstrated his fine aim, which made the young men receptive to the pointers he gave them on the proper use of a bow. The older men needed pointers, too, but he would wait on that.

He greeted the lords and ladies of three houses, two of which were new to him. The children of one couple accompanied their parents, and they threw themselves into the games like they'd done so many times. Interesting. Thomas invited the nobles to visit the manor in coming weeks, said farewell to Duke Selta, and at last rode home with Duke Prushane at his side.

They dismounted before his door and entered the hall. The first moment away from a crowd since he'd left his bedchamber. Thomas released a long sigh.

"How does it feel?" Duke Prushane asked.

Thomas considered. "It feels...delightful...and impossible,

and…" He looked at the portrait of Lady Anne Navayn. "…utterly natural."

The duke nodded, and his lower lip protruded in satisfaction. "As it should."

Thomas fingered his sash, then walked into the salon. He would have preferred to be alone just now, but the duke followed. No matter, for no one could see his heart except God. He hoped that, somehow, his father and grandfather could know his thoughts too. Thomas lifted the sash over his head, situated it on the portrait of Lord Thomas, and stared at that face. *What you and my father both deserved.*

Duke Prushane stood quietly beside him, and when he spoke, a hint of pondering laced his words. "The sash that Lord Thomas was bequeathed but never got to wear."

"Aye. He and my father both. I wish his likeness could have been painted."

"Did he look as much like this portrait as you do?"

Thomas grinned. "Almost. His hair was a shade closer to brown." It seemed that private thoughts asked to be spoken. "I once overheard my mother call my father Lord Nathan in private, and he called her Lady Esha. I didn't understand at the time. 'Twas not until recent years that I have realized my father did lead the People of the Woods in subtle ways. Lord Thomas did too. It seems only fitting to acknowledge, this day, their right to the title of Lord Navayn." Even as he said that name, his heart spoke the name of Kaituer. An echo—nay, an overlay—that he could not understand. It seemed to demand something of him.

Duke Prushane turned to him, causing Thomas to turn also. "This is one of those moments when I understand more fully what Duke Tristelle sees in you and why he entrusted much to you."

Such remarks always took Thomas by surprise, and he never knew how to respond. Jonathan was hovering in the doorway, too, with a satisfied smile, which made it all the harder to reply. "I do wish he could have been here."

Duke Prushane shrugged. "'Tis a treasure to have one friend who is close and trusted, but even better to have many friends in addition to that one."

Thomas shared a quick smile with Jonathan and said to Duke Prushane, "All treasures, indeed, and more than I ever expected." As they strolled from the room, Thomas said, "The day is not done, and yet I don't quite know what to do with myself."

"Ah, that is the sign of one who has worked without pause, whether on weighty deeds or thoughts. Remember to *rest* on the rest day. Of both efforts."

"Sound advice."

Thomas had just set his foot on the first step of the staircase when Duke Prushane said, "One question before you go up. Did Inspector Curlow depart?"

Thomas paused and looked back. "He did."

"What did he tell you of his findings?"

"Nothing."

"Nothing?"

The duke sounded...what? Shocked? Disturbed? "I assumed," Thomas said, "that his duty is to report to the king. It seemed awkward to ask what he did not offer."

"Hmm." The duke walked into the library, and Thomas continued up the stairs. What did that mean? How was he supposed to rest from his thoughts when people made obscure remarks?

Puffy clouds in a blue sky graced Thomas's morning stroll. He reached into the goat pen to stroke the kid. Then, Duke Prushane and the two Jacksens drew near, and the ewe summoned her kid to the opposite side.

"Pied goats," the duke said. "How came you by these?"

"They live wild on my property. The ewe was hurt, so she was easy to catch, and of course, the kid would not leave her."

"Ewe?" Master Jacksen said. "'Tis a goat, not a sheep, so the adults are does and bucks."

"Does and bucks?" Thomas exclaimed. "'Tis a goat, not a deer. Do you call the kids fawns?"

The duke chuckled in his subdued way. "No more than you call them lambs. I've heard this argument before. The two northern duchies use the words ewe and ram—the four southern use doe and buck. My guess is that the thicker wool of the woodland goats swayed the northerners."

Thomas shook his head. "Whatever the adults are called, I'm hoping I can make a profit from sheering their coats. You recognize them, I gather. Pied goats, did you say?"

"Aye. My grandfather once had a substantial herd," the duke said, "so they must have been worth raising. He, and then my father, tried to breed them for a solid black coat. That made the sheering more lucrative, but the breeding also weakened their hooves. The poor creatures often went lame."

"Could they not let the goats return to natural breeding?" Thomas asked.

"Not easily. The goats with white in their coats had been culled, so they were no longer available for breeding. Then, the plague struck. Untended fields, crops unplanted, hungry orphans. The weak-footed goats were edible, so they didn't survive the famine."

Thomas frowned and made a commiserating sound in his throat.

"May we all be spared another plague," the steward said. Doubtless, he remembered it.

The duke nodded, tightlipped. "Just in case you haven't lived long enough to notice, there are difficult challenges in lording any land, be it large or small."

"I have seen some of that," Thomas said, "though not as much as you."

"I will offer you some advice that aids recovery when troubles come, for you will not find this done well in Maerton

Duchy." Duke Prushane leveled a serious gaze on Thomas. "Allow the priests freedom to follow their hearts and guide folk toward truth and kindness in *good* times. When hardship comes, those who know their God find comfort and are able to help one another. Though I can never say exactly how, I've seen that such folk recover more quickly."

Thomas puzzled over his words. Why had he brought this up? "I do honor the teachings of the holy book, but I don't yet understand the customs of the church here. The priest in Navayn village came through unusual means, and the traveling priests who served Tower Woods in my youth and before could not have been sent by the Dukes of Maerton. Yet I gather that the duke appoints the priests here, which seems very strange to me."

"Aye." Prushane's pitch ground low. "He favors priests who are as controlling as he is. Women, in particular, seem to be allowed no voice. I have oft pitied the folk of this duchy. First, they had the Kaituers, who disdained the church entirely. Then, they had the Maertons, who control the church and, thereby, the people."

Thomas's ire rose at criticism of Kaituer. Though it was likely true, he could not help but counter. "Lady Anne Navayn was known for honoring God and his holy words."

"Exactly. Consider the outcome." The duke narrowed his gaze. "You don't wish to be deemed evil because of your Kaituer ancestors, but then neither can you be deemed good because of your Navayn ancestors."

"Ah." Thomas's conscience twisted—his anger had awakened at a false meaning. His own choices mattered. Not just to him, but to those who would come after. He inclined his torso. "A worthy observation."

The squires and stablemaster reached them with horses, and the party mounted up for a ride around the estate. The duke said little, leaving it to the steward and his son to comment upon the land and the use it was put to. By now, 'twas clear that the young Jacksen had as much love of stewardship as his father.

Nander followed. Did he think he was herding them? When they reached the wasteland, his true calling beckoned. While they rested their horses, he rounded up goats. Or tried to. They eluded him with ease at first. As the ride continued, he managed to gather an occasional group atop boulders, which he circled with his cocky tail flying high, while his supposed herd stared down at him.

Thomas laughed. "Good dog, Nander."

"Is this how goat herding is done in Tower Woods?" the steward asked.

"'Twould be impossible to herd anything there. We tame the little ones. I don't know if that will work here, though. Woolies seem happy to get rid of their thick coats. I'm not so sure about these. What think you? Am I chasing nonsense?"

"Nay!" the younger Jacksen said. "Nothing is guaranteed, but 'twould be folly not to at least try."

They rode through the quarries, and Thomas asked what they thought of the stone's worth.

"Unless there is considerably more," the elder Jacksen said, "I don't think you could make very much in selling it for building."

Duke Prushane shook his head. "Do not waste lynxstone on building."

"Is there a market for it?" young Jacksen asked.

"I see little of it for sale, possibly because Duke Maerton made no use of it." He lifted his brow. "If so, he may have created an advantage for you, Lord Navayn."

"How so?"

"Scarcity increases value. My lady wife is fond of collecting porcelain and other fine art. She has a couple vases of lynxeye, and they were more costly than the finest of her porcelains. You may wish to limit the quantities you sell, so the market is not suddenly engulfed with it."

"Ah." Thomas hid a smile. How long would it take Sallie to

learn to fashion desirable pieces? Later, for that. "I have need of the plain stone from this quarry. The boundary markers are crumbling, and I want them restored."

"I'd like a look at what remains of them," the duke said.

They rode on, and Thomas's companions suggested the means to make the border more obvious without need of a fence. At the last marker, Duke Prushane advised, "As for this one, re-build in the same location, with a structure symbolizing strength."

"Agreed." Thomas glanced around. "Jonathan, what became of Nander?"

"Oh, he's probably at that bare spot a few yards back. Those patches fascinate him." Jonathan walked his horse back and, after a moment, called, "Lord Navayn, come take a look at this."

Thomas went to see what interested his squire and found him squatting with reins in hand while he studied the ground. Nander dug around something pale and soon unearthed a bone, much to his delight.

Jonathan pointed at it. "That, my lord, is a butchered bone. From a ham, I would guess. And I want to know why it is buried here." He poked about the hole with a broken stick.

"Another dog, perhaps," Thomas said.

"If so, that dog also buried ash and charcoal along with its bone."

What purpose in hiding the remains of someone's stay in the woods? *Barely* in the woods, for 'twas nigh the road. Were all of these trampled spots the hidden remains of camps? Thomas had cast dirt on a fire many a time, but never hidden the traces of his stay. He looked around again, though he'd already done so. An old habit, but never would he forego watchfulness. "Scout for me, Jonathan. Has anyone been passing between here and the mansion's lawn?"

Thomas held Jonathan's horse as he walked to and fro through the woods, searching. Nander gnawed his treasure for a few minutes, then left it beside Thomas and went to see what all this walking about meant.

Jonathan returned and said, "'Tis faint, but there is a hint of a path that ends where the hedge begins at the edge of the woods. The dog snuffled all about the end of it too."

They rode out of the woods on a bridle path and skirted the trees till they reached the end of the footpath. Nander dropped the bone he carried and, once again, sniffed over an area a yard or two wide. Deer often left trampled beds, but that didn't seem right. Thomas turned his horse and looked at the manor. The front and north sides in full view. Had someone sat here watching? When? And why?

THAT QUESTION KEPT RETURNING to Thomas at odd moments, not that he had many empty moments to ponder it. None of his companions had any more notion than he as to who might watch the manor or for what purpose.

Duke Prushane's steward left the next day, though the duke and young Jacksen stayed, discussing the merits of various plans with Thomas. He got on well with Jacksen, who possessed calm confidence, without being given to overpowering certainty. Thomas learned the names of his wife and three young children, and that his chance of becoming Duke Prushane's steward would not come for decades. It seemed that he suffered under the same complaint as Jonathan, destined to remain the *younger* for too many years.

Given all that and his clear grasp of stewardship, Thomas offered him that position on Navayn Estate.

Jacksen's eyes lit. "I shall give my wife a say in the matter, but I am as certain as a man can be that I will bring my family when I give you my final answer."

That decision lifted an almost tangible burden. Far more than the hiring of a cook, the organization of servants, the extension of the kitchen garden, or the surprising arrival of a load of salt, which Duchess Selta had ordered on her way through Purthellia. The wagon even held some pots and skillets, much to the delight of his housekeeper and cook.

Best of all, was the letter that finally arrived from Duke Selta by the hand of Captain D'Jorge. Lady Sareen had found relief from her ailment at Fountain Isle. From there, they had spent some days at Tristelle Castle and were now bound for their own home.

Thomas read the letter quickly, then tucked it inside his doublet. He must greet newcomers, for D'Jorge had brought more. And these folk brought tools.

How? Five years ago, the king had provided basic tools to each family when he set the People of the Woods free of Duke Maerton's corrupt rule. But as the children matured, those tools must constantly be shared among the family and could not be brought south when some chose to leave.

"Where have you come by all these tools?" Thomas asked.

D'Jorge uttered a low guffaw with a sly look in his eyes. "Before we tell him, show him the scythes."

They were bundled together in the back of one cart, their long, curved blades wrapped in leather. These were nothing like what they used in Tower Woods, even in the northern part where they grew woodland grain. These were far too long for the contorted fields.

D'Jorge waited until Thomas turned his puzzled gaze upon him. "'Twould seem," he drawled, "that Duke Maerton has suddenly come upon a large number of tools. And though they have been used and sharpened many a time, he has been quite generous. Not even selling, but *giving* them to woodland folk."

Thomas's smile emerged, and his shoulders began to shake. "And these woodland folk now bring them—here." He tilted his head back and laughed till his sides hurt.

When Thomas's contagious mirth abated, one of the men

from Tower Woods asked, "Is it true, then, that these are really your tools, and he stole them from you, to give to us?"

"It seems likely, though I cannot say for certain where each item came from."

"Well, then, we had best give them all back to you." A determined sound in his voice almost masked the disappointment. Tools were wealth to these folk.

"Let us rather divide them this way," Thomas said. "Let me have the scythes, for, in truth, they are only useful within my broad fields. The other tools, you may keep, but I pray you will let me borrow them until I can purchase my own. Does this seem fair?"

"Oof, aye, beyond fair, my lord. And generous too."

The murmurs of approval from the small crowd merged with nods and smiles.

Jacksen cleared his throat and asked, "By chance, did any of you bring a plow?"

No plow being found among them, Duke Prushane said, "You should have at least two. There is plenty of time to get them. I can order some from the smith in my nearest town, if you like."

"I would appreciate it," Thomas said. "I shall pay for them, of course."

"I've no doubt of it. I'll negotiate a fair price for you and send you word."

The typical arrival bustle followed, and it was not until after dinner that D'Jorge said, "Let us sit outside for a bit, shall we? I have another matter to speak of."

He seemed to want privacy, so Thomas led him out the back hall door, and they sat on the benches that adorned the paved area behind the manor. "By the way," Thomas said, "I've been meaning to ask you. Did Duke Maerton's gift of tools spark any discontent among the People of the Woods?"

"I think not. His folk distributed them along with commiseration that neither the king nor Duke Tristelle have continued their earlier generosity. 'Twas a bit obvious, and some were insulted that he implied they were too impoverished to pay for tools. In fact, they haven't sought tools because they rarely need more than they have."

Thomas nodded. "So I would guess. Did you want to talk of some matter in private?"

"I do." How somber, his voice grew. "Unfortunately, I bear sad news."

Thomas's chest tightened. "What now?"

D'Jorge met his eyes in the dusk. "Your stepfather...he has passed from this life."

"Mm." Thomas stared westward and let the sad waves roll. For years, Pennot had finished the rearing of him. Taught him to make arrows, bows, and other things. Taught him to hunt. Argued with him, too, but Thomas didn't mind that so much. He'd done right by the family, though he never had the knack of getting close to one. There was no denying, this didn't hurt as much as when his father or brother died. 'Twould be an easier mourning. For him, at least. "Do you know how my mother is faring through this?"

"Not too bad, I think. She was able to tell me of his final moments. Pennot sat down heavy on the cottage porch—said he needed a rest. After a bit, he moaned and lay back on the porch. He looked at Esha and said, 'You're a good wife.' She says he murmured your name, too, but she couldn't make out what he said. Then he departed."

Thomas stared west again, taking comfort from his friend's grip on his shoulder.

D'Jorge cleared his throat. "When last I saw her, she was sitting near the graves of your father and grandfather. Pennot's grave is a little apart. You know how scattered they always are in Tower Woods. I would think there is space for another grave between your father and stepfather."

So, she planned to lie near Nathan Kaituer without dishonoring Pennot. "That is fitting," Thomas said. "Do any tend to her?"

"Certain. There seems to be plenty of coming and going. The Duke and Duchess of Tristelle brought food to her with promises of support until she is reunited with you. They have suggested that, if she finds the cottage lonely, she may wish to visit you before you are able to reach her. They even mentioned that the duchess's carriage gives a smoother ride than any she has known before."

That brought a grin. They knew his mother disliked travel of any sort and utterly loathed horses. Thomas rubbed the back of his neck. "I should go to her at once …but I don't think I can."

"Duke Tristelle advises you not to rush north. He thinks you should stay on your land. I will carry a letter to your mother, and he is more than willing to bring her to you. Or anywhere else she wishes. Tower Woods Village is an option if she doesn't want to leave the woods she has always known. She would not be alone there, and with coin, she could buy all she needs."

"I will write her a letter." Thomas stood. "Thank you for bringing me the news. Duke Prushane is likely in the library. If you see him, pray tell him I have retired for the night."

Thomas barely noticed the stairs he climbed to his chamber. Why did it always seem that bad things tried to nudge out good things?

Later, Jonathan brought him a tidbit of rumor. "I don't even want to repeat words so foul, but maybe you should know."

"What then?"

"Some in Maerton Castle Village have said that it could have been you who lit the fire in Lady Sareen's chamber."

CHAPTER 32

Days settled into a rhythm of planning, deciding, inspecting, adjusting...and wondering. All Thomas could learn from Griven was that the inspector had not discovered who lit the fire. Thomas unbuckled his wrist guard and tossed it on the table in his bedchamber as he crossed to the window. Weeks, he had waited. No word at all.

What good was an inspector, anyway? So many times, Thomas had almost sent Griven back to Selta out of sheer frustration. Still, he managed to accomplish enough work to earn some of his wages and hide his true purpose. Thomas braced his hands on the windowsill and gazed over the back lawn, stuck with the same conclusion. No one else could get around the villages nor prowl half the night as subtly as Griven. If only he had found something in all those nights. Or *had* he and just didn't tell Thomas? Or maybe no one was even trying to kill Thomas. How was he supposed to get on with life if he didn't know? When could he formally court Lady Sareen? Ever?

'Twas odd that he especially missed her during rest day festivities. Perhaps because of how he'd missed her on the first one. Hard to believe it was his fourth rest at Navayn Manor. The days of sweltering heat were likely done for the year, and his steward said they would soon harvest grain. The goats...he had three now. At this rate, he'd have gray hair before he saw a profit. They seemed destined to provide nothing but herding joy for Nander. Perhaps they would be easier to catch when the spring birthing started. But first, he must see to the harvest and the hunt.

Duke Maerton had sent the invitations, and the Seltas would be among the many guests. Thomas would finally see Lady Sareen again. The Maertons would even hold a ball on one night, and he was invited. Hard to imagine himself in Maerton Castle. Would he get much chance to talk with Sareen in all the fuss of hunting and a ball? Doubtful. Ivan would monopolize her. Besides, other men courted her as well. Only Thomas was forbidden to do so. He raked a hand through his hair. How was he ever going to find out if that prohibition was lifted?

A couple distant specks distracted him. Hard to make them out as they darted between the tree trunks. Ah, the sudden turns. Nander had found something to chase. Thomas grinned and watched. Whatever it was, it could not out-maneuver that dog, who was clearly driving it toward the manor. Was that a goat? Indeed! Thomas laughed and headed outside to see how the matter would end. If Nander succeeded, he was going to get much praise and a nice piece of meat.

Succeed he did and, with a little help, drove the tired goat into the pen. Nander was still soaking up much attention from those who witnessed his feat, when Thomas noticed Griven leaning against the corner of the stable, watching. He hadn't been there earlier. Nor did he smile. He locked his gaze onto Thomas's for a few seconds before looking away.

Thomas patted the dog again, laughed at a jest, then parted company from the little crowd and strolled to the stable.

No one was nigh, but Griven kept a casual demeanor while he chatted about going into Maerton Castle Village for the rest day. Softly, he added, "Will you send me to Purthellia? We can say I carry a message for you."

"To whom?"

"Choose whom you will. Even an order to a vendor would work."

Was Thomas's meaning not obvious? "To whom do *you* go?"

"I must give word of something to Inspector Curlow."

"Of what? I'm tired of being left ignorant of things that concern me."

"It doesn't...exactly."

Thomas held his silence.

Griven hesitated. "Pray, don't speak of it until you hear it from someone else. Duke Maerton has collapsed."

Thomas sucked in a breath. "You mean...dead?"

"I think not. Yet. They say he cannot speak. The physician calls it apoplexy. An inspector is not summoned for natural causes, but I believe Curlow should know of it."

Aye, for this, Griven must ride. Thomas reached for the leather purse on his belt. "I need stone-cutting tools, which I cannot buy here. Chisels of hard steel, large and small. Look in Purthellia for me. If you can find a stone saw, I would like that too." He handed coins to Griven.

"Aye, my lord. I'll go now, so that I may visit a smith early tomorrow. Remember—you do not know."

Thomas nodded. "Many thanks for shortening your rest day." He strolled toward the manor, keeping his face clear.

What could this mean?

DUKE MAERTON WOKE SLOWLY. Or *was* he awake? He could not move. Nor call out. A nightmare, then. Ghastly real, it felt. Yet no other horrors occurred.

He woke again. What was this? He focused on his bed curtains in the dim light. When had he gone to bed? What had happened?

He struggled for memory. He'd been in his library. Aye, the

note he'd received from his lawyer. He could not forget that. A response to his query of why the will was taking so long. The lawyer claimed he had sent it two weeks ago. Maerton's heart pounded again as it had in that moment. If it had been sent, where was it now?

He must act. He must overcome this lethargy. Must wake from this nightmare. Had his heart seized? The news of that note was bad enough to trouble a heart, indeed. But he was alive, so he could recover. He must. He would move.

His body ignored that decision.

Repeatedly, he demanded movement from his limbs. Fought for it. His fingertips brushed the sheet. Then, his toes. But only on the left. Long, he fought. Every time he awoke. With immense effort, he straightened and curled his fingers slightly. Nothing more.

He'd heard of this. The curse that could turn a strong man into a limp husk. Sometimes even dumb. He must speak the truth before it was too late. His tongue shifted but refused to form words. A dull moan reached his ears. Not this. Not this! He'd waited too long. What havoc would he watch in silence? Oh, God, no!

Sunlight had returned when Maerton woke again. He moaned, and his servant came to the bed.

How sad, the man's eyes. "Rest, my lord duke. I have water for you." The man put a wet cloth in Maerton's mouth.

Blessed water. Fed like a babe. 'Twas hard, but he swallowed.

"Good." His servant faked a cheerful voice. "I have a little broth for you in an invalid cup."

The man dribbled it into Maerton's mouth, one swallow at a time. This could not be his life. He could not endure it.

The door opened. Footsteps. Ivan stood at the foot of his bed, concern on his face, voice soft. "How are you, Father?"

Impossible to answer.

"He hasn't spoken," the servant said, "but he was able to swallow some broth, so that is a hopeful sign."

Ivan gave him an awkward nod. "Thank you." He seemed to struggle for what to say. "Don't worry about anything, Father. I will take care of all that must be done. You may just rest and recover. And...well, even if everything is not quite as it was, we can still enjoy some things together. Ah, like our morning tea. I will go and make your favorite."

He left with those words. An offer of comfort...which brought none.

Ivan returned with his steeping pot. To the servant, he said, "I will sit with him for a while, so you may have an hour to yourself."

When the door closed, Ivan leaned near. "Can you say any word at all? Please try...for me."

Try, he did. The contorted sound that issued from his lips sickened him.

But Ivan smiled. "Then, all is well." He rinsed the invalid cup at the wash basin. "A rather inelegant cup, but easier for you. I fear elegance is lost to you now. If you haven't fouled yourself yet, doubtless you soon will." He shuddered. "I cannot imagine the horror of being handled like an infant." He leaned his thigh against the bed and looked down on Maerton's face. "Don't think me unfeeling. Indeed, I grieve for you. Had I been able to spare you the agony of awakening, I would have. But nothing is perfect. Not even apoplexy."

Maerton's chest hurt. The half he could feel. Apoplexy... Hettie...nay, it couldn't be.

Ivan's voice grew silkier. "Ah, your eyes speak, though your tongue is silent. That's what it is, you know. The physician confirmed it. Just like poor Hettie, though she went sudden." Ivan smiled again. "And now, your eyes are...hmm...what words would these be? A gasp, perhaps. Shock? Likely so, for you think I don't know what you are doing. But I do, Father. You have no right to condemn me, for you are the one who caused your tragic, early death." He shrugged. "Not so terribly early. Not everyone reaches seventy, you know. At least you passed sixty.

And lately, you have become soft. Your reason is faltering. I cannot let you harm the House of Maerton."

Ivan knit his brow. "How odd your expressions look on only half your face."

The irony pierced Maerton's despair. Ivan's low-set eye skewed all of his expressions. Had there always been something wrong with a portion of his son's mind? He should have known. Should have realized much sooner. Should have required justice for his wife's death, though he loathed her. Why must that thought recur now? Did he not suffer enough?

Ivan watched him, shaking his head. "Really, Father—that will! Did you think I would let you disinherit me?"

So hard to breathe. Ivan had gotten the will somehow. The very thing Maerton had feared in his library yesterday.

"But worry not," Ivan said. "I put it on the fire as soon as I read it, so no one will ever know the extent of your folly. And though you deserve to suffer, I won't let you. No more will you be distressed over my methods. No more will you need to pretend."

Ivan poured tea into the invalid cup. "I strengthened your favorite mixture. It seems safe enough, since the physician has already diagnosed apoplexy. Very likely, 'twill be the last dose you need in order to sleep beside Mother. My final kindness to you." Ivan leaned near and slid a hand under Maerton's head for support. "Drink up now, my dear father, and the nightmare will end."

'Twas true. His son had slowly poisoned him, day after day. Was poisoning him again now. Some distant portion of Maerton's mind bade him blow the tea from his mouth. Forbade him to swallow. And live with this knowledge? Nay, he could not bear it. His folly...his shame...his son...his own son! Maerton swallowed. Every drop.

Ivan rinsed the cup, picked up the tea pot, and left, softly closing the door.

Alone. How long would death tarry?

~

THE NEWS WAS EVERYWHERE. The third Duke of Maerton was dead.

The words, "Have you heard," seemed to start every conversation. Thomas said them himself when he walked out to meet Griven as he dismounted in the drive.

Unfortunate that others had come into hearing range. Griven's face remained unmoved by the news. "That seems awful sudden."

"'Tis said in Maerton Castle Village that he collapsed yesterday afternoon and died this morn of apoplexy."

"Mm. Getting on in years," Griven said, "not to mention his girth. I bought hard steel chisels, one big for the quarry and two smaller for finer work. There were many types offered—I told the smith you wanted samples of his tools and let him choose." Griven pulled out his purse and counted coins back to Thomas. "I found no stone saw, but the smith will fashion a blade for you." He unrolled soft leather and displayed his purchases.

Thomas took the two smaller chisels and said, "Put that in the tool shed."

Disappointing to get no information from Griven, but it wasn't likely that he knew the important answers. Thomas walked back inside the manor. Everything seemed more unsettled than ever it had been. Even the hunting party would likely be cancelled...except, they must do something about those deer. What would Lord Ivan be like as duke? Better to await developments than imagine the worst. At least Thomas would get to see Tristan, for certain, the duke would attend the funeral.

Ugh. A funeral—which Thomas must also attend—and he had no black doublet. Dark brown would have to do. He went in search of the housekeeper, who had already stitched a scarf for him from the silks that had arrived, dyed in his house colors.

He found her in the kitchen hall, stitching again. "Have you need of something, my lord?" she asked.

"Indeed. Another scarf. A black one."

"Oh, the funeral." She touched her pursed lips as she did when pondering. "I fancy I'll have to go into Maerton Castle Village to find black." She began folding her work into a basket. "Might not be silk, for I daresay everyone will be wanting it, but I'll find something to fashion a neckcloth from. I'd best not delay."

She didn't exactly smile, but he guessed the prospect delighted her. She would soon gather all the latest news.

CHAPTER 33

What a depressing funeral. Why had words of hope been uttered with such solemn gravity? This tiresome lingering in the churchyard wasn't much better, but at least it spared Thomas more echoing intonations.

Days filled with rumors had given him no insight. People died, after all. Witness all the tombstones beside the church. The lords of Maerton Duchy bore the duke's coffin from that stone edifice and set it beside the grave that awaited its due. Thomas thought more of Pennot than of the late duke.

When the graveside ceremony ended, the procession formed to cover the short distance to Maerton Castle. The gray walls were nigh, but the primary gate was set in a different wall farther along the road.

Lord Ivan led upon a black horse with a black saddlecloth and black feathers standing high between its ears. Lord Sathe Maerton followed him on a dapple-gray horse without all the trimmings. His face showed more trouble than Ivan's.

Next, the king and queen rode together, with Prince Garvan following, and behind them, the royal Duchess of Tristelle and Duke Tristelle. Thomas had not even been able to greet them yet. More dukes and duchesses joined the procession, and then Thomas joined with lords or ladies whose houses were sworn to the crown. Did the nobles of Maerton Duchy resent riding behind him? He'd half expected to be relegated to the back, since Lord Ivan had the ordering of this event. Apparently, he was not in the mood for pettiness today.

Thomas rode through the gates of Maerton Castle for the first time. An imposing structure, bulging with towers. It exceeded Tristelle Castle in both the curtain wall circumference and the dimensions of the mansion, though not in beauty. Stones of mixed gray hues comprised the walls—odd to think that some of them had been part of Kaituer Castle.

What a long time, this all took. Dismounting, crossing the courtyard, and entering the vast hall was as slow as beginning the procession. Tables stood in the hall, with white linens and plate, but the higher-ranking nobility were escorted into the dining room. Its immensely long table provided space enough for the royal and ducal guests, high lords and ladies, and for the lords of Maerton Duchy. Did their wives mind being relegated to the hall?

Thomas took his place and responded to a polite inquiry about Navayn Manor. The chink of dishes had already begun as servants—a great many of them—began serving the funeral luncheon. Multiple throat-clearings brought gazes to the black-robed priest who had drawn nigh the head of the table. Lord Ivan paused and looked at him.

"Would you like me to offer the prayer, my lord duke?" the priest said.

The title grated on Thomas, but he must accustom himself.

Ivan set his glass down. "Of course."

The priest folded his hands and closed his eyes, but before he could speak, King Gairith said, "If you will not correct him, Lord Ivan, then I must. You may not use the title of duke until it has been granted to you."

The hush already begun for the prayer seemed to go rigid.

Most faces held all the expression of statues. Whatever the normal protocol, something was off.

Lord Ivan said nothing, his face also fixed.

"You may proceed," the king said to the priest.

He blinked, then began a prayer that sounded practiced. When he reached a line asking for a blessing upon the future Duke of Maerton, his delivery faltered. Doubtless, he had planned to include the name of Ivan. He closed the prayer and departed as the servants resumed their tasks.

Lord Ivan picked up his glass again and addressed the king. "Pray, pardon my servants, sire, if they commit the same error. The succession is clear, so they have already begun to address me by my future title."

"Indeed? Have you already summoned lawyers and read the will?"

"Nay, sire. Perhaps I allowed my grief too much sway, for it seemed disrespectful to speak of property before my dear father was laid to rest."

"Then, in our sympathy," Queen Ellianne said, "we shall speak no more of it today. The morrow is time enough."

Lord Maerton, seated beside the queen, narrowed his eyes and addressed his nephew. "Pray confirm that you *have* sent for my brother's lawyer to arrive by tomorrow."

"Can you not leave this for the moment, Uncle?"

'Twould have been so easy to confirm. Why had Ivan not? The queen changed the subject, and conversation resumed near Thomas. He could hear no more from the head of the table.

When the meal ended, Thomas found an opportunity to greet Lady Sareen. He must keep it formal, for Lord Ivan's gaze lingered on them. She must sense that, too, for her smile and conversation were stilted. This was not what Thomas wanted, yet for nothing in all the world, would he let Ivan see anything between them. The king and queen, seated on a conspicuously placed sofa in the hall, also surveyed the mingling company. The king's words of *court no woman* echoed in memory.

Thomas drew a little back from the cluster around Lady Sareen and listened.

A guest commented on having received the duke's invitation to the hunting party on the same day he learned of the sad tidings. He inserted a hint of question when he said, "I assume the hunting party will be cancelled."

"That was my first intent," Lord Ivan said, lifting his voice slightly, "and the ball, I shall not hold. But though the hunt will feel less joyful this year, I cannot cancel that." Lord Ivan gazed around at those who had turned to his voice. "I daresay, many of you saw deer as you journeyed through Maerton Duchy. The herd is so plentiful, it damages crops and strips the woodland. We must cull it, and I do not have the heart to hunt every day of the autumn. I pray you will not forsake our customary gathering. Indeed, I crave your presence more than ever this year, in the hope that it will lighten my grief."

Those nearest promised to return for the hunt. That manner of asking gave them little choice.

One of the lords who had attended the Navayn oath ceremony chanced to be standing beside Thomas. "What a surprise," he said dryly. "Hunting parties when his father is barely laid to rest."

"Regardless," another said, "we must do something about the herd."

"At least he acts more grieved now," a lady murmured, "than he did when his mother died."

Thomas looked across the room at Lord Ivan. Was that grief on his expressionless face? Thomas couldn't perceive it. Perhaps he let prejudice sway him. He did not show grief either, though memories of Pennot occasionally intruded. He would not speak of his stepfather's death among his peers, for they would all disdain a commoner from the People of the Woods. Better to leave them ignorant. Besides, he hadn't even gone to the grave. How could he fault Lord Ivan?

Thomas strolled past clusters of nobles, hoping for a

moment with the Tristelles. It seemed that the royal duchess was acting in her dual role as Princess Ellabeth, for she sat in a commodious chair beside the king, and young Prince Garvan sat at the queen's side. Duke Tristelle stood a few yards distant as she conversed with a couple who had just risen from their bow and curtsy to royalty.

Tristan turned to Thomas, welcoming him with a smile. Thomas bowed. "My lord duke, at last, I may greet you."

Tristan replied, then gripped Thomas's shoulder and leaned near to whisper, "My condolences to you too."

The last thing Thomas expected at Duke Maerton's funeral. He murmured, "Thank you."

Tristan spoke of ordinary things, suitable for a crowd, until the moment arrived for Thomas to make his bow to royalty.

Though she sat erect as a princess must, Duchess Tristelle's striking blue eyes were soft as she murmured, "My sympathies, Lord Navayn."

"Thank you. I speak little of it here, for none knew him."

The king and queen inclined their heads to him as the queen asked, "How do you fare on your estate, Lord Navayn?"

"Well, indeed, though I have much to learn." Such talk continued. Thomas had replied to the same question so many times, that it required little thought. Still, he appreciated the royal favor. After all, nothing of substance could be exchanged in a crowd. He described the oath ceremony—which was more than he told most—accepted their congratulations, then withdrew.

Now to pay his respects to the other ducal guests, then at last he could escape. Surprisingly, he received some promised visits before he passed from the ornate hall into the courtyard.

Just beyond the archway, Jonathan stood watching for him, their reins in his hand. Good—no need to wait. That did not prevent his habit of scanning his surroundings as they rode toward the gate. So many towers. Odd how they brought to mind the arrow that had nigh struck him amidst the Kaituer ruins. Though he imagined eyes upon him and a bow drawn, he avoided looking over his shoulder.

They'd passed beneath the gatehouse and turned toward Navayn Manor, before Jonathan asked, "How did it go?"

"Well enough. We will have visits from some dukes and duchesses as they depart over the next couple days. The Tristelles will stay one night with us. I didn't see Captain Cotrell. Is he here?"

"Aye." Jonathan's ready smile spread. "We talked a little, but he has more to tend than just holding two horses." They approached the lane that could shorten their journey, and Jonathan asked, "By road or by woodland?"

Thomas's skin crawled like it had when they left the castle. "'Tis the woodland route that I *want*. What do you hear?"

"Birdsong and deer grunts. We know where Ivan is, after all, and we have the double advantage of your eyes and my ears."

"You really should call him Lord Ivan," Thomas said as they followed the lane into the woods, "or you'll make a mistake someday that he won't forgive."

Jonathan made a low rumble in his throat. "I suppose I must get used to *my lord duke* now. Goes hard against the grain."

"Not yet, you don't." Thomas told him what the king had said.

Jonathan wrinkled both his brow and nose. "Is that how they do it in Lavaycia? Hold the title until some ceremony or such?"

Thomas shrugged. "Seems strange to me. No one said a word about it—but they couldn't then." With long vision, he searched through the Maerton estate woods. "We'll be hunting here soon, for Lord Ivan is still holding the hunting party. Best to know the trails."

"You're still planning to ride with his party?"

"No reason to change. Better in his group than alone, for we must hunt, regardless."

"True enough." Jonathan pointed to one side. "There are three of them, and the buck is exchanging insults with another I cannot see. And we haven't a single arrow. Don't see why we couldn't hook our bows and quivers to the saddles, at least."

"For a funeral?" Thomas nigh laughed through the words.

"We wouldn't have hunted on the way there."

Thomas laughed outright.

"Well, it makes no sense," Jonathan said. "I never could stand Duke Maerton alive. Why should I sit and mope when he's dead?"

"I ask for no moping. Are we not scouting unknown woods? Let us make the most of it, since we know Lord Ivan is within his castle."

The lane met a broad clearing, then left it as a mere bridle path. Trails separated and joined, eventually bringing them through Thomas's own woods, where they found a few strangers with a buck. Thomas paused to meet them. Men of Maerton Castle Village. They were cautiously respectful and spoke of sending the hindquarter to his manor.

"I have no doubt of it," Thomas said with calm assurance.

When they'd ridden out of earshot, Jonathan asked, "Do you think they will follow through?"

"Likely, but I'll give their names to Master Jacksen and confirm it. I will treat them with courtesy and deal consistently with all. We will see how that serves."

"The only thing is…with strangers on your land… how would we ever tell if someone meant you harm?"

"I don't know." That made Thomas itch to look over his shoulder. "Fields, wood, and wasteland…there is no way to watch it all." Sometimes, he felt more endangered than he had growing up in Tower Woods.

THOMAS SAVORED NEW PLEASURES. Welcoming the Duchess and Duke of Tristelle to Navayn Manor. Sitting in his own salon and conversing with his most trusted friends. Of court affairs, no less.

The duchess leaned back on a sofa and raised her brows with a knowing look. "Ah, but you see, Thomas, the late duke's will cannot be found." She took a dainty bite of a scone made with berries and a soft, sweet cheese. "Unique and quite delicious. I commend your cook."

"But would finding the will change anything?" Thomas asked. "Lord Ivan is the direct heir."

"Lord Sathe Maerton," she said, "is greatly disturbed. His brother told him several weeks ago that he was making a new will. He must have told him at least some provisions of it. Otherwise, Lord Maerton would not be so irate."

"Perhaps he would," Tristan said. "If neither the old nor the new will is found, everything will go to Ivan. Which would be rather unfair to a brother, who would be left with nothing."

The duchess sipped her tea. "Lord Ivan is acting like it is all a pointless formality." She mimicked the air of contempt Ivan often used. "He says the steward is searching and will find it—if indeed his father completed the new will—but it is a big house, and his father had begun to behave oddly of late, so it could be hidden anywhere. And then he bemoans his uncle's grasping ways when one would expect him to be mourning. To which Lord Maerton replied, 'I mourn my brother far more than you do. If no will is found, then it has been intentionally destroyed, and that is a crime.' After which, he stomped from the room, and Lord Ivan begged the king to pardon his uncle's behavior."

"What a dreadful family," Thomas said. "I'm glad I left when I did, though that bit would have been interesting to hear."

"You wouldn't have heard it," Tristan said. "Lord Ivan held off Lord Maerton's demands until well after dinner, when few remained in the salon."

"The scene was dreadfully uncomfortable," the duchess said. "Lord Maerton left early this morn—I don't think he even broke his fast. The Seltas left this morn too."

"Aye, they stopped here for a few minutes before starting their journey home." The short visit had afforded Thomas no chance for even a brief walk with Lady Sareen. Best change the subject before his disappointment showed. "Did you find time to visit my mother on your journey through Tower Woods?"

"We did," Tristan said. "She has made a decision."

"Which is?"

"She wants more time in her cottage where she can still visit the graves, but she will come to Navayn Manor before winter."

Thomas's shoulders eased. "That's a relief."

"She is worried," the duchess said, "that her woodland tunics will be despised here. I will send her clothing that is *suitable for Lord Navayn's mother*, to use her words." The duchess narrowed her eyes at the windows, where her gaze had snagged several times. "And no matter how sentimental you feel over the hangings in this salon, Thomas, I will send fabric with Tristan when he comes for the hunt—amber, perhaps. For truly, those rags around the windows are beyond hideous!"

Thomas laughed. "I have *no* affection for them, my lady. Are you not coming for the hunt?"

"Not with such a good excuse." She patted her belly. "I cannot ride with the hunt when I carry a child, and..." She daintily sneered. "...you know how *fond* I am of Lord Ivan. Tristan will come, though."

Time with Tristan—that, Thomas did long for. But why would he plan to come when his lady stayed away? Did they also fear for Thomas's safety during the hunt?

KING GAIRITH ACKNOWLEDGED the cheers from the residents of Maerton Castle Village who lined the road. Beside him in the carriage, Queen Ellianne bestowed her smile through the other window. Beyond the village's edge, they leaned back against the thick padding of the seat, and his wife sighed. "'Tis hard to smile."

He took her hand and held it loosely upon his knee. "Indeed, Lianne. We shall soon hear what the inspector has to say."

Their speed had not increased as it usually did when they left a village. Doubtless, the coachman was watching for the sign of a branch in the road. Soon, he stopped and called to one of the outriders. "Remove that from the road."

The carriage door jerked open, and the inspector leapt inside, then shut the door. They proceeded at a pace slow enough for the funeral they'd left behind. The inspector bowed from the forward seat.

"What have you learned, Inspector Curlow?" the king asked.

"With the aid of your discreet man at the nearest hamlet, I was fortunate enough to intercept the late duke's lawyer before he entered Maerton Castle Village. The lawyer tells me that there were not two but three wills."

"Indeed?" The queen murmured.

"The first, we all know of—written shortly after Lord Ivan's birth. The second must be the one Lord Maerton spoke of. It was completed within the last month, and the signature witnessed at the lawyer's establishment in Purthellia, which was contrary to the duke's habit of summoning his lawyer to Maerton Castle."

Odd, since lawyers were always summoned to noble clients. Gairith waited for more.

"At the same time that the second will was drafted, Duke Maerton instructed the lawyer to draft another will and hold it in secret. The duke sent for it shortly thereafter, and the lawyer dispatched it to Maerton Castle. Several days later, he received a note from the duke inquiring why it was delayed. He replied that he had already sent it. Then, he heard of the duke's death."

"Were you able to learn what these wills conveyed?"

"The lawyer was reluctant to state the contents without a formal public reading. Only when I asserted my authority to conduct an investigation on behalf of the crown, did he finally disclose the provisions that he considers troubling. The second will granted a considerable bequest of money to the duke's brother, to be paid on the duke's death, rather than ongoing payment from the estate. It also specified that if Ivan Maerton were deemed unfit to rule, then Sathe Maerton or his heir was to become the next duke rather than Ivan or any heirs that he sired."

A most unusual provision. That suggested something very disturbing about Lord Ivan.

The queen pursed her lips. "It has long been believed that the late duke prevented his brother from marrying. Lord Maerton has lately been staying in Othair Duchy, near the home of a certain widow. He had a long friendship with the couple and, at least in public, continued it with the widowed lady."

"Of what age is this widow?" the inspector asked.

"Thirty and some, I believe."

"What was in the third will?" Gairith asked.

Master Curlow raised his iron-gray brows. "That one declared Lord Ivan unfit to become duke and appointed Sathe Maerton as the fourth duke."

"Indeed?" The queen's accent hinted at all the concern that hardened Gairith's jaw. "Did he say why?"

"Nay." The inspector rumbled that word. "The lawyer insists he does not know the reason."

Years of shaky evidence would no longer be a problem...if only they had that will! Certain, Gairith would not make Ivan duke, but how could he legally avoid it if the will was destroyed? "How does the lawyer speak? Will he be able to make a convincing case in court?"

"I believe so. He claims to have the notes he took before drafting the wills."

"Ivan will contest," the queen said. "He has already cast doubt on his father's mental acuity of late."

"So I heard," the inspector said. "I asked the steward if that was so. He says the duke was always particular with every detail and remained so until the end. He saw no sign of mental failing. The only detail I was able to get from him was that, about a week ago, he entered the duke's presence unexpectedly. He thought the duke looked sad, though the expression passed at once."

"Everyone looks sad now and then," Gairith said.

"Quite so."

Gairith pondered for a moment. "Assuming the lawyer's words are true, Duke Maerton knew something about Ivan. That could be either madness or a crime. It would have to be severe to cause him to disinherit his son. Worse than the suspected murder of the Duchess of Maerton. Again, I worry about plans to murder Lord Navayn."

"I have not forgotten, sire," Curlow said. "I have learned that Ivan hunts quite early on most mornings. Sometimes with a friend—Newton Eberle—more often, with just the gamekeeper. If he takes down prey, he leaves the gamekeeper to clean it and rides on alone. If they take nothing, he sends the gamekeeper home, and still rides on alone."

"Does he hunt on or near the Navayn estate?"

"Nay, sire. To the west or northwest. The gamekeeper said he doesn't want to chance tracking game onto Navayn land and being obliged to send Lord Navayn a quarter fee. I am curious to know where he goes, but I cannot follow him myself. Perhaps the abundant deer could draw a few hunters to the area. Your men, of course, but in homespun."

"I shall provide them, at least through the hunt."

"Speaking of the hunting party," the queen said, "the Seltas will attend, so Lady Sareen will again be in company with both Lord Ivan and Lord Navayn. This worries me—possible fuel for Lord Ivan's jealousy."

CHAPTER 34

Sareen took care to keep irritation from her voice. "Nay, Mother, I shall take Adonna." She bent to look at a bellflower, alone on its spent stem, for her mother would be wearing her longsuffering expression. Constraints followed Sareen everywhere, even into the gardens beyond the walls of Selta Castle.

"But, dearest," her mother said, "she is not very good at arranging your hair."

"I don't care as much for that as I care that she can ride in the hunt with me. I'd think you would be glad that I have a female escort among all those men."

"I'd be happier if you didn't ride with the hunt at all. Just think if you were to fall."

"Just think if I were to be as bored as I am here."

Her mother sat down on one of the garden benches. "In truth, my dear, you need something to do. Something that matters." She extended a hand toward the dower house beyond the gardens, the current abode of her oldest brother, Joseff, and his young family. "Look how happy Marion is with Joseff and her children."

They did seem content in the well-kept house beyond the row of perfectly spaced trees and squared-off hedges. But then, they would inherit the titles of Duke and Duchess of Selta. They already tended to many things when her parents traveled. Sareen didn't begrudge them their prescribed future. 'Twas her own future she longed for. That and...the man she thought of far too often.

She had hoped...but he hadn't asked. A secret agreement would have been enough. No word from him in all these weeks. Now, she wavered between thinking he didn't truly care for her and thinking it just wasn't the right time yet. He needed to establish himself on his estate. Which made perfect sense...and didn't help at all.

Her father trod the manicured path down the slope from the castle. The sun glinted on the silver in his black hair...quite a lot of silver now, but he was still vigorous and firm-shouldered. He reached them and smiled at her. "Enjoying the gardens before they give up entirely?"

"The chrysanthemums and asters are still in bloom," Sareen said. Why was she defending flowers?

"Mm. I've received a letter from young Nardell."

Oh, dear. John Nardell had been courting her, and he'd hovered at the funeral—as much as anyone could when Lord Ivan was nearby.

"He asked my permission to offer you marriage."

"Oh, that is fabulous!" her mother exclaimed.

Sareen picked a white chrysanthemum. Silly. She had no need of it, and now it would die.

Her mother was expounding the benefits of the marriage—really any marriage, for said benefits seemed to have little to do with the husband. He would become lord of a small estate, somewhere in the south of Fennish Duchy, if she remembered correctly. Sareen felt...nothing. Best to let her mother talk it all out.

"I daresay, his estate is a little smaller than you are used to, but you must know, my dear, *all* of them are smaller than our home."

Sareen spun the flower between thumb and forefinger. "The size doesn't matter," she said.

"Really?" Her mother's voice was dry.

"Fine," Sareen snapped. "I'll admit it used to matter when I was young and silly, but it doesn't anymore. The man matters." Then, she felt guilty, for her mother's eyes had rounded as she drew her head back. "I'm sorry I snapped at you, Mother."

Her classic longsuffering look returned. "Do you perceive some fault in John Nardell?"

"Nay, no fault." Nor anything else.

"Then..." She sighed. "Will you at least think on it?"

"He mentioned in the letter," her father said, "that he will be at Maerton Castle for the hunt."

"He'd better not push his suit there," Sareen said. "Ivan had the nerve to hint at *our future* the very day his father was buried. He would be livid if I accepted another man's offer under his very roof."

"I doubt John Nardell would make such an obvious mistake," her father said. As Sareen spun her flower, her father extended a hand to his wife, who took the hint and strolled away with him.

Only two days until they would leave for Maerton Castle. Sareen wouldn't even have Beth to bear her company, and all her friends were married now. Still friends, but it wasn't the same as it had been.

She walked a garden path and turned when it did. What was she going to do? John Nardell was courteous, and if his conversation tended to be rather ordinary...well, life was just that, or it wouldn't be called ordinary. 'Twas said that sometimes husbands and wives learned to love one another after they were married. Dismal thought. Did it work if you already loved someone else? What if the person you loved didn't return your affection? Or just never reached the point of asking. 'Twas probably hard to ask, after all...considering how often Thomas had been disdained. But she would still have to give an answer to John Nardell. 'Twas not as though she could say, *please wait until I see if someone I like better asks me.*

She needed to know what Thomas intended. Whether he actually loved her. And she needed to know now. But *he* didn't realize the urgency. That left it up to her to find out for sure. Her stomach turned queasy. So dreadfully unladylike, this would be. What if he—nay! She wouldn't let doubts talk her out of this, or she'd die wondering. She would have to be brave. Like Thomas. If he could do the things he'd done against all odds, she could flout the conventions! She left the path and strode across the grass between flowerbeds…and got her feet all wet.

THOMAS FINISHED his breakfast coffee and went outside to check on the harvesting. Sunny but cool, the weather favored the laborers. No matter their normal professions, almost everyone was in the fields. If not swinging the scythes, they pitched the stalks, or bound them into sheaves, or loaded the carts, or performed one of the random tasks that the steward and reeve had settled upon. The grain would now be safe if deer fled from the woods before horsemen.

Thomas shadowed his steward for most of the day, but in the afternoon rode into the village. Rewarding his patience, Sallie placed a polished lynxeye bowl in his hands.

"'Tis a simple little piece," she said, "but I'm getting the knack of it."

Amber wound through the brown, and the satiny texture against his fingers thrilled him. "This one I shall always keep to remind me of this moment."

Sallie beamed. More so when he paid for her work and bade her polish a memento lynxeye for herself.

Thomas showed off his treasure to Jonathan, who waited

outside, then tucked it into his doublet. They rode home and discovered that Duke Tristelle had just arrived.

Captain Cotrell and Frith led horses off toward the stable, while Tristan surveyed the small herd of goats nibbling the front lawn under the watchful eyes of a goatherd and Nander.

"Your herd seems to be increasing," Tristan said, as Thomas dismounted and passed his reins to Jonathan.

Thomas did a quick count—all seven still present. "Aye, that dog finds no greater joy than fetching in new ones. After the harvest and hunt, we'll work on fencing and some structures in the goat pasture—formerly known as wasteland." He patted Nander, who'd dashed over for a brief greeting, then raced back to his duties. Thomas reached into his doublet and withdrew the lynxeye bowl. "Look. The first finished piece from my lynxstone quarry."

"Ah." Tristan took it and swept his fingers along the twining amber. "There is just something about lynxeye that begs to be touched."

"'Twas not even good quality stone that I gave her to practice on. I'm sure, now, that I can gain income from it."

"Doubtless."

After a pleasant dinner of elderbird soup, roasted venison, and a medley of fresh-harvested vegetables sauteed with herbs, Thomas invited Tristan to his library. He also included Jonathan and Captain Cotrell. "Nothing like your library, my lord," he said to Tristan as they entered.

The duke glanced toward the door, which Jonathan was just closing. "Privacy enough, with those who understand. Let us be Tristan and Thomas."

"With pleasure—Tristan." Thomas caught Jonathan's eye and nodded to the side table, where a tray with a bottle of wine and four goblets waited. Jonathan bent to his task, while the other three sat near the fireplace. "Maerton's gamekeeper stopped by yesterday," Thomas said. "Now I know why the herd is out of control. Can you believe that Duke Maerton pays a bounty on wolf and lynx skins?"

Captain Cotrell snorted, and Tristan said, "Small wonder, the way Ivan loves to hunt."

"The gamekeeper looked askance when I asked that, and he had to reveal folly to answer my question. He really came to discuss hunting strategy."

"By drive and bow, I assume," Tristan said, raising eyebrows in question.

"Aye, on the first day," Thomas replied. "They are already hemming in the deer. Tomorrow morn, the archers will take position in my woodland as the riders spread out near the castle, then begin a slow drive this way. They've obviously done this before, and he showed Jonathan and me the best archer positions."

"He plans it well," Tristan said. "He is a skillful gamekeeper and hunter—with keen ears, too, according to my own expert." He cocked his head toward Cotrell, then accepted a goblet from Jonathan. "We four will be together among the archers, then?"

"Exactly where we choose to be." Thomas couldn't help relishing that. This was his land, and the decision was his. "There will be two lines back-to-back, shooting as the deer run past on either side. Lord Ivan will be at the head of our line, with some of his honored guests between him and me." He sipped the wine Jonathan handed him.

Cotrell uttered a grunt. "That is adequate protection until we have to give chase to those deer that are hit but not killed."

"True enough," Thomas said, "but most will be flushed from the woods. The fields are cleared, and we may ride where it suits us."

"Which is far from any deer that Ivan may follow," Tristan said. "I think there is little opportunity for a foul deed when we are spread on open ground with many fellow hunters."

"There is one spot that worries me for that first day." Jonathan sat down beside his father. "The keeper showed us where they serve the meal—an area near the lane that branches from the road within Maerton's woodland. 'Tis cleared of brush, but all around it, there are places where one could conceal himself."

"I know the spot," Tristan said. "Don't be drawn alone into the brush, Thomas, but there should be no problem among the feasters."

"What of the second day?" Cotrell asked Thomas.

"Much the same, but heading north from Maerton Castle. Then, after a day to rest and scout, they will likely hunt in smaller parties."

Tristan nodded. "Typical. This is the part that worries me. Lord Ivan would not do anything obvious, but something that looked like an accident is another matter. How strong is your desire to continue riding with the hunt?"

"It matters not. I want the meat for my household and tenants, and I want to keep the herd from eating all that grows and stripping the bark from every tree in my forest. That is enough for me." Not entirely true. Only hunting with Lady Sareen would satisfy him, but he couldn't say that.

THOMAS DREW cool air into his lungs. The fair sky promised perfect weather. Though he did not hunt for sport, he couldn't deny the pleasures of his bow in hand, a quiver full of arrows, and friends at his sides beneath the forest's golden canopy. So too, he found a certain satisfaction in the clean hits that brought deer to ground. By the time the drivers reached the archers, he knew the count would be high. Better yet, the Seltas followed the deer along his side of the line, Lady Sareen riding between her father and brother.

The archers separated to track injured deer, while common huntsmen began work on the fallen beasts. Lord Ivan beckoned the Seltas to join him, but at least Thomas got a smile and a speaking look from Lady Sareen. If only he knew how to interpret it.

They had no time to talk, anyway, for quick work was needed to spare the injured prey undue pain. That done, and the deer hung from tree limbs, the party regrouped for a mid-day meal. Carriages brought the guests who didn't ride in the hunt, and carts bore the makings of a feast. Such a crowd filled the space that they had to tie the horses here and there in the brush.

Thomas washed in the stream and quenched his thirst with a tankard of ale. Rugs were spread along the ground—the one where Lady Sareen sat with her mother also included Lord Ivan. Tristan and Thomas sat down with the Duke and Duchess of Prushane and their eldest son, who was still years from manhood.

The woods rang with festive banter and laughter as appetites were sated and ale flowed. Thomas caught Ivan's loud descriptions of each of his kills. He seemed oblivious to Sareen's averted gaze. She escaped him as the guests began to stroll about, but two other bachelor nobles each found an opportunity to walk with her hand on their arm.

Thomas let his gaze drift wide, so he would not seem to stare even as he followed her progress. He would wait, for she always distributed her favor in equal measure. As usual, the servants had settled on the outskirts of the group, taking their turn to eat now. The squires and huntsmen mingled with the cook staff of Maerton Castle, while the gamekeeper moved about through the woods. Thomas would have assumed he was checking with the common hunters—if he had ever bothered to converse as he walked. Was he searching for something?

Lady Sareen flicked her gaze toward Thomas. His opportunity to get a few minutes of conversation with her. Thomas approached and bowed over her hand. "My lady, have you enjoyed the morning's hunt?"

Obvious, but he must play the game. Already, she'd placed her hand on his arm and turned from another gentleman. She strolled with him, drawing him away from others even more than he'd intended.

Her spritely voice chimed—too tense—then hurried into hushed words. "We must speak. Alone."

He scanned the area as he answered her louder words. Certain, she meant him no harm. Perhaps that bush would give enough privacy. Nay, the gamekeeper again. Thomas circled away from him and walked the trodden ground that skirted a broad tree trunk. "There is no *alone* here," he murmured. "Visit me."

"That's not private, either." She stopped and turned to him. Visible to the guests, but her back to them. "Do you know the clearing where the stream crosses your boundary?"

"Aye."

"Meet me. I'll set out at dawn. Tell no one." She turned naturally, with some genteel phrase on her lips, and drew him into conversation with one of the ladies of Maerton Duchy, which Lord Ivan promptly joined.

Thomas slipped away. What was wrong? Why did she need him? He hadn't gotten a chance to answer her, but certain, he would meet her.

CHAPTER 35

Drossin shivered beside the coals where he'd roasted a rabbit. The darkening night wasn't all that cold, but he couldn't stop shaking. The master didn't like him making a fire, but he'd told him to pretend he hunted deer in these woods. Who stayed the night in the woods to hunt and didn't build a fire? Made no sense.

'Twas often the way of it. First, he was supposed to stay nigh, then linger far away among the caves, then be nigh again. But always out of sight. Why tell him to come where the hunters were *and* stay out of sight? Half crazy, this master. Worse, he hadn't brought wine this morn.

Drossin's horse lifted its head, ears forward. Drossin stood. A moment later, soft footsteps padded on the leaf-strewn path. The master stepped from between the trees, only the outline of his cocked hat identifying him. Not even on horseback, this time. Maybe he didn't need one so nigh the castle.

"Put out the fire," he said, so quiet Drossin could hardly hear.

"Any hunter would have a fire. Why can't—"

"Quiet. You are moving to a different spot. Now."

"It's too dark, and I ain't goin' nowhere if ye didn't bring what you promised."

"Stop whining," the master said. "You'll know the spot, for you've been there before. The little clearing along the stream by the old border stone. I left the bottle for you there."

Twisting the deal again. Drossin slid his thumbs up and down the sides of his fingers as he tried to think. He was tired of this, but he couldn't figure out how to get the upper hand. "That's not what you promised."

"True. 'Tis better than what I promised. You don't want to be out here in the winter. You'd be much happier with a fat purse and going off wherever you please. You'd never have to see me again. And your final task is easy. Just make sure no one else camps there tonight. At dawn, I'll bring you coin. You can come back here for the horse and then ride as far away as you please. Just douse the fire, walk there now, and settle down with the bottle of wine that's waiting to quench your thirst."

"How do I know 'tis really there?"

The master spread his empty hands. "It isn't here."

Drossin huffed.

"Stay the night here," the master said, "and you'll never again see any of my food, wine, or coin. Go to the clearing where I left the wine, and if I find you there at dawn, you'll have a fat purse and never need to do my bidding again."

"Fine," Drossin muttered, then kicked dirt onto the fire. The master turned and strode into the moon-etched shadows.

Might as well try it, for there was nothing to drink here. Even if the cur lied, the next spot was no worse than this one. But Drossin was taking the horse, 'cause he was leaving tomorrow whether the master paid him or not.

Drossin saddled the horse, whispering to him, "I won't leave ye, lad. Daresay, he's planning to snitch ye when my back is turned. You're better off with me than him, aren't ye?"

The horse nudged him.

"Aye, ye know it too." Drossin rubbed that warm, noble nose, then slung his few belongings onto the saddle. Hard to see the trail at night, so he walked it, leading his one true friend. When he found the bottle as promised, he snatched it up. Too light to be full. He cursed the master in his thoughts, while he took a long pull.

He lowered the bottle for a few breaths. There was some truth in the master's words, so maybe he'd see coin after all. He tied the horse to a tree, loosened the girth, then took his pack and blanket from the saddle. After getting comfortable on the ground, he put the bottle to his lips again.

SAREEN WOKE a dozen times during the night, fearful she would sleep past dawn. Twice now, she'd sent Adonna to the window to check.

This time, Adonna dropped the curtain and said, "'Tis not dawn, but it must be nearing. Let us dress, since you cannot sleep anyway." She lit a candle, keeping the light shielded from window and door.

Sareen slipped into Adonna's extra clothes. They'd be recognized as servants of Selta, and with so many houses represented in the castle, the guards would not question it. A good thing the cool nights made hooded cloaks reasonable.

Adonna peeked out the window. "I fancy I see a bit of gray in the sky. Let's go down and see if that stable lad can be trusted to do as he's told."

That part of the plan worked too. Adonna gave the lad a copper coin and took the reins of their saddled horses. Maerton colors high on a mast caught a ray of the dawn, but all else fell under the shadow of the dark walls towering around them as they crossed the bailey. Sunlight etched one side of the open gate, and carts were already rattling over the cobblestones, laden with the day's produce. Sareen and Adonna fell into step behind a couple of village women heading out with empty bread baskets. Sareen kept her hood up, but Adonna's was down. If she were recognized, it would make sense that she led horses belonging to Selta. They passed beneath the gatehouse without question.

Sareen's stomach eased a little when they made the turn beyond the gate and walked along the road. Only when trees hid them from the castle walls, did they stop to mount.

"Maerton guards are lazy or stupid," Sareen said.

"Maybe they don't care as long as the horses do not belong to Maerton. Or maybe they *did* recognize you and know the horse is yours."

Sareen twisted her lips down. "If that was meant to ease my mind, it didn't!"

THOMAS WALKED QUIETLY with Jonathan to the stable. No point in bothering those who slept. He refilled his quiver with arrows and strapped it on while Jonathan saddled the first horse.

The stablemaster jerked the door beyond the tack room open and glared at them, still clad in his nightshirt.

Thomas stepped into the faint light of the open stable door. 'Tis I—no need for alarm. Just taking an early ride. You can doze a few minutes more."

Jonathan led the second horse from a stall as the stablemaster mumbled and closed the door. Thomas filled Jonathan's quiver for him, and soon they were mounted.

"I still don't like this," Jonathan whispered, "even though it was Lady Sareen who asked it of you."

They kept the horses to a walk, well away from the back of the manor, letting the grass muffle the sound of hooves. "I cannot be ambushed if Ivan doesn't know I'm coming," Thomas said.

"Unless he does."

"We'll take it slow. I watch, you listen. We have swords on our belts, bows in hand, and arrows nocked. I don't know what more we could do, but I cannot leave Lady Sareen waiting alone in the woods."

A HORSE NICKERED in Drossin's befuddled dream. It nickered louder and stamped a hoof. Harsh to his aching head. He cracked his eyelids. The highest branches glowed golden in dawn's first light. His horse shifted and blew.

Dawn. A restless horse. This clearing. Why was he here? Memory shifted sluggishly into place. The master had said he'd come at dawn. With coin. Freedom.

Drossin tried to stand and fell sideways. Woozy, but he could roll his blanket…tie it to his pack. Why did the horse keep fidgeting? It knew the master…never worried at his approach. Maybe hunters were out.

With the aid of a tree, Drossin gained his feet, took a few breaths, and staggered to his horse. "Easy, easy, my lad." He stroked its neck beneath the coarse mane…ran a hand down its nose.

He heard stirring in the forest now. A horse approaching at a walk…through the woods, not the trail. His horse held steady, so this might be the master. Drossin needed to look sober. He straightened and tugged the hem of his jerkin down.

The master, it was. Bow in hand and dressed for hunting, as he always was these past weeks. He held a finger against his lips. Drossin pressed his mouth closed to show he understood.

The master dismounted a few yards from the clearing and tied his horse. He walked soft as a fox, bow pointing at the ground, as he used his right hand to pull a leather purse from his belt. The drawstrings were tied, and it was indeed a fat purse.

Drossin's heart beat faster. It better be fat with coin.

The master lowered his arm and, with a gentle swing, tossed the purse. It arced too wide for Drossin to catch and landed beyond him with a thud and enticing chink. Coin. He'd kept his word, after all. There better be silver and not just copper. How much?

Drossin spun and took a step, reaching for it. Something smacked his back, and he pitched to the ground. He barely caught himself. Even still, his forehead struck dirt, jarring his aching head. Curses, the pain in his chest! He rolled right to relieve the other side. Tangy warmth flowed over his tongue. He coughed. Once, for the pain stopped it. 'Twas blood that sprayed over his arm.

Boots stepped past him. That snake!

The master untied Drossin's horse. He gave it a hard slap, and the horse bolted from the clearing. That lying, murdering snake picked up the purse, then bent enough for Drossin to see his face. Calm eyes stared at him. Inspecting.

Drossin longed to curse him. Tell him to burn forever. But breath—excruciating. Dawn's light narrowed until darkness swallowed the master's crooked eyes.

RAYS CUT low between the trees, flicking shadow and light across Thomas's gaze.

Riding abreast on the trail, Jonathan whispered, "There is a horse walking in the distance."

Thomas searched as far as tree trunks allowed. "I cannot see her yet."

A few paces farther, Jonathan pointed westward. "The horse is moving off that way. I hear two more coming from the northeast."

Maybe that was Sareen. Thomas hoped someone did ride with her. The trail they followed curved that way through Maerton's woodland. He could hear the stream's gurgle now, but not the horses Jonathan mentioned. They reached the point where they had recently trampled a path to the border stone. "Wait here," Thomas whispered. "If you see her, motion her toward the clearing. If you see anyone else, greet them so I know who. We are scouting, of course."

Jonathan's mouth formed a hard line. "I should stay with you."

"You're close enough. Defend this side, and I will watch the other. You know the whistle if I need you." Thomas dismounted and walked the path with the silence he'd practiced since youth. He kept his bow up, fingers on the string and slightly drawn.

He paused behind a trunk, listening for a moment. No sound from the clearing. He stepped between two trees at its edge. His breath caught.

A man lay on the ground, his back to Thomas. An arrow protruded from it. Piercing the lung, at least. Maybe the heart.

A lifetime of vigilance made Thomas scan the forest again. No movement anywhere. He whistled a sharp summons to Jonathan as he stepped forward, then knelt to see if the man was alive. Blood from his mouth made that unlikely, but Thomas felt for breath. None, but... He squinted. Could it be him?

What a lot of noise his whistle caused. Horses' hooves thudded from Jonathan's direction. Thrashing bushes and booted footsteps on the opposite side. A man dashed into the clearing from that direction, seconds before Jonathan.

Thomas leapt to his feet. He'd dropped his arrow. Too close to draw another, he cast his bow aside and grabbed his sword hilt.

The man shouted, "Hold in the name of the king!" His sword hissed out with the words.

"Who are you?" Thomas demanded.

"Curtis, of the king's men."

"You don't look it," Jonathan snarled, an arrow trained on the man.

"'Course I don't look it, fool."

Thomas recognized him now, though it had been a few years. "Lower your bow, Jonathan. I've seen him ride with the king." Thomas shoved his half-drawn sword home in its scabbard.

"You also ride with the king," Jonathan declared, but obeyed.

"Calm down," Thomas said. This was no time to irritate one of the king's men, even if he was dressed like a common hunter. "Pray pardon my reaction, but I just found a man shot in the back."

"Aye," the man growled, his eyes turning every which way. He dragged a leather thong out from the neck of his shirt and put the tube it held to his lips. A harsh whistle pierced the woodland silence and made Thomas grit his teeth. Two more men with bows came running and positioned themselves beside Curtis, who sheathed his sword.

Horses trotted through the woods from the trail. Lady Sareen! Thomas must stop her from coming. Too late. He could see her now, alarm clear on her face. Thomas held up a hand. "Stop, my lady. Return to the castle." That accomplished nothing.

"Damnation!" Curtis muttered. "How many folk are in the woods at the crack of dawn? Stay at the edge, ma'am."

'Twas likely the gruesome sight that stopped Sareen. Her mouth gaped. "What happened?" She grew squeaky, for certain she'd spotted the arrow. "Did a hunter shoot awry? Who is it?"

"Does anyone here know that?" Curtis asked.

Did the man always growl when he spoke? "I think I might," Thomas said. He squatted, hands on his knees, and peered again at the face. The light was better now, revealing a rough, reddened nose and a wide bald spot fringed with gray hair. Thomas imagined him with a hat. "I don't know his name, but I believe this is the fellow who showed me where the ruins of Kaituer Castle lay and tried to take me there. The day before I actually visited and someone shot an arrow at me."

"Is that so?"

Why did people ask that of the one who had just spoken? Thomas stood and glanced around. A pack lay on the ground. A wine bottle. Horse dung. His bow where he'd thrown it. He bent to reach for it.

"Leave that," Curtis snapped.

Thomas stopped in surprise. "'Tis mine. Did you not see me throw it aside?"

"What I saw was a bow in your hand with no arrow. Except for the one in this man's back."

Wind rushed in Thomas's ears, though none blew. Curtis couldn't actually think that *he'd* shot the dead man. "I did have an arrow. I must have dropped it when I knelt to see if he was alive." He looked for it. The elderbird feathers of the fletching blended with a few fallen leaves, but the shaft was fair easy to spot. He pointed. "'Tis there."

Another grunt from Curtis. "Half covered with leaves. Some arrows are always lost in the hunt."

'Twas true that the tip was covered, but he'd walked and knelt here. Which was so obvious that Thomas couldn't think how to say so. Curtis knelt and touched the blood on the dead man's chin. Partly congealed, but it still smeared. He looked around more as he dug inside his jerkin and pulled out a scarf of green and gold. This was about to get serious.

Curtis knotted the king's colors around his throat and tucked the ends into his jerkin. "Lord Navayn, I arrest you in the name of the king. Please hand me your quiver."

The horses fidgeted behind him. Lady Sareen hissed, "How dare you!"

Curtis remained impassive. "I dare because the king does not employ men who are too cowardly to act when the evidence demands it."

Thomas turned his head as he lifted the quiver strap over it, for he feared Sareen would be hard to silence. "Please, my lady. Berating him will not help."

"He speaks true, lady in servant's clothing." Curtis took the quiver from Thomas, though he glared at Sareen. "Who, exactly, are you, and why did you come here?"

"I am Lady Sareen of Selta, and it is none of your business why I chose to ride this direction."

Curtis grunted. "Unbuckle your sword belt, Lord Navayn."

The Navayn sword. His for a month. And his Kaituer dagger hung on the same belt. 'Twas hard to breathe. One of Curtis's cohorts had his bow drawn, the arrow aimed at Thomas's chest. He had no choice. Though his fingers were numb, he opened the buckle and held the heavy belt out to Curtis.

The king's men conferred, and one left with Thomas's weapons while Curtis asked the names of Adonna and Jonathan. Soon, more of the king's men-at-arms arrived, these dressed in the emerald-green doublets and buff trousers of the House of Fraetinloch.

'Twas strange enough to penetrate the stunned paralysis that held Thomas. Had the king arrived? When? If not, why so many of his men? And the ones in common garb, why were they here? He needed to get his brain working again.

One of the king's men bowed from his saddle to Lady Sareen. "My lady, may I escort you back to Maerton Castle?"

"Nay. I am riding with Lord Navayn."

"My lady," Thomas said gently. He waited for her gaze. "Please, if you wish to aid me, ride back to the castle now. Be with your family when news of my arrest breaks."

Her shoulders rose and fell. Though her eyes were glossy, she turned haughtily to the lieutenant with the braided cord at his shoulder. "Where are you taking him?"

"To the guard tower at Maerton Castle."

She gasped. "Nay!"

"We are not fools, Lady Sareen. Only the king's men shall guard him."

She straightened and pressed her lips to a tight line. To the man who had approached her, she said, "I accept your escort."

Some relief—a very tiny bit—slid between Thomas's shoulder blades. Curtis had untied his scarf and shoved it out of sight. He turned quietly with his companion and faded into the woods. Thomas addressed the lieutenant. "Will you permit my squire to depart?"

"To where?"

"Navayn Manor."

"If you ride straight there," the lieutenant said to Jonathan, "you may keep your bow and sword. Shadow us, and I will arrest you too."

"I'll go to Navayn Manor," Jonathan said.

"Take his horse with you."

The horses shifted behind Thomas, the beat of their gait receding. He was alone...with captors.

They bound his hands, mounted him on a horse, and tied him to the saddle. Thomas fought a wave of nausea from his dry stomach. Someone led the creature. The king's men rode on all sides of him. Guard formation—escort for a criminal...a murderer.

Entering Maerton Castle drove another jab to his heart. People gaped at him or jeered, uttering the name of Kaituer. Thomas kept his back straight and his face clear of the chaos he felt. The captain of Maerton Castle grinned broadly upon learning the guard tower was needed—and gave tongue to his outrage when he grasped that the king's men commandeered it. Thomas began to hope that the fool would keep raging, for the king's lieutenant was fast losing patience. Unfortunately, the captain must have realized his danger and withdrew in time.

Then, at sword point, Thomas was marched up the stone stairs. Within a bare circular chamber, his hands were loosed, and the thick door slammed. Arrow-slit windows provided faint light.

Thomas trod the cold stone slowly. None of this seemed real. Like shattered stained glass...the pieces all askew with no meaning...no purpose. Except to cut. His heart refuse to slow. *God...* His throat would not open. *Certain, I should have asked you for help first, but...even now, I know not what to say.* Had Sareen gotten to the castle safely? What was she doing...thinking? *God of hope...* Even his mind strangled on that word, for he felt none. *Give her wisdom and...and the serenity of her name.*

That brief prayer almost unleashed tears. By some means that he couldn't imagine, he blinked them from his eyes and held down the rising pressure. Just as well, for the blind over the door grate slid open, and a voice bade him move to the far side.

When he complied, the door opened on two guards. One watched. The other brought a few things inside. "I drew the flagon of water myself," he said. "The bread is from our food rations." He set the flagon, bread, and wooden mug on a stool, then put a bucket by the wall. The door slammed again, and iron scraped.

Perhaps Thomas should be grateful. Maybe later.

He peered through an outer arrow slit. The road toward Navayn Manor lay empty. From the inner slits, he obtained a view of the bailey and gate, though it took much shifting around. He found the top of Lord Ivan's brown, pomaded hair and discovered he was listening to complaints from his captain. Thomas strained to hear. Could he catch enough words to make sense of them?

Then, Ivan tilted his head to gaze at the tower. With a broad smile, he said, "I care not who guards him. 'Tis enough that Thomas Kaituer is imprisoned for murder in Maerton Castle."

Thomas leaned his back against the curved wall. Though Ivan's sneers were commonplace, those words cut. What would come of all this? He felt condemned already.

A nearer voice shouted, perhaps from the wall. "Summon the stablemaster. There's a riderless horse outside."

Likely, the rider had taken a fall. At least a horse could not discourage Thomas. He found it through an outer slit. 'Twas a restive creature. Someone drew it in, then an uproar ensued in the bailey, and people scurried from the kicking, rearing horse. Hooves clacked on the cobblestone as it fled through the gate again, galloped toward Navayn, then stopped to neigh and dart about. Soon, a calm rider emerged and walked slowly toward the frantic horse. It trotted out of sight, followed at a walk.

"Smart horse, to run," Thomas whispered. "Don't let them catch you."

And now he had nothing to watch. Had Jonathan told Tristan yet? What rumors would spread through Navayn Village? What was Sareen doing?

Torment to dwell on questions that could not be answered. What could he do? Not much in a cell. He paced, his thoughts spiraling in on certain aspects. He was locked up in Maerton Castle under the *king's* guard. That was strange. So, too, was the identity of the murdered man. And the fact that Thomas found him so soon after the murder. Who had murdered him? And was it far more than coincidence that Thomas found the body?

CHAPTER 36

Sareen refused to leave her bedchamber, admitting only her family and maid. Her mother sat by the fireplace and avoided all remonstrance until Sareen donned a riding habit instead of a day gown.

"I am not staying in this house and chattering with guests," Sareen declared. "I am leaving."

"Oh," her mother said, and folded her hands in her lap. "I can go with you, but your father should stay. We will see what he can arrange."

He joined them after a while. To Sareen's request, he said, "You cannot depart until Inspector Curlow has questioned you. After that...hmm. Where do you wish to go?"

"I'm not sure." She twisted her fingers together. "Certain, you must not leave, for a judgement may be needed and...and..." She gave up that sentence. "There is the village inn. 'Twould be close."

"I don't much care for that idea," he said. "Doubtless, some in the Castle Village have reason to be loyal to the House of Maerton."

"I don't like it either," she said. "Perhaps that ale house in

Navayn Village might have a room or two." Probably horrible rooms, if any, but 'twould be better than here.

Someone tapped on the door, then her brother's voice asked, "May I come in?"

"Please do." When he entered, Sareen asked, "What have you heard, Der?"

"Not much of use. Lord Ivan was angered that the day's hunting was to be cancelled, and he tried to overrule Inspector Curlow. That didn't work. Now Ivan's acting like nothing could make him happier than to entertain his guests in the mansion. Everyone else is speculating and making up theories. Oh, and the innkeeper identified the dead man as Drossin, an infrequent visitor to these parts. He doesn't seem to know anything of him except that his fortunes rose and fell."

"Strange," Sareen murmured.

Her father asked Der, "Could you tell when Curlow is going to ask for Sareen?"

"Probably soon. I told him she doesn't want to leave her room, and he said he would come up here."

When he did, Der admitted the inspector and said, "I'll wait in the corridor."

The inspector was courteous. He suggested they should talk alone, but when she declined that, he allowed her parents to stay. She told him what she knew and realized how little that was.

The only problem was explaining why she went there. "I just wanted to talk to him."

'Twas not enough to satisfy the inspector.

"'Tis hard to explain," she said. "We've been friends a long time because he was often at Tristelle Castle when I visited my cousin, the duchess. Lord Navayn is easy to talk to. He listens, and he says things that matter, instead of just compliments and polite nothings. But 'tis impossible to talk to him when Lord Ivan is around. He has such jealousies as though he owns me, I can only squeeze in a few minutes with any unwed man. I just wanted to talk with Thomas alone."

"Quite understandable," the inspector said. "When did you arrange the meeting?"

"At the midday feast, when we walked together a moment."

"Did you tell him why?"

"There was no time for that. I just named a place to meet. He didn't even have time to answer, for Ivan was watching and I had to speak of something else."

"Did anyone hear you?"

"I...I didn't think so. I whispered."

"Where was Ivan when you whispered?"

"I'm not sure. Behind me, but I don't know how close."

"I see. Thank you for the information, my lady."

She nodded, feeling that she had been no help to Thomas.

The duke said, "My daughter is uncomfortable remaining in this castle. Do you have any objection to her departure?"

"None at all, though I would like her to stay in the neighborhood." The inspector opened the door to leave, then paused to bow. "Duke Tristelle."

"Inspector. I'm told I cannot see Lord Navayn without your permission."

"Quite so." Curlow stepped back and gestured for the duke to enter. "Is there some urgent matter?"

"I brought him clothes, and since he is much like family to me, I wish to see how he fares."

"Mm. Did you know where he was bound this morn?"

"Nay. I didn't even realize he was gone until his squire brought us news. Which, I must say, is quite difficult to believe."

"I daresay," Curlow said. "You may leave his clothes with his guards." Duke Tristelle stared at him, his lips a hard line. Curlow bowed to the company, murmured, "My lords and ladies," and departed.

Dermont came back in, and soon they were rehashing things. Sareen couldn't complain, for Duke Tristelle must be told what they knew. But it all seemed hopeless. She walked to the window and stared out. All Thomas did was find a body. Someone had to find it. Why should the finest man in Lavaycia be imprisoned because he found a body? Because his name was Kaituer? Then there was no justice. And if there was no justice…he might be hanged. She patted at the tears around her eyes.

She should be paying attention, for the others spoke of a place for her to stay.

Her mother said, "'Tis most unusual, of course, to visit when he is not present, but Lord Navayn did give us an open invitation to his manor."

Sareen turned around as Duke Tristelle said, "You need not convince me. I'm sure Lord Navayn would be pleased to have you stay there." He lifted a gentle gaze to Sareen. "If that is where you wish to go, I will escort you."

"It is. I thank you."

She must look awful, for he said, "'Tis a hard time, but not a time to despair. Inspector Curlow will sift what evidence does— and does not—exist."

"Ah, the inspector!" she said. "Who failed to solve the questions of Duchess Maerton's death and the fire at Navayn Manor."

"Don't repeat that, my dear," her father said. "He has solved many other crimes, else the king would have dismissed him from his post."

"Are you staying here, sir?" Duke Tristelle asked her father.

He nodded. "I must, for I rank highest until the king comes. Or the royal duchess, of course, but I expect the king sooner."

"As do I. Regardless, I sent my courier off to my lady wife as soon as I heard from Jonathan."

"Oh, but she is with child," Sareen's mother said, "and should not travel in haste."

"I expect she will send me her proxy letter in haste and travel reasonably if she feels she can."

How slow the time passed. Thomas made use of the food and water. He watched meaningless activity through the arrow slits and paced the stone floor. At last, the door's blind slid aside, and he was told again to move away.

Inspector Curlow entered this time, and the door closed behind him. "I have some questions for you, Lord Navayn."

"I suppose so." For all Thomas looked down at the shorter man before him, he was the one at a disadvantage. He had trusted this man. Had that been wise? Curlow watched him in the dim room. 'Twas probably near noon—'twould grow no brighter.

"Before I start," Curlow said, "I have a piece of advice for you."

"I'm listening."

"Answer me with *complete* truth."

"That is my habit," Thomas said between his teeth.

"But now you are in difficulties, and it may be tempting to alter your habit. That would be unwise."

He launched into his queries then, and Thomas answered them all. None of the questions seemed to call for that strange warning. Nor did they cover the most important points. Until he asked the reason why Thomas went there.

"Have you spoken with Lady Sareen?" Thomas asked.

"That doesn't matter."

"Her reputation matters to me."

"Reputation!" Curlow scoffed. "You have a fine reputation, and you are accused of murder and locked in a tower cell. Lord Ivan has an atrocious reputation, and he preens before the highest society of the land. I care nothing for reputations. Only truth, so remember that and answer me."

Thomas rubbed his forehead. Why must everything be a conundrum! Words whispered within him. *Only a reputation built on truth has value.* Hoping that was a wise thought, he described his brief meeting with Sareen at the hunt feast.

Curlow watched him intently. "Could anyone have heard of your meeting place?"

"Before this morn, I would have answered *nay*. Now, I think it is possible."

"Who?"

"There is scattered brush around the feast clearing. Lady Sareen named the meeting place. She turned her back to the guests, but that means she was facing the brush. I didn't see anyone in that moment, but as I have been hashing over every detail, I recall that I often saw the gamekeeper moving around the outskirts of the clearing. In fact, he was nigh us when I first approached Lady Sareen. That's why I guided her to walk along the perimeter. To get away from anyone listening. But one thing, I didn't realize until today. I have watched broadly my entire life. I didn't stare at Sareen, but I kept her in view, for I could tell she was tense. And the gamekeeper was always in view too. 'Tis possible that he moved to stay nigh Sareen as she mingled. If so, he may have been in the brush, near enough to hear."

"I see."

That quick, Thomas's brilliant realization shriveled to nonsense. The gamekeeper's movement could have been pure chance, and this proved nothing. But he couldn't give up. "You haven't asked about the arrow."

"I know you said you dropped it. 'Twas fletched with elderbird feathers, as was the killing arrow. I know of your impressive skill as an archer. Do you drop a lot of arrows?"

"Very few. I find dead men less often. 'Tis disconcerting."

"Quite. So your arrow on the ground tells me nothing beyond the fact that dropping one is possible."

"What of the arrow in his back? Was it pulled out?"

"It was."

"What type of arrowhead did it have?"

"A blunt tip."

"A blunt arrow is only used for small game, not a deer or a man. The arrowhead must have remained within him when the shaft was pulled. Please do not let that poor man be buried with the arrowhead inside him."

"Why?"

"I know not what arrowhead pierced his back, but I do know what was in my quiver. Flint heads on every shaft, suitable for deer." No reaction from Curlow, but Thomas pressed on. "My quiver was taken from me in the woods. Can you get it? And make sure that no one here has access to it."

"Your weapons are held by the king's men. They will allow no one to meddle with them. Particularly after the captain of this castle made such a scene. What else did you find unusual?"

"I assume you will talk with my squire. He heard a horse moving westward from the clearing as we approached it. I did not hear it, but his ears are as keen as his nose. There was also horse dung in the clearing, but no horse."

"I saw it. Likely a few hours old."

"That horse..." Thomas murmured. He knit his brow, looking toward the arrow slit over the road. If the inspector saw nothing of interest in the gamekeeper or the arrow, he wouldn't care about a wandering horse.

"What horse?"

"A saddled horse came back to the castle without its rider. But it won't prove a thing."

"Perhaps not, but details intrigue me. Tell me."

"I saw it from that slit..." He pointed. "...and then from that one. They brought it into the castle and then it went wild and ran out again. It made a lot of noise and ran about in the road. A groom or...someone who knows horses...rode out slow after it. Then, the riderless horse ran down the road toward the Navayn estate." Thomas shrugged. That was a waste.

"What color was it?"

"A perfectly ordinary brown."

"Markings?"

"I saw none, but this is a poor vantage point to study markings on a frantic horse."

The inspector peered through the slits. "True. You are right that it proves nothing, but I thank you for indulging me. Anything else I should know?"

"Not that I can think of." Thomas rubbed the back of his neck. "Uh...how certain are you that it was murder and not an accidental shooting?"

"I pronounce certainty when I have evidence. Which do you think is most likely?"

"All I truly know is that *I* did not kill him." Thomas let his gaze wander the stone walls. "I suppose that since both murder and accident are possible, it doesn't matter which one is most likely."

"True enough," Curlow said with all the unconcern of one who was free to leave. He thumped the door, shouted, "Guard," and motioned Thomas to step to the back wall.

When the guard let Curlow out, he also delivered a bowl of stew, a fat heel of bread, crumbled cheese, and an apple. More than Thomas expected. Maybe his surprise showed, for the guard said, "We'll bring you the same rations that the king's men eat. Nothing from Maerton Castle."

Thomas was hungry enough to make short work of it. With most of it gone, he sat on the stool and leaned his back against the wall, staring at the half-eaten apple in his hand. They were in abundant supply right now, but...were prisoners fed anything more than what was needed to keep them alive? The guard's words...they fed him nothing from the castle. Why had he said that?

For a moment, Thomas felt protected. Folly. He was locked in a tower, accused of murder. Word was spreading. The people of Navayn Estate...and Tower Woods. His mother...how could she endure more loss?

And worst of all...Sareen. His throat tightened painfully. Might she blame herself for this? It couldn't have been her fault. But bad things happened to her when he was nigh. Even if he were released, he should stay away from her. He slumped, propping his elbows on his knees. He would never be safe in his own home. Just like in Tower Woods. He'd be hunted all his life. Forced to desert his estate. And his oath to his people. Lord Ivan would treat them worse than his father had.

BY THE TIME Sareen and her mother entered Navayn Manor, the duchess was complaining of a headache. Just what Sareen didn't need. The housekeeper came into the hall and stared at them with her mouth agape. The steward had met Duke Tristelle outside, and whatever trouble he'd reported took the duke off toward the stables. Though Sareen felt ready to shatter, this was up to her.

"Mother, please go upstairs and lie down. We'll use the same bedchambers as when we stayed here earlier." To their maids, she said, "See that the beds are made up and then unpack our things." She ordered the first manservant she saw to carry trunks upstairs, then turned to the housekeeper, who was wringing her hands and had been trying to interject a question. "Mistress Eldr—"

"My lady, what is happening? The rumors—'Tis terrible! They say Lord Navayn killed a man! That he's imprisoned in Maerton Castle." She ended on a squeak.

Sareen had run to this house as a refuge—and found only chaos. Her plan to shut herself up in her bedchamber would have to wait. Permanently? She could almost hear Thomas's tone. He would speak calm to his servants. So would she. Sareen drew a deep breath. "First and most important, Lord Navayn...did *not*... kill anyone."

"Well, and that is what his squire says, and truly, Lord Navayn doesn't seem like that sort, but half the village is saying we barely know him, and even if he is innocent, the Maertons will kill him and likely wreak vengeance on all who swore their oaths to him."

Oh, heavens, such a view had not even occurred to Sareen. By this time, a gaggle of wide-eyed servants had come from the kitchen corridor into the back hall. Sareen licked her lips and sought the most ordinary tone she could use. "The Maertons do not have custody of Lord Navayn. The king's men guard him, and the king will come. *He* will judge the matter."

A woman in a full-length apron—a cook, perhaps—with a face far too red, demanded, "But what if he did murder that man, and he's hanged? As soon as the king departs—"

"Enough." Sareen let silence emphasize her word, for she would not raise her voice. "If you want to worry about *what-ifs*, think on this. What if Lord Navayn returns to his home and finds the entire household has fallen to pieces because his servants deemed him a murderer?"

None ventured a response.

"If you are so fickle," Sareen said, "as to doubt Lord Navayn simply because he found a dead body in the woods, then perhaps you should leave his service at once."

The housekeeper settled her shoulders back and turned sideways to address those who had straggled into the hall. "And if ye leave now, do not be coming back here looking for work after our lord's name is cleared, for I will not have ye. And I'll not have any more talk of how he *could* have killed that poor soul or any such slander."

Her eyes rested on the cook, who muttered, "Well, I ne'er said I thought he *did* it, nor am I looking to run off...but what are we to do with a house full of guests and no master?"

"Making the noon meal is one thing you should be doing," Sareen said.

The cook exited, and a couple lasses followed her.

The housekeeper addressed those few who remained. "We still need to prepare for the arrival of Lord Navayn's widowed mother. Also, the fine amber cloth that Duchess Tristelle sent needs to be fashioned into hangings for the salon. I'll not fault ye for delay in your daily tasks, what with all this upset, but there is no more cause to dawdle."

That sent the last few servants away, and Mistress Eldred turned to Sareen. A hint of worry tightened her eyes, but she said, "I thank ye, my lady, for I fear I was too set on end myself."

Sareen tried for a smile, but her lips quivered. "I'll not deny this has been a hard morning for all."

The housekeeper touched Sareen's arm. "My lady, you're welcome here, but why did ye come?"

She pressed a hand to her chest. "I could not stay there. Lord Ivan...'tis hard enough when he is pompous and hovering around me. But now he will gloat over—" Sareen's eyelids fluttered with her determination not to cry. "I cannot help Lord Navayn at the castle, but perhaps I can help him here."

CHAPTER 37

A thin strip of light on the wall told Thomas the sun was sinking. Another empty day consumed by worry and despair. His knees ached from pacing on stone. Sitting on the stool only shifted the ache to his spine, and his shoulders never ceased hurting.

The thudding hooves of many horses drew Thomas to the arrow slit facing Maerton Castle Village. Arrivals usually came at a walk. Not these. All decked in the green and gold of the royal House of Fraetinloch, the foreriders advanced at a swift lope. They swept around the curve and under the gatehouse with nary a check. The king's carriage followed hard on their heels, and a sizable contingent followed.

Thomas crossed the cell to view the bailey. The king's men spread out and overwhelmed the men wearing the lighter, more yellowish green of Maerton. He recognized the voice of Captain Hurth barking orders and soon, the voice of Captain Benton too.

The king's carriage halted at the decorative arch leading to the courtyard and mansion, but the arrival lacked a certain air. No pomp. No royal calm. Though rigid order surrounded the king, chaos seemed to radiate outward, sweeping Maerton men aside like debris on an ocean wave. Nor did it abate.

Thomas spotted the king for only a moment as he strode through the archway of the low, inner wall. Captain Hurth must be at his side, for Captain Benton had taken charge of the bailey, which swarmed with activity. Horses were run from the stable out the gates. Maerton's men-at-arms emerged from the barracks, carrying lumpy bundles.

The king was taking over the barracks and stable. What did this mean?

～

Lord Ivan bowed before King Gairith. "Welcome to Maerton Castle."

Gairith let seconds pass. Ivan straightened from his bow. He resembled his mother more than his father, though his odd-set eyes made him look like no one else. "Have you found your father's will?"

"Nay, sire. I suspect—"

"Squire," Gairith said, "prepare the ducal bedchamber for my stay."

Ivan's nostrils twitched. "Sire, your usual suite is already prepared and will grant you the—"

"Do you object to my choice?"

"I only seek your immediate comfort. And while I would be honored to offer you my bedchamber, 'twill take time to prepare it for you."

"Squire, if you find Lord Ivan's belongings in the ducal chamber, put them in the corridor. Captain, send a man to assist my squire." Gairith relaxed his tone slightly and stepped farther into the mansion's grand hall, forcing Ivan to shift aside for him. "Lord Ivan, I am aware that bringing such a large party creates difficulties for a host. Thus, I have brought my steward, chef, and kitchen servants to relieve the imposition. They will arrive shortly."

"Thank you, sire," Whatever Ivan might be thinking, his

respectful tone hid it.

Gairith acknowledged the bows of the company in the hall, which was swiftly growing as the houseguests realized he'd arrived and came from salons or down the staircase. The ducal representatives of the houses of Selta, Prushane, and Portlen were present. The dukes of Fennish and Othair had declined the hunting party, but Gairith had sent them word of events, should they wish to be present. Doubtless, Duke Tristelle was at Navayn Manor—possibly useful, though 'twas Duchess Tristelle the king needed. Perhaps by tomorrow, he could proceed.

Thomas shivered within his damp blanket. He'd been grateful for it and the straw mat during the first night, but this night brought a storm, and the wind drove enough water through the slits to puddle on the stone floor.

Despair pursued him. He tried to blame it on the cold and wet. Darkness was always harder than daylight. He struggled to remember the encouragement that the priest from Navayn Village had murmured to him through the door grate yesterday. Some talk of comfort in a dark chasm, and that the villagers prayed for him at the rest day service. A good thing someone else prayed, because he couldn't. Why must he shiver in a dark chasm when he had dared to hope he was destined for more?

At dawn, the guards brought food. The one at the door held a lantern and surveyed the tower room with a glowering frown.

Thomas shoved himself upright, and a convulsive shiver sent an odd quaver through his groan.

"Nay, don't leave the food," the guard with the lantern said. "We'll take him down now."

Down where? And he *needed* food.

"Get up!" The guard demanded. He gripped Thomas's arm as tight as a tourniquet and said, "Don't do anything stupid," then he half dragged him through the door and down the torchlit steps. Another of the king's men eyed them, then opened a lower door.

Dreading whatever was to come, Thomas staggered through under the force of the guard's grip.

"Make room," the guard said. "We'll get no thanks for delivering him to the king sopping wet."

The light of a fire and a hanging lantern revealed benches and a table. This circular room connected to a straight wall, from which light and voices reflected. Thomas's mouth watered at the sight and smell of food. The guards shoved him onto a bench nearest the fire and slapped a bowl of stew in front of him.

Maybe his life wasn't ending just yet. They even gave him a tankard of coffee. Now that he thought about it, he probably wasn't supposed to die before his trial.

The guard who'd brought him watched through narrowed eyes and seemed to relax a bit when Thomas managed to straighten his shoulders without all the shivers. "Not as bad off as I thought, then," the guard said. "Duke Tristelle sent you clothes."

Thomas shed his hunting garb, washed with a bucket of hot water, and donned fresh trousers, shirt, and doublet. No razor to deal with his short growth of beard, but at least they provided a comb.

They were getting him presentable. To stand accused before the king. That still tied his stomach tighter than a bowstring, but he supposed he could bear it. After all, he'd stood before the king injured and condemned years before. That had ended rather well...until now. Ugh! He felt as if his spirits were being batted around like a tethered target. "When do I see the king?" Thomas asked the guard.

"We know not. Perhaps today. 'Tis said the king wants word from the north, but the weather's been bad, and the roads are mud. We'll be taking you back up the tower now."

More waiting. Plenty of time to ponder the chances of being cleared—and the certainty of future problems if he was. How could he ever live in Maerton Duchy? Or join hands with a wife? An idea occurred. Did he dare make so bold a demand of the king?

THROUGH AN ARROW SLIT, Thomas spotted Frith arriving on a tired, muddy horse. Someone must have been posted to inform him that Duke Tristelle was present in the castle. Thomas rehearsed words, for the summons would come soon.

Indeed, Captain Benton came for him and even accorded him a slight bow. "Lord Navayn, the king summons you."

"I am ready."

Beside the captain, a guard held a coiled leather thong. He stepped forward. "Extend your hands."

Thomas kept his eyes on Benton. "Is this necessary?"

"Probably not, but if it keeps you from doing anything stupid, 'twould be worth it."

"Captain, there is only one place I want to be right now, and that is standing before the king."

The captain quirked his mouth and said to the guard, "Leave him unbound. Descend ahead of us." He stepped aside, gesturing for Thomas to exit, and followed him down. They emerged from the tower entrance into the bailey.

Ah, fresh air and light! Thomas blinked in the glare. Normal mid-morning bustle was conspicuously absent. Only the king's men stood watch, and a groom led horses away. Their saddlecloths of purple streaked with white showed that the House of Fennish was represented. A scrape and bang of metal made Thomas look to the gate. It had just closed. He would have liked to ask why, but he must follow Benton. With a guard on each side, and one behind with sword drawn, tying his hands really would have been ridiculous.

They passed the arch and strode on toward the mansion. Relief carvings in the massive wooden doors depicted tower trees. The nerve of Prince Maerton to have taken that as the symbol of his house! Guards pulled the doors open, and Thomas followed Captain Benton into the vestibule and paused beside him at the edge of the noble hall. How different it looked than it had the day of the funeral. The clusters of chairs and sofas had been turned to face the center. Opposite the door, King Gairith sat upon a raised chair. Green and gold silk flowed around him, and the emerald-studded crown of Lavaycia declared his sovereignty. An ornate carpet covered the temporary dais and extended a couple yards. Two tables draped in linen stood below the dais, offset to either side. One supported tilted writing desks for the scribes. Inspector Curlow stood behind the other, which held Thomas's sword belt, quiver, and bow.

A herald intoned, "Sir Thomas Kaituer, Lord of Navayn, you are summoned before the king."

Thomas walked resolutely past the lords and ladies of Maerton Duchy and then the dukes and duchesses of Lavaycia. He caught a few key faces: Lord Ivan well separated from his uncle, Tristan with Jonathan standing behind him, and Sareen seated with her parents and brother. In the hush, the strike of his boots echoed off the stone floor. He halted at the edge of the carpet and bowed low. "My liege." He straightened and waited.

The king's deep voice carried—an address to all assembled. "A crime of murder is alleged in Maerton Duchy. Since there is no duke or duchess to lay a charge, I am come to determine whether a charge of murder is warranted, and if so, to issue that charge against the presumed murderer."

Thomas should hold his tongue. At most, acknowledge the king's words. Instead, he spoke. "My king and my liege, I, too, know of the death you speak of, and I am greatly relieved that you have come to determine the truth of the matter. I request also that you consider two other attempted murders in Maerton Duchy."

The whisper of many gasps behind him confirmed how audacious his words were, but he would not hold silent.

"The first was attempted against me at the ruins of Kaituer Castle," he said, "and the second at Navayn Manor. Though I believe the second was intended to kill me, it nearly killed Lady Sareen of the House of Selta. 'Tis even possible that the recent killing between Maerton Estate and Navayn Estate is an attempt to falsely accuse me, and by this means, kill me. Thus, I request your protection and justice, my liege."

The king raised his brows through much of this speech, and now replied, "I am honored by the faith you place in my judgement. Nonetheless, your proximity to the corpse at the time of death and the bow in your hand indicate that it was possible for you to have murdered the deceased. Before that is considered, I would know who the man was and whether the death could be accidental. Inspector Curlow, relate your investigation."

The inspector bowed to the king. "The deceased man used the name of Drossin. His place of birth and abode are unknown. He was first seen hereabouts this summer and occasionally stopped at the inn of Maerton Castle Village, where he ordered porter or wine and avoided conversation. Nothing more is known of him.

"Concerning the possibility of accidental death," Curlow said, "it is conceivable that a deer hunter inadvertently shot him. The woodland was immediately checked, without revealing any hunters at that time. Also, the area would offer poor opportunity after the previous day's hunt, and any sensible hunter would go elsewhere."

Curlow picked up an arrow from the table before him. "This is the arrow that killed Drossin." A bit of red thread was tied around it. "The entry of the arrow into his back is significant. When the shaft was pulled, the arrowhead remained within him. I had a physician remove it and study the wound. He tells me that the arrow entered between two ribs at a slightly upward angle. It pierced the left lung and heart, and was stopped by a front rib, which broke at the impact. He also believes that it was shot from a relatively short distance—near enough to decern a man from a deer. The circumstances demand that we consider murder."

Thomas wished he could see Lord Ivan. But standing so nigh the king, he could hardly see anyone except the king's attendants. At least some of them were watching the assembly rather than the inspector, who now raised the arrow. The stained shaft was tipped with iron.

Thomas's lungs made room for a full breath.

"This arrow," Curlow said, "I find interesting, though it looks ordinary, fletched with elderbird and tipped with barbed iron. There are probably hundreds of them in the arrow stands of this castle and maybe within the quivers of every hunter here." He paused. "Except Lord Navayn's." He laid the arrow down and stood Thomas's quiver upright. "This was taken from Lord Navayn when he was discovered near the body."

"What are they fletched with?" someone asked, likely because multiple colors could be seen.

"About half of them are black as a raven's wing, but some are fletched from other birds, including elderbird. That tells us little." Curlow gripped the shafts in a bundle just above the top of the quiver and lifted. The quiver fell sideways, and he propped the arrows against it, letting the bundle spread. "These are Lord Navayn's arrows—each is tipped with a flint arrowhead. I understand that they are made by the People of the Woods."

Ivan's voice interrupted the murmurs behind Thomas. "That means nothing more than the fletching, for he doubtless has iron-tipped arrows too."

The inspector said, "I checked the arrow racks in the stable of Navayn Manor and found none. I also checked the quivers of his squire, Jonathan Cotrell, and everyone else who dwells on the property. None had iron tips."

"But there used to be some in the stable," Ivan said. "He could have already used them and still had one left to murder this poor man."

"We already know," Duke Selta drawled, "that your father's steward took every movable piece of iron he could find from the Navayn Estate."

"But he—"

"I took the arrows," Lord Sathe Maerton stated. "They were mine, so they were loaded up together with my bows and horse tack."

"Thank you for that clarity, Uncle," Lord Ivan said. "Still, I find it strange to assume Lord Navayn would not have *any* quality arrows. After the hunt, there must have been several on the ground in his woodland. He could have picked them up."

The inspector raised his brows. "Oddly enough, he doesn't seem to have put them in his quiver. But worry not, Lord Ivan, I am merely stating observations, not conclusions." He bent as he spoke and lifted another quiver from behind the table linen's drape. "I also observed Lord Ivan's quiver, which I acquired on the morning of the murder." He pulled the arrows and laid them much like Thomas's on the other end of the table. "I noticed the uniformity in shaft, fletching, and barbed iron arrowheads. Such is common within a castle where arrows are made in large quantities. By their similarity, 'tis likely that the killing arrow was made in this castle."

Duke Prushane edged forward in his chair. "May I look closer?"

King Gairith said, "One from each duchy may approach—but briefly, for this does not tell us who shot the arrow."

Thomas wanted a close look at those arrows too. Best not ask. He caught a bit of talk about different shapes preferred by a couple dukes. No one challenged the inspector's conclusion.

Ivan didn't bother to approach. "Why are we wasting time with this, when he could still have found arrows lying about?"

Annoyance flitted over the inspector's face. "Jonathan Cotrell, did you or Lord Navayn pick up arrows after the hunt?"

"Nay, sir. Nor have we found any since we came here."

Ivan sneered. "He would say that, regardless."

Jonathan kept his gaze straight ahead and his lips closed. Doubtless, a difficult feat, for that silence could not sit well with his personality.

"Inspector," the king said, "have you uncovered any motive for Lord Navayn to kill Drossin?"

The inspector mentioned Thomas's recognition of Drossin's face.

Ah, a useful moment. Thomas said, "I have long wanted to find this man, for I suspect that someone sent him to lure me to the ruins of Kaituer Castle. His information would be crucial to apprehending a would-be murderer. Had I found Drossin alive, I would have questioned him—perhaps even taken him into custody and sent for you, inspector. Under *no* circumstances would I have killed him."

"What an absurd, concocted story," Lord Ivan said.

"On the contrary," Inspector Curlow replied. "If Lord Navayn murdered him, he would not admit to recognizing him. Nor would he have summoned his squire, which also alerted others to his presence with the body. Instead, he would have returned quietly to his squire and left the area."

Lord Ivan adopted an airy tone. "If only we knew what Drossin might have said to Lord Navayn before he was murdered. For instance, he could have tried blackmail. Rage or fear could have created an instantaneous need for murder. Even if we don't know the motive, that doesn't change the fact that no one else was present. Only Lord Navayn had opportunity."

Duke Prushane spoke dryly. "Blackmail is rare—outside of the House of Maerton."

"'Tis false," Curlow said, "that only Lord Navayn had opportunity. There was another rider in the woods, still unaccounted for."

"How fortunate for Lord Navayn, but you worry me, inspector. 'Twould appear that a murderer wanders my duchy, whom you have failed to find. You seem more intent on *not* identifying the criminal."

The king said, "Hanging an innocent man will not stop the actual murderer. Inspector Curlow, are there any facts upon which a murder charge *could* stand against Lord Navayn?"

"I find none convincing."

"Nor do I," the king said. "Lord Navayn, you are no longer held under suspicion, but your presence here is still required."

Thomas fought a dizzy sensation, but he bowed to the king. "I thank you for resolving the first matter, my liege. Will you consider the attempted murders today or on another day?" The king raised his brows again, and Thomas tensed. Was he pushing too hard?

"For one who appears reticent," the king said, "you have astounding determination. You may sit there." He pointed toward a vacant chair situated between Duke Tristelle and the Seltas.

At last, Thomas would be able to see the rest of the room. Walking to the chair even gave him a glimpse of Lady Sareen's face. Certain, she was trying to hide her expression, but the flush of her cheeks and the quick meeting of their eyes was enough. Thomas sat and tried to ignore how many people stared in his direction. All of this seemed off balance. Like a stone was missing from a tower foundation, and it would topple at any moment.

Once again, the king addressed the gathering. "The fire which Lord Navayn spoke of is one of several questionable events that greatly concern the crown of Lavaycia. Another is the missing will of the late Duke of Maerton, which prompts suspicion that his sudden death was not of natural causes. Now, a murder. Thrice between the full moons, the crown's inspector is needed in this duchy."

"If I may, sire," Ivan said, "I believe some instability is not unusual when authority is in question. An unfortunate ramification of your delay in confirming me as duke. As soon as that is accomplished, I will restore order, and you will find that your inspector is no longer needed here."

The king's voice ground. "'Twould be inexcusable of any king or queen of Lavaycia to confirm a new duke without investigating these crimes. Are you so self-deluded that you cannot see that these crimes all point to you?"

"To me?" Was that instant of shock on Ivan's face real or faked? "Indeed, none of them point to me! I was most sincerely attached to my father and would never harm him. The fire? I was far from Navayn Manor that night. And Drossin? I didn't even know he existed, much less have a motive for killing him. I protest this accusation, and I greatly wonder at the motive behind it."

"Interesting," the king said. "When Lord Navayn was accused, he addressed me as liege, calling our oaths to mind, and asked for my protection and justice. At the first hint that you may be accused, you protest and question my motives, which is the same as questioning the crown's justice."

Ivan delayed an instant. "Pray forgive me, sire, for shock made me speak with unclear haste. I do not question *your* motives at all—rather, the motives of others who give rise to these false accusations. As for allegiance, I will give you my ducal oath now, if you will permit."

"What good is an oath from a man I do not trust? First, we shall hear what Inspector Curlow has discovered." The king looked to the inspector. "Proceed."

CHAPTER 38

"I shall summarize," Inspector Curlow said, "and will also exclude names of my sources, for they of Maerton Duchy were fearfully reluctant to speak. Only if this matter goes to court, will they be identified."

He cleared his throat. "First, concerning Drossin. Signs indicated that he had a horse, but it was gone when he was found. Two items of interest in his pack—a curry brush and a tinderbox. That box contained a tallow candle. Being inexpertly made, probably by him, it contained impurities. All tallow candles have an odor, but some worse than others. Three individuals with keen senses of smell confirmed that Drossin's candle matches the scent of wax found in Navayn Manor. A trail of that wax led from an external side door and up a concealed staircase to the master's chamber, ending beside the hearth where the fire was lit."

Thomas's scalp tingled. Never had he expected this connection. What else did it mean?

The inspector described aspects of that fire, since many here did not know of them, and answered a few questions.

Ivan shifted impatiently. "It seems clear enough that Drossin lit the fire, so that mystery is solved, and the perpetrator is dead. Let us move on."

"Partially solved," the inspector said. "He lit a fire on a night when you had an alibi of your own creation, but he did not lay the firewood that night, nor add whatever ingredient produced apparently poisonous smoke. Its scent was already in the room when Lord Navayn took possession, but was nowhere else in the manor. It is possible that Drossin did not know what effect lighting the fire would have. He wouldn't even have known about those curious dampers in the chimneys of Navayn Manor, which made the fire doubly lethal."

This mirrored Thomas's guess that Drossin had only been tasked with luring him to the ruins. He may have been an ignorant tool. As Thomas pondered, the inspector summarized the attack at Kaituer Castle.

To this, Ivan said, "How fortunate that Thomas Kaituer came to no harm. 'Twas some time ago, of course, but he picked up an iron-tipped arrow that day." Ivan leaned forward to address Thomas. "Did you not?"

"I did," Thomas said. "How do you know that?"

Ivan waved a hand. "Some rumor, I suppose. I don't recall who relayed it."

"Interesting," Curlow said. "The event seems little known here. But as you said, Lord Navayn did pick up the arrow and carried it in his belt that day. I asked his squire about it, who informed me that his master kept the arrow in a trunk." Curlow bent to retrieve something from below the table and held it high. "This is the arrow. I marked it immediately with amber thread so it could not be confused with the others. Also, the tip is damaged from striking stone." He laid it beside Ivan's arrows.

Duke Prushane, seated nearest that table, rose to inspect them.

Thomas stood, glancing at the king, who nodded. Could he have stayed away if the king had refused? He reached the table and studied the contents. Arrows were never perfectly identical, but these were very similar.

As Thomas and a few others examined the evidence, the inspector said, "I requested sample arrows from those made in the castles." Curlow lifted a handful of arrows from below the table and laid them out. Each shaft bore an ink inscription indicating the ducal house. Varied styles were represented. "Every smith and every fletcher will work a little differently, but 'tis clear that the arrow shot at Lord Navayn—then, styled Sir Thomas—was made in this castle."

"What a surprise," Ivan said, still seated, "to find Maerton-made arrows in Maerton Duchy."

"Not at all," the inspector said, "but we do know that the arrow shot at Lord Navayn was not used later to shoot Drossin. We can now discuss whether you had opportunity to shoot it."

"Me and hundreds of others."

"Nay." The inspector sounded amused. "The question of motive arises, and you have never hidden your hatred of Thomas Kaituer."

Ivan sneered. "Everyone in Maerton Duchy hates the Kaituers."

"Nay, again," Duke Selta said. "Prince Maerton and his descendants gave no aid to those who were harmed by the fall of the House of Kaituer and the burned village. When I visited Kaituer Castle, I watched the interactions of the common folk with the Maertons, who paid for their labor but ignored them, and with Lord Navayn, who was introduced as Sir Thomas Kaituer. The local commoners may offer grudging respect to the name of Maerton, but they followed and aided Thomas Kaituer."

"I was there too," Lord Ivan said, "and noticed nothing of the sort."

King Gairith spoke with unshakable calm. "Blindness may be caused in many ways, arrogance being one of them. Returning to the point—where were you on the day that the arrow was shot at Lord Navayn?"

"I know not. I don't even know when it happened."

"And yet," the inspector said, "you heard that he picked up the arrow."

"Rumors take time to travel. I do not know the specific day."

Thomas returned to his seat, giving him ample view of Ivan's rendition of lofty boredom.

"Quite possible," Curlow replied to Ivan. "I will assist you by relating it to events of your life. You took two horses and traveled west alone. You—"

"I often ride through the Maerton Estate and the entire duchy."

"Quite so, and there is nothing unusual in that. I understand you have no squire and take no other servant with you, including the day—"

"I am a man, not a child, and have no need of a servant to care for me."

Curlow's lips tightened. "Commendable, I'm sure. If you will cease interruptions, I will tell you what day Lord Navayn was nearly murdered. On this particular journey, you took two horses instead of one. Both were saddled, and you had a pack and canvas tied to one of the saddles. After three days, you returned with only one horse. Do you remember this trip?"

"Easily. My father was displeased that I had lost one of the estate horses."

"Who could blame him? Horses are costly." Curlow tapped the arrow from Kaituer Castle. "This arrow was shot at Sir Thomas on the morning of the third day of your trip. You would have had adequate time to return here by nightfall, as you did. Now that you know what day it was—where were you that morn?"

"Riding somewhere near the cliffs overlooking the sea."

"Whom did you meet with and where, exactly?"

"I didn't meet with anyone. Remember that my father was still alive, and he—"

"I am not questioning whether your actions were reasonable.

I want to know if your location can be confirmed, which you have answered." Curlow turned to the king, "It appears, sire, that Lord Ivan could have been near enough to the Kaituer ruins to have opportunity to shoot an arrow at Sir Thomas."

Lord Ivan maintained a haughty attitude. Understandable, for proof seemed lacking, even though the inspector had discovered more than Thomas realized earlier.

"An arrow and opportunity," the king said. "What more have you?"

Instead of answering, the inspector turned to Lord Ivan. "What became of the missing horse?"

"I don't know. Apparently, I tied it poorly. 'Twas gone when I awoke. Either it was stolen, or it wandered off."

"Someone in the stables here said he would ride to search for it, and you told him nay."

"'Twas no prize steed, just a simple packhorse."

"Quite. And it carried a pack for you. Yet you bade that it be saddled instead of using a pack harness. Also, the horse knew its stable, for it did eventually return here."

"Did it?"

"Come, Lord Ivan. No one will believe you don't know your horses."

"I know my riding hacks and my hunters quite well," Ivan said, "but I have no interest in the common work horses."

"You may not know this horse," Curlow said, "but it knows you. In fact, you approached it when it came through the gate. At which point, it reared, kicked, broke free of the man who'd taken hold of its rein, and galloped out of the gate."

"Oh, *that* horse. Frankly, I didn't get a good look at it. Perhaps it was the same one. All those weeks alone must have made it rather wild."

"It doesn't seem to be wild at all. A handler followed it. He *does* recognize it and described it as 'a sweet-tempered horse but fair riled up.' It had stopped in the road heading toward the Navayn estate, but it trotted away from the handler as he approached. He suspected that it wanted to be followed, and in any event, he knows better than to chase a skittish horse. The horse led him to a certain clearing near a marker stone beside a stream." The inspector paused. "The clearing where Drossin was murdered. His remains and belongings had been removed. The horse snuffled the ground and neighed a good deal. Then, it let the handler stroke its neck and lead it back here. He tells me that it has been well cared for. Clean hooves and well-groomed. You may recall I mentioned a curry brush in Drossin's pack. The hairs match those of the horse you lost when Thomas Kaituer was shot at, and that returned here after Drossin's murder."

Lord Ivan leaned sideways as he listened, propping his chin on his hand. "So, Drossin must have found my wandering horse. How fascinating."

"He certainly kept the horse, but on the rare occasions that he visited the village, he arrived and left on foot. The innkeeper believes he was too poor to own a horse. I must wonder why Drossin didn't allow his horse to be seen."

"He probably did steal it, then, and didn't want to risk it being recognized."

"Ah. So, you believe he knew the horse could be recognized near the castle, and yet he stayed in the vicinity all summer." Curlow angled his head. "Why would he do that?"

"I know not, nor do I care."

"You do not care, but others seemed to. You must know that various members of the late duke's household gave him daily reports."

"Every morn," Ivan uttered wearily. "I was often present."

"You did not hear everything they reported. Do you know that your father made an unusual stop at the inn some weeks ago and shared a pint with the village folk? Do you know that Drossin was there at the time, and your father asked the innkeeper about him?"

"Did he?" Ivan leaned forward, fake interest lacing his words. "More fascinating yet, my father and I occasionally visited the taproom together over the years. Would you like a list of all the times?"

"Your father's sarcasm never intimidated me. Yours will not either."

"Forgive me. I find this rather tedious."

"Then I will help you understand the horse," Curlow said. "You gave it to Drossin so he could lead Thomas Kaituer to the desolate ruins. There, you could hide, and it was likely that his curiosity would bring him in range. He was too suspicious of Drossin to go with him, but the next morn, Drossin could have seen him set out alone, and then ridden to tell you. Fortunately, your arrow missed. Always a risk, for no archer hits every mark. This set several people on guard. Your father was informed that someone had shot an arrow at Thomas Kaituer. He ordered that the rumors be suppressed."

"Still no proof of anything," Ivan drawled.

"Then, the Navayn estate was suddenly released from the tight grip of the Maertons."

"The reasons were—"

"We've all heard the stated reasons," the king said. "Continue, inspector."

"Before announcing his intention to release the estate, Duke Maerton visited his brother at Navayn Manor. The duke appeared melancholy."

Thomas glanced at Lord Sathe Maerton. His receding chin never looked firm, but his lips were set in a straight line as he stared at his nephew.

Inspector Curlow continued. "Duke Maerton spoke of releasing the manor and what he would do instead to provide for his brother. The duke said he was changing his will and would settle money on Sathe Maerton directly, because the duke did not trust you to honor your family obligation to your uncle. He even went so far as to suggest that Lord Maerton should find a wife and beget heirs."

Ivan's face remained calm as ever, and his voice smooth. He

sighed as he said, "'Tis sad. Yet another indication that my father's mind was fading."

"Odd that no one else saw any change in him except sadness and the worry he expressed over you. The lawyer saw only this when Duke Maerton met with him in Purthellia. When the new will was signed, he attested that the duke was of sound mind. Your father took the will with him, doubtless to store it here."

Curlow rested his hands on the table. "While your uncle prepared to depart from Navayn Manor, the steward sent workers to perform repairs. You were seen multiple times inside the manor house in odd places. After your uncle left to stay briefly at Maerton Castle, you had opportunity to access the master bedchamber in Navayn Manor and either add to the wood already laid there, or perhaps lay the wood yourself." He leaned forward. "What leaf did you use, Lord Ivan?"

"You will have to tell me, inspector, for you are the one making up this tale—which is still rather lacking in proof."

"Had I found proof after the fire, you would already have been arrested. Your father was again disturbed. He sent for another will that he had instructed the lawyer to prepare and hold."

"Ah, the mysterious will that does not seem to exist."

"But it did exist, for the lawyer sent it, and it was delivered to this castle. But it did not reach Duke Maerton."

"I, too, find missing documents strange," Ivan said. "Regardless of others' ignorance, I have noticed my father's mind sometimes clear and sometimes not. And I am quite certain that I knew him better than anyone else did. I suspect that, in a lucid moment, he realized what a mistake he had made and sent for the will in order to destroy it."

"Except that he never received it. He sent a note to the lawyer inquiring about the delay. Then, he died."

Ivan's expression shifted to the one he'd used at the funeral. "That tragedy was a blessing in disguise, for it would have been horrible to watch him sink into a demented state."

"What did you use to help him along?"

"I don't know what you mean."

"You should," the inspector said. "I took the physician on a tour of your library, and he was kind enough to point out a certain book to me. He, too, owns a copy, for it describes dangerous plants, their effects on humans, and how best to treat accidental ingestion."

"Ah, I know which one you mean. You see, I am fond of experimenting with new tea blends, but that means I need to know which plants to avoid."

"Regardless, it provided the knowledge of how to cause apoplexy, so again, you had opportunity to kill."

"Oh, these endless opportunities! I had far too much affection for my father to do him harm."

"You sicken me," Lord Maerton said.

"Grasping after the duchy, Uncle?"

"What?"

"Did you perhaps persuade my father to make new wills on the day he visited you, so that you could steal my title and my land?"

"Never." Lord Maerton's knuckles whitened as he gripped the arms of his chair. "This duchy has been a bane upon my entire life. When I settle in a new home, 'twill not be within the borders of Maerton Duchy. I want only the legacy my brother promised me, so that I can finally be free of you."

Ivan sneered at his uncle but addressed the inspector. "Forgive me for the distraction. You probably know that my father took tea with me each morn. Do please take every tin of tea from my study and see if you can find any with this dread ingredient. You won't find proof there, but, really, I feel I should offer you some help in weeding out some of my so-called opportunities."

"There is also the matter of Drossin's murder."

"Ah, and I had an opportunity, since I ride out each morn. And he just happened to be in my path, so naturally I shot a complete stranger for no reason at all. Inspector, the absurdity of this passes all bounds."

"What *you* said does." Curlow tilted his head. "But I didn't say that. Once I realized how you use alternate tools, so that no one person knows every side of your activities, 'twas far easier to investigate you. Your gamekeeper, for instance. He always departed with you in the morning, but never returned with you. Thus, he never perceived your questionable behavior. He seems to be a guileless, loyal servant. In your defense, he even told me you suspected that Lord Navayn started the fire that nearly killed Lady Sareen. You told him of your concern for her, especially if she were to be alone near Lord Navayn during the hunt. Your gamekeeper promised to stay near her. He did hear something of interest, which he passed on to you, but he had no idea what you did with that information. In fact, you knew that Lord Navayn would—"

"Take care, inspector," Ivan snapped with noble outrage. "Do not think that I will let you raise doubts of Lady Sareen's reputation!"

That caused a stir among the Selta family. Lady Sareen demanded, "How could he, indeed, for I did nothing wrong in seeking to talk with a friend of many years. If you did not hover over me with unwarranted jealousy, I could have talked with Lord Navayn at the hunt feast. But no! I had to make an opportunity where you could not intrude, as you always do."

Lord Ivan made an odd twitch when she spoke, but he didn't turn to her. Instead, he said to Curlow, "The lady cannot see the danger she is in, but I perceive it. I did ride out at dawn to protect her, but I did not find her and assumed that she had changed her mind."

"Actually, you rode out before dawn," Curlow said, "and this brings us to your dealings with Drossin. The tap man at the inn believes he had a compulsive need for drink, but he did not come often to quench his thirst. Drossin also had a curious habit of burying all sign of his camp—including, oddly enough, corks but rarely a bottle. You were known to take wine and food on your early hunts and return with an empty bottle. You always gave your empty food pouch and bottle to a different servant than the one who handed them to you. However, you overlooked the kitchen staff."

The inspector paused, watching Ivan. "A servant noticed and repaired a damaged seam on the pouch. Thereafter, the kitchen servants realized that you used two food pouches—identical except for that repaired seam. The two pouches alternated each day the staff were asked to fill a new one. In fact, they were able to confirm that the food pouch I found in Drossin's pack was actually yours."

Lord Ivan raised his brows. "So that's what happened to it. He was indeed a thief."

"Stole it out of your hand, did he? You eat in the castle each morn and noon. Yet you take food—also in the morn—but you are never seen eating it. Nor are you seen drunk from the wine you take. In fact, you have been feeding Drossin for weeks. A man you claim to not know, who kept the horse you claim to have lost. A man who suddenly turned up in a clearing where he did not even build a fire to warm himself overnight. 'Tis my belief that you arranged for him to be in the clearing after you learned that Lord Navayn was going there soon after dawn. Then, you killed Drossin and left the body to be found by Lord Navayn."

"I tire of arguing these slanders. You still present no proof."

"Enough," the king said. "You have incriminated yourself, this day, with your many lies. Even if you are ultimately declared innocent of murder, you will never inherit this duchy."

Anger finally surged into Ivan's voice. "'Tis mine by birthright!"

"But you destroyed your father's will."

"'Tis false. He could never even have signed it."

"A moment ago," Curlow said, "you revealed your knowledge of the will's contents. Lord Maerton only knew he'd been left a legacy. He did not know of any provisions disinheriting you and your heirs. You must have read and destroyed both wills. And after destroying them, you had to kill your father, before he could make another."

Ivan breathed hard. "That is not true. 'Twas chance that he died then. I had to read the wills, for his mind was slipping. I would have talked to him. Made him understand. Helped him with the lawyer."

"Like you helped your mother understand?" Lord Maerton asked. "My brother's mind was not slipping! He'd learned that you killed your mother and that unfortunate Hettie. He must have known you caused the fire and would murder again."

The king stared at Lord Maerton with raised brows. Just when Thomas thought everything was slipping into place, a piece shifted again. No time to figure it out now, for the king spoke again.

"Ivan Maerton, the crown charges you with destroying ducal wills, with four murders, and with two attempted murders. Captain Benton, take Ivan Maerton into custody."

"Never!" Ivan screamed.

CHAPTER 39

Thomas hardly breathed through the spectacle of Ivan's arrest.

Ivan's face contorted, and he cursed a vile torrent. Though he fought, four of the king's men bound his hands behind his back and forced him from the room. A welcome silence reigned when the doors slammed and Ivan's screams no longer echoed in the stone hall. Faint, high-pitched exclamations replaced them.

If only Thomas could go to Sareen. Certain, she didn't like Ivan, but such a disturbing scene! At least she had family beside her.

A servant stepped tentatively forward and bowed to the king. "Uh, sire, a refreshment was prepared and is ready to serve. Cakes and fruit, with a light morning wine."

"You may serve."

People began to stand and move about. That and the light fare eased tension.

Thomas exchanged a grip of shoulders with Tristan, then approached the king. What words to speak? He bowed. "Your justice was as true as I knew it would be, my liege."

The king offered his rare smile. "Know that I kept you in

that tower to *protect* you until evidence could be presented. Take up your sword belt."

Thomas nodded but he had to say more. In his hesitation, Captain Hurth lifted Thomas's belt from the table and handed it to him. He drew the belt around and began buckling it. Speaking as soft as possible, Thomas said, "Sire, the day you granted my title, you placed a restriction on me, which I have honored though my heart was already bound."

"Ah." The king murmured, "I lift the restriction, for you should be safe now."

"Thank you, sire." Thomas stepped backward and turned too quickly, colliding with Duke Selta. Thomas gasped. "Pray pardon—"

"Restriction?" Duke Selta shifted his querying gaze between the king and Thomas. "Had that anything to do with a question you might ask *me*, Lord Navayn?"

"Uh..."

"Because, if so, you should ask very, very soon."

Formalities demanded that he request this in private, but Thomas would not pass this opportunity. He stood close enough to whisper, and that would have to do. "May I ask your daughter to join hands with me?"

"You may."

'Twas so easy that Thomas didn't know what to say. Certain, the duke had understood his hints, after all. Fortunately, the duke spoke to the king, so Thomas was spared the need of forming a proper response.

At last! He could walk up to Lady Sareen without feeling like he was overstepping—or breaking protocol—or defying the king —or risking her life—or any other despised hindrance. Inside, his heart cheered, *Rah!*

He joined Lady Sareen as she took the last sip from her glass and set it on the tray a servant carried. "Oh, Thomas!" She squeezed his hand as he bowed over hers. "I mean, Lord Navayn."

He smiled. "You may call me Thomas whenever you please. You already look more like your name—Sareen. Much like you did by the sea all those weeks ago."

"'Tis like a suffocating shroud has been unwound," she said. "Of course, I knew you didn't do it, but I feared that might be impossible to prove."

He let out a wry chuckle. "I suppose I should admit to some wallowing in despair in that cold, dark tower."

"It must have been awful for you!"

He shrugged. "I think I'll keep that memory as a lesson for the next time despair creeps nigh, for my worries were all for naught." A hint of her dimples showed. A sense of freedom kept coursing through him—every denied goal demanded action. "You know this mansion, do you not?" At her nod, he whispered, "Is there any place where we could have that meeting you asked me for?"

Her dimples deepened. She turned toward the back of the hall, then slipped her hand onto his arm as they began to stroll. "You see those double doors? They lead to terraced gardens."

"You did want it outside, didn't you?"

She laughed gently as a servant moved toward the doors and opened one for them. "I just need a moment of fresh air," Sareen said.

At the click of the door, Sareen drew him aside where an angled wall and trellis gave them partial privacy.

They both said, "I—" in unison.

"Would you like to go first?" Thomas asked.

She twisted her fingers at her waist. "I, um, needed to ask you something...something dreadfully unladylike. I can be patient when that makes sense, but...I need to know what I'm being patient for. If anything. So, um...oh, dear. I suppose that makes no sense, and I don't know how to say this."

His lips twitched despite his best efforts to control them. "Perhaps I should be gentlemanly and spare you the need to utter unladylike words. Sweet Sareen, I've wanted to ask this for so long! Will you join hands with me?" He held his hand out to her. "Forever."

She inhaled. "Aw, the old-fashioned words." She placed her hand on his palm.

"Did I ask amiss? That is what the People of the Woods say, and there will always be a bit of Tower Woods within me. I do realize that may be hard for you, and my estate is tiny compared with what you are used to."

"I don't care about any of that. 'Tis *you* I care about. And... you asked perfectly. Joining hands with you would be...the final joy of my early life, and the first joy of the rest of my days."

Already, they gripped hands tightly, and Thomas kissed the back of hers. Her smile...her glossy brown eyes... It just wasn't enough. He slipped his free arm behind her back and kissed her. By the quiver of her lips, she must have felt the same surge he did. He tightened his hold.

Sareen flinched away. "Ugh! Swords are awful!"

"I agree. But they are good for killing dragons."

She burst into her high-pitched laugh, like frothy music.

A throat cleared loudly behind him. Thomas looked over his shoulder. A servant stood in the doorway, looking straight out toward the garden instead of at them. "The king requests that the lords and ladies return and sit down again."

"Thank you," Thomas said. The man stepped out of sight, though the door remained open. "Stop looking overjoyed," Thomas whispered to Sareen.

"You stop."

"I'm trying." He drew her hand onto his arm again and walked as slow as possible. "We can't walk in there right after that horrible scene with Ivan and announce we're getting married."

"You picked the moment."

He gave her a quizzical look. "Do you wish I hadn't?"

Her laugh came out low-pitched. "Nay."

A smile squashed his cheeks again, but he got his face under control—he hoped—and led her inside.

Their entry was not too conspicuous, for the king still stood and chairs were being moved. Why? Ah, the dukes and duchesses were being seated in their formal positions. Three ducal houses on each side, with the royal House of Tristelle angled between the king and the House of Maerton. Sareen went to join her parents on the opposite side. Lord Maerton sat in one of the two chairs positioned for his duchy, the other blatantly empty. Was it necessary to call attention to an absence? Thomas headed toward the adjacent seating, since he ranked just below the dukes.

The king's herald stopped him. "This way, Lord Navayn. You will be seated beside Lord Maerton."

One of those chairs was for him? Did that make sense? Was it because there was no duke and Thomas was sworn to the king? Regardless, he turned to comply. Lord Maerton looked both worn down and troubled. This must be a horrible day for him. Not much Thomas could do except offer a respectful bow. "Lord Maerton."

He inclined his torso and said, "Lord Navayn."

Thomas took his place as the lords and ladies of the duchy found chairs beyond the ducal seating. Those of other duchies stayed to the rear, and privileged servants stood around the walls. Ah, Master Navayn was among them. He must have been present all along. A trusted voice to carry word to their village. That eased a worry Thomas hadn't even realized he carried.

Just then, the doors burst open. Captain Benton halted in the vestibule, with blood spattered over his trousers. He bowed. "Sire, there has been an uprising, which we have quelled."

Thomas looked past him through the doors. He saw no threat and heard only Lord Maerton's uneven breath.

"Report," the king said.

Benton strode to the center, his brow creased. "Ivan Maerton resisted throughout. When we got him almost to the tower, the captain of the castle's guard, remaining loyal to the House of Maerton, attacked us. 'Twas fought in close quarters with steel. During the fray, Ivan climbed the stairs onto the wall. His hands were still bound behind him, but he called to his men to fight, and probably made the skirmish last longer, which led to more blood spilled."

Maerton shook his head and murmured, "The fool."

"Some of the castle men did not engage on either side," Benton said. "When the last fighter fell, Ivan Maerton stepped into a crenellation and…threw himself backward from the wall. He is dead."

Silence.

At last, King Gairith said, "Captain Benton, tend to your men. Captain Hurth, collect every weapon of Maerton in the castle and lock them up. If any man refuses to surrender weapons, lock him up too."

As they departed, Lord Maerton still shook his head. Did he feel alone? Betrayed? Shamed? Thomas touched the back of his shoulder and spoke softly. "I cannot imagine what you endure this day, but I offer my condolence."

Lord Maerton looked sideways at him for a frozen second, then murmured, "Thank you."

The king seemed to ponder, which was unusual—in public, at least. "The struggles of this day seem determined to pile ever higher," he said, "as though some force wishes to stop what must come. Yet, I will finish what I have begun. I will not leave this duchy floundering, with no leader, and dividing into deeper factions than already exist."

King Gairith swept a gaze around the ducal houses. "I had hoped for all duchies to be represented, at least to witness, if not to act. I do not know if Duke Othair is yet on the road here or chose not to participate in a foregone conclusion. Duchess Tristelle sent her courier ahead with a proxy letter for Duke Tristelle to enact if called for. Thus, he represents Tristelle Duchy."

Duke Prushane said, "One duchy is without a duke. One duchy is absent, but five are present. Four are enough to confirm a new duke."

"Aye," Duchess Portlen said. "If we concur, the matter can be resolved today."

The king said, "Lord Sathe Maerton, come forth."

He stood, walked to the edge of the carpet, and bowed low. "My liege."

Thomas relaxed in his chair. Even though he did not answer directly to the Duke of Maerton, he far preferred to watch this man become duke rather than Ivan.

"A few minutes ago," the king said, "you uttered words I have never heard spoken. That your brother, Duke Naviad Maerton, discovered that Ivan killed his mother and the servant Hettie. When did you learn this?"

"The day my brother visited me at Navayn Manor."

The king set his mouth in a straight line throughout a long silence. "How long had your brother known it?"

"He did not exactly say he knew that Ivan killed the duchess, but he suspected it. He didn't know about Hettie until recently. She was old and..." His voice tightened. "...died of apoplexy."

As King Gairith watched Lord Maerton, creases at the corners of his eyes hinted at compassion behind his firm visage. The king held silence.

Lord Maerton straightened his shoulders. "My brother said there was no proof in either case. I think Lord Ivan himself must have told him about Hettie. He thought she knew what happened on the staircase when the duchess fell to her death. I did warn him!"

"Warn him of what?"

"The risk of letting a murderer walk free. That Ivan might kill again. And if he would kill his mother, he might kill his father too. But Naviad just spoke of their bond and said Ivan needed him and knew it. He kept saying there was no proof, so he couldn't do anything."

Lord Maerton kept clenching and loosening his fingers at his sides. "I don't know how much you've heard it, but my brother always said the unpleasant things without exactly saying them. Ivan did too. While my brother was with me that day, it became very clear that...though he spoke damning words regarding his son...I could never repeat them."

"Why did he tell you, then?"

"I couldn't figure that out at the time. As a warning, was the best I could think of. And I worried because, sometimes, he seemed to pursue one thing when he was really pursuing another. After he died...the same way as Hettie..." Lord Maerton straightened his shoulders again. "I thought perhaps my brother *was* afraid that Lord Ivan might kill him. And if that happened, he wanted him brought to justice. I told the crown's inspector that I believed Lord Ivan killed his father, but...thanks to my brother's accursed vagueness...I had no proof to offer. I told him of the new will and the name of my brother's lawyer. I knew of the bequest he intended to leave me, and was certain that if Ivan learned of it, he would try to prevent it. But Naviad never told me that he planned to disinherit Ivan. I only learned that today. I have *never* aspired to become duke." He drew a noisy breath. "And I daresay, all of this sounds too pathetic to believe, but it is true."

"Ah, Sathe," the king said. "Do not forget that I, too, rode with you and Naviad before we were men. Even then, he was honing his subtle mockery, and in later years, he used that and more to gain his own ends."

"A well-established fact," Duke Prushane said with low-pitched contempt.

The king nodded but kept his eyes on Lord Maerton. "Though we grew up nigh each other, I was born to be king, and you were born as the younger brother of a duke who defied the king. Thus, everything you did *must* displease either him or me."

Lord Maerton inclined his head.

"By law, you should have come to me once you knew that a

murder had been committed. In a way, your brother forced you to become an accomplice years after the murder, which technically makes you ineligible to become duke, even while he bequeathed you that title."

The king seemed to wait for a reply, but Lord Maerton said nothing.

Thomas hurt for him. He knew the pain of betrayal and disinheritance, even generations after the deed. Did Lord Maerton now feel it?

King Gairith straightened in the center of his broad chair and spoke with regal intonation. "I hereby decree…" The scribe's pen scratched with the king's slow words. "Seeing that the third duke of Maerton prevented justice for murder…seeing that his son and heir, Ivan Maerton, committed multiple murders and killed himself…now, therefore, the ducal House of Maerton is no more."

CHAPTER 40

Thomas's thoughts stuttered to a halt. The House of Maerton was no more? Could this be true? But the king had said it!

The scribe's pen ceased scratching, wax dripped onto the parchment, and King Gairith pressed his seal to the decree.

Thomas drew a few breaths to open his tight throat and released his grip on the chair's arm.

The herald bowed to the king. "What of Duke Maerton's surviving heir, sire? How shall he be styled?"

When the king did not immediately answer, Duke Fennish said, "If the house does not exist, there is no title for the name of Maerton."

Apparently, comment was permitted. Thomas said, "Sire, may I speak on Sathe Maerton's behalf?"

"'Tis a ducal matter," the herald snapped.

What was he—god of protocol? "'Tis a matter of lordship," Thomas said, "and to be frank, I have knowledge of ducal disinheritance that only a Kaituer possesses."

Duchess Portlen made a sound between a laugh and a humph. "With that much audacity, we must hear this."

"I permit you to speak, Lord Navayn," the king said.

Thomas stood and bowed to the king. "Lord Thomas Kaituer lost everything because of crimes committed by his family—not by him. He lost the courtesy title of a younger son. He bore a shame he didn't deserve. He could neither live with respect in his own land nor live in peaceful exile. That created permanent enmity, *which still exists today*." Thomas let that hang for a second. "Though the crimes of the Kaituers and Maertons are different, I cannot help but see the similarity in how they affect the last heir of each house. Rather than repeating an old mistake, I suggest that *this* heir be allowed to live in peace as the man he is —Lord Sathe Maerton."

Thomas sat down. Lord Maerton turned to stare at him, then faced the king again.

Duke Fennish also stared at Thomas, and finally said, "I suppose that if a Kaituer descendant will support Maerton's title, we dukes and duchesses must hold our tongues."

The king's gaze rested on the man standing before him. "Lord Maerton, I look forward to seeing who you are when you are not being torn in two directions. You may take a place among the lords and ladies, your peers."

As Lord Maerton gave the king final thanks and took his lower seat, Thomas's neck grew hot. Only he remained sitting in representation of the duchy—a right he did not possess. What was he to do? He looked to the king.

"Lord Navayn," Duchess Portlen said, "please tell me *why* you said what you did."

He felt terribly conspicuous but fading into the background was not an option. "I suppose part of it is just fellow feeling, but…" He straightened and looked around at the faces fixed on him. "One does not need to live here many weeks to see how fragmented the duchy is. I was surprised by resentment toward Maerton and the welcomes I have received. Yet, many also show loyalty to the name of Maerton and mistrust of Kaituer. Others seem to distrust both names. Division is dangerous for all, and I care too much for this duchy to shrug off the danger when I have opportunity to alleviate it."

That seemed to go well enough. Thomas spoke with more confidence. "When the House of Kaituer fell, that did not create peace. Only ruins and ash. No matter which side they fought on, no one could live at the castle or village when the battle was done. Even the surroundings lie in waste to this day. The fall of the House of Maerton will be no better. Already, it has endured the first skirmish and death. Peace does not come from destruction or by looking away. Peace must be created with intention. That must start somewhere, so I will start it by offering peace between the rival houses of Kaituer and Maerton. From there, we can build. Then, perhaps, no more ash heaps will rise to shame us all."

That seemed to shock. Duke Selta found his tongue first. "That is not what we are accustomed to hearing from Ma—from your duchy."

Thomas's shoulders tensed even tighter. Had he sounded presumptuous? "I am only one lord among many."

The king's voice grew dry. "You are also the only lord in the duchy with an oath to the king."

Heat surged through Thomas again.

The king gestured to the lords and ladies seated beyond the ducal families. "And there sit the nobles of this duchy, with no protection or allegiance. Nor will I let them swear to me, for I will not have this duchy divided into a score of holdings to fight with each other. They need a duke, and they need one now."

The king left a powerful pause. "Dukes and duchesses, I propose Sir Thomas Kaituer, Lord of Navayn as the new duke of this duchy."

Thomas's lips parted, but his throat closed. "Wha—" he croaked.

The king raised his brows.

Thomas cleared his throat. "Forgive me, sire, but why would you do such a thing?"

"Perhaps in part because you do *not* grasp for it. But what you do is more to the point. When you are faced with the impossible, you walk toward it. When you face loss, you move on and succeed elsewhere. You do all this without flaunting and without harm to others. The people of this land have needed you for generations."

Thomas felt as though he sat far away, listening...barely breathing. The king spoke of noble lineage and of preparing Thomas for this eventuality. Tristan said more. Then, the Dukes of Selta and Prushane said favorable things about his recent dealings on the Navayn estate. Duchess Portlen commended his desire for peace, and last, discussion came around to Duke Fennish.

"I admit, Lord Navayn," he said, "that I know you the least. Which matters little, since you have adequate support already. What I would like to know—and this is partially addressed to the king—is the plan to provide strength to support peace. 'Tis a fine ideal, but there are always some who take advantage of the peace that others offer."

"I wish you were wrong," the king said, "but we both know you are right. I shall attend that until the new duke can take it on himself. Indeed, this same need would exist for whomever takes rulership of this duchy."

Duke Fennish nodded and turned back to Thomas. "Your lineage was mentioned. 'Tis adequate, but includes commoners for two generations and—" He twitched his brow as Thomas stiffened. "Oh, calm yourself, Lord Navayn. I didn't insult them. I just want to know your plans for a wife. 'Twould be wise to ally yourself with another ducal house. No matter how much you have learned in the past few years, you are young and new to these duties and traditions. A wife who is *not* new to them is crucial."

Thomas avoided looking at Lady Sareen. He cleared his

throat to gain time. "I agree, and I promise to wed a woman who will make a perfect duchess."

Lord Dermont's chair began a rhythmic creaking and betrayed his silent laughter. Sareen looked at him, her arched brows raised high. "Brothers!"

Duchess Selta made a dainty huff. "One would think we could have had a nice party to announce this, but I suppose it will have to be now. Lord Navayn and Lady Sareen have already committed to join hands in marriage."

"Oh! I didn't mean to..." Duke Fennish pressed his fingertips to his brow. "When my lady wife hears how I stomped into this... particular tradition..."

Thomas laughed. "You may tell Duchess Fennish that I granted you gracious pardon."

Duchess Portlen, with amusement still lilting in her voice, said, "The duchy requires a name, so that we may know how to address the duke. Lord Navayn, I understand, at least in part, that you could not give up the name of Kaituer. Would you perhaps consider merging it with another name? 'Tis not unusual at marriage."

"Before that goes any further," King Gairith said, "Queen Ellianne will not allow another use of the Elle from Selta, for the royal house and two duchies already incorporate that name. 'Tis plenty."

"My sister is wise in this matter," Duke Selta said.

Duke Tristelle agreed, and then two others started to speak simultaneously.

Thomas again cleared his throat. He was going to have to find a better way to make himself heard, but it worked this time. "I believe that the name of the duchy should come entirely from within it. Upon the portrait of my grandfather, I found the name Thomas Navayn Kaituer. I believe the last duke placed it there to honor his son's Navayn heritage alongside the Kaituer heritage. Even living a short while among Lady Anne Navayn's people, I recognize more than ever her contribution to who I am. The two names that should be merged are Kaituer and Navayn. Thus, the name Kaivayn occurs to me."

Thomas swept a gaze around the ducal gathering and then looked longer at lords and ladies sitting beyond them. Hard to tell much from their serious faces.

Thomas turned back to the king. "What think you of that name, my liege?"

The king took a moment to answer. "When Anne Navayn Kaituer lay on her deathbed, she may have felt that she had failed. But she succeeded. Indeed, succeeded so well that, despite evil men, her great-grandson overcame the impossible and returned to his place. Now, it is your time to stand in your duchy and create your own legacy. This day, I proclaim you Duke of Kaivayn."

Thomas grew lightheaded. 'Twas a good thing he sat rather than stood. He breathed deep and focused on the king's words, for he still spoke.

"This duchy and its castle, I shall hold in trust for you until all documents are drawn up to create Kaivayn Duchy. When that is complete, the queen and I will summon the Assembly of Duchies to confirm the granting of your title."

A weight lifted with the words *held in trust*. Thomas wouldn't need to bear the full burden today. Just contend with a stunning fact. He...Thomas...was, in truth...a duke. A dizzying freedom rolled through him. He was more free than ever he had been. Free to fully be who he was.

The king smiled again and softened his voice. "We have many things to discuss, but for now, everyone wishes to congratulate you and your future duchess."

The king stood, bringing everyone else to their feet. Thomas made haste to Sareen, and they met in the center of the hall. He grasped her hand, and she reached her other hand up to draw his head near.

Her lips almost touched his ear as she whispered, "I knew it! I always knew it!"

What exactly she knew, he wasn't sure, but she was trembling, and her dimples pulled deep into her cheeks. She was happy—and that was enough.

The king congratulated them first. Oh, how odd *Duke Kaivayn* sounded when the king called him that!

Tristan wrapped his arms around both Thomas and Sareen. He ended his warm words by saying, "And since I didn't get to use my proxy to vote, I'll use it to tell you that Beth is ecstatic!"

Thomas laughed, then turned to the next person in a steady stream of well-wishers. They received as many congratulations on their future duchy as their coming marriage. In a moment when Sareen was occupied with someone else, Lord Maerton drew nigh and bowed low to Thomas. "I congratulate you, Duke of Kaivayn."

"I thank you, Lord Maerton." Thomas bowed and murmured, "In truth, does it bother you?"

"I meant what I said. I have never wanted to be duke of this duchy. I do not begrudge it to you."

Some sadness still lingered in his eyes, and Thomas wondered at it. "'Tis too soon for me to commit to specifics, for I know nothing of the estate or the bequest you were promised, but rest in the knowledge that I shall not leave you destitute."

Lord Maerton's eyes rounded. "You...w—"

"Certain," Sareen said, stepping again to Thomas's side, "we would never be shabby. You must visit us now and then."

Lord Maerton sketched a silent bow and withdrew. Though others approached, Thomas noted that Lord Maerton exited the hall through a side door. Likely to a private spot.

Having exchanged greetings with the higher nobility, Thomas now faced the hardest part. The lords who would someday give an oath to a new duke they barely knew. Some smiled more than others, and they didn't all rush forward.

One asked, "Will you use the same fealty oath as Maerton did?"

"I shall not answer that without *reading* it first." That got a few chuckles, and Thomas tried going a step further. "Indeed, I have much to learn before I can make decisions." No reaction. He tried a wry smile. "Except about the wolf and lynx bounties. I will not pay those, for I am heartily tired of all those deer!"

That worked better and got him a few more chuckles and some agreement.

A silver-haired lady among them asked, "Will you accept oaths only from lords, or will you acknowledge a lady's right to hold an estate?"

"I don't understand. If a lady owns the estate, what is there for me to acknowledge?"

Lord Eberle answered. "The Maertons believed land should only pass to male heirs. Even to the point of bypassing a daughter in favor of a distant relative. If a family insisted that the daughter inherit, that left the estate unsworn to the duke, since he would not accept a woman's oath. And then, of course, every person on the estate had to pay the extra half-tax."

Heat spiked through Thomas as he looked to the silver-haired lady. "He taxed you for being female?"

"Aye, until my son was old enough to swear fealty."

"I cannot imagine this." Involuntarily, his eyes turned to the king on the far side of the room.

"King Gairith," the lady said, "had not yet ascended the throne when the second duke placed that burden upon me. Others found different ways to deal with it, including marriage between a female heir and her nearest male cousin. The sort of marriage that is now heavily frowned upon."

It dawned on Thomas that this matter could stir much angst. Were there distant relatives who might fear losing an estate? "I must look closer into this, but I cannot imagine how I would look my lady wife in the eyes if I were to tax some people extra because an heir was born female."

He glanced to Sareen as he said this, and she added to it. "Even though 'tis far too soon for decisions, I have seen Lor—er, Duke Kaivayn treat women with more respect and consideration than has been common in this duchy. And um, maybe I should tell you something more. Many of you may know that Lord Ivan wished to marry me, and I would not agree to it. 'Twas not because I didn't care about the duchy. 'Twas because of who *he* was."

A young lady in the midst said, "I don't think any of us can fault you for *that!*"

Sareen flashed her dimpled smile. "From now on, I shall always view the people of this duchy as *my people*."

Lord Eberle took a step nearer, which loosened the knot of people around Thomas and Sareen. "I will admit," Lord Eberle said, "to being a member of that group you mentioned who trusted neither the names of Maerton nor Kaituer. Like you, I wish to know more before oaths are exchanged, but though I could not have bowed to the name of Kaituer, the House of Kaivayn does seem to be one that I can honor." With those final words, he bowed to the depth appropriate for a duke.

Thomas acknowledged with his own bow, not as deep, amazed that the formal gestures were already starting to feel natural. The other lords of his duchy gave him congratulations and good wishes with no one else holding back.

Eventually, Jonathan found a chance to draw nigh. "You must both know that I am wildly happy for you, true?" They assented with smiles, then he turned to Sareen. "I just want to make sure you know that the very first task I performed as squire, was to tell Sir Thomas that Lady Sareen was on the mansion roof."

Thomas laughed and said to his lady, "That is true, and I hastened to join you there."

When the greetings were done, Sareen pressed her hands to her face. "My cheeks hurt." Her father gestured to her to join him, and she returned to her family.

As Thomas looked over the mess of scattered chairs and empty dais, Tristan drew near. The hall felt enormous. Doors leading to rooms he'd never seen. A grand spreading staircase leading to levels unknown. To Tristan, he said, "I'm not sure I can grasp that this is going to be mine."

"It is. Including the stones that came from Kaituer Castle to build it. Not to mention the tower tree symbol, which has always fit you more than it fit the former occupant. Perhaps in a way, it has always been yours."

Thomas slowly shook his head. "I'm not sure I can do this."

"You've felt that before. And then succeeded."

"True." But this was bigger. The seed of an idea he'd once had suddenly sprouted. There was that surge of freedom again. Freedom to act on his thoughts. "When I formally visited the ruins of Kaituer Castle, I met a few people whose ancestors died in the fire. I want to provide a proper burial and memorial at the village site. And make it possible for folk to settle around there again." He held Tristan's eyes. "I think it likely that the People of the Woods will...leave your duchy and come to mine. I hope...I would be heartsick if that created hard feelings between us."

Tristan gripped his shoulder. "Worry not. I know full well that they have always been more *your* people than *my* people. In some ways, I feel that I have held Tower Woods in trust until some better solution could be devised."

"Do you mean...?" Thomas shifted his stance. "I cannot—"

"Nay, set this aside and make no assumptions."

Thomas closed and opened his eyes. "So much destiny seems to fall suddenly upon me that I cannot deal with more."

"There is nothing sudden about it, except the realization. Your every deed has built to this moment."

"Nothing I have done has been enough to warrant this...this blessing and responsibility."

"Not any single deed, but all deeds together have brought it to pass. Believe me in this, Thomas. Had you not solved countless small problems, nor given honor to those of both high and low estate, you would not now be granted this duchy. Remember that, whenever you feel inadequate. And should you ever fall into the error of feeling *worthy* of all your honors, then remember the amazement that came with each new gift."

Thomas chuckled in his throat. "I shall treasure both pieces of wisdom."

"Don't think too much about this tonight. We'll go back to Navayn Manor and act normal. Besides, you have houseguests there, and the king still rules this castle."

Tristan swung around and motioned to one of the nervous-looking servants who seemed glued to the wall that flanked the door. "Send word to the stable to fetch my carriage."

The servant hurried away. Not glued, after all. Thomas stared through the open doors. His estate—Navayn Manor. Too dear to give up. But his mother could be happy there, and perhaps someday, he and Sareen could bequeath it to a younger child.

She returned to his side and slipped her fingers into Thomas's hand. That changed everything inside him. "My bride to be, do you know a room where we can slip away?"

She did, of course. A salon. He gave it a quick glance as he unbuckled his sword belt and dropped it onto a chair. "Come here, my sweet darling."

She was in his arms before he finished the sentence.

He held her close, her cheek resting against his chest. His muscles began to relax. His slowing breaths made the curls of her hair jiggle. He finally asked, "Did you expect this?"

She leaned back to look into his face. "Not like this! Since I was a little girl, I always knew I would be a duchess. But this summer, I gave up that dream, because I loved you. I would be your wife in a castle, a manor, or a woodland." She tilted her head. "Naturally, a castle is easiest, so I do love this twist."

"A castle is easiest? An entire duchy comes with it!"

"Oh, Thomas, we'll do fine."

Freedom again. He started to laugh. "Ah, my sweet serenity."

"You realize my name is not spelled s-e-r-e-n-e, don't you?"

"I do, but you still bring me peace."

"Didn't you just speak profound words about the need to *create* peace?"

"I did. You create it with your smile and your own profound words like, 'we'll do fine.' You chase away my worries and leave me peace."

Her smile brought her dimples back.

He savored a slow tender kiss, then the depth of her eyes and the feel of her hair beneath his fingertips. "You are a treasure beyond anything I could deserve. And at last, I am free to love you."

SHARE THE ADVENTURE

I hope you found something in these pages that made your life a little richer. If you liked this story, maybe others would too. You can help them find it by leaving a brief review or even by clicking some stars wherever you like to purchase or review books. Those star ratings and reviews help me, too, and I greatly appreciate all of them.

Would you like to read more stories like this one? If so, I invite you to join my newsletter. I will send you some free short stories, share a little about life, and let you know about new books and an occasional sale. I won't overload your inbox or share your email address with others. You may unsubscribe at any time. Sign up at SharonRoseAuthor.com. I hope to hear from you!

ANOTHER ADVENTURE

To Form a Passage
Arts of Substance – Novel 1

Quakes isolate Devron's underground homeland, threatening starvation. He holds the only solution—and it's terrifying.

Devron sees a vision for the perfect design—to solve a problem that doesn't exist. Elegant and powerful, but why would he create anything so dangerous? The Formers' Guild will never allow it.

While he saw creative beauty, others had visions of horrific collapse. Are they warnings of disaster? Some gather their families and flee the caverns, but most shrug off the ominous signs. After all, the formers are staying. Their power to alter solid rock by command alone has kept the underground cities safe for generations. No quake can bring the cavern ceilings down.

Until it does. Countless lives are lost, and the surviving cities are cut off from the rest of their kingdom. As fear tightens its grip, looming starvation spawns one problem after another. Never again will they trust the formers they once relied on. Devron least of all.

Yet Devron knows the only solution to their survival. And even he thinks it is terrifying.

To Form a Passage is a stand-alone fantasy novel in the ARTS OF SUBSTANCE trilogy. Each novel explores one of the world's three substance gifts: forming, wind weaving, and streaming. With every ability comes risk. These gifts are neither easy nor safe. Who has the courage and wit to use their gift well? And at what cost?

Interested? Ask your favorite bookstore or library for:

To Form a Passage, by Sharon Rose, ISBN: 978-1-948160-31-5

BOOKS BY SHARON ROSE

FANTASY

Arts of Substance Trilogy:

To Form a Passage — Novel 1

To Weave the Wind — Novel 2

To Stream an Ocean — Novel 3

Castle in the Wilde Series:

A Castle Lost — An Early Days Novella

A Castle Sealed — Prequel Novella

A Castle Awakened — Novel 1

A Castle Contended — Novel 2

A Castle from Ashes — Novel 3

Castle in the Wilde — Trilogy Box Set

SCIENCE FICTION

Diverse Similarity — Novel 1

Diverse Demands — Novel 2

Agents of Rivelt — A Novel in Short Stories

More titles are coming. Get the latest news at SharonRoseAuthor.com.

ACKNOWLEDGMENTS

I have to admit that I often feel overwhelmed—in a delightful way—when I think of everyone who walks this journey with me. There are so many aspects beyond the words I write, from brainstorming the first ideas until my stories are read and shared with others. To name a few: encouragement, editing, artwork, production, marketing, early read-throughs, reviews, and encouragement. Yes, I said that twice, because after all the work is complete, personal notes from readers are pure joy!

Another blessing was having the same team through the entire series. We added some along the way, but you all stuck with me. There are too many names to list here but when you find your part below, know that I am thinking of you.

Family support is foundational to my writing. Husband, children, siblings, in-laws, even grandkids now. My thanks to all of you for everything from practical help, to encouragement, to just being your beautiful selves.

Bridgett Powers, my faithful editor and friend. Thanks for keeping up with my close releases and always being there for me. You know my books wouldn't be published without you.

Kirk DouPonce, thank you for creating cover art that reflects the story-ideas bouncing around in my head. The entire set is beautiful.

Matthew Ferguson, thank you for the medieval style maps to give substance to my fantasy world, and especially, for the vixicat in the corner.

Realm Makers—the conference, the online community, the

people: This tribe, who understands both faith and speculative fiction, has made a huge difference in my author journey. And besides, you guys are just plain fun! Many thanks to all of you.

Write Now writer's group at Living Word Christian Center: You are precious friends and encouragers. Thank you for listening to me read and giving me feedback.

Advance Readers: Though I will never see most of you face-to-face, the time you take to read, review, and spread the word, means more than you realize. Those of you who have sent me personal notes, your kind words always bring smiles to my face.

To *all* of my readers: Even though these words are printed before you read this book, I feel as much gratitude for you as for everyone mentioned above. You've taken the time to walk through this fantasy world with me, and I don't take that for granted. I hope you've found something in it to bring light and hope to your days.

ABOUT THE AUTHOR

I started writing when I was seven years old. Okay, *My Life as a Flying Squirrel* may have had a couple spelling errors, but my classmates loved it.

Plenty of life has happened since that first story, and I've come to realize the things that fascinate me. People. Communication. Culture. Personality. Viewpoints. Beliefs. Anything that makes each of us beautifully unique. Small wonder that my art spills out in story form.

It was only a matter of time, before I just had to share my stories. I've published science fiction and now fantasy, two genres that allow us to explore reality while having fun.

When I'm not writing or reading, I may be traveling, enjoying gardens, or searching for unique coffee shops with my husband. We live in Minnesota, USA, famed for its mosquitoes —uh, I mean 10,000 lakes and vibrant seasons.

To find out more, visit SharonRoseAuthor.com.

Follow me on:
Amazon, Goodreads, BookBub, and Facebook.
Find all of my links at: https://linktr.ee/sharonrose.author